DIAMONDS BY THE YARD

ELLIOTT MURPHY
MATTHEW MURPHY

MURPHYLAND
BOOKS

Cover painting by Brendan O'Connell, www.brendanoconnell.com

CONTENTS

CHAPTER 1

The sun was close to rising over the south fork of Long Island and in less than an hour the first rays of light would speckle the candy cane-like Montauk lighthouse with a radiant orange glaze as a distant glow on the horizon promised a bright mid-summer day for this affluent tip of the once irresistible *new world.* The grand old lighthouse itself was still erect and functioning since George Washington had authorized its construction in 1792 to serve both as an aid for maritime navigation and a sentry for the feared second-chance invasion by the King's fleet. Soon the new dawn would be spreading down island from Montauk to nearby Amagansett and illuminating leafy Further Lane, a two mile stretch of multimillion- dollar beach houses, shaded by century old pear trees and set back from the road with lavish, impossibly green lawns. From there it was just a hop, skip and a jump over the dunes to the seemingly endless sandy beach where Atlantic Ocean waves crashed mightily on the shore. The Hamptons, as the twenty-four villages and hamlets on the east-end of Long Island were called, was in the midst of its annual riotous influx of wealthy summer vacationers and if George Washington had known from where the invasion would finally come, he might have shone his sentry lighthouse in the opposite direction, toward the Upper East Side of Manhattan.

And our story begins here in a way, although it could have begun in oil-rich Houston, Texas, or the blue-collar Irish enclaves of the borough of Queens in New York City or even in yet another anonymous suburb of the American *heartland.* But let us say it began here on that very same fine halcyon summer morning in 1975 when a beautiful wealthy young woman still in her twenties, who had recently taken the reins of her family fortune firmly in hand, came home from a night of partying and flirtatious dancing to her own sumptuous Further Lane hideaway, champagne flute in hand as she gingerly entered her bedroom. Her husband, who had called it a night hours before, lay sound asleep on their king-sized bed and as she gently pushed open the bedroom door, the ragged sound of his snoring brought a disapproving frown to her face. Moving to the edge of the bed, she stood over him for a moment and looked down, her disappointment nearly visible, and briefly wondered *why* and *what if* ... but she had learned how to recover from life's disappointments when there was always travel and ample shopping to assuage the pain; so far, almost nothing was for *forever* in her world if she didn't want it that way. Of course, there was one exception to that rule and that was her immense fortune and the entitlement that came with it and that, without doubt, she would be wearing well, along with her fine clothes and jewelry, until the day she died.

Pulling her short silky dress over her head and absently letting it fall behind her, she walked to a mirrored dressing table, where she quickly unhooked her bra and with a steadying hand on the small flowered couch, stepped out of her panties, one high heel at a time. She was guided by the soft yellow light of a bronze bedside lamp that her husband had left on in a minimal gesture of marriage solidarity, but she hardly worried about waking him, knowing full well that he could sleep through anything. *Everyone has one good quality,* she thought, then looking at his bared crotch, *maybe two in his case.* Still tipsy from the champagne, she fell onto the couch, naked but for her elaborate jewelry - her fine watch, gold and platinum bracelets, rings on her fingers and more - which somehow made her feel almost dressed. Unbuckling the braided gold strap of her Cartier Tank watch she didn't even notice the erroneous time, for her it was just another accessory, something to wrap around her wrist and she wouldn't bother setting the time or winding the stem, preferring just to ask whoever might be close at hand, "Got the time, sugar?" and then let the conversation flow from there with her cowgirl *cum* Scarlett O'Hara accent.

Licking her fingers, she slid the three rings, ruby, sapphire and emerald, and then with a slight pull, the matching bracelets behind them. Just those rings, watch and bracelets were way beyond most ordinary people's means or dreams and yet she cared little for these *trinkets* and would barely miss any of them if they had disappeared from her jewelry box. Everything there could be replaced in a few days of shopping, everything, that is, except her cherished necklace, which was recently returned to her by bonded messenger from Tiffany and Co. in an Easter egg blue Tiffany bag from their nearby boutique in Southampton. That, she had hated being without even for the few days required for their artisans to add a new, larger diamond clasp with gold extension links that would trail down her perfectly tanned back at summer garden parties.

A few years ago, there had been a seductive Tiffany ad in the *New York Times,* which persuaded her to pick up the phone and make an inquiry, quickly followed by a personal demand to their custom jewelry department. Yes, she loved the whole idea of the necklace – chains of eighteen karat gold studded with diamonds - but she wanted something *special*, a piece that would be identified just with her, a personal talisman, and Tiffany and Co. readily obliged to make her a necklace like no other of the series. She imagined the necklace would become her personal fashion *statement*, her *signature* and her *calling card*: a solid gold chain, six feet long and studded with dozens of rare blue diamonds just inches apart, a six-figure symbol of who she was and who she would always be, which one day, would become as renown as the Hope Diamond.

When the necklace arrived it was perfect, even better than she had imagined it would be, and now with the addition of the new clasp it was even more perfect. Hating to take it off, she kept it around her neck while she stood naked and selected a short negligee from her armoire. She liked to wear the necklace casually, strung around her neck in five or six uneven loops and the sight of it was so distinctive and sparkling that most people would not even imagine that such a thing could be real. A generous handful of large diamonds strung on a gold braid, how could it be? Still, knowing that it was *real* and that it was *hers* was enough for her and admiring it brought a perpetual self-satisfied smile to her pert oval face. Finally, before getting into bed, she removed the necklace slowly and held it cupped in both her hands: spun gold and rare diamonds perhaps too outrageously opulent for a demure Park Avenue New York socialite but certainly *apropos* for a transplanted Texas heiress for whom nothing was too much, for whom extravagance was more than a style; it was a way of life. Almost reluctantly, she opened her cupped hands and let the necklace slowly unravel into an ornate three-tiered jewelry box.

"Diamonds by the Yard," she said to herself with almost girlish delight. "*Diamonds by the Yard.*"

CHAPTER 2

Lexi Langdon opened her normally sparkling green eyes, now somewhat less luminous due to the smudges of last night's party makeup, and reached for the phone on the nightstand next to her bed. In doing so she knocked over the empty champagne glass and it shattered on the floor. "Shit," she said to herself, focusing on the illuminated numbers of a bedside clock radio that told her it was just before noon. An engine-like roar, just outside her bedroom window, had seemed to grow louder and move closer all morning and was giving her an even worse headache. Getting out of bed in her see-through baby-blue negligee, she walked straight to the open window and peered out. Indeed, there were three industrial-sized lawnmowers going full blast on the huge front lawn that stretched glistening in an emerald green carpet from her immense white shingled beach house all the way to a rustic wooden fence that separated her property from the paved road of Further Lane. Lexi was not used to having her sleep disturbed by anyone, least of all those whom she was paying to keep her vast lawn manicured. Spying the lawn care company truck parked discreetly to the side of the circular driveway, she repeated, "Shit, shit, shit."

Sticking her head far out the open window she yelled, "Hey,

guys!" over the lawnmowers' incessant roar. "Could you do that some other time ... Hey, guys! Can you hear me?" But they couldn't. Her breathy voice had a precise tone of authority but little in the way of projection or volume and Lexi, unable to get their attention, backed away from the window. She searched for her pocketbook, a black alligator Hermes Kelly bag, and found it lying on the floor under her party dress. Dumping its contents right on the bed, she found what she was looking for, a crisp one hundred dollar bill, and went back to the open window. Again, she leaned out as far as she could and the bright noon sun made her negligee utterly transparent as she waved the bill in the air. The curved silhouette of her breasts to the tip of her nipples stood out like an illuminated billboard against the darkness of the room behind her.

"Hey, guys!" she called out as loud as she could manage. "Why don't you take a break ... get some lunch and do this later?" One of the three workers operating the chugging lawnmowers just happened to look up and see her waving, trying to get their attention. He quickly focused on her breasts bouncing beneath the negligee and abruptly turned off his machine, stunned into immobility. When the other two laborers saw him they followed suit, shutting down their own machines, and then, suddenly the loudest sound over that enormous lawn was Lexi herself yelling, "Guys, you're giving me a fucking headache!"

Regrettably, none of the three workers, all recently arrived from Central America, could speak anything but the most basic English, and besides that, Lexi's Texas accent was like nothing they had ever heard before and thus they were at a total loss to know what they should or should not do. Finally the head guy smiled and nervously waved back to her, the others quickly did the same, waving and smiling before re-starting their lawnmowers, getting back to work, and above all, not wanting to risk being fired for staring at the half-naked *chica muy guapa* shouting from the window. "Shit, shit, shit," Lexi repeated as she retreated into her bedroom despondent, lying back on her bed and pulling two pillows over her throbbing head.

Further Lane, Amagansett, was the kind of *tony* neighborhood where they might shoot classy magazine ads for aged Scotch whiskey showing silver-haired men in tuxedos at genteel cocktail parties. A dozen or more huge mansions were set back from the shady two-lane country road, many in plain sight, full-dress American dream palaces, easily viewed with envy and longing by passing outsiders in cars or on bicycles and not one was more impressive than the sprawling estate Lexi Langdon had paid a small fortune to use as her summer getaway. Impulsively, after one brief winter visit when she huddled in her full length fox coat, she had bought the house and property, and when she opened the house months later on an uncommonly hot Memorial Day weekend and called to inquire if there was central air conditioning, the real estate agent who had sold it to her had almost burst out laughing. "But it's a historic Sanford White mansion right on the ocean, warm at night and cool in the day. I can assure you it's *the* prime beach estate on all of Further Lane, Ms. Langdon, as well as a historically protected landmark."

"Historic or not, it's hot as hell," said Lexi.

"You'll see it's not like Texas here with all that terrible humidity," explained the agent. "You don't really need air conditioning, especially when you're next door to the ocean." With that Lexi had abruptly hung up the phone and now, as she thought of that real estate agent with her head throbbing beneath the pillow, a simple phrase came to mind. "Fuck her," she said to herself before starting to yell for someone, *anyone*, to bring her coffee and toast. And within minutes a maid did arrive and silently placed a wicker breakfast tray of coffee, toast and marmalade on the bed before starting to walk out.

"You ... wait!" shouted Lexi, not remembering the name of the young maid who had been working in her house all summer long.

"Something else, Ms. Langdon?"

"You don't expect me to clean up that broken champagne glass myself?" asked Lexi nastily.

"No, ma'am," said the maid, smiling and dropping down to her knees to pick up the shards off the floor.

"Or maybe you'd think it'd be funny if I cut myself?" asked Lexi.

The maid said nothing and stopped smiling.

"You could answer me when I speak to you. Wouldn't kill you."

The maid rose to her feet, her palm filled with glass.

"I'll have to bring up the vacuum cleaner, ma'am."

"Don't you start making a racket until I get out of here and go downstairs – I've had enough noise for one day. Now you scat, leave me alone and let me get ready. Is my husband around?"

"Yes, ma'am, Mister Arthur is downstairs."

Ten minutes later, when Lexi descended the stairs, Ray Arthur was sitting at one end of the large oval dining room table, solemnly sipping coffee while reading the *Wall Street Journal*. He had been trying hard to make sense of all those tiny figures in various stock indexes, but when he heard his wife's voice addressing the cook it broke his concentration. He looked up to see her standing in front of him, yelling over her shoulder.

"And make sure the shrimp are ... however shrimps are supposed to be," she was yelling back to the kitchen. "Last time they were all ... *gooey*, covered with sauce and I stained my dress and had to change outfits in the middle of the party." She turned her head and looked at Ray, lowering her voice. "Not that you even noticed, Ray."

"Noticed what?"

"That I had to change my dress the other night in the middle of the party."

"What dress?"

"Forget it, Ray. What are you looking at?"

"The New York Stock Exchange."

"Sugar, the only stock you ever need to pay attention to is Langdon Industries," said Lexi. "Because I own most of it ..."

"Guess what, Lexi? I've heard that before," said Ray disdainfully. "And what if I wanted to invest in some other company? Is that allowed?"

Ray Arthur was an almost handsome man with narrow eyes that never opened wide, a naturally dark complexion and shiny straight black hair. In his mid-thirties, he had looked the same since he started shaving, which he now did twice a day. Like most weekends in the Hamptons, he was dressed in a starched white Turnbull and Asser shirt, khaki pants and tasseled loafers without socks. Lexi still wore her negligee with bare feet and her hair pulled back in a ponytail.

"It's a free country," said Lexi.

"Free country or not, do you think you should come downstairs dressed – or should I say undressed – like that?" said Ray. "You know, all these servants talk to each other out here."

"Well, maybe they do talk to each other, but I only hear them talking in Spanish so what do I care what they're saying?" Lexi pulled up behind Ray and put her hands on his slicked back hair. "I thought you might join me for a little breakfast in bed." She kissed his neck. "I saved you some toast and jam."

"I had breakfast hours ago," said Ray." Up at five, went fishing and back at ten. Bet you didn't even miss me."

"What did you catch?" asked Lexi. "Anything worth ... eating?" She said provocatively as she swung around and sat on his lap.

"Come on, Lexi ... the maids are gonna see us."

"Screw the maids, sugar," said Lexi, in full-tilt Texan. "My ranch, my rules."

Lexi wrapped around Ray like a snake and soon she was straddling him, cradling his face in her hands and kissing him on the lips. Ray sat stiff, his hands on Lexi's shoulders, not knowing what to do.

"At least let's go upstairs then," said Ray.

"That was the general idea," said Lexi, taking Ray's hand and leading him up the stairs. But when they got to their open bedroom door, one of the maids was already doing the bed while another vacuumed up the broken glass.

"We could wait until they're finished," said Ray. "Or come back after lunch."

"Lunch?"

"It's just that ... I'm not really in the mood right now. Kind of tired after ..."

Lexi looked at Ray sternly. "Well, whatever mood there was, that sure killed it right there."

"Let's put it off till tonight," said Ray. "We got plenty of time."

"Tonight I'm giving a party or did you forget about that already?"

"Oh, that's right, the famous *Rebel's Ball*," said Ray. "By the way, I had one of the gardeners string those lights on the chimneys, just like you wanted."

"How sweet of you to take care of that, Ray, with your busy schedule. What did you say got you up so early for?

"Fishing."

"You fish more than we make love."

"That's not true, Lexi ... last weekend?" asked Ray.

"More like last month," said Lexi. "Ray, you ever see that film *Cat on a Hot Tin Roof*? Paul Newman and Liz Taylor?"

"Don't know ... give me a clue."

"Here's a clue for you, Ray, '*Maggie the cat is alive!*'" she declared, slamming her bedroom door behind her and leaving Ray standing in the upstairs hallway alone.

"Lexi," he pleaded through the door. "Come on, there are eight bedrooms in this house! I'm not that tired ... " But there was no reply from the other side of the door and after waiting a minute Ray walked back down the stairs, still wondering just who the hell *Maggie the cat* was.

Lexi sat on the small sofa in her bedroom watching the two nervous maids clean up, dejected and angry and ready to strike out at somebody, anybody. But before she could, the younger of the maids held up her new white bathing suit.

"*Playa?*" the maid asked timidly.

"Damn right, *playa*," said Lexi. "We're going to the beach." The maids looked confused.

"Beach," she repeated. "Fuck Ray!" This, the maids did understand and they giggled while holding their hands to their mouths as Lexi walked into her huge bathroom and shut the door behind her to run the shower.

"Fuck Ray!" whispered the younger maid still giggling.

"*Loco*," said the other maid, shaking her head and fluffing up Lexi's six goose down filled pillows.

ONCE HE WAS ASSURED THAT LEXI HAD LEFT FOR THE BEACH, Ray Arthur went alone into his study in the furthest wing of the house and quietly shut the door behind him before picking up the phone and dialing a number by memory. Thirty-three miles away in Westhampton Beach, Gloria Canasta lay on a chaise lounge on the terrace of a modern beach house in an *itsy-bitsy* flowery bikini, her dyed black hair set in large pink curlers, her eyes closed, carefully picking Wise potato chips right out of the bag one at a time. Gloria was a ripe twenty-one, petite and voluptuous, with firm round breasts that stood straight up under her bikini top even when she was lying down as she was now. She was waiting for the black polish on her toenails to dry, and hearing the obnoxiously loud footsteps coming her way, she opened her eyes to see Junior looming over her, smoking a cigarette, dressed in white loafers, high-waist checked pants held up with a white patent leather belt and a wife-beater T-shirt. Wrap-around Ray Ban sunglasses hid his eyes, but he made it obvious enough that he was focused on her feet.

"You should paint 'em red," he said, shaking his head disdainfully. "That black crap looks like something one of the Munsters would wear."

"So now you're giving fashion advice, Junior?" Gloria raised herself on her elbows. "Where'd you get that outfit? Sonny Corleone?"

"Something wrong with the way I look?" asked Junior, hiking up his pants. "What don't you like?"

"Come on, you're blocking the sun, Junior."

"You got a call," he announced, looking off into space. "Some guy. Want me to tell him to fuck off?"

"Bring me the phone, Junior," she ordered but Junior didn't move. "*Bring* me the phone, Junior ..." she repeated.

He waited, now looking at her almost menacingly.

"Bring me the phone *now*, Junior ... or my Uncle Maddy is gonna kick your ass."

"Very sweet," said Junior. "Didn't anybody teach you any goddamn manners?"

"The phone, Junior!"

All the time he had been holding the boxy Sony wireless behind his back. Moving it in front of him, "Oh you must mean this?" he said, and tossed it to her. Reaching up to catch it, Gloria spilled half the potato chips on the floor.

"I'm not cleaning this crap up!" she yelled.

"Tell your uncle to do it," said Junior as he walked away, his fiendish laugh only half put-on. "And let me know if you want me to rub some Coppertone on you – girls say I'm good at it."

"In your dreams, Junior." Gloria put the phone to her ear. "Yeah?"

"Hi, baby," Ray said softly into the phone. "Listen, things are not cool here today, think I better stay around and keep Lexi company, not raise any suspicions."

"You mean you're not coming over? Why'd you tell me you'd be back *for more* in a few hours?"

"What, wasn't this morning enough for you?" Ray tried to joke. "Don't tell me you need more of the *stingray*?

"I get it, stingray as in Ray. Very cute."

"Don't tell me I didn't satisfy you?"

"Oh ... so that was for *my* satisfaction this morning?" said Gloria. "Coulda fooled me."

"How about I take care of you next time? Scout's honor."

"Next time? Hmm ... next time, my ass."

"Sounds good to me," said Ray chuckling.

"Fuck you, Ray, believe me, I can survive without you but Uncle Maddy isn't going to be too happy about this. I told him you were coming by and he said he's gotta talk to you about business. He's doing a barbecue tonight and some of his crew are driving out from Brooklyn with a refrigerated truck from Umberto's Clam House in Little Italy with all that Italian sausage and crap he likes to grill. I think he expected you to be there."

"Hey, what can I do? I'm married, Gloria."

"You keep telling me that," she said before hanging up.

CHAPTER 3

I came east to be a musician, although maybe it wasn't the best time for such a move. Originally, I was from a safe and comfortable suburb in the Midwest like thousands of others, but there was no edge, no passion, no mystery, and still I was supposed to be happy there. But I wasn't because I wanted more. So as soon as I had the chance I packed up and left. They handed me a high school diploma and I said see you later. What I didn't know was that I wouldn't be able to go back. Ever. And in the first few years that followed, I just traveled wherever the proverbial wind might blow me, following the path of least resistance; if a place sounded good, I went there. I can truly say I had some memorable adventures but some terrifying moments as well with some repercussions that I still can't undo and learned some lessons I wish I didn't need to. But you know what they say; life makes more sense when it's looked at backwards. Because through no strategy of my own I survived it all, got lucky in Amagansett and ended up in New York City at an amazing time, when the city was leading the dance for the rest of the nation, maybe for the world. Of course, I didn't get there right away, but when I did arrive it sure felt like that was my destiny.

I hear there's a Chinese curse: May you live in interesting times.

That was New York in 1975, on the verge of bankruptcy even though President Ford had reluctantly signed legislation granting the city a slight reprieve. Still, it was the place to be and everybody sensed that; there was a burgeoning new music scene happening there, and that's where I eventually landed, although I came in through the back door, the eastern end of Long Island. I could strum a guitar and sing Beatles and Dylan or even James Taylor songs in small clubs and even smaller bars and the audience paid attention most of the time and folks seemed to like my smile and the way I closed my eyes when I strained for the high notes. Yeah, I suppose I have to say I looked good too, and perhaps that was my most valuable asset after all - my waist was slim, my dreams were wide, and I was powered by an ambition even I wasn't aware of. But all of this happened a long time ago – post-sixties and pre-AIDS, a wild time when, how shall I say, consequences were put on hold. I met rich, powerful and fabulously beautiful people and some dangerous ones too, who changed my life in serious and indelible ways from the moment our lives first became entangled. And then there was that other thing, that wild card I wasn't expecting ... I fell in love.

Of course, at the time I thought my reticent nature, my provincial shyness and my musician's coolness made me untouchable by these people, that my innocence was some kind of magic protective shield, to the point that I imagined myself somehow better than them, more morally centered or some nonsense like that. Like I was so sure that I knew who I was and nothing, not even the bright lights of New York City, was going to change that. But finally, as I look back now, I can say with a painful assuredness that I was almost entirely wrong about all of that. I've changed my mind about everything. Isn't that funny? Not really, I guess. But I changed my mind about everything I thought I knew ... everything, that is, except how utterly beautiful and captivating Lexi Langdon was that first time I saw her on Indian Wells Beach in Amagansett, Long Island.

Amagansett's picturesque *Main Street,* a brief section of Montauk Highway, curved through the town's modest business section before it resumed its way out to the very tip of Long Island.

The town's main shopping area was located there, a half-mile long at most, consisting of sporting goods and hardware stores, a delicatessen, a not-bad pizza parlor called Angelo's and finally a popular farmers' market of low green wooden shacks that abutted long and narrow potato fields. Beyond that, isolated on the outskirts of town, stood the spic-and-span red brick firehouse and the gray Long Island Rail Road train station and not much else of interest until you reached the town of Montauk, seventeen miles east to a veritable *land's end.* A few churches dotted Main Street with wooden signboards out front, quoting scripture and announcing worship and Sunday school times. And at the very entrance to the village of Amagansett, *founded in 1680,* stood the Stephen Talkhouse, a cedar shingled two-story house, set back from the road, that had been converted into a popular bar and club that drew its own congregation on a nightly basis. Stephen Talkhouse himself, the namesake of the place, had been a 19th century Montaukett Indian, famous for taking fifty-mile hikes for no apparent reason. Whether he ever stopped into the dwelling that now bore his name for a drink while pursuing his wanderlust remains unknown.

LEE FRANKLIN LAY SLEEPING ON THE RATTY COUCH OF THE Stephen Talkhouse dressing room, located one floor up from the club. He had played the Talkhouse the night before, singing "Fire and Rain" and other soft rock covers to a minuscule, but appreciative crowd. The gregarious club owner, a dapper and compact thirty-ish Irishman named Tony Hughes had told him after his show that, "You got a nice voice, Lee, but I took next to nothing in at the door tonight so I'm sorry to say if you don't drink you don't get paid," and thought it was funny, although Lee did not. Still, playing at the Talkhouse wasn't such a bad deal because Tony had agreed to let Lee and his recently acquired manager, Danny O'Connor, crash in the dressing room so they could pass their days on the nearby Atlantic Ocean beaches if they so chose. "Hey, most people pay a fortune to rent a place out here," said Tony. "And you guys are staying for free. Get a freakin' tan - go Hollywood, baby!"

Hollywood indeed! No sheets, no pillows, his rolled up jeans beneath his head, Lee nonetheless had been sleeping soundly on the couch until Danny, standing on the Montauk Highway sidewalk, hollered up to him from beneath his window. Danny's shrill Queens accent had formidable waking power and Lee opened the window widely to see him standing right below, like an old-fashioned paperboy, jubilantly waving a copy of that morning's New York *Daily News* shouting, "Extra! Extra! Ford to City: Drop Dead!"

"What are you yelling about?" asked Lee, stretching his arms and yawning. "You're gonna wake everyone up."

"You're the only one who's still sleeping. Did you hear the news?"

"What news?"

"New York City is broke," said Danny. "And Ford says *Drop Dead*."

"To who?" asked Lee, still not quite awake.

"Forget about it," said Danny. "Get your ass out here and let's go to the beach. It's fucking beautiful."

Lee Franklin peed, washed his face, brushed his teeth and then ran a well-worn comb through his longish wavy blond hair more times than necessary. He moved in close to the mirror, and bending over the sink contemplated his smile, something he did out of habit, the end of a morning ritual. Undeniable charm there and straight white teeth like Cary Grant without the tan, but there was a discernible absence of joy in his eyes and a vulnerable gaze betraying a lack of self-confidence. His advantageous good looks and lean muscular body had not entirely registered with him, he didn't *own* it yet, and a positive self-image was fighting to break through and overcome his doubts. He was sure of his talent, that was one thing, but in his *head* he was still some years away from grooming the abilities to take advantage of them. Not unlike many artists and not rare for a guy in his twenties still struggling to find himself, but in Lee's mind there was a nagging anxiety that he might never break through. And ironically, it was this same anxiety that kept pushing him forward.

Lee felt that he was always the youngest in the crowd, that others knew better and more than he did and so he was constantly looking for guidance instead of following his own instincts which were not as off base as he feared. Being with Danny did give him a certain assurance, as Danny was always praising Lee's talent to anyone who'd listen and painting a bright future for both of them even if the details of how this would come to pass were hazy. Still, even if Lee wasn't sold on Danny's managerial skills, he was as good a friend as any he'd had since he left his hometown, and he quickly dressed and came down to meet him, ready for a day at the beach.

"The beach is this way," said Danny. "You take a left at the church."

The unassuming St. Thomas Episcopal church with its squat steeple and weathered clapboard exterior stood on the corner of Main Street and Indian Wells Road, a short block from the Talkhouse.

"Sign says *Episcopalians*, know anything about them?" asked Danny. "Looks more like an American Legion Hall than a church."

"Episcopalians own everything, the banks, Wall Street, the White House, so I guess they can be discreet. Did you know there have been more Episcopalian Presidents of the United States than anything else? They're like Catholics with no guilt and their priests are allowed to have sex."

"That never stopped the priests in my parish," said Danny. "Ask the altar boys. But how do you know all of this?"

"Because I was brought up in that same church, but without the money – Midwest style Episcopalians."

They walked down Indian Wells Road, its sidewalk bumpy and broken from the invading roots of the huge ivy-covered oak trees that lined the road, passing one impressive cedar-shingled summer home after another. The houses had a windswept look about them, a kind of casual country elegance with freshly trimmed hedges, generous wrap around porches with pillowed rocking chairs and roofs accented by green, dotted with numerous red brick chimneys. One after another, these properties were a testament to the substantial wealth of those who could afford them as mere second homes.

"Old trees," said Danny.

"Old money," said Lee.

"Episcopalians," said Danny to himself, staring past the hundred year old trees to the half-hidden houses beyond and wondering what kind of people really live there.

The road ended where the parking lot of Indian Wells Beach began and the sound and smell of the crashing ocean waves filled the air. Lee had his towel and bathing suit draped over his shoulder while Danny's were wrapped up like a ball in his fist. They'd seen no one else walking on the street like them, but a steady line of cars passed, heading for the beach parking lot.

"It's probably like Beverly Hills out here," said Lee. "I heard that nobody walks around out there either."

"Nobody except us," said Danny glumly. "Tony Hughes could have loaned us his car, it's just sitting there in his driveway dripping oil."

"Speaking of Tony Hughes, why didn't he pay me anything last night? I thought the deal is I'm supposed to get paid every night?"

"Not enough people paid at the door," said Danny.

"Doesn't seem fair to me," said Lee.

"Come on, he's been paying you all along and not doing much better than breaking even, but if he had to shell out last night he was gonna lose money and maybe then you'd lose the gig. Club owners love you until they lose money, you know."

"I got that," said Lee.

"So, I told him to keep the fifty bucks or whatever. I figure he's letting us sleep in the dressing room and we drink at the bar for free so we can't really complain."

"Good move, I suppose," said Lee.

"I'm learning," said Danny.

Right before the entrance to the beach parking lot, a weathered bronze plaque was posted just off the road all but obscured by the tall reeds growing around it. It said something historic about Indians traveling on and off nearby Montauk.

NEAR THIS SPOT AT THE WELLING SPRINGS OF AMAGANSETT THE INDIANS USED TO PAUSE TO SLAKE THEIR THIRST WHEN GOING ON OR COMING OFF MONTAUK.

"Nowadays they'd go to the Talkhouse and have a Heineken," said Danny. "What the hell does *slake* mean anyway?"

"I could make something up but I don't really know either," said Lee. "Something like satisfaction?"

"*I can't get no!*" sang Danny.

"*Hey, hey, hey!*" Lee finished.

They were in a silly mood, on their way to the beach on a fine summer day, not sure if they belonged in this swanky milieu but happy enough to be there nonetheless. It was a perfect mid-August afternoon and the parking lot was full of cars with Town of East Hampton resident parking permits on their windshields. An ice cream truck served the long line of beachgoers in wet bathing suits and brightly colored towels queued in front of it and lifeguards sat on tall white wooden lookout stands like sentinels blowing their whistles, waving their arms and handing out Band-Aids for stubbed toes. Kids splashed in the surf or ran on the beach with their orange popsicles dripping onto the hot sand. Bright plastic Frisbees pierced the baby blue sky and flew over the heads of large packs of teenagers who sat on a sea of blankets and towels, tribe-like, as the noise level approached that of a high school football game.

"Let's move down the beach," said Lee Franklin. "Too much family business here. No place for outcasts like us."

Danny laughed. "No chicks here either!"

They turned right at the surf line and walked about five minutes until the beach grew sparsely populated and wild grassy dunes rose up on their right, concealing the huge beachfront homes behind them. They wrapped their white bathroom towels, borrowed from the Talkhouse dressing room, around their waists and modestly changed into their bathing suits. Lee Franklin carefully spread out his towel on the sand and lay down on his stomach waiting for Danny to do the same, but Danny stood, standing with his arms spread wide, his face to the sun, grinning.

"You're gonna get burnt," said Lee. "You're as white as mayonnaise."

Danny didn't speak for a moment, just kept bobbing his head up and down like he was bouncing some heavy realization around his brain.

"We're at the epicenter of something out here, Lee. I can feel it."

Lee looked at Danny who still had on his cordovan Weejun penny loafers and white socks.

"You can take off your shoes, Danny. You're allowed to go barefoot in the *epicenter*."

"The damn sand is too hot, burns my feet," said Danny. "Wanna go in the water?"

"Can you swim?"

"A little ... I'll go where I still got feet, where I can stand."

"I tell you, I'm kinda beat after walking all the way down here in the sun, you go in and I'll come later," said Lee as he laid his head down on a corner of his towel and closed his eyes as the sun warmed his outstretched body.

CHAPTER 4

The thing that woke him, the moment that he always remembered, was the sound of her voice, just barely shouting orders in a calm and restrained way, certain of her authority, not waiting for any discourse. Her voice seemed to originate from some cushioned place deep in her chest, rising comfortably to her throat, and the words and phrases floating like velvet bubbles out of her mouth, like this is what she did effortlessly all day long. Her verbal lists of demands and needs and desires were open-ended and she kept adding requests, things to bring to her or to do for her or to remind her to do or not to do. The ocean winds brought her voice with its lovely cadence in and out of Lee Franklin's hearing and he could only catch occasional fragments, but it was irresistible, a voice that added *please* an octave lower, as an inferred threat.

"Call Elliot James ... make it later ... put it in the cooler with the white wine ... and more umbrellas *please* ... then buy them if we don't have them! ... Tell Ray to bring my Jacqueline Susann book ... called *Once is* ... something or other ... and remind me to ..."

Lee Franklin opened his eyes and propped himself up on his elbows, looking around to find the source of this *siren's call.* It wasn't difficult to locate because just down the beach, something like a luxurious campsite was being setup; a camp with no tent, a carpet of colorful beach towels on which sat two folding beach chairs with arms and cushions and an overhead canapé to screen the sun. Two large coolers for food and drinks, not the colored Styrofoam kind you'd find down at the public beach but substantial metal cabinets that required two servants to carry, sat nearby. And above all of this regal set-up, three colorful triangular flags flapped in the wind as if to declare this spot as somebody's sandy domain. Lee blinked hard and looked out at the surf where Danny still clumsily jumped the waves, whooping and hollering with delight. Then he looked to his left again and like a mirage, the girl who belonged to that voice had appeared, lying on her stomach in a white bathing suit, surrounded by all of that beach paraphernalia. She was smoking a cigarette and looking right back at him, her head cocked to one side, grinning lightly and her one-piece bathing suit rolled down to her waist. She was fair skinned with a mild tan on her back and in one decisive motion she stood up and was bare-breasted for a moment before pulling her bathing suit up. The sight of her pale breasts made Lee feel guilty, like some kind of peeping Tom who caught a movie star naked in her trailer. Thinking she must be going down to the water to swim, he was caught off-guard when he realized she was walking straight toward him, canvassing the beach that separated them with long strides, almost comically long, and now she was broadly smiling. *Nothing shy about her,* thought Lee, sitting up on his towel just as she reached him, almost afraid she was about to confront him for staring at her.

"Hi," she said. "You're the singer at the Talkhouse?"

"Yeah, I am. Why? You were there?"

"I knew it was you!" she exclaimed. "You were singing "Honky Tonk Women" or something ..."

"Probably not, I don't really do many Stones songs when I'm solo."

"Well if you don't you *should* because everybody loves the Stones. That Mick Jagger really knows how to turn a girl on let me tell you. In fact, I met him out at a party in Montauk, my friend James

Elliot introduced us and I'm standing there and he's talking to me about Texas or something and I'm saying to myself, Lexi, *girl,* you are talking to *Mick Jagger,* can you believe it?"

"So what did he say to you?" asked Lee.

"Well, he did ask me to come upstairs and, well, you know that *word* ... have sex with him, and when I asked him why he just said *because he's Mick Jagger*. Can you believe that? But you know, I was thinking, what other reason could there be?"

"What do you mean?"

"I mean, in a way he was kinda right."

Not knowing how to respond, Lee smiled and Lexi laughed.

"Don't you want to know what I said to him?"

"Yeah, sure."

"Well ... maybe someday, sugar."

"You told him *maybe someday* you'd go upstairs and have sex with him?"

"No! I'm telling *you* that maybe someday I'll tell you what I said."

"Uh ... OK, I get it." Lee looked down.

Lexi laughed. "You're embarrassed! I always say whatever's on my mind – you just gotta get used to it."

"I guess that's a good quality."

"Too late to change now. What's your name, sugar?

"Lee, Lee Franklin."

"Well, Mister Franklin, rule number two is I don't drink alone."

"What's rule number one?"

"Ask Mick Jagger!" She smiled a perfect, well-practiced, successful smile; a smile that gets what it wants on a face with no defects save slight dimples on her cheeks.

"Don't kiss on the first date kind of thing?"

Lexi continued to smile. "Why don't you boys come over and join me for a glass of wine?"

"Well, my friend's swimming," said Lee, feeling stupid as soon as the words left his mouth.

She laughed and opened her eyes wide. "Well, I suppose he'll have to come out of the water *sometime*," she said. "We'll save him a drink."

"Yeah, of course, that'd be great." Lee stood up and she immediately extended her hand to him.

"Lexi Langdon." She smiled.

He held her hand, her skin warm and soft and there was something erotic just holding it in his own. He was thinking about her breasts which he had briefly seen just moments ago, that image still lingering in his mind.

"Y'all follow me, sugar," she said with authority. *Her voice sounds just like Texas*, he thought.

Lee walked a few paces behind her, watching her long legs stride across the sand as her hips swayed to a song of their own. She turned around suddenly and looked straight at him.

"You're looking at me," she said, pursing her lips.

"How do you know?"

"I just know," and she kept walking.

As they walked to her beach enclave, the more clearly he could see her, the more perfect she looked to him and the more nervous he became. She was slightly younger than he, early twenties, with lots of sunset red hair piled on top of her head and a body that seemed almost too perfect. He had no clue about her eyes yet because they were hidden behind big, round Jackie O sunglasses.

"Never saw those before," said Lee.

"Never saw what?" said Lexi.

"Those flags over there ... I guess you'd call them that, flags. From some country?"

Lexi twisted her head around to see the triangular colored flags draped on their bamboo poles. "From Hammacher Schlemmer, silly," she said. "What country are you from?"

"What?" said Lee.

She removed her sunglasses and stared at him. Her eyes were light green, coral green, and they drew him even closer to her with a captivating, sensual pull. Gently taking him by the arms, she twisted him around, so he was again facing the flags, and she stood on her tiptoes while whispering in his ear as her breasts pressed into his back. It felt so good, so intimate and forbidden, that he was afraid to move, afraid that she would back away from him if he did. So not knowing how to react, he stood there motionless.

"Those flags are from Hammacher Schlemmer," she repeated with her southern drawl. "Not from a country but from a store on 57th Street that sells ... *leisure items.*" She made *leisure* sound like some deliciously licentious way to pass the afternoon.

"Leisure?" he asked.

"You know, beach furniture, towels, coolers ... uh ..." she counted off the items on her fingers. "... Badminton sets, croquet sets, outdoor barbecue grills ... whatever you might need for ... *leisure*, I suppose." She softly pressed her finger to his reddening back. "And suntan lotion – ouch! Which you could really use some of, sugar. Come over here and lie down."

Lee did as he was told and lay down on one of her plush towels, which made the towels he and Danny carried feel like old wash-cloths. She kneeled over him and began to rub suntan lotion on his back.

"When was the last time you went to the beach, sugar?"

"I don't remember, never maybe. I'm more of a night owl than a ... seagull," he joked while concentrating on the circular motion of her hands on his back and shoulders and feeling her warm breath on his neck as she leaned down close.

"There you go, sugar," she said, hopping off. They both stood up although he didn't want to. "Don't move." She rubbed in a stray drop of suntan oil on his shoulder. "You're safe for a while." For his part, Lee could have stayed like that for a very long time with her hands on him and her breath so heady and sweet. Slowly, he turned and faced her. They were nearly the same height, neither tall nor short and her lips were full and he wondered how it would feel to kiss her.

"Thanks," was all he could say. "I uh ..."

Breaking the silence, Lexi said, "Listen ... Lee, before we continue our investigation of leisure flags, can I get you a drink?"

She deftly pulled a chilled bottle of Sancerre from one of the coolers and handed it to him along with a metal corkscrew before grabbing two glasses.

"Can you pour the wine ... Lee?"

"I think I can handle it ... Lexi."

Lee drew out the cork smoothly and poured the wine into the crystal wine goblets. Lexi clinked her glass on his.

"I think we're gonna be good friends, Lee," said Lexi.

"I hope so," said Lee, as they sipped their wine standing up, both moving their bare toes in the sand. Lexi instinctively led the flow of conversation and would ask Lee questions without waiting for the answers. How long had he been singing? Had he played the Talkhouse before? What music did he like?

"You should make a *demo* – isn't that what it's called? My husband is in the music business," said Lexi.

That word *husband* popped Lee's balloon, cutting short his reverie and he just nodded his head, which was almost all he could do, with her voice like a drug that he couldn't get enough of. He tried to concentrate on her eyes and mouth and then when he thought she wouldn't notice he stared down at her breasts and the point where her two legs met, a space where light shone through, like pure energy, like something sacred. And the only thing that spoiled it was the realization that there *was* a husband who had been there already. Then he noticed someone walking down over the dunes, a man in a white terrycloth robe, very dark tan, jet black hair slicked back on his head and a thin mustache like a silent film leading man. He was not smiling.

"Speaking of the devil," said Lexi. "That's Ray. He's my husband, my *current* husband," she said, smirking. "Although Ray rarely appreciates my sense of humor."

Ray Arthur trotted over to them in some quasi-athletic kind of way and gave Lexi an awkward kiss on the cheek. She did not kiss him back.

"How you doing, baby?" he said.

"So you decided to join me?"

"Just had to make a few business calls and ..."

"Spare me the details of your stressful morning, Ray," interrupted Lexi. "And say hello to my new friend Lee Franklin."

Ray glared at Lee. "I know you ... didn't I see you playing at the Talkhouse last night?"

"Yeah, I guess that was me. How you doing?" They shook hands.

"So you're staying out here in Amagansett?" asked Ray.

"Yeah," said Lee. "For a while."

"When did you get out?" asked Ray.

"When you going back?" said Lee laughing. "That's what everybody says out here."

"Yeah, funny," said Ray, not laughing. "Out here on your own?" he asked. "No girlfriend tagging along?"

"Jesus, Ray, you don't have to interrogate everybody I meet," said Lexi annoyed.

"That's still alright," said Lee. "No, no girlfriend, just my friend." Lee pointed awkwardly to the surf where Danny still swam. "And I was sitting over there and saw the flags and wondered ..."

"Say, Ray," interjected Lexi. "You're in the music business. Why don't you see how you can help Lee get a break while I get wet? I think he needs a demo or something."

Ray said nothing as Lexi ran off and Lee tried not to watch her perfectly round buttocks that almost seemed to smile back at you as she jogged away. Both men's eyes followed her as she ran to the water's edge and dove in the ocean right under the same wave Danny was jumping over. Once Lexi disappeared in the water, neither Ray nor Lee knew what to say to each other.

"Guess we should sit down, have a drink," said Ray awkwardly. They plopped into adjoining beach chairs, sitting closer to each other than either would have liked. "So, what was it you were wondering?"

"About?"

"About the flags?"

"Oh ... I forget, anyway, Lexi explained it."

"I'm sure she did," said Ray.

"Your wife said you're in the music business?" asked Lee.

"Senior Vice-President of A&R at Wes Records," said Ray. The Vice-President part was true enough although *Senior* was Ray's own invention. "And I have other interests in the city as well."

Lee smiled. "You must be a busy guy."

"You have no idea," said Ray. "But that's what it's all about. Takes a lot of irons in the fire and knowing the right people to make something pop."

"I bet," said Lee.

"And timing's everything," Ray added for no apparent reason. "Creating *synergy* is what I really do."

"Creating synergy with the right people at the right time," said Lee. "I get it."

Ray started laughing. "I am the right people so it's always the right time if I'm involved in something."

"Well, in that case, I'm very glad to meet you, Ray," said Lee, laughing along although not sure why.

Then Ray stopped laughing abruptly. "You should be," he said. "You'd be amazed how many artists want to talk to me, but I don't have time to help them."

The two of them stared far out into the ocean and couldn't help but notice what a riotously good time Danny and Lexi appeared to be having in the surf, Lexi screaming a loud Texas *Ye Ha* as she jumped wave after wave.

"They seem to be enjoying themselves out there," said Lee finally. "Perfect day for it."

Ray nodded slowly and said nothing. *He's getting jealous of Lexi bouncing around in the surf with Danny*, thought Lee. *And I am too ...*

"Lexi makes friends easily," said Ray. "Too easily sometimes."

"Oh that's just my friend Danny, kind of my manager too. He's a good guy."

"You know, a lot of women in her position would be more guarded," said Ray.

"What do you mean?"

Ray turned from the ocean and faced Lee.

"Listen, Lee Franklin, if you or your friend have any ideas about scoring with my wife you can forget it."

Lee was speechless.

Then Ray smiled widely with his awfully white teeth. "I'm just kidding you, man. It's a joke. She's beautiful, right?" He shrugged his shoulders. "Come on, let's be honest with each other. We're all in the music business, right?"

"Yeah, she's a beautiful woman all right," said Lee, still put off.

"Lexi's not only beautiful but she's from a very important family down in Texas, you know, very *tough and rich* Texans in fact. But the old man's gone now and it's all hers, the whole *enchilada*. Funny thing is, I couldn't care less about her money, but she depends on me for everything."

"Texas oil, huh?"

"That's what everybody usually thinks when you're rich and from Texas, but Lexi's father manufactured garbage trucks. Man, you would not believe how much money there is in garbage."

"More than the music business?" asked Lee.

"A lot more ... but don't get the wrong idea, I got my own thing. In fact, I'm into all areas of the entertainment field," said Ray defensively.

"What do you mean?"

"What do you mean *what do I mean*?"

"I mean what areas of the entertainment field are you into if you don't mind me asking. Besides the music business, that is."

"Well, for one thing, I recently acquired a big piece of one of the hottest clubs in New York City, just barely opened and it's already packed every night. How's that for the entertainment field?" Ray laughed aggressively. "Tell me something, Lee, have you put any records out? Ever been signed to a label?"

"No, not yet."

"And you're still at it. That's admirable."

"Admirable? What's that supposed to mean?"

"I'm just saying the music business is a young man's game – and it's tough. Believe me, I know, it takes a lot of dedication."

"Probably does," said Lee. "Guess I never thought of it as a game. I just like playing music and people seem to like it when I sing. I mean, nobody's thrown anything at me yet." He laughed. "I suppose that's admirable or something."

"Hope you didn't take offense," said Ray.

"Don't worry about it," said Lee, already thinking that Ray was definitely beginning to fit into the asshole category.

"What's going on out there?" asked Ray, suddenly standing. Lee stood up as well. Ray was the taller man but with a sunken chest and thin arms. He consciously held in his stomach and flexed his biceps, attempting to make himself look stronger than he was, but Lee was younger and better looking. Ray reminded himself that Lee was just another musician and he was a record company executive and musicians kissed his ass. *This guy has got nothing on me,* thought Ray. *I should relax.* But he couldn't.

Lexi and Danny came running back from the ocean, dripping wet and laughing uproariously about something, which they didn't share with Ray and Lee when they arrived. Lexi grabbed two towels from a large wicker basket and threw one to Danny.

Ray put on his best fake smile. "What was that all about?" he asked Lexi.

"Oh ... do you remember *Flipper?"* asked Lexi and then without waiting for Ray to reply she turned to Lee. "Your friend Danny here is hilarious."

Lexi vigorously dried her hair, threw the towel right onto the sand and sat down on her padded beach chair, lighting a *Kool* with a silver lighter and taking her time blowing out the smoke. "Danny is in the music business too," she said to Ray. "In fact, he's Lee's manager."

"Danny O'Connor. Nice to meet you ... Ray."

"O'Connor and Franklin," said Ray. "Sounds like a law firm."

Danny looked at Lee and they both broke up. "I doubt that's in the cards," he said.

"Listen, you guys, whatever you are, you must come to my party tonight." Lexi suddenly blurted out. "We're celebrating General Lee's pardon."

"Robert E. Lee?" asked Danny. "The Confederate General?"

"Believe it or not, Gerald Ford actually pardoned General Robert E. Lee just last month and we're all thrilled about it. It was a long time coming."

"You mean President Ford pardoned Lee and told us New Yorkers to *Drop Dead*," said Danny. "I read that in the papers today."

"Lexi means all the southern rebels like her are thrilled about it," said Ray. "I don't think they'll be celebrating up in Harlem." He laughed all by himself, the way it often was with Ray's jokes.

"I'm always up for a party, no matter what the occasion," said Danny, his eyes beaming at Lee. "What's the address?" He looked up toward the dunes behind them. "Is that your house right up there with all the chimneys? What street is that?" he asked.

"It's called Further Lane," said Lexi. "Just drive up Further Lane and look for my house. You can't miss it because it will be covered with party lights. Just pull into the driveway, simple as pie."

"Do we need to bring anything?"

"Aren't you sweet," Lexi said to Danny. "You guys just bring yourselves."

"Well, I guess we better start getting ready, putting this extravaganza together," said Ray, itchy to leave the beach.

"You need a hand bringing all this stuff back to the house?" asked Danny. He surveyed the towels, blankets, umbrellas, coolers and flags on bamboo poles littering the beach around them.

"Not necessary, darling," said Lexi. "We got people to do that for us." She giggled. "So I'll be seeing you boys at the party?" She looked directly at Lee.

"We'll be there," he said. "You can count on it."

"I knew I could," said Lexi and she stood up. "*Au revoir.*" She sashayed up to the wooden stairs that climbed over the Dunes that led back to her house on Further Lane. Ray merely nodded goodbye to Lee and Danny, saying nothing and following close behind her.

Strangely, Lee found himself watching Ray more than Lexi as they walked away. *How does a creep like him get a girl like that?* he wondered. Must be something about these rich people he didn't understand. While Danny turned back to face the ocean, Lee kept his eyes on Lexi and Ray and then just before they were about to disappear over the dunes, Lexi turned her head and looked right back at him with just the slightest perfect smile, raised her eyebrows and gave a little wave. And then she was gone and to Lee, the beach turned desolate. Lee and Danny walked back to their towels, looking at each other, hesitant to sit back down.

"Do you believe she brought all of that crap down to the beach and stayed, what ... half an hour or something?" asked Danny.

"I guess she can do what she wants," said Lee.

"So what about us?" asked Danny. "You want to stay longer? Go in the water?"

"What for?" said Lee, thinking, *that's the best thing that's gonna happen to me on this beach today.* "I've had enough beach for today."

"Me too," said Danny, touching his sun burnt shoulders. "Hey, we got invited to her party. Do you believe that?"

"What'd you think of Ray?"

"I don't know ... seems like a powerful guy, we should get to know him"

"Maybe," said Lee, tempted to say something about Ray but deciding not to. "We should get to know both of them."

By now it was late afternoon and as Lee and Danny walked across Indian Wells Beach on their way back to the Talkhouse most of the families and teenage kids had already packed up their blankets and umbrellas, kicked the sand out of their shoes and driven home. A small group of young mothers were already preparing a cookout for that evening and large pots of boiling water sat bubbling on charcoal fires waiting for shucked corn-on-the-cob. The ice-cream truck, now almost alone in the parking lot, was making a final sale of a Good Humor Toasted Almond Bar. The ocean had calmed, and no life-guards remained on duty as the sun began its long descent to the west. And Lee Franklin noticed none of this at all because his mind was concentrated on one vision: Lexi Langdon waving to him as she walked away. Danny talked non-stop the whole way up Indians Wells Road, but Lee was barely listening. He'd never met a girl like that before, and as much as he kept trying to remember something about her that he didn't like, he just couldn't.

CHAPTER 5

Ray was the kind of guy who took a shower in five minutes, combed back his hair and without thinking, knew exactly what he would wear. He had city clothes and country clothes, always bought the same black socks with yellow stitching at the toes at Bloomingdale's and had been using too much of the same cologne, Dior's Sauvage, ever since he read somewhere that that was what Steve McQueen wore. Organization was Ray's strong point even if he lacked flair or originality; he knew a good idea when he heard it and was always ready to adapt it as his own. Tonight's party was not a formal affair, no need for his custom-made Brooks Brothers tuxedo; no, he'd slip into a dry-cleaned pair of chinos, tasseled loafers, and a starched dress shirt with contrasting white cuffs and collar. When he peeked into the bedroom, Lexi was still in her bathrobe sitting at her mirrored vanity table.

"Should I wear a jacket?" asked Ray.

"I suppose," said Lexi. "I'm wearing a cute little Pucci dress ..." She got up and began rummaging through her large walk-in closet. "If I can find the damn thing, that is."

Ray walked over and pushed aside a few dozen hangers.

"Is that it?"

"How do you do that, Ray? Sometimes you amaze me."

"Sometimes I amaze myself," said Ray.

Certainly, one of those times Ray amazed himself was when he met Lexi Langdon for the very first time just five years before. He had been waiting to use the bathroom at a friend's party, actually more a friend of a friend. It was a party celebrating the Metropolitan Opera's new season. There would be a sanctified gala ball in the coming week which Ray would not be invited to because although he was a nobody that everybody seem to know, still, he was a nobody in the eyes of the connected New York gentry. That evening when he grabbed the handle of the bathroom door he could feel it was locked so he backed off quietly. The next thing he knew the handle dropped out of the door and landed on the floor at his feet.

"Shit!" Inside the bathroom a fine feminine voice extended that word to two syllables. "Shit!" she repeated.

Ray did not hesitate to speak softly through the door.

"Is there a problem?"

"Who's that?"

"Actually, my name is Ray, Ray Arthur, and I was standing here when a strange projectile dropped at my feet."

"The doorknob."

"Very likely."

"It fell out when I tried to unlock the door."

"Don't move," said Ray. "Help is on its way."

"Oh don't bring anybody here," pleaded the voice. "I'll be mortified."

"Mortified? Great word," said Ray. "Don't worry, this is between you and me, whoever you are." He quickly made his way to the kitchen, grabbed a slim steak knife and returned to the door, knocking softly before asking.

"Are you still there?"

"Nowhere else to go," said the voice.

"What's your name?" asked Ray.

There was a moment of hesitation. "Not saying, you'll tell everyone and make a fool out of me."

"Promise I won't."

Another pause. "Okay, my name is Lexi. But that's all I'm saying."

"Is the door unlocked now?"

"I think so, I'm holding the doorknob in my hand."

Ray got down to his knees and peered through the half-inch square where the doorknob once was. An older couple rounded the corner and looked at him suspiciously.

"Well, well ..." said the gray haired gentleman. "Party games?"

"Broken door handle," said Ray.

"Can I help?"

"Think it's a one man job," said Ray. "A lady's honor is at stake here." The couple laughed and left.

"I saved your reputation, Lexi."

"I bet you did," she replied softly. He stuck the knife in the mechanism and after a few tries managed to force open the door. When it swung open from the other side, he looked up from his knees and saw Lexi Langdon, absolutely gorgeous and laughing and her hair full of curls. His jaw fell open as he stared up at her; he wasn't expecting this and, rarely for Ray, was at a loss for words.

"Uh ... that dress is too short for this party."

"Maybe from down there," said Lexi. "If you're the kind of guy who gets down on his knees to look up a girl's dress." She laughed.

Ray stood up abruptly.

"And you better put down the knife," she said. "Looks pretty threatening. Especially when I'm standing in the toilet adjusting my skirt."

"Think I ruined the tip." Ray peered at the twisted end of the blade.

"Then you better come in. Anybody looking?"

Ray looked around, side to side. "Don't think so."

"Hope I can trust you," said Lexi, signaling him in.

"Trust me?" said Ray, shutting the door behind him. "I'm your knight in shining armor. What should I do with this knife?"

"Let's hide it someplace," she said, lifting the top of the toilet tank. "Here, I saw this once in a movie." Ray dropped the knife into the tank with a clunk.

"Guess we're accomplices now," he said. "I'm Ray Arthur."

"And I'm Lexi Langdon."

"And you're not from New York, are you?"

"How'd you tell?"

"Well, that accent to begin with, and those curls."

"You're talking about my hair?" Her fingers touched a soft coil resting on her shoulder. "I thought I might have overdone it a bit. Back home it's big night, big hair,"

"You don't need all of that," said Ray. "Where you from?"

"Texas," said Lexi. "Houston, Texas."

"Different world," said Ray. "Different set of rules, I suppose."

"I'm getting that," said Lexi. "None of the women at this damn party are talking to me. And I bet I gave more to that damn Opera than anyone."

"More what?" asked Ray.

"Money, silly!" said Lexi. "What else?"

Ray's eyes opened as wide as they got, like a crocodile woken up from a deep sleep.

"Take my arm, Lexi. I'm going to show you around. Introduce you to a few people."

She looked at him doubtfully.

"You'll see. It will be all right. Come on, I put the knife down." He laughed and she laughed with him.

"How do I know you're not wearing concealed weapons?"

"You don't," said Ray.

He walked Lexi through the party and did introduce her to people he knew and also to quite a few he didn't. The wine was flowing and soon everybody, men and women alike, were talking to her like she was their new best friend.

When they were getting their coats Lexi said to Ray, "This is the best party I've been to since I've moved here. Thanks for showing me around."

"Are you kidding?" said Ray. "With you on my arm? I should be thanking you. It did incredible things for my image."

"Can I give you a lift home?" asked Lexi.

"Share a taxi?" asked Ray.

"More like get in the back seat of my limousine," said Lexi.

"Sounds very good to me," said Ray.

They walked out onto the street to a double-parked line of limousines waiting to take people home from the party.

"Which one's yours?" asked Ray.

"The white one, over there." Lexi pointed to a stretch Lincoln that stood out from the crowd.

"Lesson number one," said Ray. "Only black limos."

"Oh ..." said Lexi.

The next week they went to lunch for burgers at PJ Clarke's on Third Avenue, Ray picked up the check.

"Next time, it's my treat," said Lexi. "Just tell me where you want to go."

"Ever been to La Cote Basque?" asked Ray.

"Sounds French," said Lexi.

"Very," said Ray.

Located on East 55th Street, La Cote Basque was the undeniable temple of high society lunches, fine French food and celebrity patrons, including Jacqueline Onassis, Frank Sinatra and most famously Babe Paley, wife of CBS owner Bill Paley and the titular head of New York society.

As Ray opened the door to the imposing restaurant Lexi nervously dropped behind.

"You go first," she said.

"Ah come on, there's nothing to be afraid of us. Just think of everybody in here naked."

Lexi, looking around the room full of middle-aged men with their young trophy wives or mistresses, along with a few tables of lunching dowager elderly ladies, made a face. "That's disgusting."

"It's just a way to not feel nervous. It's funny! Come on, you're going to love this place."

The imposing maître d' greeted them haughtily at the entrance.

"Oui Monsieur, do you have a reservation."

"Yes," said Ray. "Wes Edel ... of Edel Records."

The maître d' consulted a list of names in a large agenda.

"This way, Mr. Edel."

"But you're not ..." began Lexi.

Ray hushed her as they were led to the furthest table in the back of the dining room, close to the kitchen entrance, passing the well-dressed and elegant clientele who called La Cote Basque home at lunchtime.

"Take a look around you. Isn't this place amazing? You see those flowers? They say they spend a few grand every week just on the florist."

"And those murals painted on the wall?" asked Lexi. "Where is that supposed to be?"

"It's the Basque coast, like the name of the place."

"Where's that?"

"Southwestern France, to be exact. Didn't you tell me you went to school in Europe?"

"Switzerland," said Lexi. "On a lake."

"Guess they didn't let you girls out for much exploring."

"We went in as virgins and we were supposed to go out the same way not that any of us ..."

"Wait a minute, look who's here," interrupted Ray.

At a front corner table none other than Bill Paley, President of CBS Inc., a vast media conglomerate, which owned television and radio stations in addition to Columbia Records, was sitting with his wife, renowned socialite Babe Paley. To the surprised gaze of the stiff maître d', Ray marched right over with Lexi demurely trailing behind him. He halted at the edge of the Paley's table and Bill Paley looked up at him with a large shrimp, covered with red cocktail sauce, still speared on his fork. He was not a man used to being disturbed at lunch, especially in *La Cote Basque.*

"Mr. Paley, you probably don't remember me but we met last year."

Paley said nothing and was definitely not smiling.

"At the Grammy Awards."

Again, no response from Bill Paley, and his wife Babe was twisting her head, searching for the maître d'.

"I'm Ray Arthur, Vice President at Edel Records. I was with Wes that night. You two talked ..." Ray extended his hand.

Paley put down his fork slowly and looked to his wife apologetically. "Wes Edel, sure, yeah, I kind of remember that. How is Wes?" Reluctantly he shook Ray's hand.

"Getting along," said Ray. "I put a few of his albums in the *Billboard* top 100 this week so he's in a good mood."

"Bet he is," said Paley amused. "I offered him a top spot at CBS Records, could have been the head of the Epic label but he didn't take it, stupid move."

"He's old school," said Ray. "Likes to put the records in their sleeves himself."

"Say hello to Wes for me," said Paley, turning to his wife. "You'll excuse us ..."

Lexi was standing just behind Ray and he reached around and took her by the hand pulling her next to him.

"Uh...Mr. Paley, this is Lexi Langdon," said Ray. "Up from Texas a few months ago."

Neither Paley nor his wife said anything.

"Lexi Langdon of Langdon Industries," Ray blurted out.

"Oh, Ray," said Lexi. "Nobody cares about that."

Paley and his wife smiled widely.

"Darling," said Babe Paley. "So you're the one everyone is talking about. Apparently, without you there would be no Met season at all this year. We're all so very grateful for your support."

"Well, I like music, what can I say." Lexi blushed.

"I've taken Lexi under my wing," said Ray. "Protecting her from the riff raff here in the city." Everyone laughed.

"Great job," said Bill Paley. "I tried to do the same with Babe, but she ended up with me."

"You don't look so bad," said Lexi.

"Well, thank you, dear," said Bill Paley. His wife did not appear amused.

"Are you two ... together?" she asked Lexi pointedly. "Or are you unattached, shall we say?"

Lexi was fast to understand what she was being asked. Would she be a threat or a safe member of the club?

"Well, Ray is taking pretty good care of me."

"That's nice," said Babe Paley, now smiling.

Babe Paley was an ex-editor of *Vogue* magazine, who had risen to the top of New York's social scene with her husband Bill. Her style was impeccable and her position as the gatekeeper of New York society unquestioned. "Are you visiting us or going to settle down here, Lexi?"

"Well, I'm kind of settling in, if you know what I mean, I uh ..."

"Lexi bought the Aga Khan's old pied-à-terre on Fifth Avenue."

"All four floors?" asked Babe, astonished.

"Three of them," said Lexi. "The other was sold already."

Bill Paley looked at Ray. "Not bad."

"I'm sure you will only improve the property, my dear," said Babe Paley. "Karim's ... I mean, his Highness' taste was a bit too oriental for my taste."

"You know what Truman Capote said about my wife, Lexi?"

"I'm sure I don't," said Lexi. "But I'd love to find out."

"Truman said, and I'm quoting now, 'Babe Paley has only one fault, she's perfect.'"

"Well, I'm sure I can't disagree with that," Lexi replied.

"You're a darling," said Babe Paley, pulling a white *carte de visite* from her purse. "Give me a call, we'll have lunch, I'll introduce you to some of the girls, Gloria, CZ, Lee and her sister. You'll love them."

"Oh that would be fun," said Lexi. "Do you really eat lunch here every day? That's what Ray said ..." Ray tapped Lexi gently on the hip.

"Of course not, my dear. Who could eat at the same restaurant every day?" She looked at Bill Paley who shrugged his shoulders. "There's Caravelle and Grenouille and ... where else do we go, Bill?"

"Melon's for a burger, That's my favorite!"

"Don't let them hear you say that, here." Babe Paley laughed. "But that's where he's most happy, believe me."

"Then that's where we'll go," said Lexi, not hiding her enthusiasm. "My treat."

Babe and Bill Paley looked at each other, flabbergasted.

"She's adorable," said Babe.

"Sorry to disturb you," said Ray. "I knew Wes would want me to say hello."

"So charming to meet you both," said Bill Paley finally picking up his fork and putting that speared shrimp into his mouth.

As they were walking to their distant table, Ray whispered into Lexi's ear.

"That's CZ as in *Guest*, Gloria as in *Vanderbilt* and Lee as in *Radziwell* and her sister as in *Jackie Onassis*. That would be a nice club for you to be a member of."

"A real club?" asked Lexi. "What's the name of it?"

"Ladies who do lunch," said Ray. "And I got a feeling you're going to fit in just fine."

"I've heard of Jackie Onassis, in fact my daddy had her out on his boat one time, but the other ones – I don't have a clue."

"It's simple, if Babe Paley introduces you to someone, then they're important and rich."

"But I'm rich," said Lexi.

"And I'm going to make you important," said Ray assuredly. "Trust me. Christ, look who's sitting over there with his back to us!"

Lexi peered to see. "Looks like Johnny Carson."

"And his wife, Johanna."

"Don't tell me you know him too?"

"Not yet," said Ray.

It wasn't like Babe Paley became Lexi's best friend, but she did, almost out of a sense of duty, try to introduce her to the right people, set her on the right course, steer her clear of society's outlaws. It was almost as if she was grooming a younger replacement for herself on the New York society circuit. And when Babe Paley died of lung cancer, just a few years later, Lexi Langdon stood in mourning with Babe's best friends, CZ, Gloria, Lee, Jackie and her other most faithful lunching companions, shedding tears and kissing all her milieu in sympathy and shared grief. And no one questioned her right to be there, when she left in a black limousine.

CHAPTER 6

Back at the dressing room of the Talkhouse, Danny and Lee were pulling clothes out of their suitcases – a stream of jeans and T-shirts – and coming to the realization that trying to find something appropriate to wear to Lexi Langdon's party was proving to be a bit of a challenge. This was especially true for Danny, until club owner Tony Hughes walked in with a tall and icy gin and tonic in hand. "You boys want a cocktail?" he said. "Bar's open downstairs – help yourself."

Danny stared at Tony; they were nearly the same size, Tony looking dapper in a polo shirt, pressed jeans and a light wool blue blazer with gold buttons.

"Tell you what," said Danny, leering at Tony's fitted jacket.

"What?"

"I have a business proposition for you ..."

"I'm not sure if I like where this is going," said Tony.

"Forget about paying my client Lee Franklin for the shows this weekend and loan me your blue blazer for tonight."

"Hey, don't I have something to say about this?" said Lee.

"If Lee starts pulling in a crowd I'll pay him anyway," said Tony. "I'm not a crook." He held up both hands in V for victory signs, imitating Richard Nixon. "But what do you need my freakin' blazer for?"

"We're going to Lexi Langdon's party," said Lee Franklin.

"You're kidding me?" Tony raised his significant eyebrows and gave a long and low whistle. "You know there's two kinds of rich out here," he said. "There's *money* and then there's *real money*. And Lexi Langdon is *real money*. Her old man manufactures jet planes."

"I think it's more like garbage trucks," corrected Lee. "At least that's what her husband Ray told me. We met them on the beach today and we're invited to this, uh, soirée tonight and I suppose Danny's got to look presentable. I mean, he can't wear that," he said pointing.

Tony looked at the Hawaiian print shirt dangling on Danny's slim shoulders and nodded his head in agreement while reluctantly handing over his just dry-cleaned blazer. "It's for a good cause, I suppose. Do they know you're playing at the Talkhouse?"

Danny and Lee looked at each other.

"Yeah," said Lee. "Lexi said they were here last night and heard me sing but I didn't see them, probably came in for a quick drink and left. I would have remembered someone like that ..."

"Didn't she say something about booking a party here? Bringing all her rich friends, drinking champagne while you're singing?" Danny looked at Lee for some kind of corroboration before adding, "Of course, I said I'd have to talk to you about it, Tony. Isn't that right, Lee?"

"Anything you say," said Lee unconvincingly.

"You're both full of shit," said Tony. "But if I let you go there tonight looking like the Don Ho of Dublin, you not only give the Talkhouse a bad name but you're gonna embarrass the whole Irish race." Grimacing, he watched Danny try on the jacket. "Well...maybe not the same touch of class as when I wear it but got to admit, not bad. Tell you what, guys, I'm running out myself so I can give you a ride if you want."

"What are *you* gonna wear, Lee?" asked Danny.

"The usual, I guess, my cleanest Levi's and that pressed denim shirt hanging in the closet I was saving for the weekend. Could throw on my leather vest and shine up my cowboy boots ... but I don't have any polish. Kind of going for that Kris Kristofferson look without the beard."

"You think that's dressy enough?" asked Danny.

"Lee's not the problem," said Tony. "He's an artist and artists can wear whatever the hell they want, but you're going for another kind of image, I think, or I hope at least."

"What image?" asked Danny defensively.

"Uh ... how about rock impresario ... next generation ... the new Brian Epstein." said Tony.

"I like that," said Danny brightly.

"Thought you would," said Tony. "Except Brian Epstein was gay."

"What?" said Danny.

"Let's get going."

Tony's burgundy Cadillac convertible was parked in its usual oil-soaked spot in the driveway next to the Talkhouse, in less than mint condition, and, as on most days, with the top down, folded in the well and spotted with mildew.

Jumping in the roomy back seat, Lee said, "Nice set of wheels. What year is it?"

"You don't want to know," said Tony as he stuck the key in the ignition, the exhausted engine turning over a few times before catching, starting up and puffing out a thick burst of gray smoke through the exhaust pipe.

"Sounds more like a boat than a car," said Danny.

"Easy!" said Tony. "It's better than walking, so let's show a little respect, especially when you're wearing my jacket, eh?"

Tony threw the Cadillac into reverse and quickly backed out of the driveway without even looking. He swung the rear of the car onto Main Street, hit the brakes hard, knocked the shift into drive and went roaring off, just barely avoiding the oncoming traffic serenading him with annoyed honking.

"A lot better than walking," said Lee from the backseat, the wind rushing through his hair. "If you don't get killed."

"A fast getaway is a very useful maneuver when you're a lady's man like me," said Tony half serious, as he raced the yellow light and took a sharp left turn onto Indian Wells Road and then an equally hard right turn onto Further Lane. Tony knew Lexi's house on Further Lane, said everybody knew it, as he pointed out the four chimney stacks each circled with red party lights. They were there in minutes.

"That didn't take long," said Danny.

"Why'd you think I offered you a ride?" said Tony before he dropped them off at the head of the driveway. "Listen, boys, can I give you some advice?"

Danny and Lee looked at each other.

"Sure, why not," said Danny.

"I've been out here a long time and I'm telling you, if you're going to a party at Lexi Langdon's house then you're gonna be in with the A-list, if you know what I mean. And believe me, these are the people you want to get to know. Just watch yourself while you're trying to keep up."

"I can keep up with anybody," said Danny defiantly.

"I'm sure you can, old sport. Well, then let me give you another tip, even more important," said Tony. "Don't spill any shit on my jacket!"

Tony sped off in his massive Eldorado, his broken muffler sounding more like a tank than a yacht as Lee and Danny walked up the long twisting driveway until they stood among the Mercedes and BMWs parked on her lawn.

"You think Ray put those lights up there on the chimneys?" said Danny.

"Right," said Lee. "Ray doesn't look like a guy who does a lot of manual labor to me."

At that moment, a cream colored vintage Mercedes 280SE purred onto the grass just next to them, top town and all windows rolled up to keep out the wind. A matching leather boot, soft and supple as a pillow covered the convertible top, and a handsome black man got out of the driver's seat and graciously held his door open to let three girls, each as beautiful and slender as the next, effortlessly glide out of the car with the aid of his extended hand. You could smell the walnut dashboard and rich leather interior. Each girl kissed him once on each cheek as they passed and he, tall with glistening oiled hair and a white linen suit, ceremoniously kissed each one back. Danny noticed a chunky gold Rolex hanging on his wrist.

"You go powder your noses, girls, and I'll join you momentarily," he said in a deep soulful voice before walking the few steps to where Danny and Lee stood in envious awe. Smiling, he offered Danny the keys to the Mercedes. "Try to keep it handy, I might be cutting out early if I get lucky." He winked at him.

"Is this some kind of present?" said Danny amused. "At least I hope the girls come with the car."

"Ah...you're not parking cars, are you? Sorry, guys. Stupid of me." He took back his keys from Danny's palm.

"We're friends of Lexi," said Lee.

"Of course, you are," he said, extending his hand. "James Elliot."

"Lee Franklin, nice to meet you, James."

"James *Elliot*," he corrected. "Can't have the one without the other."

"Yes...James Elliot."

"Me, too," said Danny. "Nice to meet you ... James Elliot."

"Marvelous," said James. "And you are?"

"Danny O'Connor."

"Lee Franklin."

"Oh, a couple of Jewish guys," he said teasing. "If you know Lexi then I suppose you know Ray as well?"

"Ray and I are in the same business," said Danny. "The music business. Just met him today."

James Elliot took his time walking toward the radiant house fifty yards in front of them, stopping to emphasize various points about the house and Lexi and Ray, prepping Lee and Danny on who they might meet at the party.

"Wes Edel will probably be here tonight," he said. "That's who you want to get to know. He's a real power in your world."

"Wes Records," said Danny. "Of course, I've heard of him."

"Dear friend of mine. You smoke?" asked James Elliot. "Anyone got a cigarette? Left mine in the car."

"Sure," said Danny as he took out a soft pack of Winston cigarettes and flipped one to James Elliot.

"You can't miss Wes," said James Elliot. "I've know him for ten years and he invariably dresses in the same signature outfit: white shirt, white tie, black suit, French cuffs."

"Sounds like a classy guy," said Danny.

"But never cufflinks in the cuffs," added James Elliot.

"I bet people remember that most of all," said Lee.

"That's the point," said James Elliot. "Got a light?"

"I come prepared," said Danny, handing him a pack of Talkhouse matches. James Elliot lit up his cigarette and held the matches in his hand.

"All depends what you mean. Did you see those three young ladies who got out of my car?"

"You mean there were young ladies attached to those legs?" asked Danny.

"Models?" asked Lee.

"All three," said James Elliott. "That's what I mean by prepared." After he handed the matches back to Danny, the three men walked toward the party; the lights grew brighter and the laughter and conversation of the crowd inside louder.

Clearly, James Elliot knew his way around the house, opening the front door without knocking and walking straight through the large foyer. To their right was a large living room, packed with people and the animated ambiance of the evening. James Elliot waved and kissed nearly everyone he passed and Danny and Lee followed him like two dogs led by their master, their eyes widening as the party in full swing enveloped them, full of beautiful people and they, an unlikely pair in the center. Three large overstuffed sofas faced a giant fireplace and couples were sprawled all over them, holding drinks, deep in lively conversation:

It's a new show ... crazy young actors from all over ... still working on the first few sketches ... yeah ... Saturday Night Live *... October ... they're gonna be the new sensations of late night television ... that's what I'm hearing, too.*

"I'll catch up with you later, *Messieurs* Franklin and O'Connor," said James Elliot, waving his fingers and saying *ta ta,* as he disappeared into the depths of the house. "Be cool," his parting words.

But Lee and Danny were anything but cool, feeling so out of place that they could barely look at each other; both with the sudden realization that they were now on their own, set adrift in this strange sea by their newfound *guide and mentor* James Elliot. They floated among the waves of partygoers with the impression that each and every one here seemed to be more at ease than they were, although, of course, they'd never admit it, not to each other nor anyone else. Mechanically strolling around, they soon found themselves standing at the entry to a spacious, sumptuous wood paneled den. The French mahogany double doors were slid wide open and they recognized Ray standing inside, dressed now in a tan suit and talking with a unimpressive short and bald older man in Gucci loafers, no socks, black suit, white shirt and tie and, just as James Elliot had described him only minutes before, French cuffs *sans* cufflinks. Leaning on Wes Edel's shoulder was a very *impressive* tall, blond and beautiful woman, dressed in raspberry capri pants, balancing on stiletto heels with a silk blouse straining hard at the buttons holding in her formidable breasts. Wes Edel was talking animatedly about politics and war, and each time he looked away, Ray furtively peeked down her décolleté. Alana, Wes' young girlfriend, didn't seem to mind.

"Three months later and I still can't get over it – U.S. Army helicopters lifting Americans off the freakin' Saigon embassy roof. Never *shoulda* happened."

"You're right, Wes, it never should have happened," repeated Ray.

"In my opinion, that's when this country started going to hell ..."

Just seeing Ray, a face they recognized, brought the glimmer of a smile to their faces. When Ray noticed them standing in the entrance and beaming at him he couldn't decide if he should just ignore them or invite them over. But he was bored with Wes Edel's pontificating about the Vietnam War, couldn't even hold his own in that conversation, and so he waved over Lee and Danny. "Hey, guys, come on over!"

"Who's that?" asked Wes suspiciously. "Should I know them?

"A couple of guys I met at the beach today," said Ray. "Not heavyweights but the one guy's not a bad singer."

"Oh shit, not musicians," said Wes.

"Don't worry, they're not gonna ask you for a deal tonight," said Ray just before Danny and Lee joined them. "Wes, this is Lee Franklin who's performing at the Talkhouse and this is his manager ... uh."

"Danny O'Connor," said Danny, shaking hands vigorously with Wes.

"This is Alana," said Wes. "My ... assistant." Alana smiled and looked away.

"Lexi and I caught some of Lee's set last night," said Ray. "Nice voice – and then, what do you know, if we don't meet them on the beach today. They're trying to break into *our* business," he said with a laugh.

"Music business – worst business in the world," said Wes glumly. "I don't even know what music is anymore and I've been in this freakin' business all my life. Someone sent me a record of this new *punk* singer ... what was her name, Ray?"

"Smith," said Ray. "Something Smith."

"That's it. Anyway, I didn't understand it at all. And her publicist was calling her a punk, like that's a good thing. For me, *punk* is some kind of insult, isn't it? Imagine if I started calling any of my artists punks? They'd quit the label."

"The *punks* all play at this dump called CBGB," said Ray. "It's the new hot spot."

"Where is it?" asked Wes.

"The Bowery."

"You're fucking kidding me," said Wes. "The Bowery? Down on skid row with all the bums?"

"Don't ask me," said Ray. "But I heard Clive Davis was sniffing around down there, shopping for bands, and some other major labels too. I had some of my people check it out."

"Who are *your* people?" asked Wes. "Do they work for *my* company?"

"Well ... me actually," said Ray self-consciously. "I checked it out myself, went to see a couple of bands play."

"Can I say something, Uncle Wessy?" interrupted Alana.

"Sure, baby," said Wes. "Jump right in."

"Well, all I know is that all my friends in fashion are buying Doc Martens shoes in London and putting safety pins all over their clothes."

"Your fashion friends? More like fashion victims and drug addicts," said Wes. "Stay away from them."

"And they all hang out downtown at CBGB, so there!" She plopped a kiss right on Wes' bald crown. "I'm gonna go circulate, baby," she said. "But *please,* save my place in this discussion. It's *soooo* fascinating." She made a sick face, putting two fingers in her mouth and walked away.

At once, Danny started peppering Wes Edel with arduous questions about the music business, recording contracts, publishing deals and agents – anything he could think of. And he just kept pushing, oblivious to the obvious fact that Wes' patronizing monosyllabic response was clear enough evidence that he was not in the least bit interested in enlightening Danny on the ins and outs of his own industry. Ray jumped on the bandwagon, even more condescending than Wes, but even this didn't stop Danny, who seemed oblivious to their sarcasm and mockery as he just kept pumping Wes and Ray for information and names.

"... I'm just saying that because I read this book all about record deals called *This Business of Music* written by this really famous entertainment lawyer. Ever heard of it?" he asked them enthusiastically. "I tell you; I really learned a lot just from reading that book."

Ray and Wes didn't bother to hide their amusement.

"Do I know the book?" said Wes. "Are you kidding me? The guy who wrote that book was my lawyer, *is* my lawyer and still some moron is always trying to sue me. Lawyers," he said disparagingly. "Now that's the real problem. If I was you I'd stay away from them, kid."

"Or become one," added Ray. "Maybe think about a different career. It's not too late." He laughed with Wes.

Lee could tell that Danny was embarrassed now and he didn't like that at all. Something in him, some primordial urge was pushing him to come to his friend's defense; a kind of solidarity that he knew well from back in Rome when a jail cell door had slammed shut and there sat another guy, his age, on the upper bunk who looked over and gave him a knowing shake of the head.

"I think he's got the right career," said Lee, looking at Danny. "He got me a gig this summer."

"You got him the gig?" asked Wes.

"Got him the gig and a place to stay and now we're at this party talking to big-shots like you," said Danny genially. "I must be doing something right."

Wes Edel was moved by Danny's moxie and shrugged his shoulders. "True enough. What'd you say your name was again?"

"Danny O'Connor."

"Okay, Danny, here's the best advice I can give you – don't listen to anything anyone says to you, kid. Find your own way."

"Speaking of which, I'm going to cruise the party, get something to eat," said Lee, eager to get away.

"Start with the shrimp," said Wes. "Fucking delicious."

Lee excused himself and walked out onto the large deck patio, which bordered the well-lit kidney-shaped swimming pool, surrounded by blossoming gardens and manicured trees, all dressed in an array of glistening golden lights. Flaming torches surrounded the pool and winding footpaths headed out over the dunes and to the nearby pool house, itself the size of a small cottage with white shingles and green shutters, matching the main house. A tall young waiter strolled about the crowd, serving effervescent champagne in Baccarat flutes, crowded together on a shoulder high tray as a good hundred or more *well-heeled* revelers partook of an extravagant buffet laid out on a series of long rectangular tables. A chef in checkered pants, white double-breasted jacket and a *toque* on his head carved slices of filet mignon, honey-glazed baked ham and turkey while the next table offered a mountain of peeled jumbo shrimp on crushed ice, next to porcelain platters of smoked salmon and prosciutto. A smaller table, dedicated to caviar and *foie gras*, was presided over by another waiter who grilled accompanying toast. Finally, came the dessert spread where crystal bowls of chocolate mousse, silver trays of pastries in the shape of angels and an amazing three-tiered *Frasier,* topped with the reddest strawberries you could imagine sitting on the whitest whipped cream in existence, competed for cholesterol hierarchy. Everybody seemed to be tan, laughing and having the time of their life, standing around on that patio, next to the sparkling blue pool, plates, forks and glasses in hand. It was as if someone had choreographed this scene for a *Vanity Fair* shoot, the perfectly stylized rendition of what surely went on every summer night out in the Hamptons.

There was music coming from somewhere and Lee picked up on it as soon as the Rolling Stones' *Black and Blue* album came on. He pretended to be listening or *grooving* or concentrating on something important, but in his heart, he was lost and didn't know whom to talk to. Then like an auditory hallucination, he heard a sweet and tempting voice calling out his name, but unable to find its source he began swinging his head around searching until finally, at the far side of the pool he saw her, Lexi Langdon herself, looking like a Dallas Cowboys cheerleader, dressed in a handsome Stetson hat, cowboy boots and a short, very short, party dress.

"Hey, Lee, sugar!" She waved to him. "Get over here!" Lee smiled and waved back, weaving a path through the crowd and around the pool to reach her. At the sound of her voice, suddenly he felt transformed and his mood changed in the most sudden and remarkable way. It took all of his self-control not to trot. "I was just talking about you," said Lexi, taking his hand when he reached her. She began introducing Lee to the guests standing around her, but names and places came so fast and furious that Lee could hardly keep up. There was Lisa de Kooning, the beautiful daughter of the famous abstract expressionist standing with Carlos, a suave South American who couldn't stop dancing and had known Picasso and asked Lee if it was true that all musicians always carry some *marching powder*. There was a tall French restaurateur from Manhattan with a thick handlebar mustache and his equally tall and beautiful German model wife, and Peter Beard, a suave, handsome and legendary photographer who spent half the year in Africa and had been photographed up to his waist in the jaws of a giant crocodile. And super-model Alana Horst who Lexi squealed was her best friend and Lee knew already as Wes Edel's tall girlfriend. Lexi was raving about Lee to anyone within range of her inimitable voice, saying how he was playing at the Talkhouse and how great a singer he was and insisting they all come to see him perform. Of course, everyone nodded, smiled and said they would definitely be there next weekend, although Lee had his doubts. Still, he had no doubt that Lexi was making a big fuss over him.

Then in a flurry of conversation, Alana dragged Lexi away to meet someone and Lee, alone again, spotted one James Elliot, way over on the other side of the crowd offering a glass of champagne to a nice looking girl, young for this party, with short blond hair, miniskirt and sandals. They were standing alone at the edge of the sprawling terrace, which spread to the vast backyard surrounding the illuminated swimming pool behind the house. But James Elliot didn't stay with her long and soon came over to see Lee.

"Hey, *lucky*," said James Elliot. "Having fun?"

"You called me *lucky*?" asked Lee amused. "What's that about?"

"When I'm at a party I call all the men l*ucky* and all the beautiful women ... *sweetheart*," said James Elliot. "That way I don't have to remember names and worry about getting them wrong."

"That's a good one," said Lee. "Have to remember that. Hey, what happened with that blond over there? She was cute. Couldn't get anything going?"

"Listen, *lucky*, her name is Shirley and she's got a boyfriend – for the moment – and that boyfriend has gone to find the men's room. Now, of course, she has never modeled before and she is sure that she is too short, too fat, too old – too everything – to ever be a model. And maybe she's right. But I gave her my card and she *will* call me and then we *will* see what does or does not get going."

"And what if she doesn't call?"

"She *will* call," said James Elliott. "What beautiful girl doesn't want to be a model? Anyway, I'm just playing the odds."

"The odds?" asked Lee.

"Exactly, the *odds,* as explained to me by this guy I met when I moved here from Milwaukee about ten years ago. Called him lucky just like you. And he had more *pussy* than any man I ever met before or since."

"If you're good looking and rich, it's not so hard," said Lee.

James Elliot laughed. "Short, bald and worked in Bloomingdale's Cosmetics Department, so the only thing he had going for him was that he dealt with all kinds of women all day long. But he knew about the odds and he understood the power of perseverance; said every day he made a point to ask three beautiful women to have a drink with him after work. That's about a hundred a month. So, let's say ninety told him to forget it and nine had a drink with him and that was it. But that *one* who had that drink and then gave him her phone number, well, that was plenty for him. In fact, he told me it was almost more than he could handle."

"But, man, all that rejection from the other ninety-nine. How did he handle it?"

"He took it in stride."

Lexi had returned and was presiding over a large group now, holding court and seemingly oblivious to the rest of the party around her until, as if on cue, her group dispersed, and she walked straight over to Lee and James Elliot. She didn't wear a bra under her silky wraparound party dress, and her signature Diamonds by The Yard necklace, loops and loops of gold and diamonds, glistened on her *décolleté*. Lee must have been grinning like the Cheshire cat.

"What are you so happy about?" asked Lexi.

Of course, Lee didn't say it was the way he could see her nipples poking through her dress. "Just great to be here at your party, that's all."

"In the realm of Lexi Langdon," added James Elliot, "happiness is the prevailing mood." He smiled at Lee. "We're just enjoying the view."

"So, you fellows know each other?" asked Lexi. "The famous photographer James Elliot who, by the way, I wanted to tell you this, James," - she grabbed James by the hand - "Your last Vogue spread was just brilliant – I opened up that magazine and wanted to buy every piece of clothing you shot. You make it all look so irresistible."

"That's what they pay me for." He laughed. "It's a dirty job, Lexi, but somebody's got to do it."

'What? Shoot the models or buy the clothes?" asked Lee.

Lexi and James Elliot looked at each other, "Both," they said nearly in unison.

Lexi pointed out a few of the better-known personalities standing nearby. "Well, it looks like I've got the *crème* of the Hamptons here tonight – celebrity photographers, handsome singers." She looked at

Lee. "And a load of TV folks ..." She gazed around. "Oh my God! He's balancing one of my Baccarat champagne flutes on his head!"

Sure enough, there was a tall young man entertaining an enraptured crowd, balancing a full champagne glass on his head.

"Who is that guy?" asked Lee.

"His name, and I kid you not, is Chevy Chase and he's part of a crew of young actors and comedians putting together a new TV show, *Saturday Night Live.* Everybody's betting it's gonna be a huge success. And Chevy's got a friend...John something, who's even more outrageous than him and..." She stopped mid-sentence. Burt!" she exclaimed. "You made it."

Lee and James Elliot both turned to see a short *Young Turk* of Wall Street dressed in a sharp English cut chalk-striped suit that was better suited to a man twice his age.

"Lexi, how wonderful to see you here in all your power and glory!" responded his rather formal sounding deep voice.

"Gentlemen, let me introduce you to the man who I am confident is increasing my fortune while we stand here enjoying ourselves on this balmy evening. Burt Bateman – Lee Franklin and James Elliot."

Burt firmly shook hands and quickly and confidently dominated the conversation. In truth, he was very well spoken, interesting, funny, a born raconteur, and within minutes Lee knew most of his vital information: Ivy League graduate turned Wall Street whiz kid who referred to his boss, the head of a well-known investment bank, by his first name.

"So," Burt went on, "I told George that if he didn't think investing in a private company that would deliver packages more reliably than the U.S. Post Office, picking them up at your office and actually getting them to their destination on time is a good idea then I don't know what an investment banker is supposed to do. So, of course, he went for it and the stock has split twice already."

"What's the name of that company?" asked Lexi. "I should remember these things."

"Federal Express," said Burt. "Sounds like the Mexican Army -

Faster Federales!" he barked. "And you don't have to remember a thing, Lexi, because you already own a substantial amount of their preferred stock."

"Well, that's comforting, Burt. But you left out the most interesting aspect of your life, at least that I'm aware of anyway," said Lexi.

"What's that? My game of five-card stud or Texas hold 'em?"

"Both are very impressive," said Lexi. "But what I always remember about you is that you were born in Las Vegas and I never knew anybody that was actually born there."

"I thought that's where they conceived babies," said James Elliot. "Not where they were born."

"My father ran a casino," said Burt. "Still does in fact."

"How'd you end up in New York?" asked Lee.

"Got packed off to military school and then marched right into Princeton and soon enough I realized that you may see the cash on the gaming tables of Las Vegas, but the major money, a least in terms of real capital, is down on Wall Street. And I remembered what my father said is the golden rule of making money."

"What's that?" asked James Elliot. "Own the casino?"

"That helps, but what he said is if you want to make money you have to be where the money is."

"And I suppose that's why you're all at my party?" quipped Lexi and they all cracked up.

"Have things calmed down on Wall Street since that *Equity Funding of America* mess?" James Elliot asked Burt. "I suppose lots of folks got burned in that."

"Surprised you knew," said Burt. "Imagine that – a guy making up fake life insurance policies naming himself as the beneficiary and then killing off people who didn't even exist and collecting the proceeds."

"What do they think of him now down on Wall Street?" asked Lee. "I guess he's a real pariah now."

"Are you kidding me?" scoffed Burt. "They think he's a genius, of course."

CHAPTER 7

The tide of the party ebbed and flowed as Lexi floated gracefully from group to group, *working the room*, and Lee often found himself unable to keep up with her and set adrift in her wake. Even when stranded, he would observe her from afar, studying every move she made, every word she spoke for she had suddenly become the most interesting thing in the world to him. It was easy for him to see what drew people to her, her core attraction obviously her wealth and all the *accouterments* that went with it, but there was more than that, something like the dazzling charisma of a film star coalesced with the smooth way a politician presses the flesh and wins votes.

In less than five years in New York, Lexi Langdon had metamorphosed into a very self-confident hostess by carefully observing her one-time mentor Babe Paley and literally copying the style and grace of these *grand dames of* society, especially the way they handled themselves at parties. *Parties are a woman's workplace,* Babe Paley explained to her, *at least for women like us*. Lexi was a quick learner and now she had it all, poise and sophistication, an unflappable cosmopolitan flair and seemingly tireless and endless generosity. Tonight, as at every party she hosted, she made a point of sharing a few gracious words with as many of her guests as possible. *No matter how high and mighty they may seem,* Ray had once told her, *everybody loves to be flattered and told they're beautiful and smart.* Ironically, once Lexi became a member of the set that Ray tried so hard to make her a member of, he became something of an outsider to her, his own wife.

Lexi had quickly discovered that she had an innate talent for keeping the conversation popping with compliments, getting people to laugh and *ohh* and *ahh* and to graciously accept acknowledgement for who she was, *Lexi Langdon, hostess par excellence.* And Ray taught her how to use all of those skills for her – and his – benefit. *The best party gift you can give anybody,* he said, *is a Lexi Langdon quote to bring home to their own boring lives.*

In the main salon, three white leather couches were arranged semi-circle around a fireplace and Lexi was sitting on one drinking, laughing and holding court as the center of attention. Lee stood a bit on the periphery and when she noticed him she discreetly motioned with her head for him to come sit next to her and made just enough room for him to squeeze in.

"You must be following me," she whispered to him as he sat close. "But that's OK."

Slightly embarrassed, he said, "I don't really know anybody else here."

"Well then, here's someone you should know," said Lexi, grabbing the hand of a guy with curly red hair strolling by, introducing him just as *JP*, nothing more. Another Irish guy from Queens like Danny, solid and unpretentious, JP owned a club on New York's Upper East Side and Lee immediately liked him.

"It's a music business club," said JP. "Ask Ray about it, he's been there plenty of times."

"Never brings me," said Lexi with a pout. "But listen, JP, you're going to be hearing big things about Lee Franklin."

"What's he done now?" asked JP.

"He's a fantastic singer, for one thing. Has a voice like...velvet. Well, I can't think of a better word." She looked at Lee intently. "But he's really good."

"You should be my press agent," Lee said to her a bit abashed. "Always thought of my voice as more sandpaper than velvet."

"Either way, I'm sticking with you, pal, if you got Lexi Langdon promoting you," said JP. "You should come in the city sometime and play at my place, hang out, meet some people."

"What's it called?" asked Lee.

"What do you think? JP's!" he said with a twinkly smile.

"I don't know about the rest of you," said Lexi suddenly. "But I'm famished."

She squeezed Lee's hand and discretely pulled him with her as she got up from the couch.

"Want to take in a little ocean air, Lee?" asked Lexi with a hand to her mouth. "Get away from the riff-raff for a while?" she joked.

"Sure," said Lee. "Lead the way."

Several torches lit a path from Lexi's patio over the dunes and all the way to the beach. Lexi and Lee walked single file on the wooden-planked footpath; she in front while he couldn't take his eyes off her legs, from ankle to thigh and everything else. She had a natural rhythm when she walked, swaying her hips with her hands in little fists in front of her; something he first noticed on the beach. While they walked, she talked and would turn around to face him when making a point about Texas or Ray or New York or whatever and when she did the dazzle of her smile almost stopped Lee in his adoring tracks.

"Oh, this is far enough," said Lexi, pointing to a smooth place on the sand dunes. "And these Lucchese boots may be fabulous, but they're killing my feet." She plopped to the ground and held her leg up to Lee. "Could you?"

At first, he didn't know what she meant, and he could see right up her short skirt to the darkness between her legs. *Does she realize I can see all the way up to her panties? Should I be embarrassed to look?* But then he got it. "OK ... take off your boots, yeah, sure."

"What did you think I meant?" Lexi coyly asked.

"Better not say," said Lee.

Lexi just smiled and shook her head. "Musicians."

A little later Danny, wandering around on his own, came upon Lee sitting with Lexi in the dunes. "Hey, everyone's looking for you," he said.

"Me?" asked Lee.

"Not you! Her!"

"I better get back to work, guys." She planted a tender kiss on Lee's cheek, grabbed her boots and scooted off.

"What was that all about?" asked Danny.

"I think she meant she better get back to her party."

"Not that, man. I mean what were you two doing? Lost in the dunes?"

"I don't know, we were just talking about things," said Lee, still feeling Lexi's lips on his cheek. "Nothing important really, just talking. How's the party going? These people are from another world."

"What do you mean? People are people," said Danny.

"People are people except rich people," said Lee. "They're different."

"I've heard that before," said Danny. "But I don't buy it. Dress me up in a nice suit, silk tie and you'd wonder what kind of bankroll I had behind me."

"Or where you borrowed the suit," said Lee. "Hope you're taking good care of Tony Hughes's jacket."

Danny spread his arms like he was preparing the sacrament. "Like it was my own parish priest's vestments, speaking of which, look what someone gave me." He took out a domino-sized chunk of dark hashish. "Some guy was rolling it into his cigarette and saw me watching and just broke this off and gave it to me. Do you know how to smoke this shit?"

Lee took the hashish in his hand, broke off a tiny piece and rolled it around in his fingers, took it to his nose and breathed in its unmistakable scent. "This is the real deal. There's still part of the seal on that chunk you're holding. Must have come from Afghanistan."

"What are you?" asked Danny. "Some kind of expert?"

"I don't know about that, ..." said Lee. "But I know how to smoke it. You need a hash pipe or some tinfoil over a glass or mix it with tobacco like the guy who gave it to you and roll it in a joint. Not sure if I want to though, this stuff can get you in a lot of trouble."

"It gets you higher than weed?"

"Didn't mean that," said Lee.

CHAPTER 8

The first time I got stoned on hashish, the same kind of high-quality shit that I held in my hand at Lexi's party, was in Amsterdam's fabled Paradiso club, a one-time Dutch religious center turned rock concert palace. In 1971, the Paradiso was a must-see on the international counter-culture circuit, a publicly subsidized venue where both the using and selling of soft drugs were tolerated. I was three hours off the plane from Chicago and after dropping my back-pack off at the Brouwer Hotel on Singel Canal, I took a stroll through the city. To my naïve amazement, the Red Light District was high-lighted right there on the tourist map of Amsterdam I had picked up in the hotel lobby, so I have to admit I made a slight detour there. The girls sat right in the front windows, lining the block with temptation and I knew I was a long way from Kansas ... or Ohio. Then I started asking how much it cost and decided I couldn't afford it and so I found my way across town to Leidseplein, Amsterdam's answer to Times Square. The Paradiso stood right off the main square, a dark brick building with a line of kids in front. Gotta say, it felt like home.

Just a few months out of high school, I had talked my stepfather into buying me a plane ticket to Europe. He wasn't that hard to convince, because flights were cheap back then and he just wanted to get me the hell out of the house. Since graduation, I was sleeping well into the afternoon and nearly every dinner erupted into some kind of argument. The month before school ended, I remember coming home to see the Kent State shootings all over the news. "Those bastards," I remember saying, and I also remember my stepfather's sullen reply, "Yeah, they should have used machine guns." You see, from the moment my stepfather had entered the house, my standing there had gone down until I was definitely the stepson non-gratis. And since it was only getting worse, I was eager to get away to Europe, even with just the vaguest of plans to hook up with high school buddies who had gone over before and meet them someway, somehow at the Paradiso. That never happened; my friends never showed up and after two days of waiting around I was getting nervous just sitting in the Paradiso balcony alone watching a Dutch band Golden Earring play, when two rough looking older guys approached me and sat down on either side.

"So, you're the one that ripped off our friends," the one on the right with a three-day growth and bright red & gold oriental vest said right into Lee's ear. "Stupid thing to do, man. You're gonna pay for that."

Jet lagged and confused, not knowing a soul in the Paradiso and with the music was as loud as anything he'd ever heard, Lee had a bad feeling about these guys; they looked deadly serious and threatening. "What are you talking about?" he protested. "I just got here. I bought a ticket to the show like everyone else."

"And before that you sold them that crap," said the other one, a somewhat smoother character with a full red beard. "Where'd you get that? Scraped some tar off the road or some shit?"

"I don't know what the fuck you're talking about," said Lee. "I just flew in."

"We know that, asshole," said the other one, even more aggressively. "But you were supposed to fly in with five kilos and instead you showed up with this bullshit."

"I'm telling you, you got the wrong guy," said Lee.

"Do we? I don't think so. You American?"

"So what?"

"Wearing a Levi's jacket, big cowboy-buckle on your belt?"

"This place is full of guys wearing Levi's jackets."

"Maybe I should just take care of you right now," he said menacingly, taking a pearl handled switchblade from his pocket. "Show me what's in your pockets or I'm gonna open this." He moved forward and Lee pushed back in his chair.

The one with the red beard put his hand on his friend's knife. "Hey, cool down," he said. "You crazy? We're in the middle of the Paradiso." He looked at Lee. "You say you're the wrong guy? Tell you what we're going to do. Our friends, the ones you ripped off are gonna be here soon enough and then we'll see if you're the right guy or the wrong guy. Until then don't move."

"See what?" protested Lee. "I don't know what the fuck you're talking about."

"Just don't move from this chair until they show up. Got that? If you're the wrong guy you got nothing to worry about, but if you try to run you're not getting far. We'll be watching you."

The two of them stood up and moved to some empty seats down the row from Lee, never taking their eyes off him. Lee was flipping out, panicking, wanting to get up and make a run for it, not knowing what the fuck was happening and now these maniacs seem to be threatening his life.

So, he had no choice but to just sit there and watch the band, but he couldn't really concentrate; he wondered if there was a way to call the police, if they would even come into a place like this – and would they even speak English? It seemed that everyone around him was smoking hashish in small ceramic or wood pipes wrapped in colorful pieces of cloth and cupped in their hands. It was wide open here, like nothing he had ever seen before and he was almost getting high just by being there. And he felt totally outside the law and now that wasn't such a good feeling.

About half an hour later, three guys came in and joined the other two who were still staring at him. Some conversation went down, whispering in the ear, and something passed between them. Then they all got up and split except for one, the guy with the red beard and the double- breasted suit jacket. He looked at Lee and smiled and walked over.

"So, you're not the guy after all," he said.

"I know I'm not the fucking guy!" said Lee. "I just got here, I told you."

"They found the right guy, took what little money he had on him and threw him in a canal. Seemed he turned into a junkie in Afghanistan, never bought the hashish, came back with nothing. Fucked up big time."

"You think I give a shit?" said Lee. "Your friend pulled a knife on me, you think that's okay?"

"Cool down, man, he was just trying to scare you. My name's Gallagher, Richard Gallagher, what's yours?"

Lee hesitated. "Lee," he said.

"Just Lee?"

"Yeah, just Lee for now."

Richard Gallagher reached into his jacket pocket and came out with a piece of hashish the size of a Hershey Bar and handed it to Lee.

"No hard feelings," he said.

"What's this?" asked Lee.

"Peace offering," said Richard. "Want to smoke?"

"Why don't you guys just leave me alone," said Lee.

"Hey, come on, nothing happened and you handled yourself pretty well with my friend there. Kept your cool, I was impressed."

"Right," said Lee. "Is that a compliment?"

"Of sorts."

"You're British?"

"Irish," said Richard. "That's why I got a sense of humor." Out of his other pocket he took a small conical carved piece of wood and expertly wrapped it tightly with a cloth.

"What's that?" asked Lee. "Some kind of pipe?"

"It's a *chillum,*" said Richard as he mixed some hashish with tobacco in the palm of his hand and stuffed it into the bowl, then took out a Zippo lighter and flamed it up like a torch.

"Take some," he said, holding his breath and passing it to Lee who tried to copy the way Richard had held it, cupping his hands underneath and breathing in the cool smoke.

"Wow!" he said, also holding his breath.

"Wow is right," said Richard. "All's well that ends ... high!"

Richard Gallagher was an experienced drug dealer, although he liked to refer to himself in the less derogatory way as a *smuggler*, more *panache* to it. He was well dressed, charming, with the Irish gift of gab and he knew his way around Amsterdam and, it seemed, the rest of Europe too. When the band was finished and they couldn't get any higher, Richard and Lee left the Paradiso and bought some fries at a stand outside the club.

"Mayonnaise?" said Lee. "You put mayonnaise on the french fries?"

"First lesson, Lee," said Richard. "When in Rome do as the Romans do, so put some mayonnaise on your fries It's great - trust me."

For some reason, Lee did trust him and having given up on his friends, just started hanging out with Richard Gallagher who seemed to have plenty of spending cash and willingly picked up the tab for everything they did, even treating Lee to a *ménage-à-trois* in the Red Light District. Lee fell in love with Amsterdam, which was like hippie heaven and he was surprised when Richard told him that they should split to Paris and finally down to Rome.

"But Amsterdam is great," said Lee. "No hassles."

"Amsterdam is for kids. Wait till we get to Paris, man, it's really classy, whole other world. You'll dig it, man," said Richard. "You can throw away your backpack, makes you look like a hippie – I'll give you a suitcase, I've got an extra."

And that he did the next day, handing Lee a nice old leather valise with shiny brass fasteners and separate compartments for his shirts and ties, if he had owned a tie. They took the first-class train to Paris, got off at Gare de Nord and were soon walking down the wide Champs Elysées and visiting Napoleon's tomb at Invalides. Lee had never seen anything like that in his life; majestic buildings seemed to line every street and he learned to use a Turkish toilet in the cafés, putting his feet on each side of the drain hole.

Paris did make Amsterdam look provincial and quaint, but you had to take it on its own terms. Everyone in Amsterdam had seemed to speak English, but in Paris you had better at least try to speak some French if you wanted to get by or even order wine in one of the fancy restaurants that Richard favored. After having their photo taken on top of the Eiffel tower, they ate dinner at the famous *La Coupole*, the vast flamboyant and noisy Montparnasse brasserie full of bustling waiters and beautiful women. After dinner they moved to sit on the terrace of *Le Select*, the café across the street where Hemingway and Fitzgerald drank.

"Thanks for that dinner, man," said Lee. "Never ate snails before. Don't know how I'm gonna repay you for all of this."

"That's easy enough," said Richard. "You want to pay for that dinner?"

"What do you mean?"

"This is what you do, Lee, you jump into one of those taxis right out front here and go back to the hotel room ..."

"By myself?"

Richard put his finger to his lips. "You go back to the hotel and you take all of your clothes and stuff out of that suitcase I gave you and then you bring the empty suitcase to this address." He passed a small piece of paper across the table. "And the person who takes the suitcase will hand you an envelope and you'll bring it back here and we'll order another bottle of champagne. Simple enough?"

"What's in the empty suitcase? Or shouldn't I ask?"

"Better not to ask," said Richard. "But if you want to know I'll tell you. Nothing big, just a couple of kilos of Afghani hash."

"I've been carrying around a suitcase full of drugs?" asked Lee. "Crossing borders?"

"Kind of," said Richard smiling. "Like I said, it's easy. And it's even easier when you don't know what you're carrying."

"You fucker," said Lee cheerfully. "And what would have happened if I got busted?"

"I'd take care of it," said Richard. "Give you my word."

Lee looked out to the broad Boulevard Montparnasse where a line of taxis sat waiting right in the middle of the street. He took a deep breath and put the paper in his pocket.

"I'll be right back," he said. "I hope."

And it was just as easy as Richard said; after dumping all his stuff on the bed and going back to the taxi with the empty bag, he went to the address on the paper and rang an apartment off Champs Élysées and whoever answered must have been expecting him because he was buzzed right in. When the door to the apartment opened there was an attractive young woman standing there dressed in a pale blue Pan Am stewardess outfit.

"Richard's friend?" she asked.

"Yeah."

"Name?"

"Lee,"

"Right, so I guess I'll take that off your hands now and you'll take this." She handed him a sealed brown envelope and then went to take the suitcase.

"You can let go now, sweetheart," she said.

"I can?" asked Lee.

"Yes, you can." She kissed him quickly on the lips. "That's for Richard." And the apartment door shut.

Lee was back at the Select barely forty minutes after he had left and the champagne was still cold. Discreetly, he handed the envelope to Richard, who opened it, peered inside and smiled. Lee could see it was full of five-hundred French franc notes and before placing the envelope in his inside jacket pocket, he handed Lee a bunch.

"Stick it in your pocket, walking around money," he said.

"Feels good," said Lee, stuffing the bills into his jeans. "That was easy enough."

"Told you," said Richard. "Welcome to the company, son."

But they didn't stay in Paris long because Richard always wanted to keep moving. "We're going to Rome, I gotta meet some people. You'll like it, best looking chicks in the world. That is, until they hit thirty and then they dress in black and gain forty pounds. Overnight."

Richard seemed even more in his element in Rome than anywhere else. A good-looking woman, mid-thirties, was waiting for him when they got off the train: Lorraine, British and stacked with dark hair and a mischievous smile like Diana Rigg. She and Richard took a room together at a small hotel off the Campo de Fiori, a rectangular piazza and marketplace, the surrounding buildings all shades of ochre, and a busy neighborhood hangout not far from the better-known Piazza Navonna. Lee took his own room a floor above and from his windows heard the sound of neighbors yelling and smelled their pungent cooking. The Campo de Fiori quarter was lively and off the usual tourist beat, a gathering place where locals hung out near a huge statue of a 17th century philosopher right in the middle of the piazza.

"Wonder why I never heard of this guy," said Lee, reading the inscription below the statue. "Giordano Bruno."

"Burned at the stake," said Richard.

"What for?"

"Probably smuggling," said Richard. "Let that be a warning." He laughed.

When the weather was fine, they took leisurely dinners on the terrace of *Da Luigi*, an Italian cinema haunt; Richard pointed out Federico Fellini sitting at a table next to them and told Lee he could get him an audition if he liked. Life in Rome became a pleasant routine of waking late and taking café at a hole in the wall café in Campo de Fiori, where they stood and read the *International Herald* Tribune while eating gooey *cornettos*. And later, they sat on the fountain in the center of Piazza Navonna, eating chocolate *tartufos* from Tres Scalini. There was always something to do, people to visit, just sit and smoke hashish, and wander around the city's endless winding *viales*, most often as a threesome with Richard's girlfriend Lorraine tagging along between the two of them, arm in arm.

"Do you really like it over here in Europe, Lee?" asked Lorraine. "I imagine it must be quite different from Illinois ..."

"Ohio," corrected Lee. "Yeah, nothing like it. Wish I could stay here longer."

"What's stopping you?" she asked.

"Actually, I'm running out of funds," said Lee. "I know you've been paying for most of these dinners, can't expect that to go on forever. I gotta figure out a way to make some money over here if I'm gonna stay."

"Why don't you play on the streets?" asked Lorraine. "You always pick up a guitar when there's one around."

"I guess I could do that..." began Lee.

"You could do better than that, my friend," said Richard. "I got some shit coming in tomorrow. Why don't I front you a couple of kilos and you pay me after you sell it? Keep the rest for you. You could make a few grand."

"Who do I sell it to?" said Lee laughing. "I never did anything like that before."

"That's the easy part," said Richard. "You'll find someone in ... Ohio, who wants it I'm sure. The tricky part is getting it back to the States."

"To the States?"

"Yeah, man, that's where you can make some money. Maybe ten times what you paid for it."

"And how do I get it back there? Send it with a postcard to my parents?"

"Not quite," said Richard, "but close."

He showed Lee where to buy the two Gucci cosmetic cases and afterwards they sat in his hotel room with razors and glue and balsa wood and hollowed out the bottoms and fitted in the hashish.

"You know where the post office is?" asked Richard.

"Right around the block," said Lee.

"After you come back, we'll go out to lunch."

"Oh please, not Da Luigi again," said Lorraine. "We've been going there every day since you got here."

"Except Monday, when they're closed," said Richard. "But we'll go wherever you want, sweetheart, wherever you want. Let Lee get on his way here."

After the police nabbed Lee at the post office, they took him back to the hotel on Campo di Fioro to get his belongings and searched his room. On the way up the stairs, handcuffed, Lee passed by Richard's room and saw that it was empty with the door wide open, bed made and not a sign of him or Lorraine. When the police asked if he had accomplices staying in the hotel, Lee said no, he was on his own, sure that Richard would find a way out of whatever mess he was in. But weeks later, still sitting in jail, he realized that he was on his own, back to square one, just another American caught up in a foreign legal system, scared and alone.

"What do you say we smoke this shit later," Lee said to Danny. "Little too obvious here in the middle of the party. Let's get a drink."

Feeling slightly invisible as they stood at the bar, two guys around their age approached them. One, tall with chiseled good looks, the same guy who had been balancing champagne glasses a short time before, seemed overly friendly while the other, short, pudgy and in costume looked manic, his eyes darting all over the place.

"Say, we've been meaning to ask you fine fellows something, if you don't mind. Exactly what field of endeavor are you men in?" The taller one asked earnestly while trying to signal the bartender's attention.

"Well, I'm a singer," said Lee. "If that's what you mean."

"And I'm his manager," said Danny.

"Okay, now we got that straight, don't we, John?"

His friend burped loudly.

"So, listen up, this is my friend John Belushi and we're television and your music." he said. "And we're taking over."

"You're Chevy Chase the actor, aren't you?" asked Danny. "Someone said you're gonna be big."

Jesus! Thought Lee. *Danny can't stop.*

"I'm Chevy Chase and you're not," he said and then he tripped and fell, and everybody broke up laughing, while his partner Belushi, dressed in a Union blue Civil War uniform, hid behind a paste-on beard.

"I think your buddy here is in the wrong army," said Danny while helping Chevy Chase to his feet. "This party is called *The Rebel's Ball*, and you look more like Ulysses S. Grant than Robert E. Lee. They were on different sides, you know."

"Knew it," said Belushi. "Should have worn my samurai outfit."

Around two in the morning, the party was winding down fast and again Danny and Lee found themselves standing at the patio bar, practically alone with the bartender, who was already packing away glasses into storage boxes, when James Elliot approached them.

"Word to the wise, gentlemen, don't be the last ones to leave the party," he said. "You guys need a ride?"

"What about your girls?" asked Lee.

"Two of them disappeared into that gentle night," said James Elliot. "But Kathy is coming with us."

"Kathy!" declared Danny. "Really? Wow, she's gorgeous, I was talking with her for a while, what a babe."

"I sent that *babe* over to talk to you," said James Elliot with a chuckle. "You looked like you were dying for some female company."

"You did that?" asked Danny surprised. "Why?"

"I thought you two would get along," said James Elliot. "And you did – she told me she likes you."

"Are you shitting me?" exclaimed Danny. "She likes me? Did she really say that?"

"Stranger things have happened, my man," said James Elliot.

"Hey, speaking of strange things, you mind if I ask you something?" asked Danny. "No offense intended."

"Shoot."

"What are you doing at a party celebrating the pardon of a Confederate General? Isn't that a little out of place?"

"Is that what this party is about?" James Elliot laughed uproariously. "I bet half the people here had no idea. Man, I'm getting out of here before the Klan starts burning crosses on Lexi's lawn. You guys coming?"

"Shouldn't we find Lexi to say goodbye?" asked Lee, still remembering her kiss on his cheek.

"Maybe not," said James Elliot. "She and Ray seemed to be having some kind of a tiff tonight and I saw Lexi disappear upstairs a while ago. She didn't look happy then and I doubt if she'll come back down."

"Do you know what it was about?" said Lee, wondering if Ray had seen them talking together out on the dunes.

"The argument? Who knows? Maybe Lexi was upset that Ray was doing too much coke ... or she might have been pissed at him for not giving her any." James Elliot replied with a smile. "When it comes to the lifestyles of the rich and famous, take my advice, don't even try to figure it out."

They were smoking next to James Elliott's creamy Mercedes when Kathy came sprinting out of the house on her very long legs with her compact braless breasts bouncing right along. She had that smile only models have, somehow a little wider and more radiant than other women and short, stylish blond hair that looked good no matter where it fell. All of that without an ounce of fat on her body, poured into Fiorucci jeans and a midriff baring T-Shirt with Keith Richards' stoned face on it.

"Sorry, guys, you been waiting long? Had to use the little girls' room."

"No problem," said Danny. "Good things are worth waiting for, like uh ... Christmas." He immediately felt stupid. "Christmas in August!"

"You're so adorable," said Kathy, bending down to kiss him and leaving a red outline of her lips on his cheek.

"God must love me," said Danny. "I told you it's like Christmas in August."

"He's the funniest guy I've met in a long time," Kathy said to James Elliot. "Cracks me up!"

"But looks aren't everything," said Danny. "They're the only things!" Kathy hugged him tightly and squealed with laughter.

Lee sat up front while Danny and Kathy, squeezed into the back seat, talked low. James Elliot took the long way home, cruising down Further Lane past the exclusive Maidstone golf club, an ivy-covered series of low buildings with peaked slate roofs shielded by tall dark hedges.

"That's where the old money parties," said James Elliot, as he turned left and stopped by the beach to admire the night sky, bursting with stars.

"Come on, I want to see the ocean," said Kathy. "Get my feet wet."

"I'll come with you," said Danny, winking at Lee. "Just in case there are any land sharks."

"Dada-dada-dada-dada," said James Elliot, humming the ubiquitous *Jaws* theme while he pulled out a slim joint from his silver

cigarette case, engraved *JE*. "You two want a hit of this before you say hello to some twenty-foot killer shark?"

"Sure," said Danny and Kathy almost in unison.

"You smoke, Lee?" asked James Elliott.

"Rarely," said Lee, "but I love the smell of it."

"It's good," said James Elliott. "Mellow."

"I'll take a hit," said Lee. "It's been quite a night."

James Elliot passed the joint around and everyone except him immediately started coughing. "Mellow?" said Danny as he tried to hold the smoke in.

"Come on, let's go," said Kathy. "That's enough for me." Kathy and Danny ran giggling down to the beach, trailing off into the darkness while James Elliott and Lee sat in the car.

"Man, didn't they see *Jaws*?" said James Elliot. "That flick ended my night swimming days *pronto*. What do you think, Lee, something starting up between those two?"

"Looks that way," said Lee. "I never saw Danny so well behaved. That party might have changed his life."

"You never know what might happen at one of Lexi Langdon's parties," said James Elliott. "There's magic in that rarified air."

"My first time," said Lee. "Pretty impressive ... I take it you've known Lexi a long time?"

"Actually, I met Ray first, through Wes Edel and his girlfriend Alana. I shot some photos of her that Wes really dug so he hired me to shoot a cover for one of their artists and Ray came along to the session and started bossing everyone around. I thought it was funny, didn't pay him any mind. Just trying to throw his weight around. Then, a short time after that, Alana introduced Lexi to Ray, and they started hanging out and the next thing you knew, they were getting married. Lexi's a lot of fun and Ray is...well, Ray's just Ray."

"How long ago was that?"

"When I did those photos of Alana? Maybe nineteen-seventy? Seventy-one? But I remember even then Alana talking about her fabulous new friend who inherited a fortune. I think the deal was that Lexi had just moved to New York and was starting a new life and, you know, Ray won the *dating game* being a music biz head honcho, and totally connected to everyone that mattered in the city. Might have come from some money himself, had some class, but I'm not sure about that because I think Lexi is paying the bills. But one thing is for sure, that man is a first-class hustler. Can't take that away from him." James Elliot took a big drag from the joint.

But does she love him? Lee wondered.

"But don't get me wrong. Lexi needed Ray to show her the ins and outs of the Manhattan *glitterati*," said James Elliot as he held in the smoke. "Make sure she didn't fall in with the wrong crowd in the big bad city. Hard for a girl to erase that kind of mistake."

"But what did Ray know about all of that? I mean, come on, the music business is not all that classy in itself."

"Oh, Ray's been around, believe me, and he traveled in the right circles. He's a night bird, so he meets everyone and knows which fork to pick up first at a formal dinner. He was always willing to give a helping hand to the right unattached heiress. So, like I said, he knew his way around the crowd that Lexi wanted to be part of."

"What do you mean by that?" asked Lee. "What crowd are you talking about? You mean like ... rich people?"

"It's not just about being rich," said James Elliot, leaning back in his seat, resting his arm on the steering wheel. "Although you definitely need some serious cash to run with them. Let me give you an example, you got Ahmet Ertegun, chairman of Atlantic Records; his wife's a Rumanian aristocrat, and he's partying with Giovanni Agnelli, chairman of Fiat, and they're all hanging out with Andy Warhol, Mick Jagger and Liza Minnelli. It's not like you got to be from the right family anymore, although that doesn't hurt," said James Elliot. "But you still have to find a way in, to be invited to the right soirées. And I guess Ray did that for Lexi, like her guide, making sure she wasn't wasting her time in swinging singles joints on the Upper East Side, standing at the bar of *Maxwell's Plum* and *Looking for Mr. Goodbar*."

"So, Ray was Lexi's *Mr. Goodbar*?"

"Well, he hasn't murdered her yet," said James Elliot. "Although tonight it looked like the other way around."

"And what was in it for Ray?"

James Elliot looked at Lee like he was the stupidest guy on the planet. "I hope you're kidding me, man."

"I guess," said Lee.

"Listen, Ray Arthur is no dummy and he knew a good thing when he saw it and hooked onto Lexi from the moment they met and kept her occupied mind, soul and body twenty-four hours a day. And somewhere in that whirlwind he talked her into marrying him and it's been a wild ride ever since. The two of them made a name for themselves as a couple right away, cover of *Interview*, Lexi getting her portrait done by Warhol, Truman Capote's black and white ball at the Plaza, all of that. You know what I mean, Lee?" James Elliot nodded his head as if reading Lee's mind. "You gotta be a couple to make it with the kind of people they hang around with, single women are dangerous to the status quo."

"What about you? You're not a couple and you seem to fit in."

"You could call me the *black sheep*," he said with a laugh. "But I'm still the photographer to the high and the mighty. Someday, I'll tell you my story."

"Hey, I just noticed something, you're not calling me *lucky* anymore."

"Guess I got your name now ... Lee."

On the beach, Kathy and Danny sat close, on a washed-up packing crate with Tony Hughes's blue blazer draped over Kathy's shoulders. They kissed and Danny gently stroked her cheek. "Your skin is so soft, I never felt anything like that before."

"That's nice ... thanks," she said growing shy.

Danny looked at her. "Tell me what you're thinking."

"Well, really, if you want to know, I'm thinking that I really shouldn't be sitting on the beach in the middle of the night kissing some guy I just met at a party whose name is..."

"Danny," he said quickly. "Danny O'Connor."

"I know, Danny. And I'm Kathy, Kathy Muller."

"I know that too ... so is there something else?

"Something else?"

"I mean like, do you need to know something else? Or can I start kissing you again."

She laughed. "You're too much, Danny O'Connor! That's your call, I'm not gonna tell you what to do." Their eyes locked and they started to kiss again and didn't stop. Danny's hand was under Kathy's T-shirt now and each time they came up for air she noticed he was smiling.

"What's so funny?" asked Kathy.

"Nothing's funny ... I'm just so happy being here with you. You're like nothing I every felt before ... "

"You mean my breasts?"

Danny got embarrassed and took his hand out. "Oh no, that's not what I mean ... I don't know how to say it, but there's this big chemistry between us, something like that anyway. I don't know ... I failed chemistry."

"Not tonight you didn't," said Kathy. "You know what I like about you, Danny? You're a *what you see is what you get* kind of guy."

"Not so fast," said Danny. "That's not even my jacket."

"I didn't think so," said Kathy. "Doesn't suit you."

"You know, today I was on the beach with Lee and I felt something was about to happen and I told him and now here I am with you. It's like I was meant to meet you tonight," said Danny.

Kathy touched her finger to his lips. "Don't talk about it, Danny, just let it happen. We better get back to the car or they're gonna start wondering."

They stood up and Danny stepped on Tony's blazer, now fallen on the ground and covered in sand.

"Oh shit!" he said out loud.

"Next time wear your own clothes," said Kathy. They ran up from the beach laughing and jumped into the back seat. James Elliot started up his car, slid it into reverse to pull out of the deserted beach parking. Checking the rear view mirror, he saw them whispering low into each other's ear.

"Any great whites out there?" asked James Elliot.

"Only one," said Kathy. "And he was wearing a blue blazer."

"Man, what a night!" exclaimed Danny as he and Lee walked up the dark driveway to the outside stairs leading to the rank Talkhouse dressing room. "I got Kathy's number, gonna call her tomorrow."

"You can thank James Elliot for that," said Lee.

"There's something about that guy I really like. He's cool, knows what's going on and just stands back and lets it all happen. He's got this really confident thing about him, like he could handle anything. I wonder what he does?"

"Lexi told me he's a fashion photographer, shoots for *Vogue* – must be kind of successful with that vintage Mercedes and all. Suppose that's why he's got all those nice-looking girls hanging onto him like your Kathy there. So, what's her story?"

"Well, she's a model, not a star, but she works all the time, travels all over the world. Said she wants to give it a few more years and then do something else, sell French Antiques or something like that. Grew up in Purchase, a rich *wasp* town up in Westchester County, in that kind of family you see on TV shows but never really meet in real life." Danny laughed. "You know I was kissing her down on the beach back there - I still can hardly believe it – and she really kissed me back. I never was with a girl like that before, so beautiful and hip and ... willing."

"What makes models different from other girls?" asked Lee.

"How do I know? She's the only one I ever met. But I'll tell you, nobody kissed me like that before," Danny admitted shyly.

"Well, Danny," said Lee as they entered the Talkhouse dressing room and flipped on the corner lamp. "All I can say then is if you want to make it with a girl like that you better *step up your game*."

"New clothes?" asked Danny. "She said I should wear my own next time." He took off Tony's wrinkled blazer. "Man, look at this. Now I'm gonna have to get it dry-cleaned."

"That's the price you pay for love, Danny."

"So what do you mean, *step up my game?*"

"Look at James Elliot," said Lee. "Silk shirt, pressed jeans, lizard belt."

"Gimme a break, man. You think I can afford to dress like him?"

"It's not about money, Danny, it's about style. And style is something money can't buy ..." His words trailed off as their eyes were fixed on the small dingy room in front of them, still in the same disheveled state they had left it in, clothes thrown over a rundown couch, half drunk beer bottles with cigarette butts floating in them and a bathroom you wanted to get out of as quickly as you could. They looked at each other haplessly and both started to laugh.

"Hey, what are you talking about?" asked Danny in between howls of laughter. "Look at our suite here. Do we have style or what? Come on!"

"I take it all back," said Lee, unable to control himself. "It *is* about the fucking money! Wow, you know what? I'm starving. You wanna get a slice? I saw Angelo's is still open."

"Yeah, man! That weed made me hungry as hell. Hey, you know what I'm gonna tell Angelo when I order my pizza?"

"What's that?"

"Give me a slice with style!" And they both fell onto the couch laughing hard.

"That's a start!" said Lee.

CHAPTER 9

I could have easily stopped right there after that party and never seen Lexi Langdon again. Just disappear from her radar, and man, that was something I was already good at. Could have, should have, that's what the road to tragedy is paved with, isn't it? But obsession became a major player in this drama and as hard as I tried, I just couldn't get her off my mind. Maybe the best thing would have been just to let Danny and Kathy have their summer fling while I hung out around the Talkhouse, trying to write a few decent songs and use some of my existential angst for inspiration. But I was lonelier than I looked or anyone around me suspected and that, coupled with my feeling that I was already a major failure in the eyes of my family, made me susceptible to anything that felt as good as Lexi. I mean, just looking at her made me believe that I could start over, reinvent myself. I had no police record here and no routine stop by a Suffolk County cop was going to show that I'd spent time in a Rome prison, sharing my cell with an Afghani drug smuggler until my stepfather blew all his retirement savings on lawyers and bribes to get me out of there and back to the States with the caveat that I would not bother to come home. He and Mom had had enough of me and I can't say I even blamed them. If I could do it all again, I should have stayed in Europe and actually started playing on the streets, not gone for the easy money trying to deal hash, not drained my parents' bank account ... could have, should have ... but that was another continent for Christ's sake, the old world. Not like Lexi's world, which renewed itself every day according to her whims. It was so damn irresistible! But I wasn't really running to Lexi as much as I was running from this nagging suspicion that everything in my life was turning to shit, this profound disappointment in myself at such a young age. And I swear, every time I looked into Lexi's coral green eyes I wanted to stop running, stop moving, stop the clock.

From that night on, the summer moved along at a delicious and intoxicating pace. There were more parties at Lexi Langdon's Further *Lane* mansion and Lee and Danny passed leisurely, long, lingering afternoons with Lexi, James Elliot and Kathy on the beach, drinking white wine and eating smoked salmon sandwiches for lunch. Sometimes Ray was a part of it, sometimes not, but when he joined in, he was more and more unbearable, always having to be the smartest guy in the room and compelled to constantly stake out his own turf in what was obviously Lexi's domain. By nature, Ray was a competitive son of a bitch and that was with nearly everyone he came into contact with, especially Lexi. At first, she could laugh it off, pretending to feel some kind of grudging respect for Ray, that he was proud of his own achievements and income and not willing to be totally dependent upon her. But Ray wanted it both ways, with Lexi generously supporting his luxurious lifestyle, his custom-made suits, fishing boat and everything else, while he was to be treated as king of the castle even if it wasn't his castle at all. More and more Lexi was becoming fed up with his bragging and found herself avoiding Ray, making her own plans and not caring if Ray showed up or not. She made impromptu trips into the city for shopping and even began appearing at those charity events that craved her patronage, charm and, of course, generous donation without Ray.

Naturally, there were other Hampton parties to go to as well that summer, but Lexi Langdon's parties were on another level, so much more extravagant than anybody else dared or could afford. Her lavish *soirées* were marked with an unmatched opulence, buffet feasts fit for a gourmand army and continuously flowing champagne served by formally attired waiters, a clear step up from the decidedly more informal social life of the rest of the East End. And thus, all the interesting people, the people everyone really wanted to socialize with, were always there and so just being in this exhilarating atmosphere made you believe that you were a part of it. But above all, Lexi Langdon was the star of her own show and that summer of 1975, among the A-list from Southampton to Montauk, she was *the* hostess of the season, and people coveted her invitation. Rumors came and went about her marriage to Ray - would they stay together or was it already over - and that remained an enigma to anyone who met them that summer. Some evenings they would stroll arm in arm, appearing deeply in love, with Lexi hanging onto Ray's every word and then just a few days later she might ignore him completely, paying less attention to him than to one of her staff. Naturally, Lexi's friends put the blame squarely on Ray and there were spiteful rumors of his infidelity, but nothing of this reached Lexi's ears, no one wanting to go so far as to risk upsetting the status quo. As rocky as their marriage might be, they were still the *anchors* of that summer's social scene and the action revolved around them like a whirlwind.

In addition, there was ongoing speculation about the precise source and size of Lexi's wealth. Nobody knew much apart from the apparent limitless supply, which presumably kept coming from somewhere in Texas. Lexi spent freely on herself, friends, and entertaining and more than anything else seemed amused by all the gossip, even taking pleasure in fueling the fires herself, often starting a party conversation with comments like, "Did you hear what they're saying about me now?" And, rest assured, all ears tuned in ...

That summer a parade of celebrities, TV stars and gay fashion designers all came to her Further Lane *fêtes* and without exception they all *kowtowed* to her, wanting to be her new best friend and hoping to be invited back. It was as if the good times were at Lexi's beck and call; it was she who created the magic while rarely appearing in the same designer outfit twice. The two constants of Lexi's *look* were her Diamonds by the Yard necklace and her long strawberry blond hair; always in the limelight, a charismatic spotlight focused on her wherever she was, illuminating the ground she stood on or the chair she sat in with an aura of pure allure. At parties and wine tastings, at tennis matches or polo games, *wherever* she was, Lexi's presence turned the excitement level up a few notches. She joked about herself with a charming languid Texas accent in a self-deprecating way where *sugar* was sprinkled liberally in the *faux* intimacy of conversations about subjects as banal as the dew on the grass beneath her sandals. But she did have her own unconventional way of looking at the world, a combination of *noblesse oblige* and down-home Texas earthiness that even the most cynical New York socialite found irresistible. Lexi could pretend to be making fun of a particularly outrageous and costly outfit she might be wearing, say, crocodile cowboy boots with a silver metallic mini-skirt, and her guests would out-do each other rushing to her defense.

"Oh no, Lexi!" someone might say. "You're the only woman here tonight with any style at all!" And then they'd nod along knowingly while she recounted decades' old Houston tales, herself only having heard them second and third hand. Grand events such as the opening of Glen McCarthy's Shamrock Hotel in Houston, excitedly reminding her audience that the *Chroni*cle described the night as "A Bedlam of Diamonds" even if they had never heard of the oil-rich cast of characters she spoke of. And even more baffling was her announcement of the imminent arrival of a mysterious *Yellow Rose.* Most people, although listening intently, couldn't figure out if Lexi was talking about a work of art, a precious pet or a close relative from

Texas. Although in some fashion *The Yellow Rose* was all of those things and more.

Juxtapose time and place and imagine Sag Harbor, one-hundred fifty years ago, back when it was a picturesque and thriving whaling center, where sailors roamed the numerous bars and brothels of the town and the wharf extended far out into the harbor, accommodating a hundred whaling ships at a time. Wind was the energy source for those vessels and yet fortunes were still made in *oil,* just as they were in Lexi Langdon's time, although back then it was *whale* oil. The first *oil crisis* came when *uber*-merchant John D. Rockefeller began selling kerosene from his newly created company Standard Oil, which was called that so folks would know his product had the same *standard* as the whale oil they were accustomed to. Ironically, when oil deposits were found underground in Pennsylvania, many unemployed whalers found themselves working in the oilfields as a new era began. In 1975, oil prices were still high and not yet stabilized from the OPEC crisis of three years before when oil producing countries put the screws to the west with great effect, causing long lines at gas stations while making Texas oil barons even richer and raising the stock of the ancillary companies like Langdon Industries that served their needs.

Back in Sag Harbor's whaling heyday, the ships' captains built white shingled three-story box-like Victorian homes for themselves, topped with railed *widow's walk* terraces perched on the roof, where anxious wives would search the horizon for signs of a returning ship. If you were standing on one of the remaining *widow's walks* this historic night, staring out into the harbor lights, you would see a much shorter wharf straddling a packed marina which catered almost exclusively to the yachting set. And you would also see in the distance, just entering the harbor, an imposing black ebony hull, over one hundred feet in length, majestically making its way into the docile marina like the ominous arrival of William Butler Yeats's *rough beast ... slouching toward Bethlehem.*

THREE STORIES HIGH AND LIT FROM BOW TO STERN LIKE A floating Christmas tree, one late June night, *The Yellow Rose* cruised into Sag Harbor around midnight. Her engines churned and gutted the sea as its *basso-profundo* horn alerted the harbormaster of her arrival. Since arrangements had to be made exactly where she might fit, it was impossible for a ship of such size to enter the harbor furtively. Finally, she was assigned a spot at the far end of the wharf itself, in plain sight for all to see, a gargantuan object of desire beyond nearly anybody's means, except Lexi Langdon's. People came to gawk at the sight of the *unobtainable* with their fingertips touching the hull of the ship, forced to be content to stand before this floating mansion without ever going inside.

Contemporary Sag Harbor was a vacation village on the same circuit of such *star* East End locations as Amagansett, East Hampton and Southampton; and, accordingly, full of pricey antique shops and fine seasonal restaurants where hungry diners tried to catch the eye of the maître d'. Strict zoning laws had kept much of the eighteenth century look of the town proper intact, dotted still with many of the historic Victorian homes built a century before. Once the sun set, Sag Harbor's main drag came alive, like any other beachside town, where all kinds of characters migrated on hot summer nights to grab an ice cream cone and just hang out. The incredible sight of *The Yellow Rose* maneuvering onto the wharf, quickly drew a reverent crowd who watched the boat in awed silence. It was, by far, the most impressive yacht in the marina that summer and dwarfed all the fine teak sailboats resting nearby, making them look like mere wooden toys. Whole families of summer vacationers stood and stared, licking their ice cream while *The Yellow Rose*'s crew fit tenders and secured dock lines to sturdy brass cleats far into the night, polishing up everything that was meant to shine, so Lexi Langdon, the de-facto ship's owner, would not be disappointed when she arrived to inspect what was perhaps the most tangible and visibly impressive symbol of her legacy.

Lexi, so wound up at the thought of the boat's arrival, left Further Lane alone very early the next morning. She drove swiftly up Route 114 into Sag Harbor and parked in the clearly marked "No Parking" zone right in front of the yacht, leaving the car keys dangling in the ignition and impatiently pushing through the small breakfast crowd that stood there on the dock gawking. With her head held high she waltzed right onto the boat and every eye followed her. Captain Jack Henderson of Galveston, Texas, dressed in a starched white shirt decorated with modest gold epaulets, waited for her at the receiving end of the short gangplank. He was all you would imagine the captain of such an impressive yacht to be: smartly trimmed gray beard, lined tanned face and authoritative manner. Dressed in white from head to foot with a black brimmed captain's hat shielding his face from the morning sun, he smiled with confidence, knowing that there would be no unpleasant surprises for Lexi, that everything on the boat was as flawless as could be this morning. At sea nearly all his adult life, Captain Jack was a stickler for command structure and only Lexi rose above him when it came to *The Yellow Rose*. He might be the captain, but she was the boss, *The Yellow Rose* an extension of her identity. He was never more aware of that than when he stood impatiently on the deck of the boat in his softly polished white bucks, nearly at attention, awaiting her arrival.

In addition to Captain Jack, there was a uniformed crew of three, two all-around hands and a helmsman, standing respectfully in place at the top of the gangplank waiting for Lexi to board. Down below in the galley, the cook was already busy preparing a delectable lunch. The boat crew might change from voyage to voyage but Captain Jack had been part of *The Yellow Rose* since it was launched into Galveston harbor a decade ago and he was as integral a part of the boat as any of its luxurious fixtures.

Built near the great lakes by Burger Boats in Manitowoc, Wisconsin, the boat had been freighted to Texas on a wide-load tractor-trailer, traveling by night and taking up two lanes of the highway. Captain Jack had overseen the final equipment installations at Galveston Yacht Club and Marina and taken her out on a few trial runs in the bay before reporting to Lexi's father, Alexander "Lex" Langdon, that his new yacht was ship-shape and ready to sail at its owner's convenience. Not being a man prone to wait for anything he had already paid for, Lex Langdon immediately drove down from Houston that very afternoon with his teenage daughter Lexi in tow. She was with her father because the two had been in the middle of one of their rare lunches together when Lex received the call from Captain Jack. Almost immediately, he put his fork down and they left the restaurant, Lexi still chewing on her steak as she tagged along after him. When they arrived at the Marina an hour later, Lex Langdon regarded the boat with silent reverence and then proceeded to inspect every inch of it, every plank and every fitting, above water. As a man who expected to get exactly what he paid for, nothing more and nothing less, he asked Captain Jack quite a few questions, as if it were he who built the boat for him, before finally bobbing his head in delighted approval and proclaiming to his daughter, "Well, Lexi, I think this little lady is gonna be a fine new addition to the family. What about you?"

"What family do you mean, Daddy?" asked Lexi puzzled.

"Our family, you and me," said Lex. "That's all there is since your mama died."

"Oh," said Lexi.

"Yeah," said Les. "You and me and now this big beautiful boat."

"I didn't even know you liked boats, Daddy," said Lexi with a distinct teenager's lack of enthusiasm. "What if I get sea-sick?"

"Then you can sit on the dock here while I'm out cruising," he said gruffly. "Don't tell me you don't like it."

Lexi felt his coldness and it sent a shiver up her spine. "Of course,

I like it, Daddy. It's a fine-looking boat, probably not another one as fine as this in Texas."

Lex put his arm around her and hugged her firmly. "That's the idea, baby. Now you're getting into the swing of things. Just as long as none of my Saudi partners show up with any of their own floating palaces, I should be the top dog around here for a while, don't you think?"

"What you gonna call it? Doesn't a boat need a name?"

"I was thinking of naming her after you, calling the boat *Lexi,*" he said. "What do you think of that?"

"Well, that's sweet, Daddy, but I don't know," said Lexi. "I think a boat like this needs something more ... historic. I'm not even grown up yet. People might think it's kind of, you know, funny ..."

"What do you mean *funny?*" he said curtly.

"I don't know, like I'm too young to have a big old boat like that named after me."

Lex Langdon weighed her words carefully, just like he had done with every important business move in his life. He was at his best when operating in a defensive mode and got most animated at football games when the opposing team had the ball. Knitting his eyebrows, he sucked in his lips and rubbed the palm of his hands together. He was a tall man in his 60s, overweight but still spry, and able to move around at a pace that surprised everybody, not least of all his numerous and ever-changing lovers, both professional and otherwise.

"You might have a point there, baby," he said more gently. "Wouldn't want folks making fun of you or the boat for that matter, didn't spend that kind of money to get laughed at now, did we?"

"I don't suppose so," said Lexi.

"This boat needs a name that every man, woman and child in Texas will take seriously."

"How about *The Alamo*?" suggested Captain Jack who was standing nearby. "Everybody in Texas takes that name seriously enough."

"Too obvious," said Lex. "And I do business with some Mexican politicians, including the goddamn President of Mexico himself, who might not appreciate it. But maybe it should be a name that has something to do with Texas," he said. "Something splendid and beautiful like ..."

"Like *The Yellow Rose of Texas*," said Lexi. "That's a song that everybody likes and it's about Texas."

"Well ..." Then Lex Langdon held his breath before exhaling loudly which was what he always did when a deal was signed and delivered. "Let's just call her *The Yellow Rose* then," he said with glee. "This damn boat is big enough already without getting the entire state of Texas involved." He looked behind him to Captain Jack. "That'll be it then, *The Yellow Rose*."

"Yes, sir," said Captain Jack. "I'll have *The Yellow Rose* painted on the escutcheon tomorrow morning."

"Jesus Christ! Where the hell is that?" asked Lex Langdon.

"Right on the bow, where it should be in big gold letters. By the way, she's ready for her maiden voyage, Mr. Langdon. You just give me the word – beautiful day for a cruise around the gulf coast, don't you think?"

"Hell yeah, let's take her out for a spin, see what she's made of. Crank her up. And, Captain Jack, I hope there's something to goddamn eat here," said Lex Langdon. "I don't expect to shell out a million bucks on this damn thing and end up eating out of a can of chili."

"We're fully stocked," said Captain Jack with a smile. "Just about anything you could want. Although I'll have to fix it myself today."

"I'll go check out the kitchen," said Lexi.

"Galley," corrected Captain Jack. "It's right back there."

After Lexi disappeared down below, Lex pulled Captain Jack aside. "Listen, I might need your help with a ... delicate matter."

"Anything I can do, sir."

"Well, the thing is ..." Lex peered around the boat, making sure Lexi was out of sight. "The thing is, I plan on doing some serious business entertaining on this boat, especially when the Saudis come to town. So I might need your help with that, if you know what I mean."

"What kind of entertainment did you have in mind?" asked Captain Jack.

"Well, you know, plenty of booze, maybe get a nice poker table set up here and we're gonna need some broads, definitely some real lookers for those Saudi princes. And I'd prefer to use the local talent, if you know what I mean, not bringing in the usual girls from Houston who will be blabbing all over town."

Captain Jack almost blushed. "Well, can't really say that's my line, Mr. Langdon, but I know there are a couple of strip joints in town. I'll get a few phone numbers and you can decide what you want to do."

"Sounds good, just keep my name out of it. Did they put that safe in the master bedroom like I ordered?"

"I believe they did, sir."

"Well, there will be plenty of money on board to keep everybody happy ... and quiet."

"Aye, aye," said Captain Jack. "We'll put blindfolds on the *entertainment* until we're far out to sea." He laughed.

"Even better," Lex said grinning. "Throw 'em overboard after we're done!" he added, putting his finger to his lips as Lexi approached them.

"What are you two gentlemen talking about?" she asked.

"Business," said Lex. "Just business."

While Lex Langdon's original intentions may have been all business, the boat often served as the common ground where he and Lexi could come as close to bonding as he was capable of. Sunday afternoons, they would cruise to nowhere with Captain Jack at the helm and Lexi would sit on the deck with her father while he explained the *family business* to her. It was here, on this boat with her daddy, that Lexi acquired the substantial business acumen she still possessed. Lex Langdon was a hard taskmaster and if he explained something once he didn't like going over it again, a man who didn't suffer fools gladly, and he grilled Lexi on stock prices and cost ratios until her head spun. His intention might have been to groom Lexi to take over someday after he retired, although he never told her as much. Sometimes, in between these informal tutorials he might digress and even talk about Lexi's mom briefly before getting back on track, back to *business*, his favorite subject.

"Your mom was with me when we met those astronauts in Houston at that NASA dinner," he would say. "And she just charmed them, like she did everyone else. I should have brought her along on more trips, would have had I'd known..." His words trailed off.

"Known what, Daddy?"

"Oh, you know, life goes on, that's all. So, do you remember what I said about the difference between preferred stock and common stock? Which one is better to have?"

Lexi thought hard. "Well, I think you said whichever paid the most dividends, but if you're making a deal try to leverage your stock options at the lowest point in the past thirty-six months. Wasn't it something like that?"

He chortled proudly. "That's my girl, that's Lex Langdon's daughter talking now!"

Nonetheless, *The Yellow Rose* also gained a reputation as a floating bordello and casino, where deals and girls were put to bed. Once they were out to sea and beyond the territorial limit, a very high stakes baccarat game often began with topless waitresses serving the drinks as Lex Langdon collected signatures on million-dollar deals. Naturally, Lexi was not invited on those business cum pleasure excursions.

LEXI SPENT THE SAD AND SULLEN MONTHS FOLLOWING Alexander Langdon's sudden death sitting in her Houston bedroom, waited on by maids and visited by relatives and business associates but incapable of going anywhere near *The Yellow Rose.* In fact, just mentioning the name could bring her to tears. So, the boat remained idle in her berth at the Galveston Yacht Club while Captain Jack waited patiently, day after day, and kept her *shipshape* and ready to go with the hope that Lexi would keep both the boat, *and him*, in her employ.

Since Lexi could remember, her father had always been more than busy; his social life and business interests intertwined with meetings and deal making often lasting well into the night. He was a man usually on his way to a flight or just getting off one; being constantly on the move had been his *modus operandi and* even when he was home in Houston, he rarely returned to his River Oaks mansion until Lexi was already sound asleep. Then she went off to school in Switzerland, and the memory of those summer days when he had found time to spend a few hours with her on *The Yellow Rose* were all she had to hold on to, besides, of course, her vast inheritance of nearly a quarter billion dollars and rising. But now, thought Lexi, just when she was finally getting to know him, when she had reached an age when they could start to understand each other, he was gone for good. But that special day, when Lex Langdon took his only child down to Galveston Harbor to inspect *The Yellow Rose* and select its name became a cherished memory etched into Lexi's consciousness better than a hundred birthdays rolled into one. It came to her in one of her most anguished moments of grief, almost like a message from another world, that her father was gone but his spirit could live on for her in *The Yellow Rose.* When, some days later, she finally returned to the boat and gazed upon its fine lines, she could immediately feel his spirit. She climbed up to the bridge and, putting her hands upon the large chrome steering wheel, at that moment she was transfixed, knowing whom she was and what she had to do. She was the late Alexander Langdon's daughter, titular head of Langdon Industries – *largest maker of waste disposal vehicles in the United States* and a true heiress; one of the richest women in the country and *The Yellow Rose* was a significant component and emblem of her empire.

Although technically *The Yellow Rose* was an asset fully owned by Langdon Industries, corporate bylaws stated that the major stockholder in Langdon Industries had the ultimate say over the boat's itinerary, and that clause literally put it at Lexi's beck and call. This huge floating pleasure palace boasted a climate-controlled wine cellar, large walk-in wardrobe closets made of pungent cedar and a matching black hulled motorized launch, and everywhere Lexi looked she found traces of her father's personality: from the felt-topped poker table to the hidden Sentry safe to the black marble bathroom/sauna. That boat had been outfitted to his personal tastes alone, and she could feel his presence everywhere on it and nowhere else did Lexi Langdon feel as safe and secure as when she was there on his custom-designed yacht.

"SOME FRIENDS WILL BE COMING ON *THE YELLOW ROSE* FOR lunch," Lexi told Captain Jack later that morning in Sag Harbor as they sat on the bridge. "A wonderful new designer I met named Calvin Klein; he just won the Coty Award, although I doubt you know what that is ..."

"You got me there."

"And one of his friends and perhaps the most important woman in the fashion world, Diana Vreeland, you know, the fabulous editor of *Vogue*. Anyway, Calvin is making these fantastic blue-jeans that everyone is dying for."

"In Texas they're still wearing Wranglers," said Captain Jack.

"Well, don't tell Calvin that! Anyway, I think there'll just be the four of us, so I thought we could go for a nice day cruise somewhere, have a little lunch on the deck since the weather's so nice and take a swim, have some fun. What do you think?"

"Well, I don't really know what these *fashion* folks like to do, but we could circle Gardiner's Island," replied Captain Jack. "And I can tell stories about Captain Kidd's buried treasure. Put on my pirate outfit, if they'd enjoy that."

"You're kidding me."

"Yes, I am, Lexi," he said straight-faced.

"Funny you should say that because I'm friends with one of the Gardiner girls now," said Lexi. "The family lives in East Hampton, but they still own that island, held on to it for centuries. Can you imagine that?"

"Oh, well in that case, I'll leave out the part about her ancestor Earl Gardiner, another pirate, if she ever comes on board," said Captain Jack.

"Oh no, she'd love it," Lexi said with a laugh. "Why, she thinks she's some kind of pirate herself! Tell me, Captain Jack, who do you have working on the boat this summer? I didn't recognize a soul besides you when I came on board."

"That's correct, it's a whole new bunch from the University of Texas and that reminds me, one of the guys plays guitar," said Captain Jack. "Nice kid, but he's always strumming something down below, so I'll make sure he won't disturb your lunch."

"Is he any good?" asked Lexi.

"Truth be known, not so hot," said Captain Jack with a frown. "And still getting his sea legs to boot."

After a brief pause, Lexi exclaimed, "Hey, that's a great idea!"

"You mean you *want* him to *play*? He's not really that ..."

"No, no, not him," said Lexi. "But I do know someone who *is* really good, I mean, someone who can really sing. Great guy and he performs at a local hangout called the Talkhouse. But I think it's only the weekends, so maybe he's free today."

"Talkhouse?"

"Steven Talkhouse, in Amagansett. Everybody out here knows it."

"If you want, I'll give a call over there and see if I can roust him, send one of the crew around to go pick him up," said Captain Jack. "What's the name again?"

"Stephen Talkhouse," said Lexi.

"I was talking about his name."

"Of course, his name is Lee," said Lexi, who couldn't suppress a smile. "Lee Franklin, good-looking guy too."

"So, are you bringing him on board for his looks or his talent?" teased Captain Jack.

Giggling, Lexi admitted, "Well ... both. But he can really sing, trust me."

"Maybe you want to call him yourself?"

"No, you go ahead, Captain Jack," said Lexi.

"I'll have to go down below to make the call," said Captain Jack as he stood. "Be right back ..."

"Wait a second," Lexi said coyly. "One thing, when you speak to Lee, tell him it was your idea, keep it on a professional level."

"Aye, aye, my lady!"

Captain Jack got the number of the Talkhouse and sure enough, Tony Hughes rousted Lee out of bed to take the call at the telephone by the bar. Danny was already there, drinking his second cup of coffee when Lee got on the phone.

"Yeah, I'm Lee ... sure, I'm free today. Well, yeah ... I'd love to come and sing on the boat," said Lee to Captain Jack. "I don't know, whatever you want ... fine ... I'll be ready." He turned to Danny in astonishment. "You're not gonna believe who that was, some guy named Captain Jack, calling from Lexi Langdon's yacht *The Yellow Rose* in Sag Harbor. He wanted to know if I could come down with my guitar and sing for Lexi and some of her friends today while they're cruising around. Even said they're gonna pay me!"

Danny got even more excited than Lee. "Wow, Kathy told me that boat is fucking incredible, probably takes up half the harbor. I've never been on a boat like that before. Wonder who's gonna be there?"

"I don't know," said Lee awkwardly. "But ... I got a feeling I should go alone, Danny. This Captain Jack didn't say anything about bringing anybody along. It's like a job, ya know?"

Tony Hughes jumped in, as if on cue.

"Hey, Danny, do you know how to tend bar? I really need someone to fill in today. My regular guy called in sick."

"Do fish swim?" said Danny. Which was the parting shot for him and Tony to go off on a tangent of one-liners regarding such matters as *what bears do in the woods* and the *religion of the Pope* while Lee went back upstairs to get ready. He knew what looked good on him, how his jeans should fit and when a T-shirt was worn-in just enough to be sexy on his slim torso. And he knew soon he would be seeing Lexi.

Arriving at the boat, Lee stopped in his tracks, standing with the rest of the gawkers on the wharf, transfixed by the enormity of the yacht, unprepared for this floating *Taj Mahal*. "Don't tell me this is it?" he said to Justin, the guitar-picking member of the crew who picked him up.

"Yes, sir, sure is, *The Yellow Rose*. Every kid at Texas A&M wants to work on this boat."

"And Lexi Langdon owns this?" Lee asked, standing frozen. "All of this?"

"Not the water," joked Justin. "Just the boat. Uh ... we better get on board, sir. I think they've been kind of waiting for you to get underway. Go ahead and I'll stow your guitar below. You know, I play a little myself, what's in the case?"

"Gibson Hummingbird," said Lee. "Nineteen sixty-five, sunburst finish, Grover tuners."

"Wow, that's kind of vintage."

"Only valuable thing I own. Try it out if you like," said Lee. "It's been banged around plenty but still tunes up perfectly."

"Better not," said Justin. "I don't think Captain Jack is a big fan of my playing or my singing either. Said I sounded like a *whale in heat* and I don't think he meant that as a compliment."

Lexi and Ray were standing on the large deck at the bow of the boat, sipping cocktails with Calvin Klein and Diana Vreeland. When Diana was asked what she wanted to drink, her cryptic response had been, "Have I told you that I think water is God's tranquilizer?" Her dangling earrings tinkled in the wind, like Zen wind chimes, and her gold and silver striped metallic caftan was as glamorous as the boat itself, while Calvin, informal in a T-shirt and jeans looked as young as the crew. Ray was explaining the sights of the harbor, but when he saw Lee coming on board he turned sharply to Lexi.

"What's he doing here?" he asked, sounding more annoyed than surprised.

"Oh ... you mean Lee Franklin?" Lexi's eyes brightened just at the sight of Lee coming toward them. "Captain Jack thought it would be nice to have some *entertainment* while we cruise around Peconic Bay, so he called over to the Talkhouse," she said dismissively before handing Ray her glass and moving to greet Lee warmly. "Will y'all excuse me while I welcome him on board?"

"Captain Jack called the Talkhouse? How did he even know about that place? Or him?" Ray asked, pointing his finger accusingly at Lee. "Listen, Lexi, if you wanted to hire some talent all you had to do was ask me ..." But Lexi had her back to Ray and the roiling engines of *The Yellow Rose* as it prepared the leave the harbor, and it silenced him anyway.

"Good-looking guy," observed Calvin.

"But that cowboy vest has got to go," criticized Diana.

Watching Lexi kiss Lee on both cheeks and hug him much longer than Ray thought necessary, he said nothing.

Captain Jack had been enjoying the whole scene, Lee's arrival and Ray's consternation, discreetly from the upper bridge. Suddenly he cried out with glee, "Cut and run!" But no one among his startled crew, who were ready to cast off, moved. Finally, Justin, standing next to him and looking utterly perplexed, asked him, "Captain Jack, are you saying you want us to actually cut these ropes?"

"Jesus Christ! And you call yourself sailors? That's what a pirate captain would order after they'd be through raping and pillaging and trying to get out of town before the law caught up with them. So they'd cut the ropes and sail away as fast as the wind could take them. *Cut and run!*" Captain Jack heartily explained.

"I get it, from *back in the day,*" said Justin, taking out his Swiss Army knife.

"For Christ's sake, we don't really cut them!" Captain Jack bellowed with an exasperated sense of urgency.

It was one of those perfect mid-summer mornings, the sea was glassy and calm as *The Yellow Rose* strove forward as effortlessly as a duck on a pond. In fine weather like this Lexi preferred lunching on the spacious aft deck, so a formal table for six was set with a white linen tablecloth, napkins, engraved silverware and crystal glasses, etched with the monogram *LL.* A large marine blue canopy was pulled taut over the deck, warding off the sun, and Captain Jack read aloud the day's menu, including terrine de *foie gras,* cold lobster salad and chilled *Sancerre,* for Lexi's approval. She turned to Lee who stood nearby.

"I hope you like lobster as much as I do, Lee."

"I hate to drop them in boiling water and hear 'em thrashing around," said Lee. "But I gotta admit, I love to eat them."

"I could tell you were the sensitive type," teased Lexi.

"Yeah, sensitive ... but I'll eat anything." Lee was not sure of his place on Lexi's boat, because he had thought he would be performing and now his guitar had been put away somewhere and it looked like he was sitting down to lunch with everybody. "Lexi, you don't have to worry about me eating or anything. Just let me know when you want me to play."

"Of course, you'll join us for lunch, sugar," said Lexi, picking up on his uncertainty. "And you can sit right next to me, Lee, because you're my guest here, just like Diana and Calvin. And if you feel like singing, well, that's even better. Personally, I'd love to hear it. But maybe later, sometime after lunch, how does that sound?"

"Sounds perfect," said Lee.

"Anything you need, just ask Captain Jack."

Even with Lexi's assurances Lee still felt awkward and Ray couldn't have been less welcoming. He was sullen and withdrawn around Lee, barely talking to him and finding any excuse to get between him and Lexi when they were together. Finally, when the silence just became too awkward, as they were staring out across the bay, he looked icily at Lee and said, "You know it was my idea for you to come on the boat today – you owe me one, buddy."

"I appreciate that, Ray," said Lee. "When's your birthday? I'll send a card or something."

"Don't get cute," said Ray walking away.

"Hey, just kidding," said Lee.

WITH SHELTER ISLAND DIRECTLY IN FRONT OF THEM, *THE Yellow Rose* pulled out of Sag Harbor and turned north, following the inlet that ran by Barcelona Cove.

"That cove is where whalers would carve up sperm whales before bringing everything to market," explained Captain Jack. "Blubber, whale oil, even the bones that were used in women's corsets." Everyone looked over to see, except Ray. "They didn't waste anything."

"I'd like to try on one of those whalebone corsets myself," joked Lexi, putting her hands on her tiny waist. "I heard you couldn't breathe in those things."

"You'd look fabulous in anything, Lexi," said Calvin Klein.

"I never thought of a whale as a fashion statement," retorted Diana Vreeland. "Quite the contrary."

"I've been meaning to ask you, what do you think about the way most people dress?" asked Ray.

"What do I think about the way most people dress?" said Diana dismissively. "Most people are not something one thinks about."

"Everyone dresses in blue jeans now," said Ray. "All the elegance is gone."

"Blue jeans are the most beautiful things since the gondola," said Diana, moving away from Ray with Calvin and whispering in his ear, "That man is the most narcissistic person I've ever met," she hissed. "I loathe narcissism, but I approve of vanity."

"I'm crazy," said Calvin. "And I don't pretend to be anything else."

"You're perfect, darling," Diana said with finality as Captain Jack walked by. "Where are we headed, Captain?" she asked. "Out to Montauk? Will we pass Andy Warhol's house?"

"Montauk?" said Ray very concerned. "Who said anything about Montauk? Don't you think that would be too far? I mean, we'll get back much too late."

Everyone looked at Ray, surprised that he was already talking about returning when they were just out of the harbor. "I mean, it's up to you, Lexi," Ray backpedaled. "But I mean Montauk is a long way ..."

Lexi said nothing, not even acknowledging Ray, looking straight out to sea with a secret superficial smile.

"What's our itinerary, Captain Jack?" she asked with authority. "Perhaps you could show Calvin and Diana, and Lee too, of course, on that chart you're holding."

"Exactly," said Captain Jack, pulling open the rolled-up map with everyone but Ray gathering around. "First, I thought we'd circle Gardiner's Island which is right here," he said pointing to it with his finger. "There's a nice spot where you can take a swim if you want before lunch, good snorkeling spot. And then we'd come back the other way, by. We should be back by early evening..." He looked behind him where Ray was sulking. "If that's OK with you, Ray?"

"Well, of course, it's up to Lexi," said Ray.

"How considerate of you, Ray," Lexi said sarcastically. "Hope we're not keeping you from anything important."

Diana Vreeland shook her head and looked to Calvin.

THE YACHT GAINED SPEED ONCE IT CLEARED THE HARBOR, ITS dual propellers causing a fearsome wake on each side of the boat, witnessed by the frowning faces of nearby day-sailors as they dealt with the rough ride over the waves the big boat generated. The *Yellow Rose* circled Gardiner's Island in just over an hour and slowed down as it came around to the island's western shore with a clear view of the impressive manor house and a restored 17th century windmill.

"We should drop anchor here if you want to swim on the leeward side of the island," said Captain Jack. "The water will be smoother, probably warmer too, and then you can all have lunch on deck."

"If Ray thinks we have time," said Lexi, her first words to him in all that time.

"Be nice," said Ray. "I was just ..."

"Can you believe that one family still owns that island and has it all to themselves," interrupted Lexi. "Now that's what I call real privacy. Wonder if they're allowed to shoot trespassers?"

"Not sure about that," replied Captain Jack. "That kind of thing is frowned upon these days, except back in Texas, of course. Actually, I read the island was a gift from the king sometime before the revolution."

"Why don't you look into buying an island for yourself?" Ray asked Lexi. "Wouldn't that be fun?"

"Depends on who was on the island with me ... and what time they had to leave."

Ray went on, "I'm sure you can find one for sale somewhere. Say, Captain Jack, I've been meaning to ask you, what was that smaller island we passed on the way around? Looked almost uninhabited."

He turned to Lexi. "Maybe we could buy that one." Lexi glared at him. "I mean *you* could buy it, darling, of course."

"Did some research on that before we cast off today," said Captain Jack. "That's Plum Island. Some people say that they test germ warfare there. Not sure anyone would want to set up house there, no telling what would crawl out of the sink."

Lexi looked glumly at Ray but spoke to Captain Jack. "Things are toxic enough on this boat already," said Lexi before diving into the water.

"If you don't mind, Captain," said Calvin. "Diana and I are going to sunbathe while everyone swims. You know, catch up on the changing taste in fashion and all that."

"Too much good taste can be boring," said Diana.

Deeply engrossed in conversation about the fashion world, Calvin and Diana sunbathed on the bow of the boat while Lexi swam near the boat and Captain Jack handed down snorkeling gear. Lee and Ray stood on deck watching.

"You're not going in?" Lee asked Ray.

"Don't think so," said Ray. "Not in the mood."

"That water looks pretty good to me, can I borrow a suit?"

Ray looked at him frostily. "You didn't bring your own?"

"Forgot."

"I suppose so. Ask one of the crew to show you where I keep my clothes."

"Don't worry, I'll take an old one," said Lee.

"There are no old ones," retorted Ray.

Lee went down below with Justin, leaving Ray alone on deck to brood. He changed into one of Ray's suits and quickly returned, diving directly into the water. Lexi was already fifty yards from the boat in snorkel and fins and Lee swam to her with long powerful strokes. On deck Ray stood with his arms folded next to Captain Jack who said, "If that boy can play guitar as well as he swims, we might be in for something special."

"What's so special about that?" replied Ray defiantly. "Who can't swim?"

Captain Jack just smiled as Lee dove under the water, reached Lexi and surfaced right beside her.

"Hey," said Lee as they treaded water together.

"Hey, yourself," said Lexi, taking off her diving mask. "So, you found a bathing suit."

"Ray lent it to me."

"I bought him a bunch and he's yet to get one wet. Isn't this water just *delicious*? You know, if I were swimming out here all alone, I'd probably swim naked. Nothing feels as good as that. I love that."

Lee smiled. "Me too...I used to do it on the Island of Ponza, just off Naples in Italy. The water was so clear you could see all the way to the bottom."

"That must come in handy when you're swimming naked," said Lexi. "Will you look at Ray standing there? He doesn't look very happy."

"Hope I didn't take his favorite bathing suit," said Lee.

"I don't know what's got into him," said Lexi. "Just don't pay any attention to him 'cause that's exactly what I'm trying to do. Come on, let's swim around the boat."

Lexi was a good swimmer too with a fine practiced stroke, and Lee had to make an effort to keep up with her. As they made a wide circle around the boat, he couldn't help but notice that Ray would shift his position on the boat to keep them in view.

"Hold up a minute, Lexi," said Lee as he grabbed one of her flippers. "You're too quick for me."

"Learned how to swim at a Swiss finishing school," Lexi explained. "In fact, I was on the swimming team, thought it would keep my figure in shape while I was eating all that fondue. Swimming, skiing, a little French and *voila* we girls were finished!" She looked toward the boat. "What the hell is Ray Arthur doing now? He's worse than the chaperones that followed us around back at that school. Watch this ..." She waved to Ray and he meekly waved back, forcing a smile. "I believe he's getting jealous," said Lexi giggling.

"Oh ... sorry," said Lee.

"Don't you be sorry, sugar. That's the whole point. Come on, I'll race you to the boat."

"What does the winner get?"

"Maybe a kiss ... sometime."

She swam to the boat with smooth, strong strokes and nimbly climbed up the boarding ladder draped over the railing. Captain Jack stood ready with a large fluffy white towel. Lee didn't race her to the boat, treading water, he wondered what she meant by *that's the whole point* before finally swimming to the ladder himself. They towel dried and lounged on the aft deck with Calvin Klein and Diana Vreeland, already there with Ray, taking in the sun as lunch was being spread out on a serving table.

"You look great in that suit," Calvin Klein told Lexi. "French?"

"I don't know," said Lexi. "Cheryl Tiegs was wearing it on that *Sports Illustrated* cover and I went right out and bought a few."

"*Sports Illustrated* is now a fashion magazine?" said Diana Vreeland. "Isn't that just marvelous."

"You should design bathing suits, Calvin," said Lexi. "It's so hard to find one with any style."

"Well, I'm thinking of doing a line of underwear next season – it's almost the same thing."

"Is that what fashion has come to?" said Diana Vreeland. "Jeans and underwear?"

"Sounds good to me," said Calvin.

Lunch was announced and Lexi took her place at the head of the table while everyone was seated. "I hope everybody's hungry," she called out to Lee and her guests. "Captain Jack says our new chef is so good that *The Yellow Rose* might be getting a Michelin star."

Justin served them delicate slices of terrine de *foie gras* and copious portions of fresh lobster salad, pouring chilled white wine whenever a glass was half empty and stood by while they ate, drank and talked. Dessert was *coupe colonel*, a mix of lemon sorbet and vodka and a silver coffee service. Captain Jack ate with them, excusing himself before dessert arrived and took his coffee up to the bridge. As soon as he could manage it without Lexi noticing, Ray joined him and started right in about getting home soon because, he believed, the weather was about to turn nasty and the seas rough. Captain Jack, pointing to the nearly flawless blue sky and calm bay, assured him that was not the case, but Ray persisted, saying Lexi was in a hurry. Captain Jack didn't pay Ray much mind and just kept about his business, only taking his orders from Lexi and he knew that she was in no hurry to go anywhere, certainly not while Lee Franklin was on the boat with her.

WHEN THEY DID FINALLY PULL BACK INTO SAG HARBOR, JUST before dusk, it was a veritable *rush hour* in the marina. There was movement all around as smaller boats came in from Peconic Bay, restless to get home to their berths before darkness fell. The harbormaster was forced to keep *The Yellow Rose* anchored just outside the marina until she had the wide berth she needed to maneuver. Ray paced the deck anxiously while Lexi disappeared down into her stateroom to shower and change clothes. Lee stayed on deck, using the outside shower to rinse off the saltwater and thinking it strange that he had never taken his guitar out of its case or sung anything nor had anyone asked him to.

He strolled through the well-appointed dining room, finished in rare blond woods with contrasting geometric in-lays, and stepped down a short flight of stairs that, he supposed, led to the engine room. As he ducked his head to clear a low ceiling in the passageway there, a voice from a half-closed door called out to him.

"Who goes there?"

Lee stopped and gently pushed open the door just the slightest bit to see Captain Jack sitting in his cramped but handsomely finished cabin. He had his official *whites* off now and was dressed in tan shorts, canvas belt and pink polo shirt.

"Excuse me," said Lee, holding his clothes in front of him. "Just looking for someplace to change."

"The crew room is right there," said Captain Jack. "You can change in there. Does Lexi need anything?"

"No, I don't think so," said Lee. "I think she's in her stateroom."

"Then come back and have a chat after you're done."

"Sure thing." Lee took his clothes into the small crew quarters and when he returned Captain Jack was stretched out on his small bed.

"Thought I'd take a rest until we can dock," he explained. "Harbormaster said we better wait for all the small fries to get home to their births or one of them might run into us. Any sign of Ray up there? I wouldn't be surprised if he swam to shore."

Lee laughed. "I don't know, probably up top somewhere. Ray doesn't seem to enjoy being out on the water too much today. Strange guy."

"Never bothered to figure Ray out," said Captain Jack dismissively. "Do you know him well? You guys good friends?"

"Not really," said Lee shaking his head. "I don't know if you could even call us friends."

"But do you *like* him?" asked Captain Jack directly. "That's what I was getting at."

Lee didn't know how to respond. "Well, I don't really know Ray well enough to answer that. I'd have to say I'm more friendly with Lexi ... I mean, I'm more Lexi's friend," said Lee.

"I thought so," said Captain Jack smiling. "Took a chance even asking you that, didn't want to put you on the spot or anything. Ray's friends, at least the few I've met, are always kind of full of themselves, trying to let you know how important they are. You don't fit into that category. Makes sense, it was Lexi's idea to call you up today, bring you on board."

"Yeah? Ray said it was his idea."

"Why doesn't that surprise me?"

"But I never even played a note."

"Not sure if that was her intention," said Captain Jack. "Hope I didn't put my foot in it."

"Don't worry," said Lee, somewhat pleased, although curious as to why Captain Jack was telling him all this and giving him the distinct impression that Ray was not one of his favorite people. He hardly knew the captain of Lexi's yacht and definitely did not want to get caught in some feud between Ray and Captain Jack. "Hey, *The Yellow Rose* is quite a boat, never been on anything like this before. Saw some nice boats on the Italian coast but nothing like this. You've been working here long?"

"I don't *work* here, son," said Captain Jack with a note of condescension. "I'm the goddamn captain of *The Yellow Rose.*" He laughed heartily. "Captains don't work – we tell everybody else to get to work and what to do and when!"

"Or they walk the plank?" said Lee.

"Something like that. Lexi's dad would have gotten a kick out of you saying that."

"This was his boat, I take it?"

"Until the day he died. I mean, to begin with, he had her built for him to his exact specifications, designed the stateroom himself, and loved showing her off to his Texas friends. I don't believe anything made that man happier than this boat."

"Not even Lexi?" asked Lee.

"Well ... sure, Lexi made him happy as well. Let's just say Lex Langdon was complicated."

"He made garbage trucks, right?"

"Yeah, Langdon Industries - they're still my official employer."

"There's something I can't figure out," said Lee. "Hope you don't take it the wrong way."

"What's that?" said Captain Jack.

"How can you make so much money from ... garbage trucks?"

Captain Jack laughed uproariously. "Guess that's what everyone would like to know! Well, the truth is they make *waste removal vehicles* – that's the official term – and that means everything from garbage trucks to exhausted rocket fuel collectors and a host of other stuff I don't understand. Let me tell you, Lee, that man had his fingers into everything that ever-made money in Texas; I'm talking oil, missiles, real estate and servicing that huge army base Fort Hood. Did you know it's the biggest U.S. military base in the country and yet it's named after a Texas Confederate general? Lex taught me a song about him one night when we were both in our cups." Captain Jack belted out in his deep baritone:

My feet are torn and bloody,
My heart is full of woe,
I'm going back to Georgia
To find my uncle Joe
You may talk about your Beauregard,
You may sing of Bobby Lee,
But the gallant Hood of Texas
He played hell in Tennessee.

"You sing better than I do," joked Lee. "But isn't that the melody to 'The *Yellow Rose of Texas?*'"

"You bet," said Captain Jack. "I think it was Lyndon Johnson who named that base and Lex Langdon got involved because of him, they owned some of the land together or something, you know, *silent partners*. And then it was Lex's construction company that built the damn base, or at least a lot of it. And now Langdon garbage trucks pick up all the trash there."

"He knew Lyndon Johnson?" asked Lee. "The President?"

"Thick as thieves," said Captain Jack. "Lex Langdon was a proud member of the *military industrial complex* and it was LBJ who personally brought him into the club. I'd do these sunset cruises on *The Yellow Rose* and there'd be nothing but Army brass, Congressmen and Saudi Sheiks clinking their glasses together and making deals for God knows what, while some good-looking gals made them comfortable."

"When Lexi was on the boat?" asked Lee astonished.

Captain Jack looked at Lee like he was beyond dumb. "What do you think?"

"So, Lex was pretty well connected politically."

"Lex Langdon knew how to *milk the steel cow* and was an early backer of Lyndon, helped put him into the Senate and remained a close friend and supporter during his years in the White House. Told me he was about to go to the reception in Dallas the day JFK was shot, that's how thick he was with the Democratic Party. Also said they should have done the reception anyway. That's how much he didn't like Kennedy."

"Jesus."

"Lex Langdon, he was a southerner through and through; Texas family for many generations, fought the Comanche, fought the Mexicans, fought the Union and was fighting the IRS until the day he died." Captain Jack gurgled up a laugh like a broken water pipe. "You had to take Lex as he was, that man wasn't about to change after the millions he'd made for himself and his friends. Do you have any idea how many garbage trucks the U.S. government buys every year? Some say LBJ moved the space center to Houston just so Lexi's Dad could haul away the garbage, make millions more and give a nice chunk to the Democratic Party."

"But he never ran for office himself?"

"Hated goddamn politicians," said Captain Jack. "Except Lyndon, of course. Hey, bet you didn't know why Lyndon Johnson named his daughters Lucy Baines and Lynda Bird?"

"Never really thought about it," said Lee.

"So, they'd all have the same initials – LBJ!"

"That's crazy," said Lee.

"I believe Lex Langdon was copying him when he called his daughter Lexi."

"That's right," said Lee. "There are LLs all over this boat." With his head bowed, he stood there in Captain Jack's cabin, cramped for space.

"Not much room to stretch out down here," said Captain Jack. "When the boat's empty I camp out in one of the forward staterooms, much more comfortable. But when Lexi's on board I like to let her have the run of the boat and stay out of her way as much as I can. When she was a teenager, she'd have slumber parties with a bunch of her friends and I'm talking about seventeen-year-old girls in nightgowns on every deck. I'd pour myself a tall Scotch, come on down here and lock the door." Captain Jack stood up and carefully selected a cigar from a dark walnut case. "Let's go up to the bridge and I'll show you how we dock this thing. You want a cigar? They're *Montecristos, straight from Havana.*"

"No cigar for me," said Lee. "But I'll take some fresh air."

"That we got, and plenty of it," said Captain Jack. He led the way from his cabin to the spacious rear deck and up three narrow staircases to the flying bridge where he piloted the ship. Ostensibly a work area where courses were plotted and weather checked, the bridge was also a luxurious lounge with wrap-around white Naugahyde sofas and a matching pilot's chair mounted behind an enormous polished wood steering wheel with chrome spokes. An impressive control panel spread out in front of the wheel with the latest technical innovations in super-yacht motoring – multiple radios and radars, a gauge that measured the rudder angle – anything you could imagine when money was no object. Once Captain Jack got the okay from the harbormaster, he skillfully brought the boat to rest dockside as his crew secured the lines. In a second, all went quiet when he shut down the engines and he went down to bid goodbye to Calvin Klein and Diana Vreeland with Lee following close behind. Ray was nearly off the boat the moment the engines stopped, standing impatiently at the top of the gangplank.

"Don't tell us you're leaving, Ray?" asked Captain Jack.

"That's right, Jack," said Ray. "Otherwise, tomorrow morning I'll have to go back to the house to eat breakfast and pick up my clubs. I'm teeing off at eight a.m. sharp."

"If you and Lexi would like to stay on board tonight, I'm sure the cook can bake some fresh croissants for you in the morning. Breakfast is not a problem. And I'll send Justin to pick up your clubs."

"I'm sure Lexi would love that, but I can't sleep with the boat rocking underneath me," said Ray. "Guess I'm not a natural born sailor like you, Jack."

Captain Jack nodded and said nothing. Ray turned to Lee.

"So, the party's over, Lee. Lexi's gonna stay on board but we're all leaving. Calvin could drop you off at the Talkhouse."

"Or if you want, Lee," interjected Captain Jack, "we can continue your tour of *The Yellow Rose* and I'll have Justin drop you off later. Up to you, of course."

"Well, in that case, I guess I'll stay," said Lee. "If it's no problem." He could see Ray clenching his jaw and the apprehension in his eyes, clearly not keen on the idea of leaving Lee on the boat with Lexi. But he quickly turned and started down the gangplank, "Suit yourself, man," he said and briskly walked away.

Maybe not a natural born sailor, thought Captain Jack as he watched Ray get into the two-seater Mercedes 450SL Lexi had bought him, *but a goddamn pirate nevertheless*.

"Shall we climb back up to the bridge?" Captain Jack said to Lee. "Have that drink?"

Captain Jack filled two glasses with ice from a chrome bucket before settling back into his customary place in the pilot's chair. Pulling out a bottle of Scotch hidden behind a row of charts and commenting, "My private stash," he filled their glasses and told Lee to get comfortable on the couch. From the bridge, the modest lights of Sag Harbor were spread out before them like a dark blanket of twinkling jewels and every docking space in the Marina was taken with yachts, sailboats, day cruisers and speedboats of every sort. Captain Jack looked it all over carefully. "Nothing like *The Yellow Rose* here," he remarked. "But then it's not so showy up here like in St. Tropez or Miami Beach."

"This boat has been to France?" asked Lee astonished.

"Three ocean crossings," said Captain Jack. "We'd go in the summer when the weather was good, about two weeks to reach the Canary Islands and then pass by Gibraltar right into the Mediterranean. Of course, Lex Langdon would fly to Cannes, set up shop in his usual suite at the Carleton, fill it with the best-looking hookers in town and start doing deals with the Saudis with his boat out there in plain sight of his hotel veranda. He liked showing off the boat, all lit up like a Polish church off the beach down there on the Riviera almost as much as he did being on it himself."

"What about Lexi's mother?" asked Lee. "Where was she when all this was going on? Back in Houston?"

"I never met Lexi's mother," said Captain Jack. "She was gone before I came on the scene."

"Divorced?"

Captain Jack shook his head. "Dead at thirty-five, still a young woman. Some disease called Lupus got her while Lexi was just a little girl."

"What's Lupus?"

"Attacks the immune system. Lex told me it was Lexi who noticed it first, all sitting at breakfast one morning and Lexi saying something about her mother having a rash on her face shaped like a butterfly. Apparently, that's an early symptom, dead in less than a year. Like I said, never met her, but they say she was beautiful, like Lexi, I suppose. Being married to Lex Langdon must have been quite a trip for that poor woman; he didn't take the *faithful* part in his wedding vows too seriously."

"And what about him after that? Did he remarry?"

"No, not Lex ..." Captain Jack hesitated. "It's kind of complicated," he said while puffing on his cigar. "I probably shouldn't be telling you all of this, you know."

"No problem," said Lee, backing off. "It's none of my business, really."

"Can I speak to you confidentially? Man to man?"

"Sure, I won't write a song about it, promise."

Captain Jack laughed slyly. "The ballad of Lex Langdon, that would be a good one! But what I'm trying to say here is that Lexi didn't have it so easy when she was growing up as folks might imagine with all that money and everything. People see a girl at her young age, all this ..." He gestured around the boat. "And everything else, they might think she always got what she wanted. But the truth is she really didn't."

"What didn't she get?" asked Lee.

"Well, how about enough love for one thing?" Captain Jack responded. "And not much time with either of her parents, for another. They shuttled her off to school over in Europe at a pretty young age and then her mother dying like that ... well, it was pretty rough on her. And Lex Langdon was not what you'd call a model father. I mean, he did love her in his way, but sometimes he treated her more like a nuisance than a daughter. I don't want to judge the man, he had other priorities."

"Never remarried?" Lee asked again.

"Like I said, Lex Langdon was not a one-woman kind of man. And once Lexi's mother was gone, he was even less so. He had *pit stops* all over Texas, and Mexico, too." He started laughing and coughing on his cigar smoke. "Got to hand it to him though, desperado 'til the end, died in the saddle."

"Here? On *The Yellow Rose*?"

"No, not here. If it had happened here, I doubt if Lexi would have set foot back on the boat. No, it was back in Houston at the Shamrock Hotel. Thing was, Lex Langdon could have had just about any woman in Houston he wanted if he took the time to make a phone call or go out on a date, but the man had no patience. When he got horny, he'd just cruise down Bissonet Street and pick out whatever hooker struck his fancy and take her back with him to the hotel.

Spotted this little Mexican whore he had apparently been with before, took her back to the Shamrock and started to go at it ..."

Captain Jack leaned to his right and peered down the bridge's chrome ladder to ensure no one was within earshot. "Thing was," he continued in a hushed tone, "Lex Langdon was a *large* man in every way and was probably carrying close to three-hundred pounds, so when his heart gave out he just collapsed right on top of that gal and she started screaming bloody murder, and they had to bust right into the room to pull him off of her! No chance of keeping it quiet after that and next thing you knew Langdon stock tanked and the board of directors wanted to change the name of the company or sell the whole damn thing to some outfit up north."

"Surprised that's such a scandal," said Lee. "Guy has a heart attack while screwing a prostitute. What's the big deal?"

"Well, a couple of things made it a big deal, Lee. First of all, Houston ain't New York, it's the gold-plated buckle of the Bible Belt. And secondly, this was a man who attended breakfast prayer meetings with the President of the United States, and ..." said Captain Jack barely controlling his glee, "there were *two* girls in that hotel room with him and one was just shy of 15 years old – two sisters I believe. Man, they got them the hell out of Houston and back down across the border to Nuevo Laredo, pronto."

"Jesus, how did Lexi handle all of this?"

"Well, how *does* any girl handle it? She grew up real fast. Lexi loved her daddy more than anything and when it came to family, he was *it*, so when she lost him, she was devastated. But she was determined to carry on the Langdon name. And that wasn't easy because it was like a war down there in Houston after Lex died, everyone aiming to take Langdon Industries down and grab all those juicy government contracts. I heard Lexi had a pretty hard-hitting meeting with the board, but she stood her ground, barely a major at eighteen years old, saying the company had to go on and there'd be no scandals from her. It didn't hurt that she had one of LBJ's daughters standing by her side all the while."

"They're friends?"

"Since they were kids," said Captain Jack. "The board took her at her word and gave in, and Lexi gave a big donation to the Democrats out of Lex Langdon's estate. She's still the majority shareholder and the status quo today is just where Lex left it. Nothing's changed except now she lets the board take care of the business and mostly stays out of their way. And that's how it's been ever since."

"What a world." Lee gazed past the darkness of Sag Harbor Sound out to the flickering lights of Shelter Island.

"What a world is right," repeated Captain Jack. "That's why I like it here, Lee, floating on the water. Hey, I wonder what's happening down below, better go check if Lexi needs something before I turn in." He looked at Lee ruefully, hesitatingly, as if he wasn't sure what he was about to say next.

"Don't take this the wrong way, but I'd appreciate it if you kept all that stuff I told you about Lex to yourself...wouldn't want folks gossiping up here as well. That's what Lexi was trying to get away from."

"Don't worry," said Lee. "I don't want to see Lexi get hurt either."

Captain Jack smiled knowingly. "I didn't think so, Lee. I saw the way you look at her. Guess that's why I talked so damned much ... that and the Scotch." He gave a belly laugh and flicked the stub of his cigar out into the harbor water below. "Lexi needs people who really care about her. Not sure if Ray fits into that category."

"I know what you mean," said Lee.

"Hell, I don't know what I'm saying here, but I tell you what, Lee, I love that girl like she's my own daughter, don't want to see any more harm come to her if I can prevent it. Let's just leave it at that."

CHAPTER 10

Ray drove recklessly along the back roads of East Hampton, speeding down Scuttle Hole Road and overtaking cars as he passed the darkening farm fields of Bridgehampton, many of which now sprouted sumptuous mega-mansions instead of the celebrated Long Island potatoes of yesteryear. At this hour of early evening with stores just closing, the streets of the sober-looking village of Southampton were clogged with traffic. Ray impatiently honked his horn and ran a few red lights while nervously peering down at his watch. Not only was he stressed out at being late, but now he was extremely anxious about leaving Lexi alone on *The Yellow Rose* with Lee Franklin whom she *seemed* to have some kind of attraction to. But he couldn't figure that out, wondering what she could see in this guy who was just two steps away from standing on some street corner busking for quarters. But he knew he had left the boat in too obvious a hurry with Captain Jack giving him the evil eye and leaving nothing but suspicion in his wake.

Still, he just couldn't stop himself even though his inner voice kept imploring him, *don't go there, don't screw up, don't blow it.* But Ray was not a guy who listened to any voice but the one he spoke out loud, never analyzing his motives, just calculating his next move and trying to come out on top wherever he was. What was pulling him now to Gloria besides the illicit sex and cocaine was a self-destructive force rising like a beast within and that was something he'd never look at or admit to. To Ray, any kind of introspection was just a sign of weakness and he never went *there.* What he craved was the rush of risk, taking it to the edge and not getting caught. Proving to himself, over and over again, that he was the smartest guy in the room. So smart, in fact, that he could slip away to see Gloria and her uncle Maddy the Horse, hopefully throw in a few lines of cocaine and some *quickie* sex and still keep Lexi, his marriage and all the perks that came with that *well-capitalized* setup intact. Ray looked at himself in his rear-view mirror while running his fingers through his shiny dark hair and he couldn't help but smile. *What was he worrying about, a guy like him? Come on, this rock star wannabe was no threat. You're the man,* he said to himself as he stroked both hair and ego. Arrogant and proud of it, he had maneuvered himself to be right where he wanted. *On top of the world, Ma!*

Ray had taken credit for a run of good luck and even convinced himself that he was *the man of the moment*, the kind of guy who made things happen, managed a record label, married the richest girl in town and even got in bed with the Mafia. But being Lexi's full-time escort was starting to get old; he was sick of her setting the course of their marriage and running their lives according to her whims. She had dragged him to a recent charity event and someone there had the nerve to greet him as *Mr. Langdon.* It took all his self-control not to explode, but he knew that would be a fatal mistake because as long as he was married to Lexi Langdon people treated him differently, with an addendum of respect, ready to extend favors, both personal and in business. He was not so naïve that he didn't understand that all of that would be over in a heartbeat if things with Lexi ever disintegrated and he was back on his own. He'd seen that happen once already, down in Virginia, when a messy divorce had left his mother with a pile of debts, a lover who disappeared and a telephone that barely rang, least of all from her son who'd gone to New York.

But now, with this new *thing* he was getting going all by himself, he believed that whatever happened between him and Lexi, he'd be fine, a man of means who could snap right back at her if it came to that. Really, the only thing that unnerved him was that it had all happened so fast. He could hardly believe that it was just last winter, coming back to his office at Edel Records after wolfing down a pastrami sandwich at the Stage Deli, when he came upon the receptionist arguing with this cute young female *very* punk rocker who was more than insisting that someone at Edel Records should listen to her demo, that they'd be sorry if they didn't. Dealing with pushy artists looking for a deal was a common enough task at almost any record company and if not for the impressive outline of her breasts, her erect nipples jutting against her T-shirt, Ray might have walked on inside to his office without getting involved, but just that was enough of a lure to divert him. Besides, he was always horny after lunch.

"I'll take care of this, Rosalyn," he informed the receptionist while motioning Gloria to step his way. "Listen, sweetheart, Edel Records doesn't accept unsolicited material. But maybe I can help you out. I'm Ray Arthur, Vice President of A&R, and I bet you're a singer and that's your demo you're holding there, and you want somebody to listen to it. Am I right?" He smiled ironically.

That day, like most days, Gloria wore a very short plaid skirt with ripped pink fishnet stockings, Doc Martin steel-capped boots and a washed-out T-shirt with Keith Richards' stoned grinning face on it. Her black hair and kohl eye makeup were in sharp contrast to her clear pale skin and dark red lipstick covered her generous lips. She might have looked trashy, but definitely the sexy kind of trashy.

"Yeah, I got a band - Gloria and the Obnoxious ..."

"And you're Gloria," said Ray.

"Very sharp, Ray Arthur. I see how you got your job."

"Look, Gloria, we don't accept demos that we don't ask for. It's company policy. Get yourself a manager and have him call us."

Gloria moved just inches from Ray in an obviously provocative pose and her hungry stare zeroed in on him. A bouffant of spiked blue-black hair stood high on her head, with a faint bouquet of Halston perfume, and now Ray was thinking that she probably wasn't wearing any underwear at all. At least that's what he was hoping.

"Any other company policies I should know about, Mister Arthur?" she said softly.

She draped her hand on his shoulder and left it there. "Well, there *are* exceptions to every policy," he said timidly. "You can call me Ray."

"Then that's what I am, Ray. I'm the exception," said Gloria, not backing down. "I'm clearly an exception, can't you see that?" She bent forward and he looked down the torn neck of her T-shirt to gaze upon her breasts.

"You are ... exceptional," he said. "Okay, give me your tape and write down your name and number. I'll give it a listen just because you're so ..."

"*Fuckable?*" she mouthed the word, just barely whispering it, but loud enough so that the stunned receptionist could hear.

"Uh ... something like that," he said, pulling out his gold Cross pen. "Here, write it down on the box and I'll get back to you."

"I'm counting on it, Ray," said Gloria, taking the pen from him, scribbling on the cassette label and tucking the pen back into Ray's inside jacket pocket.

Back in his office Ray threw the cassette in an ever-growing pile of demos on his windowsill, where it might have stayed forever if not for his obsessively efficient secretary who, while straightening his office later that afternoon, noticed the name on the tape box in large block letters.

"Isn't that the name of that mobster? DiGeronimo? The one I always see in the news?" she asked Ray. "He's got a funny name. Something *the horse*."

"Let me see that tape." Ray took it out of her hand. "I don't know, probably a lot of DiGeronimo's around." Then, after driving himself crazy for an hour he finally picked up the phone and dialed Gloria's number.

"Yeah?" she answered.

"Tape's not bad," he lied, having barely listened to more than the first thirty seconds.

"That didn't take you long, Ray," she purred.

"So, when can I see the band live?" he asked.

"The band or me?"

"Both," said Ray.

When Gloria hung up the phone she was sporting a huge smile. *Gotcha Ray!* She thought, giggling with delight.

Just two weeks later, on a dreary Sunday afternoon with the sun blanketed behind thick gray clouds and last night's rain pooling in toxic puddles, Ray sat brooding in the backseat of a chauffeured Lincoln on his way downtown thinking, *What kind of a club has a band playing a gig on a Sunday afternoon?* Even if, as Gloria had explained to him, this Hilly Krystal who owned CBGB and personally booked all the bands, told her this was the best he could offer, he still didn't get it. "Call him back," he had told her. "Tell him a record company VP is coming down. He'll find a better slot for you." But Gloria said she'd already done that and Hilly had been less than impressed.

"Take it or leave it," Hilly had said to her. "Bands audition on Sunday to play at CBGB. If this *suit* wants you to play some other time than he can book you a showcase somewhere. And you know why he won't do that?" he asked rhetorically. "Because they're too fucking cheap, that's why."

So Sunday afternoon it was and coincidentally Lexi was out of town that day, over in Colts Neck, New Jersey, giving out ribbons at a horse show. *Another good sign that this was supposed to happen,* thought Ray, because with Lexi gone he could make of the day what he wanted, rent a limo and try to get alone with Gloria somewhere. But to do that in style, he'd need some *blow*, so he made a cryptic telephone call to his most reliable dealer who confirmed that he was indeed holding the goods, *another good sign.*

"How's the weather?" was the question.

"Stopped raining, think I'll take the dogs out for a walk," was the reply, all code of course - if the dogs needed to walk then there was cocaine, *Columbian marching powder,* to be had. Ray's first stop before CBGB was a top floor apartment in a modest Jane Street doorman building down in the Village. Phil was a dealer to the stars and his well-tipped doorman screened all his *friends,* of which there were many, with a series of ever-changing passwords. Between the phone and the door, it was hard to keep up without a codebook.

"How do I know you're Ray?" asked the doorman.

"Because Ray is my name and Phil is my friend."

"Right. And what does Phil like to do?"

"I don't know ... walk his dogs?"

"You got it, go on up," said the doorman.

"Some security," said Ray.

"Phil's idea," said the doorman.

Ray was announced and sent up on the elevator. He rang the doorbell and waited in front of a steel reinforced door listening to the dogs growling on the other side while Phil unlocked three massive locks, finally swinging open the door and letting him in. What Ray would have liked to have done was just go in, get the drugs and leave, but there was a protocol that had to be followed, a kind of ritual between client and dealer that involved a warm hug, a kind of *faux-friendship* chat, and, in Ray's case, promises of concert tickets and free albums next time he came by. Phil *worked* in his black silk dressing gown day and night and had two large, suspicious German shepherds constantly prowling around the apartment. He measured out cocaine on a double balance scale before pouring it into a glass vial and handing it to Ray while stashing the cash in his top desk drawer, chock-full of hundred-dollar bills. Phil's emaciated girlfriend, *Dot,* in her own silk robe, silently haunted the apartment and Phil seemed to be always annoyed with her about one thing or another.

Phil's wall-mounted shotgun did make Ray nervous, but he got over that as soon as he took a sample hit, nodding his head in approval and snorting the cocaine deep into his sinuses. As if by instinct, Dot came in right after the coke was laid out and bent down with her own handy straw perched to her nose.

"Hey, Dot, feed the dogs," Phil ordered, moving the tray of coke away from her. "No more blow till you feed the goddamn dogs."

"That's why I don't have a dog," said Ray nervously, pulling another bill from his wallet. "You better give me another gram, Phil. This stuff is too good." He glanced at his watch. "Got to run, I'm going to a show."

"On Sunday afternoon?" said Phil, shaking his head. "Isn't anything sacred anymore?"

Ray briefly considered that it might have been *too much* to hire a white stretch limousine to take him down to some club on the Bowery, Manhattan's skid-row, but that's where CBGB was and what the hell, he could put it all on his expense account. Besides, this way he could slump down in the back seat behind the tinted windows and take a few hits without fearing that some cop might pull up next to him and notice. But just as he was doing exactly that and pulling his head up from the small mirror resting on his knee, someone was indeed tapping on his window. *What the fuck!* Ray stuffed the mirror into his pocket and pushed the button that brought down the window and to his horror a greasy hand thrust itself right in, inches from his face, with the grizzled face of a local denizen of the quarter, a real down-and-outer, peering at him with bloodshot eyes.

"Spare change, mister?"

"I don't have any change," said Ray. "Can you take your hand outside my window, please?"

But the bum didn't move. "I'll take bills as well," he said. "No problem."

Fuck! Ray reached into his pocket and pulled out a fiver. "Hey, if I give you this five, you make sure none of your buddies bother the car, OK?"

"Security will run you extra," said the bum who deftly snatched the bill out of Ray's hand. "Have a good day now."

Ray was hoping that Gloria's band would do a short set – four or five songs max – and then he could take her in the backseat with him for a long ride around Central Park, the tinted window that separated them from the driver rolled up tight. Yeah, that would be nice; plenty of room back there to get Gloria on her knees in front of him while he stretched out and undid his pants. Or at least that was Ray's fantasy based on his belief that her coldness, her toughness, her outrageousness was just a front, a mask he'd surely be able to crack. Since their *torrid* if brief encounter up at Edel Records, they had talked quite a few times on the phone; in fact, Gloria called him nearly every day. And as much as Ray tried to tilt the conversation into something personal, Gloria was serious about her career and seemed to know what was going on in the growing punk scene, saying her biggest influence was Wendy O. Williams and her band the Plasmatics whom Ray had never even heard of. When he asked what she liked about them, what made Wendy so special, Gloria replied matter of fact, "She plays with her tits out, little pieces of black electrical tape crisscrossed over her nipples. I think that's kind of cool, don't you?" Cool, he couldn't say, but that was enough to titillate Ray and get him out of his Fifth Avenue Penthouse where the doorman saluted him and down to CBGB, smack dab in the middle of the Bowery, New York's last stop for alkies and down-and-outers, buttressed by flop houses and closed restaurant supply stores on a grim Sunday afternoon.

Ray left his raincoat in the car and hurried out. A few more grimy panhandlers loitered right in front of the club and Ray stepped up his pace, anxious to dash past them, afraid their grubby hands might soil his tan suit. Maybe that was a mistake, he thought, wearing a suit to CBGB, but the suit went well with his *chocolate* Gucci loafers and casual was something Ray did not do well, having almost worn a tie. Four nearly identically dressed guys in tight ripped jeans, Converse sneakers, T-shirts and black leather motorcycle jackets were standing in front of the entrance, gloomily shadowed by the white awning above. They all had matching, almost *Beatles-esque* haircuts, like they were posing for a photo.

"Hey, Tommy," said the tallest of the four as he squinted over his rose-tinted *granny glasses*. "Look at that, it's Sunday and Jimmy Swaggart has come to see us play."

"Who the fuck is Jimmy Swaggart?" asked Tommy Ramone.

"Moron," said Joey Ramone, a sneer on his face and even with his exaggerated slouch towering over the other three. "Jimmy Swaggart is Jerry Lee Lewis's cousin - he's a preacher on TV. Don't you ever go to church?"

"Who goes to church?" said Johnny Ramone, the toughest of the group. "But I watch TV and I never heard of him."

"That's 'cause you watch cartoons," said Joey and they all laughed. "Nothing but cartoons." Then, as if it were planned that way, they got stone cold quiet as Ray approached them, their silence daring him to speak.

"Hey, guys," said Ray, as he stood unsuccessfully trying to slide past them and into the club. "Mind if I go in?" he joked.

"He looks like that A&R guy Gloria said was coming down," said Johnny Ramone, not even addressing Ray directly.

"Yeah, looks the type," said Dee Dee Ramone. "Look at those shoes." All eyes went to Ray's loafers.

Now blocking the door with their arms folded in front of them, the four didn't move, just stood there looking at Ray. Finally, he spoke.

"Yeah, I'm Ray Arthur from Edel records."

"Got your checkbook with you?" asked Joey.

Ray laughed nervously. "Well, not really ..."

"Still time to go get it," said Joey. "They don't go on for a while."

"So you know Gloria?" asked Ray. "She's pretty good, huh?"

"Fuck Gloria," said Dee Dee Ramone, "We're the Ramones, we're the band you should be seeing."

Ray handed Dee Dee one of his cards and said, "Call me at my office."

Dee Dee looked at the card. "We'll be there tomorrow morning when you get in, okay?"

"You should call first because ..."

"Hey, can we wait in your limo while you go inside?" Joey interrupted. "Getting cold out here."

"Why would you want to do that?" asked Ray, smiling self-consciously. "Why not go inside?"

"Because it's full of punks!" said Joey and they all guffawed like *The Dead End Kids*.

"We're the *Ramones*," Johnny emphasized. "So, if we sit in your limo nothing will happen to it. What do you say, Ray?" Then, without waiting for an answer, all four Ramones sprinted to the limo, falling over each other as they jumped into the back seat. Ray shook his head in disbelief and slipped into the club, hoping that his driver would take care of getting them out of there.

HILLY KRYSTAL SAT JUST INSIDE THE FRONT DOOR OF THE CLUB, collecting admissions and checking names off a sloppy, handwritten guest list. He wore a sleeveless flannel shirt, cut down like a vest, and a black T-shirt underneath, the only person in the club with a beard.

"Ten bucks," he said without looking up.

"I'm Ray Arthur from Edel Records, I'm on Gloria's guest list," said Ray, extending his hand.

Slowly, Hilly shook Ray's hand. "Oh yeah, you're the record company guy Gloria said was coming down, said you want to sign them," said Hilly.

"Oh, that's a little premature," said Ray. "Just want to see them on stage."

"Premature? Like a baby?"

"Yeah, I guess," said Ray.

"The bands don't have guest lists, but I do," said Hilly. "So you can be my guest. Hey, we should talk, I'm thinking of starting a label myself, I already got the CBGB's logo, just need some distribution. Been selling a lot of T-shirts too."

"T-shirts? That's interesting," said Ray patronizingly. "Not really my line ..."

"More profitable than interesting," said Hilly irritably, checking Ray's name off the guest list. Even on Sunday afternoon *CBGB* was packed and Ray had to push his way to the front of the club, moving slowly up the center aisle with the long bar on the right and a dozen paint-chipped tables on the left. He found Gloria standing by the mixing board, talking with the soundman.

"Hey, Gloria," Ray called out, waving as he walked toward her. She didn't wave back and gave him the once over when he reached her.

"What's with the suit?" asked Gloria, hardly acknowledging him.

"What do you mean *what's with it*?" asked Ray defensively. "Me ... I'm what's with it."

"You look like my Uncle Maddy, he'd wear a suit in the bathtub."

"So, what's the story on this famous uncle of yours? Even my secretary has heard of him."

"Who doesn't know Maddy the Horse?" said Gloria. "He's in *The Post* like every other day, gets accused of, like, everything ... but actually he owns a bunch of discos and gay bars down in the Village."

"They say he's like some kind of a..." Ray shrugged his shoulders.

"Gangster?" said Gloria, finishing Ray's sentence. "Yeah, he's probably some kind of criminal, but the less I know the better and he's good to me so what do I care. Says I'm his favorite relative, only one who's not a *mooch*."

"Is he gonna be here today?"

"Unfortunately, no," said Gloria. "Said he'd like to come but he's gotta go dump some bodies in the Jersey swamps."

Ray said nothing and gulped.

"Look at you! You believed me," said Gloria laughing. "I'll introduce you sometime, if you want. You'd probably like him 'cause he likes to make money, just like you, I bet. Just one thing when you meet him, Ray ..."

"What's that?"

"Don't keep staring at my tits like that or he'll think it's disrespectful 'cause I'm family."

"I'm not staring..."

"Right, Ray. Be a good boy while I go get ready."

Gloria disappeared into the dressing room. Ray was itching to do more coke, but he certainly wasn't going to share it with Gloria's band or anybody else. He checked out CBGB's bathroom, but there was piss all over the floor and no doors on the stalls, so Ray searched for another place to get high. Finally finding the basement door, which he covertly opened, he descended the stairs in near darkness, his lit Cartier lighter held in front of him like a torch. There was some light at the bottom of the stairs and as he stepped into the shadows his shoe slid on something, but he regained his footing and got down to the business at hand; pouring some coke on the back of his hand and snorting it hard and fast, leaving telltale white rings around his nostrils. *There, that feels better,* he thought, although now aware that it really smelled terrible down in that basement. He went back upstairs, wiped his nose and discreetly opened the door to join the crowd in the club.

Joey Ramone was standing with Debbie Harry when Ray walked past them. "Hey, man, your driver threw us out of your car," said Joey. "Not very hospitable."

"Bet he'd let me sit in it," said Debbie.

"I bet he would," said Ray.

"Jesus, what's that smell?" asked Debbie.

"Yeah," said Joey. "It smells like dog shit. Did somebody step in something?" He looked at the soles of his sneakers but there was nothing there. Then they all looked to Ray. "I think it's coming from you."

"I don't even own a dog," Ray protested, checking his own shoes.

Immediately Joey and Debbie's eyes bore down on his Gucci loafers, and sure enough, Ray's left shoe was smeared with dog shit.

"Jesus," said Ray. "How the fuck did that happen?"

Joey looked closely at Ray's eyes and belly-laughed loudly. "I'll tell you what happened, you went down to the basement to snort some blow, didn't you?"

"No," said Ray. "I don't do coke."

"Right," said Debbie. "So, what's that on your nose? Flour? You've been baking a cake for us?" She looked to Joey. "He went down in the basement to do cocaine so he wouldn't have to share it with anybody. But he didn't know that's where Hilly keeps his dogs!" They laughed uproariously.

"What's so funny?" asked Hilly as he joined them. "Jesus, it smells like shit around here."

"He's been down in the basement snorting coke," laughed Joey Ramone. "Stepped in dog shit."

Hilly looked hard at Ray. "Which foot?"

Ray looked down. "Looks like my left shoe got it. I was looking for the dressing room."

"You're lucky," said Hilly. "Left foot is lucky, else I would have to throw you out of the club. Hey, Ray, no hard drugs here, and do me a favor and stay out of my basement, okay?"

"Sure, no problem with me," said Ray. "Just looking for the dressing room."

"Toilets and dressing room are in the back," said Hilly. "And while you're back there will you clean the shit off your shoes before you track it all over the club?"

"Oh, yeah, sure ... gonna go say hello to Gloria," said Ray awkwardly. *Jesus, how am I gonna clean this shit off my shoes?* He thought to himself as he headed into the men's room where naturally there was no toilet paper.

Ray left CBGB with Gloria soon after her short set. "That was quick," said Gloria when they were settled in the back of the limo. "Thirty minutes including set up and getting all our gear off the stage. Fuck, not much time to get into it. So ... what did you think, Ray?"

"I'm thinking that I can't believe that dump is the famous *CBGB* everyone is talking about."

"Actually, Ray, I meant what did you think of our set."

"Oh ... you were good, Gloria, lot of stage presence and your voice cut through," said Ray, secretly disappointed that Gloria's tits weren't on display like Wendy O. Williams.

"One thing about CBs," said Gloria. "They got a good sound system so everyone wants to play there."

"That Hilly Krystal wanted to do business with me, but I'm not interested in getting involved with a club like that. If it were me, if I had my own club or disco, I guarantee you it would be classy and exclusive, and I'd draw the celebrities and the rich crowd. I'd get the right clientele."

"Then you really *should* talk to my uncle Maddy, because I heard him say he's opening up a new disco downtown. I'm gonna introduce you two."

"Anytime," said Ray. "You want a little blow?"

"I wouldn't mind," said Gloria, pulling closer to Ray as he pressed the button to roll up the screen between them and the front seat, telling the driver to take a ride around Central Park. The long way...

ALL OF THAT JUST SIX MONTHS AGO, THOUGHT RAY, *AND NOW everything's happening just like I planned it.* "You're the man!" he exclaimed to himself as he finally arrived in Westhampton Beach. Night had fallen fast and things were quiet on the strip of beach homes of Dune Road but the house Gloria was staying in, on the bay side, was still well lit, with four large cars, Mercury and Lincolns, parked in front, forming a protective wall. A group of men stood at the entrance of the driveway smoking cigarettes, talking and blocking Ray from pulling his Mercedes more than halfway in. After gunning it the whole way there, Ray was in no mood to wait and he lightly tapped on his horn. The four large men standing there immediately stopped talking and turned to stare at him. They didn't look happy and the least content of them all was the shortest of the crew, a skinny guy in his thirties wearing an ill-fitting sharkskin suit with long, dark, greasy hair and sideburns, known as *Junior*.

Shouldn't have done that, thought Ray immediately. He started to get out of the car to explain when Junior pointed his finger at him, slowly waving it side to side while shaking his head disdainfully. The message was clear, and Ray didn't move. Junior took a last drag of his cigarette, dropped it to the ground and stomped it out with his foot, all the time his eyes fiercely fixed on Ray. Slowly, he walked over with the three tough-looking men right behind him.

When Junior reached the car, he gestured for Ray to lower his window, which Ray obediently did, outnumbered and definitely in the presence of violent men.

"Who the fuck you honking at?" Junior asked Ray.

"I'm here to see Gloria," said Ray. "You can ask her, she's expecting me."

"I didn't ask you who you was here to see, I asked you who the fuck you was honking at. 'Cause if you was honking at me then we got a problem."

"I wasn't honking at anybody in particular," said Ray meekly. "I just thought you didn't see me."

Junior turned to the biggest of the men standing behind him. "Sal, he thought we didn't see him. Like we don't see who's driving a fucking Mercedes right into Maddy's driveway.

"I was just in a hurry," said Ray. "That's all."

"Well, let me tell you two things. First, I don't give a rat's ass if you're in a hurry and second, I don't like getting honked at – you got that, asshole?"

The enormous guy he had called Sal butted in, "Junior, maybe we should go ask Maddy if he wants this guy to come in. I mean, he says he's a friend of Gloria but who the fuck knows."

Junior turned sharply. "Sal, shut the fuck up, OK?"

Sal shook his head and said nothing while Junior deliberated his next move, chewing on his lip, the whole time staring at Ray. Then he turned to Sal. "All right, I'll tell you what. Why don't you go in and ask Maddy what I should do with this asshole whose beeping his horn at me and waking up the whole freakin' neighborhood." He steadied his glare forcefully back onto Ray. "And you stay in your fucking car until I tell you different."

Sal, the big guy, trotted into the modern, white beach house and was back out within a minute.

"Gloria said you should let him in. He's a friend of hers. Says his name's Ray. He's okay."

"So, it's Gloria who's giving us orders now?" said Junior. "Well, fuck me."

"Maddy told me to ask her. He's watching TV, so I did what he said."

"So, get the fuck out of the car... Ray," said Junior.

"Just leave it like this? Sticking out into the road?"

Junior said nothing and Ray timidly got out of the car, walked up to the house and knocked on the door while still keeping an eye over his shoulder on Junior and his crew who were now leaning all over his car and following his every move. Gloria answered the door wearing a turquoise tube top, no bra and hot pants with chunky platform heels that almost brought her up to Ray's height. She held the door open for him and Ray was about to walk in when Junior yelled at him.

"Hey! You gonna leave your car sticking out in the middle of the road? There's no fucking valet parking here ... Ray."

Gloria shook her head, looked at Ray and said, "*asshole,*" under her breath. "You better move it. Don't get Junior going. He can be a real pain in the ass." Ray turned around, walked back to the car, started it up and drove the five feet up the driveway. He set the break and turned off the ignition, the whole time Junior standing right there staring at him stone-faced.

"Jesus, what's his problem?" asked Ray when he got back to Gloria at the front door. "It was like he was going to shoot me or something right there 'cause I beeped my horn."

"That's Junior," said Gloria. "He's working for my Uncle Maddy now, moved here from Cleveland, that's all I know. But he's a *made* guy, so he's trying to show everyone how tough he is. Don't worry about it, I'm family so he won't bother me or Maddy will give him a load of shit. Hey, you took your time getting here, Ray. I thought you were coming for dinner?"

"Gloria, I couldn't just leave and jump off the boat. I mean, Lexi had friends there."

"What kind of friends?" asked Gloria.

"This fashion designer Calvin Klein and the editor of *Vogue* magazine or something. And then there was this musician friend of hers and that was it. I don't know why the hell she invited him."

"Maybe she likes him," said Gloria teasing. "What's good for the gander is good for the duck, eh?"

"Goose," corrected Ray, annoyed. "And she doesn't like him."

"Whatever," said Gloria. "You better say hello to Uncle Maddy. He's in the back watching some old gangster movie on TV. So*ooo* boring!"

Gloria led Ray to the screened-in terrace at the back of the house. The lights were out and her uncle Maddy was relaxing in a beige recliner, his feet up, and watching the big TV before him. Barrel-chested with large arms and a corpulent belly, his body almost spilled over the chair. He was barefoot and dressed in his suit pants and a sleeveless white undershirt.

Ray started to speak, "Hi, ya Maddy, I ..."

"You wait," said Maddy impatiently. "I love this fucking scene. Look at this."

It was *Public Enemy* with James Cagney, a black and white gangster flick from the 1930s. In the film a happy mother was fluffing the pillows in her son's bedroom while "I'm Forever Blowing Bubbles" played on a scratchy Victrola. There was a knock on the door, then the screeching sound of car tires pulling away. A young man walked to the door, her other son, *the good son*, and opened the door wide. Standing there was Cagney, wrapped in hospital sheets like a mummy, dead. He rocked back and forth on his feet and fell into the foyer, flat on his face.

"Cagney, *Top of the World Ma*," said Ray.

"Wrong movie," said Maddy giving Ray a dirty look. "That was *White Heat* and this is *Public Enemy*. Cagney was the fucking best. Think I'm gonna end up like that, Gloria?"

"A movie star?" said Gloria. "I doubt it. You'd need more hair on your head and less on our back."

"Not a fucking movie star," said Maddy annoyed. "I mean wrapped in sheets like Cagney, whacked by some scumbag."

"I certainly hope not," Ray interjected. "Not while Madame Rue's is still going. I'd have to find a new partner," he joked. "And this is just our first venture together."

Maddy didn't laugh. "You can bet your ass I'm not gonna end up like that – anyone tries to move in on me I'll whack 'em first. And my partnerships don't end until I say they do," he said to Ray.

"Just kidding," said Ray. "The club's going great, Maddy, believe me, nothing to worry about. And the stars are becoming regulars, Warhol, Bowie, Liza Minnelli, Bianca Jagger ... all of them. You get the stars there and the *bridge and tunnel crowd* follows, just like I told you, and that's when the cash starts coming in because the VIPs expect everything to be gratis. Soon we'll be starting to rake it in - there's gonna be plenty for everybody – everybody."

"Who the fuck is Warhol?" asked Maddy. "Some faggot friend of Stanley's? Why don't you get Tony Bennett down there, some real stars?"

"Warhol's a pop artist," said Ray. "A very rich pop artist who hangs out with other rich people and they all come down to the club and spend money. Isn't that what we want?"

"Faggot?" asked Maddy, as he got out of the recliner, almost knocking it over with his bulk in the process.

"Well, yeah," said Ray. "I think he's gay, if that's what you mean."

"They're all fucking faggots," said Maddy. "I've been running these fairy clubs for years down in the Village. Never had a problem. What the fuck do I care!"

"Warhol did a painting of an electric chair," said Ray. "It sold for a ton of money."

"You trying to be funny again?" asked Maddy. "Hey, with all these big shots you think we've got enough security there at Madame Rue's?"

"There's a couple of big guys at the door with Stanley, off-duty cops."

Maddy was stuffing his face with pretzels and his burst of laughter sent crumbs flying all over the room. "Maddy!" cried Gloria. "For Christ's sake, I just cleaned this fucking place."

He ignored her. "Now that's funny. I even got the cops working for me. You just taking cash, right? Everything in cash, no fucking credit cards."

"As much as I can, yeah, cash."

"Hey Ray, you met Junior, right?"

"Can't say he really introduced himself to me formally," said Ray. "But I heard somebody say his name out front. He gave me a hard time."

"That's what I pay him for, giving people a hard time. Junior's gonna help you out at Madame Rue's, keep an eye on all that cash you're gonna have coming in now that we're getting so fucking popular with the *jet-set*."

Great, just what I need, thought Ray. *That psycho looking over my shoulder.*

CHAPTER 11

The Sag Harbor marina was quiet now and Lexi had showered and was getting ready to settle into bed with Jacqueline Susann's *Once Is Not Enough.* But before she did, she wanted to come up on deck and towel-dry her hair in the warm night air. Slipping on a fluffy, white terry-cloth robe she put her hair up in a towel, walked out of her stateroom and came up on deck where she heard Lee and Captain Jack talking on the bridge above her.

"I thought everyone had gone home with Ray," said Lexi, obviously pleased, as she climbed the few steps to the bridge. "Speaking of which, can someone explain to me why that man suddenly can't sleep on a boat? I mean, I sleep better on *The Yellow Rose* than anywhere."

Captain Jack stood up to welcome Lexi and offered her his hand when she stepped up onto the bridge while Lee stayed in his seat.

"I believe Ray said something about a golf game tomorrow morning."

"So now he's a golfer," said Lexi disdainfully.

"I was showing Lee here around the boat and letting him finish his drink," said Captain Jack. "Me too." He jiggled the ice in his glass. "What can I get you, Lexi?"

"Actually, I came up to dry my hair, but you know, I wouldn't mind a nightcap myself," said Lexi, sliding onto the couch next to Lee. "Scoot over, sugar."

Lee made room while Captain Jack went down to fetch that drink. "So, you're still here," she said to Lee with a smile.

"Hope we weren't keeping you up. Captain Jack was just telling me the history of *The Yellow Rose*."

"I know it's hard to leave when he gets going," said Lexi. "My daddy and him could sit for hours, right at this table, just going on and on about everybody and anything. And finishing a bottle of bourbon between them."

"He's a great story-teller," said Lee. "Can't imagine him being anything but a ship's captain."

"Captain Jack is as much a part of *The Yellow Rose* as ..."

"You are," finished Lee.

"I suppose."

"This boat means something very special to you. I can tell you feel good here."

"I can't imagine being without it. When I come on board, I leave all my troubles behind."

"You've got troubles?" said Lee. "You don't look like it."

"Everyone's got troubles," said Lexi before adding softly, "*The Yellow Rose* ... it's the best memory I have of seeing my father really happy – the day he got this boat."

"Must have been quite a guy," said Lee.

"Had his own way of getting things done, that's for sure. Old school, I think you'd call him, friends with LBJ and all that Texas political crowd. Said he never went back on a handshake in his life. Never be anyone else like him."

"I guess he lives on in you somehow," said Lee.

"How's that?" asked Lexi intrigued.

"Well, for one thing, you've got the same initials as him and they're everywhere you look on this boat, on the towels, the glasses ...

all over. So, some things do live on. I bet you're more like your father than you realize."

Lexi's shrill laughter cut into the still night air. "Well, I'm not sure if that would always be a good thing! I got to confess I inherited his bad temper ... but only on rare occasions."

"Sounds scary," joked Lee. "Hope I never see that."

"Stick around, sugar, and I'm sure you will," said Lexi. "You should ask Ray - I can be pretty ornery. But in his case, he deserves it most of the time. I mean, was he a real pain today or what? And he's been like that all summer, always in a rush, can't relax anywhere. I swear, next time I go out on *The Yellow Rose* I'm gonna leave him home to mope by himself."

Captain Jack came back carrying a flute of champagne.

"How'd you know?" she asked.

"Captain's intuition." He handed it to Lexi, and she raised her glass. Lee and Captain Jack followed suit.

"Well, here's to..."

"Us," said Captain Jack.

Lexi clicked Captain Jack's glass and looked straight at Lee as she repeated his toast: "Here's to us."

"To us," said Lee, holding Lexi's gaze.

"Hey, Lee," said Lexi, breaking into a mischievous grin. "I got an idea. Weren't you supposed to play something for us today? You got your guitar with you, right?"

"Yeah, I do. It's downstairs somewhere."

"Captain Jack, I hate to ask you to go down again but could you be a darling and bring up that guitar so Lee can sing me a little lullaby before I go to bed." Without a word of complaint Captain Jack got himself back up out of his chair and returned within minutes, this time with the guitar still in its case. Lee took it out and checked the tuning.

"What do you want to hear?" asked Lee.

"Surprise me," said Lexi. "Something soft and sweet for a beautiful night like this. Maybe a love song?"

Lee thought for a moment while he fingered a few chords and got comfortable with the guitar in his lap.

"Listen, I've been working on this new song, guess it's finished enough to play. Never sang it before ..."

"Oh, go ahead, Lee!" Lexi encouraged.

Lee played a few intro chords and tenderly started singing in his low baritone:

As I lay down with my lady
The sounds of the night keep us warm
I'm living a city life called maybe
But tonight there's no reason to be strong.

Somewhere in these night-lights lies the answer
And you can get Diamonds by the Yard
And Tiffany dreams and Porcelain dancers
And an old man playing blues guitar.

It was a softly sung ballad with a chorus that built it just short of being an anthem, three repetitive chords and it suited Lee's voice very well, as if he had written it, which of course he had. He wasn't used to singing in front of just one or two people, but he wasn't nervous or self-conscious when he sang in front of Lexi. He just locked into her eyes while she sat next to him, visibly delighted. When the song was over Captain Jack burst into loud applause, but Lexi remained motionless, transfixed, glowing.

"That was just beautiful," she said finally. "It almost felt like it was written for me. You mentioned Diamonds by the Yard! You know that's what Tiffany calls this necklace I'm wearing."

"I know that," said Lee.

"You know more than you let on, Lee," said Lexi.

"Sometimes the songs know more about me than I know about the songs," he said.

Lexi just smiled.

"Have you ever been serenaded like that before, Lexi?" asked Captain Jack.

"Not like that," said Lexi, thinking that if Captain Jack had not been there she would have kissed Lee right then and there and kept kissing him until somebody told her to stop which, of course, on her yacht at least, nobody ever would.

CHAPTER 12

The three acts of the Hamptons summer *season* were staged around three pivotal holiday weekends. *Curtain rising* on an often chilly Memorial Day in May, then the story building momentum through the thermometer busting July 4th blowout and finally hitting a bittersweet climax over the long September Labor Day weekend, the last blast before autumn set in, a time to go wild, have a final fling, do *something* unforgettable. And in that same spirit, on the tiny Talkhouse dance floor, riotous dancing and accompanying lunatic shrieks were being led by none other than Danny O'Connor himself, party ringmaster *par excellence*.

Lee Franklin had already left the stage, cutting his set short when Tony Hughes gave him a nod and a wink. "Let the privileged class boogie for a while back on the dance floor," said Tony. "Work up a sweat and buy some drinks. Listening to sensitive guys like you only makes 'em cry."

"Sure, I'll take a break," said Lee. "Twenty minutes?"

"Take the rest of the night," said Tony. "You've been bringing in a good crowd for a while now, you deserve it. Say, Lee, have you thought about next summer? Coming back with a small band? I tell you, man, I think we've got something good going here. The *regulars* love you and now you've got Lexi Langdon and her bunch coming in and they spend money like ... they've got a lot of it, which they do. I'm telling you I've never sold so much champagne in my life. Or drank so much either!" he added with a burp. "Miss Vicky says her tips are over the top but come to think of it so are her tits!" Tony laughed. "She's probably the biggest draw of the Talkhouse this summer ... next to you, that is, Lee."

"You mean Vicky the waitress?" asked Lee.

"I mean Miss Vicky with the most incredible, amazing rack of tits I ever saw on a nineteen-year-old girl in my life," exclaimed Tony. "If you missed that you must be blind, old sport." He lowered his voice. "Never seen her wear a bra yet. Goes to Bennington College and needed a summer job. And you know what the best thing about her is?"

"What's that?"

"I'm sleeping with her!" said Tony.

"Good for you," said Lee half amused.

Tony feigned ecstasy. "Man, if you only knew. Hey everybody!" he screamed. "Let's get this party moving!" He cranked up the Wurlitzer jukebox to maximum volume, slung a slew of quarters in it and punched in every Stones, Credence and Donna Summer track it held. The teeny dance floor of the Talkhouse was squeezed between the bar out front and the kitchen in back, separated by horizontal wood beams that gave an artificial semblance of privacy. A hidden spot for lovers to slow dance and cuddle on a dead winter's night, but tonight it was pulling in Lexi's crowd like they were caught up in a religious frenzy with pairs of expensive women's sandals strewn around the edges, kicked off after the first guitar riff of "Brown Sugar."

Standing at the far end of the bar alone now, Lee watched the tumult in back where Danny was leading a riotous conga line. Tony must have punched in "Ruby Tuesday" on the jukebox, and when it came on it slowed things down and Danny escaped to the bar to grab a drink, squeezing in next to Lee, perspiring and out of breath.

"Looks like you've got everyone going berserk back there," said Lee. "You do a better job entertaining them than me."

"Are you kidding?" said Danny. "They love me! I'm teaching these blue bloods how to party hardy." The bartender came to give Danny his drink. "You see that bald guy on the dance floor?" Danny said to him.

"Yeah!" said the bartender. "His name is Dexter Kay.

"Right," said Danny. "Dexter said to put whatever I'm drinking on his tab."

"But Tony said you drink for free, Danny," the bartender replied.

"Don't tell Dexter Kay that!" He turned to Lee. "I'm telling you, these people *really* love me."

"And Kathy, too," said Lee. "You can see that each time you two come within arm's length of each other."

"Oh, Kathy, man, she is so incredible," Danny swooned. "It's getting serious. I'm telling you I'm doomed, she's all I can think about."

"Must be something in the air," said Lee. "Tony Hughes is *shtupping* his teenybopper waitress and now you're over the moon with Kathy. What's going on?"

"*Love is all around you*," sang Danny before trotting back onto the dance floor as the opening chords of "Fortunate Son" blasted from the jukebox. This was Danny's moment of glory, his place in the sun, and Lee had never seen him so elated. Everyone back on that dance floor was following him like the Pied Piper, but Lexi wasn't among them. In fact, she was standing right behind Lee as he felt a hand caress his shoulder.

"That feels good," he said. "Right where the guitar strap digs in."

"Why'd you stop playing?" Lexi asked. "I was waiting for my favorite song."

"Tony Hughes thought your friends wanted to dance, drink champagne and kick off their shoes. And me singing "Just Like a Woman" wasn't gonna do it for them."

"So, you're through for the night?"

"Looks that way." Lee pointed to the dance floor. "All the action's back there."

"Your friend Danny is a riot – getting everybody crazy. He told me he's gonna take everyone skinny-dipping at a pool he knows nearby."

"You're kidding," said Lee. "Never knew Danny to be such a rabble rouser."

"Think he rises to the occasion when anyone pays attention to him," said Lexi. "He always makes me laugh though, he's like your kid brother, Lee."

"Kid brother? He's supposed to be my manager."

"He can still be your manager, I suppose, but he's a kid, Lee. There's a world of difference between you and him, anyone can see that."

"Is that a compliment?"

"Take it any way you want, sugar. I'm usually pretty good at figuring people out, but I can't figure you out at all. Maybe you can help me." Whenever Lexi started talking to Lee and her green coral eyes focused in on him, it was like they were all alone someplace, like anything could happen.

"I can't figure you out either," said Lee. "So we're even."

"Is that what you'd like to do? Figure me out?" asked Lexi teasingly.

"Right now," said Lee, "I'd like to get out of here for a while, take a ride or something."

"That could be arranged," said Lexi.

"What about your friends? Won't you be missed?"

On the dance floor, Danny had tied somebody's silk tie around his head and held two bottles of champagne high in the air like he was leading the Dom Pérignon parade. "I think Danny can take care of them," said Lexi.

"Yeah, they'll be OK, I guess," said Lee. He hesitated before adding, "And what about Ray?"

"Ray!" Lexi laughed. "Ray is at Swingo's!"

"What the hell is Swingo's?"

"It's some kind of rock and roll hotel, restaurant ... whatever, in Cleveland. This famous radio DJ from out there, *Kid Leo,* is hosting some soirée and Ray and Wes Edel and Alana went out there to be a part of it."

"So why didn't you go?"

"You really want to know?"

"I do," said Lee, "if you want to tell me."

"Well, it's Labor Day weekend and I didn't know when I'd have another chance to hear you sing, so I'd rather be here ... with you."

"Thanks," Lee said meekly.

"Can't believe the summer's over."

"Not quite," said Lee. "Still have this weekend. The official end is Labor Day and that's not until Monday."

"You're an optimist," said Lexi. "I don't suppose either of us will be hanging out here for long, Lee. What are your plans after this, anyway? You have another gig coming up somewhere?"

This was the very thing that Lee had been trying not to think about, that soon everything would be coming to an end out here and this summer would just fade away and him with it. Even standing there at that moment, flirting with Lexi Langdon at the Talkhouse bar, it still seemed so unreal to him. Was he just imagining something between them that didn't exist outside of his own fantasy? Or was she just playing with him, maybe that's what girls like her did, but it was no game to him because since the first time he had seen her she had not left his waking thoughts. And what if he never did see her again after this summer, then what?

"Honestly, I don't know where I'm going once this summer's over, no idea, Lexi." Looking at her, so close to her now, he had just had one thought, *I can't let this go.* "Right now, standing here, talking to you like this, it just seems this is where I should be. Am I making any sense?"

"Makes sense to me, sugar."

"So what happens after this," he said, "your guess is as good as mine."

"Well, my guess is ... it's a nice night for a ride, like you said. Up for a little adventure?"

"Sounds good."

"So?"

Lee smiled. "I imagine you have a car?"

"That I do, a few in fact, but tonight let's just get in the *Stang* and drive and drive and drive some more and see where we end up. Still sound good?"

"What's the *Stang*," asked Lee.

"*Stang* as in *Mustang*," Lexi replied as she gathered up her bag and started to head out of the Talkhouse.

Eagerly, Lee abandoned his barstool to follow her.

"Do me a favor, Lee?"

"Sure."

"Count to ten slowly and then meet me in the parking lot across the street. I'll be in the white convertible."

"No problem," said Lee, thinking, *pretty safe way to start an adventure.*

He actually counted to ten a few times in the midst of the noise and the music and the loud drunken shrieks, standing by the door and hoping that nobody would ask him where he was going. Then he ducked out fast, crossing deserted Main Street, and walked into a small parking lot that fronted a string of one-story stores, among them a two-chair barbershop with a candy cane barber's pole. He wondered how he had never noticed that before and then like a vision, like something that had just driven in from another world, there in the gleaming moonlight was a white *Mustang* convertible with red interior, same color scheme as that barber pole, with Lexi at the wheel, beckoning him.

"Sexy car," said Lee. "Sexy driver."

"And I do love to drive," said Lexi. "Get on in."

She pulled out of the parking lot looking both ways before

turning right onto Main Street, picking up speed as she headed out of town.

"You always leave it parked with the top down?" he asked.

"And most times with the key still in the ignition," she added giggling. "Pretty irresponsible, eh?"

What if somebody stole it?"

"In that case, I suppose I'd just buy another one."

Lee laughed. "The same year? What is this one, sixty-five?"

"Sixty-four," said Lexi. "It was the car I was longing for way before I got my driver's license, used to cut out pictures of it and put them on my bedroom wall when I was away at school. So, when I finally did get my license, Daddy bought me one in mint condition. Walked out of my house one morning and there it was in the driveway with a big red ribbon on it."

"And this is the same car?"

"Well, it looks exactly the same, I suppose, but I cracked up the first one after Daddy died. I'm almost ashamed to admit it, but this is my third *Stang*. I cracked up the second one, too."

As they drove into the steamy August night, Lexi shifted the *Hurst four on the floor* like a real pro and they zipped past the Amagansett Fire Department with its empty white flagpole.

"Four-Twenty-Seven, bored out and stroked, quad-carbs, dual-exhaust, Hurst Shifter, *positraction*," blurted Lexi. "Bet you didn't think I knew about any of that. My daddy was an engineer, you know."

"You're full of surprises."

She cruised in fourth gear along the deserted Nepaguage stretch of Montauk highway, a sandy slice of land between Amagansett and Montauk, once under the sea, where Montaukett Indians canoed to the fresh water of Indian Wells. The road ran parallel to the Long Island Rail Road tracks beside it and Lexi sped confidently along, a good twenty miles per hour over the speed limit.

"And what about you?" asked Lexi, as she placed her hand on Lee's thigh. "You got any surprises in you?"

"Are you flirting with me?" asked Lee.

"Who me, sugar? I'm just the driver." She laughed. "Out for a joy ride." They passed a low-slung red and white seafood joint, at this hour long since closed.

"That's the lobster roll," said Lee. "Tony Hughes took me and Danny there once, nothing can beat their lobster salad on a hot dog bun."

"Better than you had on *The Yellow Rose*?" asked Lexi.

"Well, maybe not – Jesus!" exclaimed Lee. "Look over there, that house is on fire! Holy shit!"

Lexi pulled off the road onto the sandy shoulder and turned off the engine. Perhaps a half-mile away, across the road, gold and yellow flames were pouring off the roof of a beach shack, silently filling the night sky with billowing dark smoke.

"Is that for real?" asked Lexi. "That house couldn't be burning up like that, could it? Why don't I see any fire trucks?"

"Should we go check it out?" asked Lee.

Lexi thought a moment. "I don't know. We're not going to put that fire out by ourselves. What do you think we should do, Lee?"

She turned to him and he leaned toward her and kissed her on the mouth, and she put her hand on his cheek and they opened their mouths and entwined their tongues. And then there was the shriek of the sirens, but they didn't stop kissing, didn't even look up when three red fire engines from Montauk came rushing by, passing them and turning onto the dirt road that led to the burning house. Their lips parted, they opened their eyes and they looked at each other, knowing that something profound had happened, neither knowing what to say. Then before starting up the car, Lexi kissed him again.

"Suppose they'll take care of it," she said, pulling back onto the highway and looking at him seductively. "Let's drive, keep our own fire burning, what do you say?"

They cruised along the rolling hill road of old Montauk Highway until they arrived at the well-lit Gurney's Inn - the famous Montauk beachfront resort. While she drove, Lee continued to kiss her neck and caress her hair and now *his* hand was on Lexi's thigh.

"Suppose we could pull right in here to Gurneys and get a room ... talk things out," said Lexi softly. Right then a string of cars pulled into the driveway and she jerked her head away from him. "I thought I knew that car, Lee. We better keep moving, this is a little too public for me."

"I'm fine," said Lee, putting his arm around her. "I just want to kiss you more."

"If I start kissing you, I may never stop," she said seriously.

"That's the idea," said Lee.

On the edge of the village of Montauk there was the more modest Memory Motel. "Why don't you pull in here?" said Lee and Lexi pulled off into the beach side parking lot and turned off the engine. They looked at each other and renewed their kissing.

"Think it's still open?" asked Lexi.

"I'll find out," he said.

Lexi watched him walk into the motel office. After she looked into the rear-view mirror to fix her lipstick, he was back holding a room key. She got out of the car and followed him to room 102.

"The guy in the office was a surfer," said Lee. "And stoned on something, didn't even ask my name. Said they just had a cancellation which never happens on Labor Day weekend, said I must have some heavy karma working for me tonight. I don't know what he was smoking, he was something else." Lee nervously dangled the key in his hand. "Memory Motel, Montauk, NY ... Says here we can just drop it in any mailbox, and it will get back to them. Do you believe that works?"

"I don't know about that," said Lexi impatiently. "Let's just hope this key opens the door to the room and gets us off the street here with all these cars passing by - see if your karma is still working."

Lee opened the door for her and then closed it behind them, attaching the security chain on the inside. The room itself was what you might expect from a beachside motel probably build in the early sixties and not redecorated much since. There were two easy chairs, a beige shag carpet and a long cabinet along the wall with a Motorola TV on top. Like something out of a *Beach Party* movie, a little worn and torn from a decade of summer vacationers. First thing Lexi did was throw open the window and the sound of the sea came rushing in.

"Oh, that's so wonderful," she said. "I can't get enough of it."

"What's that?"

"Oh, just the ocean," she said. "There's no ocean in Houston and it's a good hour drive to the Gulf."

"Just an ocean of oil," said Lee.

They were standing before the king-sized bed now and both laughed to break the awkwardness of the moment.

"If this room had been a little bigger I could have carried you to the bed like Rhett Butler," he said. "But you really need a grand staircase to pull that off properly."

"At least, I hope there's a toilet," said Lexi. "Why don't you see what's on TV?" She kissed him once softly and went off to the bathroom. Lee turned on the TV and watched the thin line of light beneath the bathroom door. He stood nervously flicking through the stations and then the bathroom light went off and the door opened, and Lexi was standing there in her bra and panties and heels with her Diamonds by the Yard necklace coiled around her neck. Her breasts were pushing out of the top of her bra as she walked toward him.

"What did you want to talk about?" asked Lee.

"Nothing," said Lexi. Then they fell into each other and embraced. She put her hands under his T-shirt and felt his skin while he pulled it over his head and tossed it onto a chair. He unhooked her bra, which fell silently to the floor and pulled her close, so her breasts pressed into his chest. They stood and kissed for the longest time until suddenly and without warning Lee had the distinct perception that she was gradually resisting him in some way, that her kisses were not as deep; that she was no longer passionately into him like only moments before. Lexi pulled away from him and got into the bed, pulling the covers around her.

"Is something wrong?" asked Lee.

"Tell me something, Lee. Am I lovable?"

"That's a strange question," said Lee.

"Come get in the bed," said Lexi. "I need to talk for a while before we ... you know."

"Anything you say." Lee lay down next to her, as close as he could, and she traced his lips with her fingers. "You're a good kisser," she said. He took her hand in his and wanted to squeeze it harder than he should, as if that would somehow convince him that this was all real.

"You asked me if you're lovable ... are you asking me if I love you?"

"No, I'm not asking that, Lee ... I don't want to know that ... yet. I mean, am I really lovable, just me alone, without everything that goes with me?"

"What goes with you?"

"Don't play dumb, Lee."

"Okay, but I never knew anybody like you before, Lexi, so how do I begin to answer that? When I kissed you in your car, you were just a girl I really wanted to kiss, who I've been wanting to kiss since the day I met you on the beach. Is that what you mean?"

"I don't know. I'm not even sure myself. But I'm scared."

"Tell me what you're scared of, Lexi? Not me, I hope."

"I'm scared of getting into something I won't know how to get out of," she replied. "And I'm scared of the way you make me feel."

"How do I make you feel?" asked Lee.

"Good ... too good."

Then, slowly, she let their lips touch again and Lee could only hear the sound of the waves and their breathing. He pressed his lips harder to hers and they rolled and shifted until he was on top of her, holding himself up on his elbows with his hands in her hair and they were kissing deeply until again she stopped, and turned her head.

"Oh, God," she moaned. "I shouldn't even be here with you," she said. "You know that don't you?"

"We've both seen this coming for a while, haven't we?"

"I'm not denying that ... but I don't think I can do it like this, Lee, in a motel room. It's like I feel that any moment someone will bust in and start taking photos of us.

"That's crazy," said Lee.

"I know it's crazy." She pulled away and sat up. "I made my mistake and I have to live with it for a while before I start something like this - I just have to figure things out or wait for Ray to make the first move. I thought I was ready for this, Lee, but I wasn't. I'm sorry."

Lee lay on his back and felt all the magic of the moment dissipate like sand through his fingers, like smoke in the air. "So, what you're telling me is that you're in a marriage you call a *mistake* and you can't fix it? I don't get that."

"There's nothing to get," said Lexi, irritated. "It's just the way it is. I said I'm sorry, what else do you want me to say?"

AT THREE IN THE MORNING WHAT REMAINED AT THE Talkhouse were the dance floor survivors, the hardcore, all now sitting at the round back corner table. Danny, Kathy and Tony Hughes with the *talented* Miss Vicky, his waitress of the month and another slightly older couple, Talkhouse regulars, along for the ride, drunker than they thought they were. They all were pretty well into their cups by now and an open bottle of Mount Gay dark rum sat on the table before them.

"I'm hot," Kathy complained.

"It's August in the Hamptons," said Tony Hughes. "What do you expect? Snowstorms?"

Decidedly, in a more sober atmosphere that was not funny at all, almost moronic in its irony. But this crowd was eager to laugh, ready to party and up for most anything –wanting neither this night nor the summer to end.

"Hey, guys, you want to get cool? I got an idea," said Danny.

"You gonna make a snowstorm?" quipped Tony, still laughing at his own joke. "This I gotta see."

"Listen to me, there's a big house behind that church on Indian Wells Highway just over there." He drunkenly pointed in the general direction. "And you know what's in the backyard of that house?"

"Fucking igloos!" said Tony still laughing.

"A swimming pool!" announced Danny, and within minutes they were all gone from the table, making their wobbly way across Main Street and then huddling next to the side yard of the house Danny had led them to, hidden by the bushes.

"OK," said Danny whispering. "We all strip down right here, put our clothes in a pile and when I give the signal we run and jump into the pool."

"Is there anybody in that house?" asked George, the male half of the older couple who tagged along. "Wouldn't wanna get in trouble or anything. Maybe we should just ask them if we could buy them a drink or something before just barging into their pool." He looked to his wife for approval.

"For Christ's sake, George, have a little fun," she said sternly. "We're only going for a little swim. What's the harm?"

"It'll be all right," said Danny. "I come here all the time to swim and there's never anybody here. Now listen, everybody strip." He started to undo his belt and untie his shoes and there was the slightest moment of hesitation and embarrassment and then all at once, as if on cue, everybody began to peel off jeans and shirts and skirts and blouses, kicking off flip-flops and running shoes until the lot of them were standing there stark naked.

"Let's go!" yelled Danny and out they came, running fast from the bushes, their penises and breasts bouncing in the moonlight. Danny, Kathy, Tony Hughes and young Miss Vicky rounded the side of the house at a slow trot while George and his wife trailed behind. Once they had arrived in the middle of the backyard and all eyes had adjusted to the darkness, they realized they were standing before a very impressive ... badminton court, with no swimming pool in sight.

"Where the hell is the pool?" asked George's middle-aged and embarrassed wife, covering her sagging breasts with one hand and her crotch with the other. "Didn't somebody say there was a swimming pool, George?" she asked her equally dumbfounded husband.

"It wasn't me," George answered defensively. "But somebody said that ... I heard somebody say that back at the Talkhouse." He looked angrily at Danny. "Didn't you say you've been here before? That there was a pool here?"

"Well, I thought there was a pool here," Danny sheepishly replied. "Don't all these houses have pools? Christ, if I owned a house like this, I'd have a pool, wouldn't I, Kathy?"

Kathy was totally comfortable to be naked and beautiful and spread her arms wide. "Danny, if you had a house like this, you'd have two pools."

Danny picked up a racquet lying a few feet away and faced everybody. "Since we're all naked, why not play badminton?" he asked enthusiastically. "Somebody help me find a *birdie*."

Suddenly, Danny's accomplices didn't feel as drunk as they had just minutes ago, frivolity was replaced with sheepish looks until Tony Hughes stepped in. "Hey, I got a better idea, let's all get dressed and go back to the Talkhouse for champagne ... on me."

And just that generous and jovial offer got everyone cheering, laughing and even patting Danny on the back for being the instigator of this wild prank, although you could see the disappointment on George's face when Miss Vicky began to dress. After struggling back into their clothes, they moved across the street, back to where their party had begun and returned to their seats around the table so recently vacated, the ice not yet melted in their rum cocktails. Everyone, that is, but Danny and Kathy, who stayed behind in the backyard of the dark house.

"I really did think every house out here had to have a pool," said Danny. "But you know what, I knew it would be funny either way."

Kathy smiled softly. She looked perfectly desirable and not the least bit self-conscious as the moonlight highlighted her lithe, sweet body. "We don't need a pool," she said. "We just need a blanket. And I'm not sure we even need that." Then, with eyes fixed on Danny's, she slowly dropped to her knees.

Salivar's was a dockside seafood restaurant, painted green and white, in the heart of Montauk harbor, where the after-hours crowd would converge at 4 a.m. to mingle with early-bird fishermen on their way out to sea. Nuzzled next to the fleet of charter fishing boats that crammed the piers, it was a well-known local hangout decorated with photos of deep-sea fishermen weighing their impressive catches of sharks and tuna on immense scales. Salivar's served breakfast at all hours for the vacationing city fishermen who crowded the day boats going out for bluefish and flounder as well as for the scruffy crews who baited the hooks, cleaned the fish and kept the beer on ice. Come the wee hours, night owls seeking a cure from carousing the Hamptons' bars would also appear, hopeful that a plate of scrambled eggs and toast would cure their spinning heads. Mounted above the bar was the head with gaping jaws of a huge great white shark, caught just a few nautical miles offshore and, some said, the inspiration for the novel "Jaws," now a blockbuster film playing at the local cinemas.

Lee and Lexi drove into the dirt parking lot next to Salivar's, her Mustang creating a cloud of dust.

"Jesus," said Lexi, as she got out of the car. "I feel like I'm driving into some desert barbecue joint back in Texas. Don't they believe in paved roads out here in Montauk?"

Inside, they took a booth and the weary waitress put two glasses of ice water in front of them. Without looking at the menu, both ordered steak and eggs and coffee with home fries on the side. Conversation was difficult and stiff, something that had never happened to them before.

"I guess I should apologize even more," said Lexi, finally getting to the heart of the matter. "I still don't really know what happened back there at the Memory Motel, it all felt so right kissing you in the car and then suddenly it all felt so wrong once that door shut behind us. It was like one minute I could totally forget about being married and then, it just hit me like a ton of bricks."

"Lexi, you don't have to explain. It's all right," said Lee. But it wasn't, really.

"It's not all right, Lee, because I *want to* and I'm feeling really confused. Maybe this will sound naïve to you, but it's like I just started a new life here in New York with Ray and I don't know if I'm ready to start running around behind his back.

"You don't think Ray's doing the same thing? Or at least thinking about it? He doesn't seem like the faithful type to me, Lexi. Maybe you're being naïve."

"I don't even want to think about that tonight," she said with a flash of anger. "Ray may not have turned out like I dreamed he would, but he is my husband and I hope he's not doing that to me ..."

"Doing what?" asked Lee.

"What I was about to do back at the Memory Motel. I know myself, Lee, and that ... well, it just would have changed everything from the next time I looked at Ray until the next time I looked at you and the next time I looked at myself for that matter. Am I making any sense to you, sugar? I guess you just about hate me now," she said pouting.

"No chance of that," said Lee. "I understand, you just want to keep things the way they are."

Lexi grew quiet, reached across the table and took Lee's hands into her own. "I lost my mother when I was just a little girl, hardly remember her, and then my daddy kinda disappeared into his business and traveling and I was waiting for it to be all right again, like a family, even if it was just the two of us. And that started to happen a little bit ... and then he died, and it all came crashing down on top of me, his reputation most of all. The things people will say behind your back, the rumors ... it's so ugly. And now, up here in New York, even with Ray, I had a chance to start over."

"Starting over at what?"

"Just being happy, for one thing, and putting all that behind me. I'm someone different now, I have a place, I have a ... guess you could call it a status here, I'm not just the sad little daughter of the mighty Lex Langdon."

"You can't change the past, Lexi," said Lee.

She looked at him incredulously, like he had said something traitorous to everything she believed in.

"Of course you can, Lee. I already have."

DRIVING BACK TO AMAGANSETT, LISTENING TO LATE NIGHT talk-radio, sometimes, when she wasn't shifting gears, Lexi put her hand on Lee's and smiled tenderly at him. Little had happened between them physically and yet, something profound and irreversible had transpired between them emotionally; they were caught in the middle of something now, conspirators at the point of no return. The radio news reported that Labor Day weekend 1975 had so far been the safest in memory, but Lee didn't feel safe at all because Lexi was sitting right next to him and he was missing her already and that felt like love.

CHAPTER 13

The Vietnam War had ended on April 30, 1975, and the pundits and historians called it the defining event of a generation, but the only thing that had ever concerned me was not being defined by it in any way at all. When I had turned eighteen and got my draft notice, first thing I did was contact the local anti-war organization which put me in touch with a so-called draft counselor, who told me not to eat, shower or brush my teeth for at least two days before going in front of my draft board. He also gave me the number of an anti-war shrink who wrote a letter saying I was incapable of socialization and it all worked; I was out. Got my 4F in the mail and next thing I knew I was on my way to Amsterdam on a lark. In Europe, the good life looked easy to get if you were smart enough not to play by the rules or at least that's how Richard Gallagher made it seem as we traveled from Amsterdam to Paris and finally ending up in Rome. Richard had a connection for hashish there, smuggled in from Kabul, and he taught me how to put a false bottom in a package, how to send it home to the U.S. without raising any suspicions. But my first try at being a drug smuggler was a total fiasco. I'm still not sure if I was set up or followed, but the police grabbed me right away as I was standing in line at the Rome post office, just blocks away from Campo Di Fiori where I had been staying in a two-star hotel. I had two kilos of hash hidden in two Gucci cosmetic cases, wrapped and ready to mail back home. I ended up in a Roman prison waiting for Richard Gallagher to bail me out or something, but he never showed up. In fact, I sat there for about a month before a guy from the U.S. Embassy appeared and finally my stepfather got me out of it, spent all his retirement savings, meaning no more move to Florida for him and mom, and deleted the Welcome Home *clause from our relationship. I can't remember my stepfather and mother ever agreeing about much of anything, but finally they found common ground: I had ruined their lives.*

And then Lexi Langdon came along, swept me right off my boots so to speak, and I was sure my destiny had finally arrived, thought the gods were smiling on me again. It was the same kind of elated feeling that I had when I was traveling around Europe with Richard. But the gods weren't smiling; in fact, they were laughing at me again.

LABOR DAY WEEKEND PASSED LIKE A SPEED BUMP IN THE ROAD and the hot and hallucinatory summer slowed and screeched to a halt as the temperature dropped. You could almost hear the echo of summer cottage shutters, slammed shut all over the East End, while white sheets covered the furniture. Traffic thinned, the ratio of pickup trucks to Mercedes inversed itself and the excitement of the season got packed away into Louis Vuitton and Mark Cross bags, drawn back into the teeming whirlpool of New York City, a mere ninety miles away. Accompanying the early signs of autumn, falling leaves and chilly nights, the Hamptons returned to its off-season normalcy, the villages along Montauk Highway growing quiet while corn and potato fields were plowed under. The locals came out of hiding and took charge once again; Southampton's Main Street shops held discount sales of pricy bathing suits and plenty of empty seats were to be had for films at the East Hampton Cinema. On a brisk October afternoon, Lee Franklin stood in front of the Talkhouse and watched the nearby traffic, now unencumbered and mostly local, whiz by him on Montauk Highway. The autumn air was filled with the sharp odor of burning leaves, fallen from the trees and piled high on the side streets of the village. His gig at the Talkhouse had ended right after Labor Day, but Tony let him stay on up in the dressing room as long as he could get by without heat. Lee was playing with the idea of getting lost again, taking what little money he had and making his way to a warmer playground – Florida or even Southern California – and nurse his *terminal* heartache. As hard as he tried, and as tough as he imagined himself to be, he could not erase Lexi Langdon from his mind nor forget about the touch of her lips, the delicious smell of her hair and that one night at the Memory Motel where almost nothing happened and everything changed. He hadn't heard a word from Lexi in over a month and it tormented him more than he would have thought possible. Could she really have forgotten him that easily?

Danny had already left Amagansett for the city weeks before and the two of them had a brief goodbye and *catch you later* on the Long Island Rail Road platform before Danny boarded his train. Their moods couldn't have been more different and Danny, sensing this, tried to be reassuring. "Kathy's got her own place in the city and I'll be there a lot," he said. "You should come in and have dinner, hang out. Don't be down, man, the good times have only just begun."

Lee nodded bitterly. "Maybe for you they have, but for me, I'm not so sure," he said. "Sounds like you got a great gig, so don't fuck it up," he added laughing. Danny had mentioned to Ray, in a highly exaggerated claim, that he was once the director of a string of airport bars and out of the blue Ray had offered him a job at Madame Rue's.

"How can I fuck it up?" asked Danny, raising his hands. "I think I'm just a glorified bartender, anyway. Ray says he's part owner of this place, and he wants to bring in some of his *own people* as soon as possible.

"So, you're one of Ray's *own people* now? Congratulations."

"Hey, it's just a job," said Danny. "A stepping stone to bigger and better things for both of us."

"Just don't turn your back on Ray," Lee warned.

"I got eyes in the back of my head," said Danny. "You know that." When the train arrived, they did a high five, and Lee walked slowly back through town, not passing another soul he knew by name except Angelo, who leaned on his counter reading the *Daily News*, his pizza place empty with stacks of white cardboard pizza boxes piled high over the ovens.

The door of the Talkhouse dressing room banged open and shut and Lee, who was lying on the couch strumming his guitar, turned to see Tony Hughes, dressed in a pale pink button down Oxford shirt and his signature blue blazer, his salt and pepper hair wet and slicked back, just out of the shower and adjusting his dangling steel wristwatch.

"Can't keep time for crap," said Tony. "Supposed to be a Rolex, but I got my doubts. Bought it from one of my Chinese cooks."

"They make Rolex watches in China now?"

"That'll be the day!" Tony laughed. "With a little paper that tells your fortune inside. But you know what – I don't need a freakin' watch because I always know what time it is."

"So what time is it?" asked Lee. "I don't wear a watch."

"It's time for a cocktail," said Tony. "We're going into Bridgehampton for cocktails and dinner, you and me, sport, and I'm buying 'cause we're celebrating."

"What's the occasion?"

"You'll find out - grab a jacket and let's go."

"Can I borrow your blazer?" joked Lee.

"Last time I gave it to one of you guys, it took two dry cleanings to get the sand out of it!"

They jumped into Tony's hefty Cadillac, top still down, pushing the season a few more weeks. The car had that musty smell of too many nights left out in the rain but nonetheless gave a formidable *King of the Road* ride as they drove from empty Amagansett, through sleepy East Hampton and then through the even more deserted tiny hamlet of Wainscott. They sped past the closed *pitch and putt* golf course and the Greek restaurant whose sign, which once boasted *"The Best Steaks in the Hamptons"* now announced *"Closed for the Season."* In Bridgehampton they rounded the gray granite Civil War monument that divided the road and pulled into one of the many available parking spaces. Lee didn't say much on the way, just sat there with the wind blowing his hair while Tony, who had had a great season and was ready to kick back for a few months, talked of his winter plans.

"Maybe I'll drive up to Vermont and visit Miss Vicky, spend some time in the mountains." said Tony.

"You ski?" asked Lee.

"I doubt if we'll be doing a lot of that this time of year."

"Lucky guy," said Lee half-heartedly. "So it wasn't just a summer fling. Those sure disappear when the weather changes."

"Are you referring to yourself?" asked Tony with a smile.

Lee didn't smile back and found it hard to hide his hurt feelings of being abandoned by Lexi and left behind by a dazzling domain of all the beautiful people he had partied with. A world he had a brief peek at, that of the rich and glamorous, had suddenly disappeared, moved on and had taken Lexi with it.

"Cheer up, Lee. I know how you're feeling; the action gets a little slow out here after Labor Day, but at least you can find a place to park now," said Tony. "That's one good thing."

Like a yacht being pulled into a dock, Tony inched the Cadillac close to the curb, switched off the engine and suddenly everything became quiet.

"All's ashore who's coming ashore," he said.

"Looks like this island is deserted," said Lee.

"It's spooky, isn't it?" said Tony. "Every year I think the summer is just not gonna stop, not gonna give up. But it always does. And then it's so damn quiet out here. Could drive you to drink."

"So what are we celebrating?" asked Lee.

"You know who JP is?" asked Tony.

"Yeah, he owns a bar in the city, right?"

"That's right, and I got a call from him," said Tony smiling conspiratorially. "And he had some good news for you, my friend."

"What kind of news?" asked Lee.

"I'll tell you when we're inside. It's happy hour!" exclaimed Tony as he pushed open the front door of the restaurant.

Bobby Van's was crowded enough to make you think the summer might actually be holding on for a last gasp. The dark restaurant featured a carved mahogany bar with a thick white marble top and brass foot rail where waiters scurried back and forth to an adjoining terrace, carrying trays of drinks to boisterous tables. Among its occupants who were laughing louder than anyone else in the place and capturing the attention of all, Lee recognized a distinct whiny, melancholy voice and knew immediately to whom it belonged: Truman Capote, sitting at the head of a table of six and holding court.

"Truman's sitting there with James Jones," whispered Tony. "He wrote *From Here to Eternity* with Sinatra."

"You mean the *movie* was with Frank Sinatra," corrected Lee.

"Don't be a smart ass," said Tony. "Come on, let's go say hello." Tony starting walked directly to the table.

"You know Truman Capote?" asked Lee, astonished.

"I know everybody," said Tony.

Tony put his hand on Truman's diminutive shoulder. "Why aren't you home writing?" he said.

To Lee's surprise Truman Capote actually seemed to know Tony, greeting him warmly and introducing him all around.

"Lee Radziwell and I spent a marvelous night at the Talkhouse," explained Truman by way of introduction. "Never danced so much in my life and that was a sight to behold, I can tell you."

"Glad I didn't have to witness that," said James Jones.

"You only wish," said Truman. "Tony Hughes is the local impresario of the place."

"*Impresario?*" Tony laughed off the compliment. "That's a big word for you, Truman." This caused gales of laughter all around and Tony invited Truman and his party back to the Talkhouse for champagne after dinner. Tony stayed there just long enough to make sure they'd all remember him, and then he and Lee slipped into a green leather booth at the back of the restaurant.

"Tony, can I ask you something? You won't get mad?" asked Lee.

"What do you got to lose? This summer is over and you've already been fired," Tony said with a laugh. "I don't need you serenading the local drunks with "American Pie." Tell me what you want me to know?"

"Well ... I've been playing in bars for years now and I never saw anyone give away as many drinks and bottles of champagne as you do. So, my questions is... how do you make any money?"

"I depend upon *the kindness of strangers*."

"You and *Blanche Dubois*, I suppose. But what does that mean? People give you money? Women? Forgive me, but you're a pretty unlikely gigolo, Tony."

Tony nearly fell out of the booth laughing before he could recompose himself and explain what he meant. "You know who Willem De Kooning is, right?"

"The painter?"

"Right, the freakin' painter. Used to be quite a drinker too and the Talkhouse isn't far from his house in Springs. Back in the day, it was almost like his car knew the way by itself. He was running quite a tab with me and then one day he decides to get sober and wants to settle his bar bill which had gone on for years," he said. "So, he offered to give me a handful of his drawings to even things up between us. I didn't know shit about art, but we were buddies back then, so I didn't argue with him. He sure didn't look like he had any money, white overalls covered with paint. But since then, with De Kooning getting so famous and all ... Boom! It's like I'm an art collector and everyone wants to buy those drawings! Just selling one of those sketches has kept me afloat for quite a while."

"Wow," said Lee. "Nice to have friends like that."

"You too, sport," said Tony. "And JP is a nice friend to have."

"So, you gonna tell me what he said or just keep me squirming?"

"OK, here it is. JP calls me up and asks me if the guy who was singing at the Talkhouse over Labor Day was named *Les Franklin,* didn't even get your freakin' name right. Said he was calling to offer you a gig at his club and a place to stay. I guess you're pretty hot, Lee – word's out. I should get a commission."

"Jesus, when did this all happen?"

"Actually, he called this morning and asked for you, but I didn't know where the hell you were."

"You mean, you didn't want to climb the stairs to the dressing room to wake me up."

"Something like that, sport. Anyway, he left a pretty detailed message which I had to promise to give you verbatim – that's his term *verbatim* – I thought he was gonna start talking dirty to me or something!" Again, Tony nearly fell over laughing. "Almost pulled my pants down." Lee didn't get the joke.

Tony continued, "So the message is, you got a steady paying gig playing at JP's as long as you want it and a pad to crash in," said Tony.

"Wow! What's JP's like?"

"Kind of like the Talkhouse, a bit smaller and no real stage, but it's a real music business hangout. The pad is a little apartment upstairs over the bar. And it looks like it's all yours, sport. Not bad, eh?"

"Do I have to pay for the apartment?" asked Lee.

"That detail I was not made privy too, but JP added one thing he said was important for me to tell you."

"What's that?"

"He said to tell you *not to worry about anything,* don't even bother to call him, just get your ass to the city and he'll explain everything when you come by JP's tomorrow afternoon."

Then Truman Capote called Tony over to his table and Lee sat there by himself wondering why JP said he should not worry about *anything*, which was a strange thing for a bar owner to say. When Tony returned the waitress brought them fresh drinks.

"What did Truman want?" asked Lee.

"Said I seemed so quiet, so withdrawn, asked me if I was in love so I said I was. Wants me to stand up and make a toast to the whole restaurant, tell the world about it, so to speak. Look at him sitting over there with that shit-eating grin, just waiting for me to make a fool of myself. What should I say?"

"Don't ask me," said Lee.

"Well, here goes nothing." Tony stood up and raised his glass high, tapping it loudly with a spoon.

"Here's to Miss Vicky!" he exclaimed. "Best set of tits east of the Shinnecock Inlet!"

Truman Capote nearly fell off his seat with high squealing laughter.

CHAPTER 14

Funny how you can connect things that presumably have no connections: September 5th, 1975, Sacramento, California, Lynette Fromme, perhaps the last follower of Charles Manson not in prison, tries to assassinate President Gerald Ford, but a Secret Service agent courageously steps in and takes the bullet. For a moment it was like the 60s nightmare all over again with the Manson thing, crazed hippies and political assassinations all rolled into one. And then, that very next year of 1976, a new TV series called Charlie's Angels began a five-year run and introduced Hollywood poster queen Farrah Fawcett with her miraculous hair and thousand-watt smile to prime time America. The "Angels," as it were, were LA investigators working for the all-knowing and never seen "Charlie" who sent them on dangerous crime-busting missions. It was like no one but me made the connection with Charlie Manson and I wondered how out of step I was with the rest of America. On the same day as Ford's assassination attempt, the London Hilton Hotel was bombed by the Provisional Irish Republican Army with 2 people killed and 63 injured. Danny said they celebrated in his Queens neighborhood with free-flowing Guinness Stout at many of his neighborhood pubs.

But the thing that everyone, including the media, was wrong about in 1975 was how harmless cocaine was; they were calling it the preferred drug of the rich and famous while books about Sigmund Freud's coke habit hit best-seller lists. New York was teeming with the drug, had been for years, especially way uptown in Harlem jazz spots, but journalists didn't write much about that until the privileged class took on the white powder as their own preferred party-favor. Soon, anyone who liked to party loved getting high on coke even if no one liked coming down.

Both One Flew Over the Cuckoo's Nest and The Rocky Horror Picture Show were hit films about crazy people while at the same time America was discovering it's not so innocent past in the best- selling novel Ragtime. The zeitgeist was extreme, the new decade may have been mirroring the Roaring 20s just fifty years before but nobody felt the crash coming. Except me...

LEE PUT ALL HIS BELONGINGS INTO AN OLIVE-GREEN DUFFEL bag, grabbed his guitar case, said his goodbyes to Tony and the Talkhouse staff and walked out the door. Lee waved to Angelo who spun pizza dough high into the air as he continued walking down the street past Gordon's restaurant, a place he could never afford to eat at with the rich bluebloods who frequented the place. Pausing in front of the volunteer fire department's red brick façade with the grand old flag flapping majestically in the wind atop the lofty white flagpole, Lee put his guitar case down and saluted.

He was cautiously hopeful about this move to the city and the prospect that this gig at JP's that came out of nowhere, might finally give him the *shot* that had always eluded him. In all his years playing clubs up and down the East Coast, Lee had never gotten that one great gig where someone with a little clout might have spotted him and offered him a deal, an entry into the music business and an exit from the *chitlin' circuit*. But he had little faith in his own abilities to self-promote, it just wasn't in his nature. On his own, he had never been able to open that golden door, even find the goddamn handle. Still, what did he have to lose? And besides, it was a step closer to Lexi, who still lingered in his dreams and kindled his anxieties. If his heart was a compass, *due Lexi* was his fixed point.

"To the American dream, long may she wave," he said to himself, picturing him and Lexi in her white Mustang convertible rounding this curve just a month ago and thinking, *she was mine there ... for a moment.*

Lee picked up his gear and hurried down to the railroad station past the closed and shuttered Farmers' market and barren potato fields. Like all Long Island Rail Road trains, his was a no-frills commuter train, rickety cars pulled by a diesel locomotive that should have been retired years before. A grim-faced conductor in a stiff round, gray cap punched a series of cryptic holes in his ticket, saying nothing and moving on down the aisle. The coach was nearly empty as Lee gazed out the grimy window watching the East End pass by. The country's borders may begin here on these far eastern shores, but he was moving inward to the real port of entry, the masses' turnstile into the harmony and discord of the republic itself. All of that and more – *New York City.*

Once the train crossed the trim Shinnecock Inlet, the vista quickly turned suburban and predictable, classic pink, green and blue, cookie-cutter houses protected by chain link fences, identical strip malls offering every service from *Poodle Grooming* to *Adult Books.* It was impossible not to laugh at that, thinking that all other literature must therefore be meant for children. He found himself holding his breath, realizing that he would never live in a place like this again, if he could possibly help it. *It's like they put a slice of the Midwest between the city and the Hamptons,* he thought. Whatever happened, he knew he wasn't going back there; that was no longer an option.

Dozing off, he had the troubling dream that haunts most musicians, of being caught unprepared onstage before an impatient audience. Lee awoke in a sweat when the train was deep into the borough of Queens, passing row upon row of attached houses. Then, suddenly it grew dark as the train dipped into a tunnel under the East River and soon screeched into Manhattan's Penn Station. He walked up a crowded staircase leading out of the station, having the distinct impression that the intensity of existence itself had just been kicked up a few notches. He stopped on the sidewalk just to take it all in, to adjust his perceptions: the crazies, stumbling along in tattered rags, ranting at invisible demons; the untouchable skyscrapers whose thousands – *millions* - of windows looked out like the eyes of the *megalopolis* itself. Here, even the buildings seemed alive. Looking around he had the impression that everyone else was moving faster than him at a frenetic clip and he felt some sort of collective energy invading his nerves. He got into step and joined in the march, taxi horns welcoming him like a chaotic brass symphony.

JP's was on the Upper East Side of Manhattan in the East 70s on First Avenue, an unlikely neighborhood for such a place, which traditionally bred singles bars not music clubs. Lee walked into the darkened mid-afternoon bar and, like all bars at that hour, the place smelled of stale beer. No one seemed to be around and so he waited in silence until a toilet flushed and JP came out of the swinging doors that led to the bathrooms in the rear, zipping up his fly.

"Wondered when you'd get here, pal," said JP. "Nice to see you again."

"Well, glad to be here," said Lee.

JP smiled and shook his hand.

"I bet you are. I was tempted to string a *Welcome Lee* sign across the door, but I thought it wouldn't be too discreet." JP laughed.

Well, now I've moved from one wise-assed bar owner to another - hope I'm making progress, Lee thought. But the funny thing was that out in Amagansett, Tony Hughes had dressed like a city dandy, blue blazer and button-down shirts, while here in the city JP more resembled a hip yacht club member with boat shoes, polo shirt and khaki pants, in sharp contrast to his handlebar mustache and curly, shoulder-length, blond hair.

"Follow me," said JP, without explanation as he took Lee back outside, showing him the separate street entrance to the apartment over his bar. "This is home now, pal." JP talked quickly while they walked the two flights of stairs. "You'll be playing downstairs," he continued, not looking back. "I don't know what nights yet because sometimes the record companies like to showcase their new artists here at the last minute so I leave the schedule kind of loose. But when you do play, do three short sets, not too loud, and take long breaks so my bar gets some action. There's a small PA and Jim Reeves is the tech - he does the house sound and will record your show if you're nice to him - he'll help you out. Who knows, pal, maybe you'll end up getting a deal yourself."

"And is there any ... uh?" asked Lee warily.

"Money? You're wondering if there is any money in this for you? Here's the deal, I'll give you a piece of the door and you can drink and eat for free in the bar but no steaks or lobster. But the best part for you, and if you know anything about apartment rents in this city, you'll understand what I mean, is that you won't be paying a dime for this apartment. That's what I told ... Ms. Langdon. Or should I say, that's what Ms. Langdon told me. Probably a losing deal for me, but who can say no to Lexi Langdon, eh?"

Lee stopped abruptly on the stairs. "Lexi Langdon? What does she have to do with this?"

"Everything, pal," said JP, fumbling with the keys in the door of the apartment, before he and Lee walked in. "I should fix this goddamn lock..." His eyes grew wide as he surveyed the apartment, still smelling of fresh paint, newly laid wall-to-wall carpet under his feet. "Wow! Her people really fixed this place up," exclaimed JP smiling broadly. "You asked me what Lexi has to do with it? Are you kidding me? This was all her idea." He walked around the newly decorated apartment, commenting on everything, clearly delighted at the transformation. "Wow, will you look at this place now. Maybe it's not such a bad deal for me after all."

Lee was standing there, duffel bag draped over his shoulder and guitar case in hand, with his mouth hanging open, wondering if JP was talking about the right Lee Franklin.

JP looked at him, "So what do you say, pal?"

"It's nice, it's really nice," said Lee. "I wasn't expecting this."

The place was basically a modest New York *railroad flat* and nothing could change that, but Lexi, or whoever Lexi had hired to decorate it, had turned it into a real gem, not overlooking a thing. There was new furniture, including a handsome black leather couch, new towels and sheets, a great Marantz stereo with JBL studio speakers, even a few framed psychedelic posters from the Fillmore East.

"Jesus, she put a half-dozen bottles of Dom Pérignon in the refrigerator," JP called out from the kitchen.

"Lexi likes Dom Pérignon," responded Lee, immediately regretting having said it.

On his way to the door, JP handed Lee the keys. "I bet you'll get used to that Dom Pérignon," he added sarcastically. "Let's go downstairs and have a drink, pal, maybe not Dom Pérignon, though," he snickered. "And while we're down there I want to show you something," he added with a wink. "Think it might explain some things to you."

Back inside *JPs*, Lee sat at the empty bar while JP went behind the bar and pulled out a bottle of Johnny Walker Black. "Scotch?"

"Sure."

JP poured two glasses with ice and they clicked their glasses without saying a word.

"Let me tell you something, Lee. My whole life I've only done one thing right," said JP. "Just one thing but I do it very well."

"What's that?" asked Lee.

"You know, tend bar, pour drinks, owning a joint like this. And you want to know why I'm good at it?"

"You take care of your customers?" asked Lee.

"I keep their secrets, pal," said JP. "And this deal here and the apartment and whatever Lexi Langdon has to do with this – this is our secret, right?"

"Okay, JP, I can appreciate that," said Lee awkwardly. "Suppose I should thank you."

"That's not the point," said JP. "The point is, that whatever you do, we don't want Ray Arthur to find out anything, do we? Because that wouldn't be good for either of us. Who knows, maybe he'll be the one to sign you to a deal. Wouldn't that be ironic as hell?" JP roared with laughter as he bent down to grab something. "Now, speaking of Ray, look at this. This is what I wanted to show you." He pulled out a folded *New York Post* from behind the bar. "This paper is from a week ago, right before *Mrs...*" he emphasized, "... Langdon called me." JP turned to page six where the town's gossip was laid out in bold print. There was a large photo, nearly a quarter of the page, of two men in sharp suits and a small cute brunette. It was not clear if one of the guys was putting on his fedora or trying to shield his face with it.

"That's Maddy the Horse holding the hat," said JP. "And that dumb bastard smiling with his arm around the babe is ..."

"...Ray," Lee said astonished. "Ray Arthur."

"And I hear the chick is some relation to Maddy the Horse, his niece or something. Anyway, can you believe that? Ray gets his picture taken next to this mobster, cuddling up to this cute babe and he's smiling like an asshole?" He handed Lee the paper. "Wes Edel must have loved that," he said with glee.

REPUTED UNDERWORLD BOSS MADDY THE HORSE EXITING MADAME RUE'S DISCO WITH EDEL RECORDS VP RAY ARTHUR

"I don't get it," said Lee.

"What's not to get? Maddy the horse is a big time Mafioso and for some ungodly reason, Ray was hanging out with him and if I know Ray Arthur, he was especially hanging out with that babe with the nice knockers hanging onto his arm. So what do you think happened next?"

"I don't know," said Lee.

"Well, Lexi Langdon, charity heavy-hitter and serious Democratic Party backer, who just happens to be Ray Arthur's wife, sees this over breakfast while sipping tea in her Fifth Avenue penthouse and hits the goddamn roof. Here she is, queen of the Hamptons and her husband gets caught, both messing around on her and hanging out with a known criminal."

"But why should I care what Ray does?" asked Lee.

"*Because,*" JP emphasized, "the day after this photo appeared in the *New York Post* was the day Lexi Langdon called me and set up this sweetheart deal for you." JP raised his eyebrows. "Or maybe I'm stupid and it was just a coincidence, what do I know?" He smiled and took another sip of Scotch.

"I...uh..."

"Didn't anyone ever tell you when to shut up?" asked JP as he put the paper back under the bar. "Just one last thing."

"What's that?"

"She said to be ready at eight."

CHAPTER 15

At 8:15 that night the intercom in Lee's apartment buzzed. Lee panicked when he couldn't locate the damn button to answer the buzzer; it was the first buzz since he moved in that afternoon. Finally, he found a small intercom panel hidden in the tiny kitchen next to a cabinet and picked up the receiver.

"Hello, hello?" he said breathlessly.

"It's me," she replied quite calmly.

Lee let out a deep breath. "I'll be right down," he said.

"Not so fast, sugar." She spoke with that same Texas twang that had been haunting him since the Memory Motel. "Let me come up and see this swinging bachelor pad that I ordered, see if I got what I paid for."

Instantly, the sound of her voice made him both anxious and excited, like a chemical reaction taking over both his mind and body. Just the way she hesitated between words, like she owned the very air she was speaking into, in her every pause he felt an unmistakable sexual tension building in him. He buzzed her up, waiting just inside the door, not sure if he was hunter or prey and uncertain how to act when he saw her. Dodging into the bathroom, he checked himself out in the mirror, quickly undoing his belt and re-tucking in his T-shirt.

Lexi was making a steady and determined stride up the stairs, in a far cooler state than Lee, mostly thinking that her new Charles Jourdan shoes were killing her feet and looking forward to taking them off once she was in the apartment. She had told her driver Armando, that she might be a while and that was about all the preparation she had made for her encounter with Lee that evening. For the briefest moment, just before she raised her hand to knock on Lee's door, she thought about what she might really be starting. Calling JP, hiring her decorator to renovate the apartment, all of that had been easy and done mostly out of anger at Ray who had made a fool out of her with that little tramp rocker. However, once she walked in Lee's door, she was well aware that things would change fast, maybe permanently, but even so, she could care less. Her main concern was that this would be the same Lee Franklin she remembered from *The Yellow Rose,* the Talkhouse and especially the Memory Motel. She made the softest of knocks, just tapping on the door with her fingernails and he slowly opened the door. The smell of her perfume hit him like a drug; she was dressed in boots and a skirt, a smart, black, glove-leather jacket over a thin sweater, one hand clinging to her Diamonds by the Yard necklace at the base of her neck. Neither of them moved.

Lee breathed in deeply. "You smell good, Lexi," he said as he leaned on the doorframe. "Really good. And you look...uh..."

"Nervous? Well, I'm trying not to show it ... how am I doing, Lee?" she said softly.

"You're doing fine, probably better than me."

"Been a little while."

"Yeah ... a while."

"Guess you've been wondering what happened after that night ... I kind of disappeared for a couple of weeks."

"Closer to a month," he said. "I didn't know what happened ... not that you owe me any explanation."

"Well, I'll tell you anyway. I went back to my house and, of course, Ray wasn't there, and I was torn in two between what I thought I was supposed to do and what I wanted to do."

"Which was?"

"I think you know. Couldn't sleep all night and I almost drove back to the Talkhouse to find you. But I didn't, just couldn't, and I left early the next morning for the city."

"No goodbye?"

"That's why I'm here."

"To say goodbye?"

"More like hello. So ... can I come in now?"

Lee stepped forward and kissed Lexi on the mouth gently, hardly moving or thinking, just feeling.

"Yeah, come on in."

"Thought you'd never ask," she whispered as she squeezed past Lee, very close, and again, her perfume enveloped him. She gave the apartment a quick once-over, stopping at the entrance to the small living room and nodding her head in approval.

"Not bad, sugar," she said. "My decorator told me how he planned to make it ... inhabitable. Gotta say, looks nice."

"Just like the lady ordered," said Lee. "Who picked out the posters?"

"The concert posters were my idea; thought you'd like them. Jimi Hendrix at the Fillmore East, Rolling Stones at Madison Square Garden. Wanted you to feel at home, you're a rocker, right?"

"Suppose so."

She stood there, just looking at him. "You know, I think you look just about the same as when I left you, a pair of jeans and a black T-shirt. You haven't changed, Lee."

"If that's a compliment, I'll take it," he said.

"I bet I know what's that way." She pointed toward the front of the apartment.

"The East River?" joked Lee.

"Exactly," she said taking his hand and leading him into the bedroom. "Shall we take a dip?"

"You've been here before?" he asked.

"Not really, but I know the layout." She turned around to face

Lee and stood just inches away. "Didn't know how it would turn out, but having you here changes everything."

"You got that right," said Lee. "I'm here."

"Yes, I guess you are."

"Are you here too ... completely?"

"You already kissed me, what do you think?"

"Maybe I better kiss you again, just to make sure."

"Can't be too careful," she said, while putting her arms around his neck and then kissing him deeply. She pulled out his T-shirt and rubbed her hands along his bare chest, then started to unfasten his belt buckle, undoing the buttons on the fly of his Levi's 501 jeans one by one. "This feels very real to me," she whispered teasingly as she reached inside his pants. Lee moaned and gently pulled her light cashmere sweater over her head. Lexi stepped out of her short skirt and now, just in her bra and panties and chocolate brown Chelsea Cobbler boots, sat down on the bed. "Do me a favor Lee?"

"Help you with the boots?"

"How'd you know?"

"Because you asked me that once before," he said, as he removed them. On his knees in front of her, he opened her legs and came forward and lay on top of her and they began to make love ferociously, stripping off what was left of each other's clothes with impatience, and soon he was inside of her. They flipped over and then she was on top and his hands were on her waist lifting her up and down until they both exploded and collapsed upon the pile of clothes that lay around them. Reaching up, Lee pulled a pillow from the bed and put it under their heads while Lexi found her bag and snuggled next to him as she lit a cigarette.

"I don't ever want this to stop," she whispered. "I knew it would feel this good with you, I was always sure of that."

"You did all of this, the gig at *JPs*, this apartment, decorating." Lee motioned around him. "All of this, just so we could be together?"

"Why else would I do it?" Lexi gazed at the ceiling. "I thought I might never see you again," she said bashfully. "And I couldn't let that happen."

"Why couldn't you let that happen?"

"I think you know why," she said, kissing him gently on the lips. "You know I like you."

"So what's changed since the Memory Motel?" He smiled. "Guess you didn't like me back then."

"Don't be silly. Just something happened that brought me back ..."

"Back to me?" asked Lee.

"Well, to you, sugar, of course ... and my senses too. There was this stupid photo of Ray in the newspaper ..."

"Yeah," he said. "I saw it."

"You saw it?" she said, surprised. "Then why are you asking me all these questions?"

"I just wanted to hear it from you."

"I don't care, I'm over it ... but when I saw that picture, it was like a wake-up call. And when I asked Ray about it, his reaction just made it worse."

"What did he say?"

"Oh, at first he said it didn't mean anything, not to make a big deal, you know, and I just knew he was lying and that he would go on lying for as long as I let him. And the funny thing was, the whole time I was talking with him all I could think about was being with you again."

"Glad you figured that out."

Lexi hit him with the pillow. "Hey, I'm from Texas, and a wife is supposed to be faithful to her husband or someone might get shot." They laughed.

"And now?"

"All bets are off as far as I'm concerned."

"How are we going to do this, Lexi?" asked Lee. "Can I call you? When will I see you?"

"I think it's best if I call you, for now," said Lexi. "We'll figure it out, I've done pretty good so far, huh?"

"Can't complain," said Lee. "Guess we just have to be careful, that's all."

"Lee, we're in the big city now, there are millions of people running around out there, nobody's going to be watching us."

"There are not millions of beautiful women running around New York in Mustang convertibles," he said.

"Not me either, sugar," said Lexi. "When I'm in *town,* I have a car and a driver. What do you think? I'm going to spend my days looking for a parking space?"

"I have to tell you something, Lexi. This last month after you left the Hamptons, I kept thinking it might have been my fault, like I made some mistake at the Memory Motel, I moved too fast or something."

"No mistakes, Lee, I just wasn't ready. You knew I was drawn to you the first time I saw you on the beach. You saw me smile at you when we were walking up to the house. I remember that."

"Me, too."

She put her arms around him and kissed his ear. "There's a stillness about you that just starts me tingling, even when you're just listening to me going on about something ..."

"Well, I know I made one mistake," interrupted Lee. "I didn't pick you up like Rhett Butler and carry you to the bed."

"Well, you can't do that now either," said Lexi, pulling him closer to her. "Because we've already been on the bed."

"Next time, Scarlett."

They drank champagne and made love again and then slept briefly, awaking in each other's arms. Lexi asked Lee to throw on his clothes and go ask her driver to pick them up some cheeseburgers at JG Melon's over on Third Avenue. The girl was hungry.

"You mean, your driver has been waiting out there the whole time we've been making love?" asked Lee.

"That's his job," said Lexi. "To drive me where I want to go and to wait for me while I'm doing what I want to do."

So, Lee put on jeans and shirt and shoes and no underwear and went downstairs and told the driver, who didn't seem to be the least bit surprised to see him, what they wanted to eat. "Please tell Ms. Langdon it will take about thirty minutes," he replied. "Does she want anything else besides cheeseburgers?"

"What else do they have at Melon's?" asked Lee with a newfound confidence. "What's good?"

"I know Ms. Langdon enjoys their cottage fries and cheesecake, too."

"Well then bring us some of that, too," said Lee. "Two of each."

"Yes, sir," said the driver. Lee liked that and he stood on Third Avenue as the limousine pulled away, watching its red taillights disappear around the corner. *I'm here,* he thought to himself. *And up in my apartment is a beautiful heiress who only wants me to make love with her. So why am I so nervous?* He walked slowly back upstairs and into his apartment to find Lexi dozing on his bed. He knelt on the floor next to the bed and looked at her, listening to her breathing. She opened one eye.

"Aren't you going to get undressed and get back into bed Lee? That food will take a while."

"Yeah, suppose I should. But I love to watch you sleep."

"You're too romantic for words," said Lexi. "Come on in."

He slipped off his jeans and crawled in next to her and they lay as close as two lovers can, they slept like two spoons in a drawer, only dreaming of each other. And next thing Lee knew the buzzer sounded and Lexi's driver had returned with a large brown bag full of burgers and cottage fries and he was putting on his jeans again.

After they had eaten, Lexi said she should be going back home, she had a big lunch the next day and started to pick up her things to get dressed, always coming back to Lee, still reclining on the bed, to give him tender kisses on his neck. Then she disappeared into the bathroom, and when the door shut, Lee jolted upright and a wave of panic shot through him.

"I'll be seeing you again soon?" asked Lee when Lexi came out of the bathroom.

Lexi laughed. "I may be an extravagant Texan," she said, "but I didn't decorate this apartment for a one-night stand." She kissed him. "Don't you run away either."

"Tell me where would I run to...and why?"

"I don't know...aren't you guitar players known for being on the road?"

"Maybe my road ends here," he said.

Minutes later, Lee was standing alone in the crummy foyer of his building, still holding the door open and watching Lexi as she darted out to the running Lincoln Town Car parked snugly at the curb. The dark-suited driver had been standing attentively by the rear door and opened it smartly with a smile when Lexi reached the car. Lee thought about the driver waiting there the whole time they were making love, going to JG Melon's to bring them back dinner, and then waiting some more and shook his head in wonder. But now, he couldn't just go back upstairs to that apartment and sit there all by himself with Lexi's scent still permeating the sheets and her voice still echoing in his ear and her taste on his tongue. So instead, he walked the few steps to JP's, hesitating a moment to look down the Avenue where her car had just pulled away and then entered the bar which was jumping. It was nearly eleven now and the New York night was well out of the starting gate; the crowd around the bar buzzed and most of the tables were already filled. JP himself was perched at his usual spot at the large round table closest to the bar from where he could keep an easy eye on the cash register. He called Lee over.

"Hey, guys, I want to introduce to my new house band, Lee Franklin and the ... Lee Franklins." That got a few snickers and then JP presented Lee to his friends sitting around the table, one of whom was a familiar face indeed.

"This gentleman to my right, Lee, this is Billy Joel, he's on Columbia Records – that's where you will be too, if you get lucky. Billy just put out a new album, *Streetlife Serenade*."

"Bought it as soon as it came out," said Lee eagerly.

"Well, *Columbia* told me somebody bought it," Billy Joel kidded. "Must have been you." Billy was dressed in a dark, wide lapelled suit with a yellow paisley silk tie, sharp and Sinatra-like, with quick, darting eyes.

"I not only bought it," said Lee. "But I play 'The Ballad of Billy Kid' sometimes, great song."

"Hey, Billy, there's something I want to ask you about that song," said JP.

"Shoot," said Billy Joel.

"In the song you say Billy the Kid robbed banks, but you know, I don't think he did."

"It's not about *that* Billy the Kid, it's about a bartender I knew out in Oyster Bay on Long Island ..." Billy Joel looked around the table and did a perfect Rodney Dangerfield imitation. "What, here I am having a few drinks, trying to relax and now I've got to explain the lyrics to my songs?" he joked. "Today, everybody's a rock critic! Can't get any respect."

JP pointed to the bearded guy in the ski sweater across the table from him. "Lee, this is Billy Beatty, some say he runs SIR rehearsal studios, but mostly he's sitting here with me shooting the shit."

"Nice to *meetcha*, Lee," said Billy. "And, JP, you got it wrong again because I gotta get back to SIR. Aerosmith is coming in at midnight to rehearse and I better make sure that everything's set up right for them. Last time they were here, Steven Tyler was complaining about the monitors all night and Joe Perry blew out two of my Marshall stacks."

"Sit down, pal," said JP glibly. "What's your rush? If Perry and Tyler get there by three in the morning, you'll be lucky." He pointed to his right. "And of course, Lee, I think you already know James Elliot, best dressed photographer in Manhattan."

"Hey, man, good to see you," said Lee warmly. "James Elliot and I closed the Talkhouse together on many a night."

"Nice to see you again, my friend," said James Elliot, turning to address the table. "Let me tell you something and this is serious - this guy's good."

"I know," said JP. "Why do you think I hired him? Saw him play at the Talkhouse this past summer and he knocked me out."

Lee looked at JP and said nothing.

"Hope he's not that good," said Billy Joel. "Gonna put me out of business."

Lee had never met a *rock star* like Billy Joel before, and now, to find himself casually sitting around drinking with him, he couldn't resist the chance to talk with him but couldn't think of much original to say. "So how's the new album going?"

"I guess it's going OK, just out and the reviews aren't terrible. For me this is always the toughest time, in between when the album gets released and the tour starts. Don't know what to do with myself. Maybe I should get away somewhere."

"Hey, just sit tight and put yourself in a New York State of mind," said JP.

"'New York State of Mind,'" said Billy Joel, humming a soulful melody. "Good name for a song."

"Be my guest, pal," said JP. "Have another drink, kick back, you'll like this, Lee, we've been talking about the music business. These guys can tell you anything you want to know, isn't that right, Billy?"

"In that case, then I really will need another drink," said Billy Joel, waving for the waitress. "What are you drinking, Lee?"

"Johnny Walker Black on the rocks."

"Man's got style," said Billy. "While we're at it, JP, ask them what they want to drink over there," gesturing two tables away where Carly Simon sat with her husband James Taylor. "And tell her to record one of my songs, please."

"So you were talking about the music or the business?" asked Lee.

Billy Joel replied, "Well, when it comes to the music business, as

Bill Graham always says, '*it's not the money...*' - then raising his voice and causing heads to turn – '*It's the MONEY!*'"

"You know, I'm a businessman," said JP. "So, I love to talk about art. But you guys are artists, so all you want to talk about is money."

"The music is the easy part," said Billy Joel. "Getting paid is more difficult."

Sitting there, listening to these guys talk about record deals, advances, publishing companies, and the music execs that had *ears* and those with lavish expense accounts, all of this was a first for Lee. They were really talking about the *business* of music, big numbers and big names, not the fantasy that he and Danny imagined it to be when they would dream and scheme in the Talkhouse dressing room. This was not the Hamptons anymore, where doors were open to nearly everyone who wanted to party. Now, Lee was seeing these people in their element, in the very real world of the city, where status had meaning, where a career was a way of life. Even James Elliot had an air of seriousness about him that was not so apparent those late nights at the Talkhouse *a*nd JP was clearly more in his element as a bar owner than a partygoer. Only Lexi had been exactly the same as when he last saw her. Because it made no difference where she was, town or country; she lived in her protective bubble and traveled in a secured universe that knew no boundaries; the only thing she had to modify was her wardrobe.

Lee looked around the table at JP, James Elliott, Billy Beatty, Billy Joel and he felt like he just had become a member of the *Rat Pack.*

CHAPTER 16

Many afternoons, Lee would wake up in his flat over JP's and just stare out the window for the longest time, not even getting out of bed. Gazing up and down First Avenue, he had the heightened sense that all that motion and energy was carrying him along with it like a surfer on a great wave. He had a crazy desire to know exactly where everyone was going, every soul down there on the street on his or her way to somewhere, everybody moving. While spellbound by it all, he didn't really feel part of it but still believed he was in the right place at the right time and luck was on his side.

In Europe, Richard Gallagher had once told him that the most precise definition of an expatriate was someone who felt more at home when he was not at home and that description, he had to admit, fit him like a glove. Yet he didn't have much to show for his freedom, with too many years now of playing in small bars, never sticking anywhere, always looking for but never finding a reason to stay in a place once his gig was up and romances grew stale. But now, against all odds, he had found a place in this pulsating city, *the* capital of the world, in love with another man's wife who seemed to want him too, although in ways he still didn't clearly understand. All of this happening suddenly to a guy who never made things *happen* before, never gifted with a clear direction or motivating force. So how had he managed to arrive at this undeniably fortuitous situation? Had fate suddenly taken him under her wing? Good looks, charm and obvious talent had served him well so far, better than most of his kind, by the fact that he was able to make a living singing and playing guitar. Just as his high school guidance counselor had branded him so many years ago, Lee still thought of himself as an *underachiever* in the classic sense of the word; the one who effortlessly put one foot in front of the other when he should have been sailing above the crowd, leading the way. But the only time he really had stepped out, he ended up behind bars and that took the wind out of his sails, big time.

The seasons changed while Lexi Langdon and Lee Franklin often made love with a passion that didn't diminish as the traffic cruised continuously uptown beneath his bedroom window. For the first time he could remember, Lee didn't want to be anywhere but where he was and more significantly, he didn't want to be alone anymore even if it was his need for solitude that had drawn him to playing music in the first place; a very public place where he could hide. Since he got out of jail, Lee had *survived* with nobody's help but his own, with no cushion to fall back on if he failed and that had been all right with him. The thing he was sure of, his *ace in the hole*, was that he was confident he could take care of himself whatever happened. And now Lexi and love and *The Big Apple* itself had all come into his once simple but controlled life and were moving him along at a dizzying pace and he was inclined to go with it. In spite of all the encouragement along the way, pleased club owners and applauding audiences, he hadn't on his own strengths been able to take his career, let alone his life, to the next level. But chance had been on his side lately and so his trust was growing. *This is an Unreal City,* thought Lee. *You can be anybody you want to be ... when you're alone ...*

AND THAT'S EXACTLY WHAT HE HAD BEEN, *ALONE,* WHEN HE HAD first encountered Danny O'Connor, less than a year before, totally by accident, in New York's LaGuardia Airport of all places. Just thinking of the randomness of it all made Lee grin because, after all, how many friendships that began over a conversation struck-up in an airport bar actually stick? Lee had been changing planes, on his way up to Boston when a freak spring snowstorm had delayed his flight and sent him to the shelter of the airport bar with his guitar case and a definite shortage of funds in his pocket. Another guitar player, a friend, had asked him to fill in while he went out on the road. The gig was at Johnny Dee's, a college hangout in Somerville, Massachusetts, right outside of Boston, where he'd be playing for the lunch and dinner crowd. Lee was sure, even before he got there, that the gig would be a drag, but hell, it paid. So, he gave up his tiny sub-let in Washington DC and headed up to Boston, another college town.

In the airport bar he sat down on an upholstered barstool, pulling his guitar case close where he could keep an eye on it. With not much wiggle room in his budget he was in no hurry to order anything, having just about enough extra cash to nurse one beer until his flight finally boarded. The rumpled sports section of the *New York Times* had been left on the bar and he began reading it:

Casey Stengel, Yankee & Mets Manager Dies at 85

"It's not over until the fat lady sings." Looking up, Lee saw the young bartender leaning over the bar peering down at the newspaper he was trying to read.

"What's not over?" asked Lee.

"I guess Casey Stengel was talking about baseball," replied the bartender. "But really it's about life in general, don't you think?"

"Guess you could say that," said Lee. "Is this your paper?"

"Naw, I don't like sports. You a musician?" he asked.

"Yeah, I guess the guitar case gives that away."

"So, what do you want to drink?"

"Well ... "Lee looked at the line of premium Scotch Whiskeys behind the bar and the snow coming down in thick white flakes outside. "What the fuck, give me a Johnny Walker on the rocks."

It was mid-afternoon and The Jetlag Lounge was empty. After pouring Lee four fingers of Scotch, Danny came out from behind the bar and sat down on the empty stool on the other side of Lee's guitar. He was clean-shaven and a few years younger than Lee, whose three-day growth exaggerated his own age. Danny had that kind of pale boyish face with light freckles that defied adulthood and his curly dark hair, slicked back for the job, was spilling over the collar of his white shirt. But the most impressive thing about him was his wide-open smile, which hardly ever left his face and only got wider when he became truly amused; the kind of guy who turned just being alive into a daily, joyful adventure.

"Mind if I join you?" he asked.

"Sure. That's a generous drink you poured me, thanks."

"It's on me ... well, sort of," said Danny. "Hey, I could give you the whole damn bottle and nobody would know. It's just a part-time job, so what do I care? I won't be here for long."

"Still in school?" asked Lee.

"I hope you're kidding me. School's for accountants, I'm starting my own artist management company. Music business is where the money is these days."

"That's too bad," said Lee sarcastically. "I'm just trying to lower my own tax bracket."

"You should talk to my brother about that."

"Don't tell me he's an accountant?"

"Something like that ... hey, what do you play? You a professional?"

"I play guitar and sing, and I guess you'd have to define that term *professional*."

"You know, like is that what you want to do to earn a living?"

"Oh ... no, it's just a hobby."

They stared at each other for a moment and Danny just kept smiling.

"You're shitting me," he said. "That guitar case looks pretty battered. And you too," he laughed. "You look like you've been around, no offense."

"You pinned me," said Lee. "So next question is what do I play and where do I play? I play in little bars and clubs and I play what people want to hear. A lot of James Taylor these days, I don't know why."

"Fire and Rain?" asked Danny.

"And snow, my friend," said Lee, looking out the window. "Lots of snow."

Sitting together at the bar, they talked for several hours, before Lee's plane finally took off. Every once in a while, someone would come into the bar and Danny, acting like it was almost an inconvenience, would get up and serve them a drink, tell them to make a sign if they wanted another, and return to his place with Lee. Easy to talk with, optimistic and full of jokes, Danny kept telling Lee he had good looks and lots of charisma.

"Rock stars got to be tough," said Danny. "A loner, like John Wayne with a guitar. That's what Elvis is."

"You think Mick Jagger looks like John Wayne?" asked Lee.

"Mick Jagger's English, it's a whole different set of rules. Those guys gotta look like they came out of a book by ... what's his name ... Dockins."

"*Dickens,*" corrected Lee. "*Oliver Twist.*"

"Yeah, that's what I mean. Mick Jagger sounds like *Oliver Twist,* right? Same kind of name, a name that describes the guy, and the way he looks. Don't you get it? So, what's your name?"

"Lee Franklin. What do you think? Is it all right? Tell me if I got a chance in hell with a name like that."

"Are you kidding me? With a name like that you could go anywhere," said Danny. "Lee, like Robert E. Lee – a rebel! And

Franklin, like Benjamin Franklin, a solid guy. A stand-up guy who's still a rebel, like *Marlon Brando* in *The Wild One*.

Lee liked that. "And what's your name?"

"Danny O'Connor," he said.

Lee laughed. "With a name like that you could ..."

"Own an Irish pub or be a cop?" Danny suggested. "Don't you see? That's what I'm trying to avoid. I want to be a manager like Colonel Parker with Elvis, Brian Epstein with the Beatles. I got a lot of great ideas. Hey, you got a demo?"

Just for the hell of it, Lee gave Danny a cassette of one of his recent performances recorded right off the soundboard, which he just happened to have in his guitar case.

"I promise I'll let you know what I think," said Danny.

"I'm grateful already," said Lee ironically.

"Listen, Lee, is there a number I can get in touch with you?" asked Danny. "I got a friend, a musician like you, a real studio cat, sings and plays guitar. He told me he had a message left on Radio Registry about a summer gig out on Long Island that he can't take. I can try to hook it up for you."

"What's Radio Registry?" asked Lee.

"It's a big-time message service that musicians communicate with each other through for work and stuff. *Professional* musicians, I mean." He pointed his finger at Lee. "Like you. I'm surprised you don't have a number with them with a name like Lee Franklin."

"I don't even have a telephone number," said Lee, shaking his head and smiling. "But if you can remember the name Johnny Dee's, outside of Boston in Somerville, you can reach me there for the next couple of months."

Danny promised that Lee would be hearing from him soon, said he had a good feeling about Lee and told him they were going to go places together. "Don't forget my name – Danny O'Connor."

Lee laughed. "It's already etched in my memory." He slung his guitar case over his shoulder, waved goodbye and started walking to his gate, but by the time he arrived in Boston he had forgotten he even talked to Danny. The gig at Johnny Dee's was just as disheartening as Lee feared it would be, playing for the lunchtime crowd, people pretending they were listening while they wolfed down burgers and fries and then scurried back to work or school. Why they even had him playing there, at that time, was a mystery to him. The owner said he didn't get it either, but whenever they had live music, they sold more booze, even at lunch. Nearly a month into the gig, Lee was called down to his office.

"Your manager called, left a number, said you should call him back right away. He's got a gig for you in August out in the Hamptons.

"My manager?" said Lee, surprised. "I didn't know I had a manager."

"Well, that's what the guy said, anyway. I think the number is from Queens, New York," said the owner. "You can use my phone if you want but keep it short. I got a business to run."

"You sure do," Lee replied. After the owner left his office, Lee picked up the phone and dialed Danny's number.

Looking out on First Avenue, Lee was thinking about what Danny had said to him at that LaGuardia airport bar last spring, how they were going to go places and it just amazed him. In fact, Danny was right because he *was* going places, places he had never dreamed of going before, yachts and mansions, and now hanging out with rock stars. But as thrilling as all that was, the main thing was that he was falling perilously in love with Lexi, and he worried that if he kept falling like this he would hit the *ground*, as hard as the First Avenue pavement outside his window. This impossible situation was unsustainable, but despite all of that, he had no intention of walking away from it.

The intercom buzzer rang, breaking his reverie and anxiety. It was JP telling him to come down to the bar because he had a phone call. "I bet you know who's calling," said JP, lowering his voice conspiratorially.

Lee threw on the nearest clothing he could find, no socks, untied Adidas running shoes and flew down the stairs and into the bar. JP was standing at the high bench at the end of the bar where he took reservations, holding the phone and giving Lee a knowing grin. "All yours, pal," he said. "I'll give you some privacy." JP walked to the rear of the restaurant and Lee waited a few seconds, then put the phone to his ear.

"Are you busy tonight?" asked Lexi. "Want to keep me company?"

"You know I want to do that. What time are you coming over?" he asked in a soft voice.

"Tonight we're doing something different - we're going *out* to dinner, and I know a place that's gonna knock you out, sugar. But I believe there's a dress code and you'll need to wear a jacket."

Lee laughed. "OK, will a Levi's jacket do?"

Lexi laughed too. "Well, in that case it might be better if I pick you up one? Tell me your size and I'll send Armando."

Lee hesitated. "My size? I'm a forty-four, I think, haven't bought a suit in a while."

"Forty-four," said Lexi enticingly. "Sounds like a gun."

"Bang- bang."

"I suppose you're standing there in JP's talking to me like that on the phone?"

"Well ... right."

"Remind me of something tonight, will you please, sugar? To get a phone line put into your place upstairs."

THIS TIME, IT WAS LEXI'S DRIVER, ARMANDO, WHO BUZZED LEE and came up to his apartment, handing him a suit bag from Barneys Men's Store, telling him he'd be back in a half-hour to pick him up.

When Lee came downstairs, dressed in a black Armani suit and a new crisp white shirt, he caught a glimpse of himself in JP's window as he ducked into the limo; he looked and felt like a superstar and with the chauffeur holding the door open, Lexi mouthed a silent *wow* and immediately kissed him while her free hand pressed the button that raised the dark tinted glass, separating them from Armando.

"Where we going?" he asked.

"Ever heard of Windows on the World?"

"Can't say I have," said Lee. "But I guess it's a restaurant, right?"

"It's more than a restaurant," said Lexi. "It's an experience in itself, on top of the World Trade Center – a hundred and six floors up in the sky. On a gorgeous night like tonight, we can sit at our dinner table with Manhattan spread out beneath us for a backdrop. I'm expecting it to be just spectacularly romantic."

"Just kissing you in the back of this limo is what I call *spectacularly romantic*. But aren't you afraid of us being seen out together? Doesn't sound like the most discreet little *bistro* for a rendezvous with a name like that, Windows on the World."

Lexi settled back into her seat and pulled her red fox coat around her shoulders.

"First of all, Lee, I think the chances of Ray being at this place are next to nil because he's up in Boston looking at some group called The Modern Lovers of which, believe me, he is not one. And secondly, I invited James Elliot to join us for dessert, so we're covered. Besides, we're just friends out for dinner together. What's naughty about that?"

"I guess nothing's wrong with that ... but what if Ray ever found out we were more than friends, Lexi? Do you ever think about that?"

Lexi laughed. "Honestly? I try not to, and not now anyway because Ray's not here, it's a beautiful night and you look like a leading man."

"Hope so," said Lee, not knowing if he should be concerned. Dropping the subject of Ray, they were soon whizzing past Union Square and crossing over to lower Broadway, on their way downtown.

"I don't know if I've ever been this far downtown before," said Lee.

"Don't suppose musicians spend much time on Wall Street."

"Not really, and you?"

"Well, more than you'd think. The law firm that represents Langdon Industries in Houston, Williams, Connolly & Califano, they've got a branch down here right next to the New York Stock Exchange. Sometimes I've got to sign some proxy or something or other about Daddy's estate or have lunch with some visiting member of the board. And you never know what kind of interesting folks you'll run into up in their office 'cause they represent everyone from Mafiosi to movie stars to the governor of Texas. It's a hoot just sitting in their reception! And every Monday they send a messenger to me with a manila envelope of spending cash for the week."

"So that's how you people do it," laughed Lee. "Even cash gets delivered."

"And signed for," said Lexi.

"Do you count it before you sign?"

Lexi looked at Lee with amusement. "Armando, my wonderful butler, he signs for it, silly. What do you think?"

"I don't know what to think ... do you even count your change when you buy something?"

"Depends."

Lee shook his head. "It's not my world."

"So, let's talk about your world for a change, Lee. How's your music going?"

"Pretty good, I suppose. JP seems happy, thinks I'm building a little following, says the place fills up whenever I'm playing. But maybe you're paying people to come down and see me. Maybe that's what you need all that cash for."

"Stop it!" Lex laughed wholeheartedly. "You don't need me to get an audience. You're a great singer." She kissed him tenderly on the cheek. "That's how you hooked me."

"Hey, did I tell you I met Billy Joel?"

"Wow," said Lexi, her eyes opening wide. "Now he must have some connections to the right people in your field. And by right people I definitely don't mean Ray."

"I'm sure he does," said Lee. "I should be making some calls, inviting some record companies down to my shows or maybe I'm just not hungry enough ..."

"We'll see just how hungry you are when we sit down to dinner, sugar," Lexi interrupted as the limo pulled beneath the two enormous light gray blocks of steel and glass, lit up like gargantuan beacons penetrating far into the night sky. The towers looked monumental, like the last buildings that would be left standing when the end of the world came, and everyone took off for another galaxy. After getting out of the car, they tilted their heads back to peer up at the distant flat roofs of the World Trade Center Towers.

"Feels like we're standing in front of the Great Pyramids of Egypt at their creation," said Lee.

"Kind of," said Lexi. "They say these buildings are so high that up on the top floors you can feel them sway in the wind. Shall we go for a visit?"

A dedicated elevator in the North Tower sped them directly to Windows on the World and the suave maître d, with an indistinct European accent, greeted Lexi by name and quickly led them to their reserved table. Normally seating four, the table had been set up for two intimate diners, right next to the colossal series of vertical window slabs facing north to all of Manhattan, the two rivers that outlined it and far into New Jersey and the boroughs of Queens, Brooklyn and the Bronx as well. Lee watched traffic crawl on the main arteries of the city as boats stood motionless on the river. He could see planes taking off and landing at all three of New York's major airports. The many bridges that crossed the rivers, each one outlined by a necklace of lights following their spans, seemed majestic, connecting gloriously luminous Manhattan to the darkened skies of its surrounding *colonies*. Lights danced all around him, just outside his window, like nothing he had ever seen before and Lee grinned like a boy gazing at a Ferris wheel for the first time.

"Wow! That's an amazing view," he said. "I feel like Zeus sitting on Mount Olympus." But Lexi wasn't looking at him or out the window either. She was busy waving to a distant table.

"Why, that's Dick Cavett," she said to Lee. "He was a regular at my parties this summer. Did you meet him?"

"Don't think so," said Lee. "I met so many people, should have taken notes."

"Well, he always left early, I think he must write in the morning or something ... and I think he's with Tom Wolfe," said Lexi even more eagerly. "I don't know which I love more, his books or his wardrobe. All those white suits! I bet they're having the same conversation they were having at my party out on Long Island, arguing the merits of contemporary art. One of them is for it and one against, but I can't remember which is which."

"I read Tom Wolfe's *The Kandy-Kolored Tangerine-Flake Streamline Baby* back in high school," said Lee. "Kind of changed my life."

"You did?" asked Lexi. "I didn't imagine you a reader, Lee. I thought all you rock stars read ... comic books," she teased him.

"First of all, I'm not a rock star ..."

"Not yet, sugar."

Lee smiled. "And yeah, I've read a few books, I guess, but never the ones I was supposed to. They were making us read *The Good Earth* in high school, like I can relate to Chinese peasants, and then Tom Wolfe comes along and he's writing about California hot rods and Phil Spector and race car drivers and taking it as seriously as anything else. Made me think that there was a whole other world out there waiting for me."

"There is a whole other world," said Lexi. "And it feels like we're sitting on top of it all right now, no?"

Lee turned in his chair and saw Manhattan shine beneath him, tracing Broadway as it cut diagonally across the island.

"Look at the Empire State Building down there in Midtown. Looks tiny."

"Big enough for *King Kong*," said Lexi.

"So how much of the city belongs to you?" asked Lee, kidding.

"Just you," said Lexi as she slipped off her high heel and rubbed her foot on Lee's leg under the table.

It was the first time that Lee had eaten in such a distinguished atmosphere, every man in a jacket and tie and women definitely dressed to be seen. A formal waiter in a burgundy Eton jacket took their food order, followed by an ancient, dour-faced *sommelier* that inquired about what wine they would be drinking. Lexi suggested a Nuit St. Georges red with the meat and a bottle of chilled Sancerre, her favorite white, to complement the fish. When the white wine was brought to the table the *sommelier* showed the bottle to Lee before pouring a small amount into his glass to taste, something Lee was not used to doing. *Maybe this is a test,* he thought. But he rose to the occasion, swirled the wine in his glass and brought it to his nose before swishing it around his mouth and swallowing slowly.

"Greets the palate like an old friend," said Lee and the *sommelier's* frown almost turned to a smile.

"I'm sure it does, sir. Thank you."

Lexi broke out laughing.

"You handled that well," she said. "I had no idea you were such a wine connoisseur."

"I'm not really," said Lee. "I spent some time in Europe, so I know how it's done. But nobody ever returns a bottle."

"I did once," said Lexi. "Just to be nasty." She giggled.

"Nobody but you, then," said Lee. "Anyway, I actually remembered that line from *Gilligan's Island* when I was a kid. *Thurston Howell III* was this rich guy on the island, always saying posh things like that. Cracked me up."

"I used to watch that show too," said Lexi. "I liked Ginger, the movie star. She was so glamorous."

"That's funny, we watched the same shows as kids," said Lee. "Never thought about that."

"Don't be ridiculous, Lee," she said. "Everybody gets the same thing on their television set no matter who you are."

Then dinner began to be served by a team of nimble waiters who sliced Lee's Chateaubriand and deboned Lexi's Filet of Dover Sole Amandine.

"But not the same thing on their plate," said Lee.

"Maybe not," conceded Lexi. "Bon appétit, sugar."

WITH IMPECCABLE TIMING, JAMES ELLIOT WAS STANDING AT the edge of their table just at the moment a waiter was handing them dessert menus.

"Am I late?" he said. "Thought I'd take the stairs to get some exercise."

"You're kidding?" gasped Lexi.

"Yes, my dear, I am indeed kidding." James Elliott moved just inches from the window. "Wow! There it is, right in front of you, it's like you're sitting on top of it all."

"That's exactly what I said!" said Lexi.

"Kind of takes your breath away," said James Elliott as he unbuttoned his coat.

"Hope you're wearing a jacket," said Lexi. "They're very strict about that."

James Elliot peeled off his overcoat and underneath was a black blazer almost identical to Lee's own Armani.

"Same dress code?" he said to Lee. "Nice threads, my man, where'd you get it?"

Lee looked to Lexi who said nothing, not changing her expression. *Now, this is a test,* he thought.

"A present," said Lee modestly. "From an anonymous admirer." Lexi gently kicked him under the table.

"I like that," said James Elliott grinning. "Especially the anonymous part."

As Dick Cavett and Tom Wolfe were exiting the restaurant, they veered their course to stop by Lexi's table and Dick greeted her warmly, kissing her on both cheeks. Tom Wolfe was dressed in a bespoke white suit with a black and gold polka dot silk tie knotted low on a high Victorian starched collar.

"I saw you two over there deep in discussion," said Lexi. "So I didn't want to interrupt. Don't tell me you gentlemen are still fighting about modern art? Will I have to take down my Picassos next time you all come to a party?"

"What I love about you, Lexi," said Dick Cavett dryly, "is that when you say *my Picassos,* you use the plural and you're serious."

"I've only got a couple of ... small ones." Lexi modestly clarified.

"That's reassuring," said Tom Wolfe.

"But that's because my two *De Koonings* take up so much room."

"*Touché,*" said Dick Cavett.

"Read my book *The Painted Word,*" said Tom Wolfe. "I dethrone the kings of *Cultureburg.*"

"Oh, don't get him started," said Dick Cavett. "I'm still trying to digest."

After dinner they dropped off James Elliot at his Soho loft on Greene Street and soon they were back at Lee's apartment. When they walked in, as if by habit, Lexi headed directly for the bedroom.

"Wait," said Lee. "There's something I want to do."

"Right here?" she said teasingly. "Or out in the hallway?"

"No, Scarlett." Lee bent down and put one arm around her back and another around her legs and swooped her up in one motion, lifting her off the floor in his arms with her luscious mouth just inches from his.

"Whoa! You're strong, Lee," said Lexi.

"Call me Rhett," he said, walking the few steps to the bedroom with Lexi in his arms, laying her gently down on the bed before he covered her, and they kissed for a very long time before removing each other's clothes and touching. Lee was kissing Lexi's erect nipples to the sound of her sweet moans. They were too impatient to completely undress, too many buttons, snaps, belts and stockings, and Lexi was pulling Lee's penis clear of his suit pants and taking it in her mouth, and Lee was hiking up her dress and pulling off her black lace panties and then...and then he was inside and they were kissing even more passionately until he exploded within her. If someone had been walking down First Avenue at that moment just under Lee's windows, he might have smiled at the unmistakable cries of ecstasy audible from Lee's apartment. Every time they made love now it grew in intensity, the awkwardness and shyness of that first time having completely vanished. In bed, at least, they were truly together.

Later, they lay there watching the Sony Trinitron TV that Lexi had installed. It was indeed Saturday night and they watched the new hit TV show *Saturday Night Live* which had premiered just weeks before.

"I can't believe it," said Lee during one of the opening sketches. "I met a couple of these guys at your party, that one who's always falling down ..."

"Oh, that's Chevy Chase," said Lexi.

"And the crazy guy dressed up like a bee. I remember him from that party."

"John Belushi," said Lexi. "Ray knows all of them, says he hangs out with the whole cast down at this club Madame Rue's he's got himself involved in." She looked at Lee and kissed him. "Sugar, you gotta do me a favor, come to my rescue and be there at my dinner party next week. I need you for moral support."

"You think that's wise? Won't Ray be there?"

"That's the whole reason I want you there. I can't face a night of Ray and his *BS* alone. I'm afraid I'll lose it in front of all my guests."

"I can't imagine you doing that," said Lee.

"You know we've been fighting a lot lately, it's gotten to the point where I can hardly stand to be in the same room with him when he starts bragging ..." She shuddered. "I can't stand a man who brags. He wasn't always like this, I don't know what happened, but now he's so full of himself. I don't know what he's trying to prove."

"How are we going to do it? asked Lee. "Might be awkward if I just show up alone."

"James Elliot is coming – I'll ask him to bring you along with Kathy. Ray won't suspect anything."

"But what if he does?"

"In the words of your hero *Rhett Butler*," said Lexi breaking into a laugh, "'Frankly, my dear, I don't give a damn!'"

CHAPTER 17

Kathy ran down the steps of her apartment building and jumped into the cab waiting on the curb whose door swung open for her. With some difficulty, she maneuvered her very long legs into the cramped back seat and gave James Elliot a big kiss.

"Don't you smell good tonight?"

"Don't I always?"

"Of course, darling. So where we going?" Kathy asked James Elliot. "Up to Nirvana on Fifth Avenue? Visit the queen?"

"Lexi's no queen," said James Elliot. "If she was, she wouldn't hang around with me."

"What's wrong with you?"

"Queens don't hang around with gay, black photographers."

"Are you kidding me?"

"You're right, that's exactly who they hang around with."

"And besides," said Kathy. "You're not really gay, I've seen you with a lot of girls, some of them friends of mine."

"I'm like an atheist who prays before he goes to bed at night, like to keep my options open. Just in case I might want to change my mind."

"You're one of a kind, James Elliot."

"That's what I'm trying for. Speaking of which, how's your sex life going?"

"My sex life? Well, quantity wise it's severely been reduced to one prime candidate. But quality wise, I can't complain."

"I should get a little credit for that," snickered James Elliot. "Taking you two down to the beach that night."

"I owe you," said Kathy. "Never saw it coming ... but Danny is kind of ... solid? Know what I mean? Maybe that's what I was looking for."

"That's what we're all looking for my sweet angel. Someone to grow old with ... not that I will *ever* grow old, mind you."

"Who's gonna be at this shindig?" asked Kathy. "And why was it so important that I come? Danny's working tonight, I could have stayed home and worked on my beauty sleep."

"You, my dear, have been cast in the role of *beard*."

"For you? Who's going to be there? Your parents?"

"Don't even go there," said James Elliot. "This is all on a *need to know* basis, mind you, but we're picking up Lee Franklin and he's coming with us to Lexi's and you two are officially on a date, as the young people say. And tonight, discretion is definitely the better part of valor."

"Lee Franklin? I don't get it. Who's he trying to hide from?"

"Begins with an R as in *are* you really her husband and ends with a Y as in *why* the fuck did she ever marry you?"

"Ray Arthur? I don't get it... you mean..."

James Elliot raised his eyebrows and put a finger to his lips.

"Holy shit!" cried Kathy. "Lee Franklin and Lexi Langdon are doing it!"

"I wouldn't call that being discreet."

"Does Danny know?"

"I doubt it, and don't you go telling him. Leave that to Lee."

"If you say so, James Elliot. That Lee Franklin is turning out to be more than some shy singing cowboy I guess."

"A lot more," said James Elliot smiling.

WHAT BLEW LEE AWAY FROM THE GET-GO WAS NOT SO MUCH that the elevator in the elegant Fifth Avenue building opened right onto Lexi's foyer, although that was surely impressive, but that the congenial young Filipino in a black turtleneck sweater, who was standing there ready to greet Lee, Kathy and James Elliot as the elevator doors parted, was the same man who had waited in front of Lee's apartment many times, brought them burgers from Melon's and delivered Lee his Armani suit before driving them to Windows on the World. Lee stared at him not knowing what to say but to his relief the driver, now butler, gave absolutely no sign of recognition.

"Lexi's other guests have already arrived," he said as he turned around and led the way into the apartment. "Please follow me."

"That's Armando," whispered James Elliot to Lee. "He's Lexi's butler, driver, whatever. Keeps this queen-size *pied-à-terre* running like a Swiss clock. He's very smooth. She brought him up from Texas with her. *Very* discreet."

"I got that," said Lee, not going into detail.

The apartment was enormous; Lexi had bought the top three floors with dozens of windows overlooking Central Park and the sheer amount of space was overwhelming.

"Wow," was all Lee could say.

"Wait until you see the whole layout," said James Elliot. "There's a sweeping staircase connecting all three levels that you are absolutely not going to believe."

The butler took their coats and led them into the library of Lexi's home, which seemed more like some aristocrat's palace than an apartment. Long hallways led to larger rooms and that circular stairway suggested upstairs bedrooms and more. Built-in walnut bookshelves lined the library walls and a Mary Cassatt portrait of a beautiful young girl hung over the fireplace where three fragrant logs burned in perfect unison. A few guests sat on a leather couch and easy chairs before the fire, chatting, smoking cigarettes and drinking champagne. With Lexi and Ray were Wes Edel and his girlfriend Alana, Jann and Jane Wenner, the creators of *Rolling Stone* magazine, and Margaux Hemingway, the great writer's granddaughter with her escort Errol Wetson, himself heir to the New York version of McDonald's - Wetson's Burgers. When Lee walked in, Errol was explaining to the gathering of beautiful people that once there had been more Wetson's than McDonald's in New York. "But now, thanks to them and Burger King and the union strikes, we're on the verge of bankruptcy," he announced bitterly.

"You'll get back on top," encouraged Margaux Hemingway. "Remember what my grandfather said."

"What's that?" asked Errol.

"*Courage is grace under pressure.*"

"I'll remember that tomorrow morning when I'm crossing the union picket line to close my flagship – *ex-flagship* - store in Hempstead."

Of course, when Lexi saw them, she rose to her feet, so everyone else followed her lead and there were kisses all around except for Ray, who stood his ground glumly next to Wes Edel as Lexi introduced the late arrivals to her assembled dinner guests.

"Let's see," said Lexi. "Who doesn't know each other here?" On that deliberate cue, names were exchanged, and hands were shaken and Kathy and Margaux who knew each other from the modeling scene kissed and screeched with joy. More champagne was brought in and within minutes the enlarged party was sitting back down, amiably conversing, all a few decibels higher than before. Lee found himself drawn to Jann Wenner, clearly the most *rock 'n roll* guy there.

"I thought *Rolling Stone* was in San Francisco. Why the move to New York?" Lee asked.

"Because New York is where the publishing industry is," said Jann Wenner, in his hip yet direct fashion. "And where most of the major record labels are, and where a lot of the artists live, too. When we started in the sixties it was all happening in San Francisco, for a moment in time it was the *epicenter* of ... everything, but now the energy center has shifted. It was the obvious right move."

"I remember your first issue," said Lee. "Saw it in some *head shop* back in the Midwest, it was like the first magazine I ever read that took rock 'n roll seriously, that wasn't just for teenage girls. John Lennon was on the cover, right?"

"Dressed like a soldier for some film he was making," said Jann. "Why do I think you're a musician?"

"Because I was late to the party?" asked Lee.

"Funny guy, maybe you'll make it into the magazine some day."

Jann's wife Jane was dressed in a white and blue striped French boating sweater, like Jean Seberg or Picasso. "We just started setting up the office here," she said. "I've been decorating Jann's space."

"I've got Pete Townsend's guitar," Jann interrupted. "The red Gibson SG he smashed at Woodstock – got it encased in Plexiglas and I'm going to hang it on the wall right across from my desk. It looks amazing. You should come up and see it sometime."

"That's about as far as we've gone with the decorating scheme," said Jane Wenner laughing. "Hanging smashed guitars on the wall."

Silently, butler Armando quietly appeared at the door and announced that dinner was ready, and Lexi thanked him, but no one got up until she did. Dinner was served at a long oval table with place cards for the seating arrangement. Couples were separated and Lee found himself sitting between Jane Wenner and Lexi; Ray was at the far end of the table and Lee was almost sure she must have planned it that way. The service was relaxed but very correct as Armando brought the large platters of food from the butler's pantry to an intricately inlayed ebony and ivory credenza and then served each person individually. Lee felt like he was eating in a restaurant, better than that, where you called your waiter by name. He tried his damnedest to keep one thought out of his head, *I could get used to this,* because he knew that was impossible, at least for the time being. Ray hadn't taken much notice of Lee since his arrival, not acting overly suspicious or hostile, but it did seem to Lee that each time he found himself engaged in a conversation with Lexi, Ray would find an opportunity to interrupt, to butt in, to draw her away from him, asking Lexi an inane question or her opinion on something unimportant and nearly shouting from the far end of the table, "Hey, Lexi ..."

When dinner was over, linen napkins were left on the matching tablecloth and there was more champagne awaiting everyone in the library. Ray made a point to sit right between Lexi and Lee on the leather couch and Lee had to slide over to make room.

"You guys sure had a lot to talk about at your end of the table," he said. Lee started to say something about how Jane Wenner was reminiscing about the early days of *Rolling Stone* in San Francisco, but Ray wasn't interested. "Hey, why don't we go out on the town tonight?" Ray interrupted. "Thursday night, best night of the week, don't have to deal with the tourists coming in from the *burbs*. How does that sound to you, Lexi?"

"How does what *sound*? She replied coldly. "I thought we were quite comfortable here."

"Let's expand our horizons, get out on the town like we used to do. You like Ashley's, don't you? We used to hang out there all the time."

Lexi looked to Lee. "I think I went there twice," she said coolly, "if that."

"After Ashley's we can all go down to Madame Rue's," said Ray. "Show you my baby."

"Your baby?" repeated Lexi, not in the least amused. "Madame Rue's is your baby?"

"You know what I mean."

"Sounds like a plan to me," said James Elliot, trying his best to inject some enthusiasm. "I'm up for it if everyone else is."

But the Wenners had just flown in from the West Coast and jetlag was getting the best of them, so no nightclubbing for them, and Margaux had to get up for a model shoot at 5 a.m. the next day and even *bon vivant* Errol Wetson had to be out in Hempstead, Long Island at the crack of dawn so at last it was left up to Lexi, Lee, Ray, Kathy and James Elliot to carry on. And as much as Ray insisted what a happening downtown club Ashley's was, full of music biz movers and shakers like him, he couldn't convince Wes Edel to come down there with them either.

"Listen, Wes, we don't have to stay long at Ashley's, just have a drink and say hello and then we'll head over to Madame Rue's and I can guarantee you that will be a lot of fun. I think Liza Minnelli is supposed to show up tonight."

"Include me out," said Wes Edel adamantly. "I know all about that joint and I don't know why you'd want to be tipping your glass with those hoods. Keep going like that and next thing you know, they'll be trying to take over my business."

"You just gotta know how to deal with them," said Ray. "They're reasonable people– just businessmen like anyone else."

"Except for one thing," said Wes.

"What's that?" asked Ray.

"They don't sue each other – they shoot each other." He looked toward his young girlfriend, Alana. "You don't want me to get shot, do you?"

Alana thought about it for a moment and then said in absolute seriousness, "It would depend where, Wessy." Everybody laughed.

"And another thing, Ray," said Wes pointedly. "Somebody's got to be in the office in the morning, eh? Minding the store?"

"I'm there when I need to be there," said Ray. "You know that. But you know, Wes, that's where I meet the artists, in the clubs at night. That's the only reason why I'm out there," he added defensively.

"Never made a deal at a nightclub in my life," said Wes. "And never will. You can hang out and bullshit until dawn but when the artists and their managers come into my office the next day, on my turf, where my chair is higher than theirs, that's where the business gets done."

"You don't really put your chair higher than theirs, do you?" asked Alana.

Wes laughed. "Bet I do! Hey, I'm the one signing the checks."

"What about us? We met at night," said Alana, and everyone laughed again.

"Then let's go home, before our contract runs out, Alana," said Wes. He stood on tiptoes to kiss Alana. "Now she's the best deal I ever made," he announced.

"But I don't do hit singles," said Alana.

"Doubles," said Wes, glancing at her very nice breasts. "Hit doubles."

Just before they left, as Wes was putting on his coat, he turned to Lee. "Word on the street is your shows at JP's are going well – that you're a crowd-pleaser."

"I try my best," said Lee.

"I might be looking for a good opener for some of my acts. Interested?"

"Sure," said Lee. "I mean ... yeah, great, thank you."

"Talk to Ray about it," said Wes.

Danny was nervously smoking a cigarette, suit jacket collar flipped up rakishly and standing outside the door of Ashley's, excited as hell to be there to greet them all when they arrived. When Lexi's limo pulled up to the curb right next to him, Lee exclaimed, "Wow, look at Danny!" both amused and proud, never having seen Danny O'Connor dressed up like that before, in a fine suit and shined shoes, grinning as if he owned the place or something.

"Look at Danny in that suit!" Lee went on. "He's all decked out for us."

"Everyone who works at Madame Rue's has got to dress right. I set the standards myself," said Ray with his usual bravado. "Building an image for the club is everything in this business. And that goes all the way down to the bartenders right up to the boss, me."

"Really? Is that what that photo in the *NY Post* was about? Building your image?" asked Lexi, but Ray didn't respond and the tension was only broken when Danny rushed over to the limousine, beating the driver to open the door.

"Welcome downtown!" said Danny. "Can I see your passports?"

"My faithful employee," said Ray to Danny. "Hope you got us that nice round table I asked you to? I don't want to be sitting in the back with the tourists."

"I thought you said the tourists weren't out tonight?" remembered Lexi. "Maybe *we're* the tourists, Ray?"

He ignored her. "Something up front, Danny?"

"You bet, I took care of everything with Ashley himself," said Danny, as Lexi, Ray and James Elliott proceeded to walk in while he hung back to give Kathy a discreet kiss.

"Is this a secret or something?" said Lee, nodding toward Kathy.

"Just don't want Ray Arthur to see too much, the less a guy like that knows about you the better."

"Getting smart and looking pretty spiffy, man. Where'd you get that nice suit?" asked Lee.

"Some guy brought in a rack of them to Madame Rue's the other afternoon - said take your choice. A hundred bucks each - can you believe that?"

"Probably fell off of a truck in Brooklyn," said Lee.

"Hey, feel this fabric," said Danny defensively. "Armani, imported from Italy."

"Sure, it's not a knockoff?" asked Lee. "You want to feel real *Armani*?" He felt the lapel of his own suit; the one Lexi had given him."

"Not too shabby yourself," said Danny, impressed. "That JP's gig must be paying all right if you can buy clothes like that."

"Good enough," said Lee, quickly changing the subject. "How long has it been since I've seen your smiling face?"

"Too long," said Danny, patting Lee on the back as they caught up to the rest of the crowd entering Ashley's. "This is your table," said Danny to Ray, leading the way. "Is it okay?"

"It will do," said Ray, plopping down in the prime seat at the reserved table. "But when we leave, make sure Ashley just sends me the bill, I don't want to see a check on this table."

"Already took care of that, too," said Danny. He and Lee sat across from Ray. "So how are you, man?" he said to Lee. "I miss you, never see you anymore."

"I know," said Lee. "You're downtown and I'm uptown."

"That says it all," said Danny. "How are the gigs going?"

"JP's is cool, my shows are going over well, and definitely more of a listening crowd than the Talkhouse so I can play some original stuff too. And I've got a nice little pad over the club."

"You got a place there?" Ray glared at Lee, more interested than he should be. "You'll have to show it to me sometime." Then he waved Lexi over to him. "You sit down here, darling, right next to me," and conspicuously took Lexi's hand in his.

"We should talk with Ray about your career tonight," Danny suggested tactfully to Lee. "He's in a good mood, showing Lexi off to everyone. You know, normally she won't go to these places with him. Must be because you're here. She liked you from the start, I could tell that day at the beach."

Lee said nothing.

Although Ashley's was a music business hangout, no one paid much attention as a DJ blasted out the latest hits and the crowd just raised their voices to be heard over the clamor of drums, bass and guitars. Perhaps ironic in a club that catered to artists, managers and record company executives but understandable in the same way that comedians rarely laugh at each other's jokes. Ashley's was downtown on lower Fifth Avenue, the gateway to Greenwich Village, and a place to party, not to work. Ashley Pandel, a charismatic and well-liked industry figure was the spirit, soul and namesake of the place; a smooth-talking whiz kid from LA who had charmed and cajoled his way into the upper echelons of the entertainment business. And Ashley was very good at what he did: treating everyone in his place like a star and making the stars themselves, whose careers he promoted, feel even more *celestial.*

Ashley himself served as the congenial nightly host to the famous and not so famous and even if he couldn't get you a table, he did it with panache and a smile. He had made his career as the publicist of multi-platinum recording artist Alice Cooper. Ashley's genius in garnering publicity had been an integral part in creating a media darling and had saved Alice from languishing as a talented cult artist. Alice himself, born *Vincent Furnier,* had of course been an important part of the mix with his ghoulish stage theatrics and catchy kitschy choruses, but it was Ashley's instinct that had created the safe personage that Middle America embraced. Soon enough, Alice was hosting golf tournaments with a cuddly George Burns and cracking jokes on *The Tonight Show* with Johnny Carson. America liked friendly monsters and there was nothing threatening about a male rock star with makeup and a girl's name as long as sex was taken out of the mix and replaced with on-stage guillotines and other horror film props. Hits like "I'm Eighteen" and "School's Out" cemented adolescent rage onto a demon-headed, golf-playing rock star and the money just kept pouring in. And when it was time to diversify with a *clubhouse* all his own, Ashley's was born.

Ashley, tanned and smiling, was soon standing right at Ray's table, making sure there was room for everybody while a solemn faced Alice Cooper *sans* makeup sat nearby drinking Budweiser and engaged in serious conversation with his wife. No one seemed to recognize him.

"Ray Arthur," said Ashley. "What brings you down here? Checking out the competition?"

"Hey, man, I could never compete with you, Ashley." Ray looked toward the table next to them. "Isn't that Alice sitting there? Hey, Alice!" yelled Ray.

Alice looked up briefly and nodded without really acknowledging Ray.

"It's Ray! How you doing, man?"

"Probably figuring out his next move," said Ashley. "Wants to get back to Arizona and ..."

"Play golf, I bet," said Ray. "Tell him to call me, I'm a member of a club up in Westchester."

"Actually, Alice owns his own club," said Ashley, enjoying having said that.

"Oh...yeah?" said Ray, looking around. "Well, then I'll come play with him. Good business tonight, Ashley, the place is packed."

"That's the idea," said Ashley. "How's Madame Rue's doing?"

"We're gonna drop in later," said Ray. "Gotta see Liza Minnelli."

"Count me out," said Lexi to Kathy.

"Ashley, I forgot to introduce you to my beautiful wife. This is Lexi ..." Ashley bowed at the waist.

"Beautiful, indeed," said Ashley. "Pleasure to meet you, Mrs. Arthur."

"I still use my maiden name, Langdon," she said, looking sternly to Ray. "But, Ashley, please call me Lexi like all my friends. It's a pleasure to meet you as well," she added graciously.

"Lexi's from Texas," added Ray. "Her father owned half the state before ..."

"That's enough of my resumé, thank you very much, Ray," interrupted Lexi, rolling her eyes.

"That good-looking guy next to my wife is Lee Franklin, a singer I discovered out in the Hamptons this summer."

Lee smiled, feeling embarrassed.

"And you know James Elliot, who does some work for my label..."

"Of course, I know James Elliot," said Ashley, moving around the table to shake hands.

"Any decision on Alice's cover shots?" asked James Elliot. "You know I'm ready, willing and able. Just give me the green light and we'll make some magic."

"You got to talk to the *head magician* over there," said Ashley, nodding to Alice. "He's been at war with the label over everything, you know, artistic control and all that crap."

"Artistic control," said Ray. "I allow as little of that as possible. Artists don't know what's good for them. That's the problem with ..."

"Hey, guys," interrupted Lexi. "I know how you love to talk shop, but Kathy and I are just dying for a drink."

"You are so right," said Ashley as he signaled a pink-haired waitress to come to their table. "I see anyone pen a copy of *Billboard* in here and they get thrown right out."

The waitress sashayed over to the table, chewing gum.

"Sweetheart, can we order some drinks?" said Ray.

She looked at Ray. "I'm not your sweetheart. But I'll take your order."

"Everybody is a punk nowadays," said Ashley. "Even my waitresses."

"I've been to CBGB," said Ray. "I know what the scene is like. Talked quite a bit with the Romans ..."

"I hope you mean the *Ramones,*" corrected the waitress.

Ray held court. Talking loudly and ordering a magnum of champagne for everyone, when he mentioned *his club* and *his* record label, he spun his head around, looking to make sure those sitting at nearby tables were taking notice of him. When the waitress returned with the champagne, Ray insisted upon opening the bottle himself, standing up as he theatrically popped the cork and then looked around like he was expecting applause. Most people, of course, ignored him and the waitress just shook her head. Lee stood up and excused himself to the men's room, needing to take a break from Ray. But the worst of it for him was seeing Lexi sitting next to

Ray with him holding her hand and sometimes kissing her on the cheek. He was sure that Lexi didn't like it, that she was just keeping up appearances. At least he hoped it was like that.

Lee was about to climb the wide staircase connecting the two levels of Ashley's, when a slim and pale young guy actually came walking down the polished walnut banister, balancing himself with a bottle of wine in each hand. Reaching the end, he deftly jumped off as the room erupted in applause just as Danny was joining Lee at the bottom of the stairs.

"Did you see that?" Lee asked Danny. "That guy walked down two flights on the banister in his bare feet."

"Philippe Petite," said Danny. "You know, it's the same guy who threw a wire between the two World Trade Center Towers and walked right across it, like he was crossing the street or something. Blew everyone's mind. He's been partying all over town ever since because now he's a real celebrity himself, toast of the town and a regular at Madam Rue's."

"Jesus," said Lee, thinking of his recent dinner with Lexi at Windows of the World. "I heard about it, that's way up there almost in the clouds, gotta have balls to do that, I'm telling you."

"Or wings," added Danny. "But now he drinks for free all over the city. And they gave him a free pass for the World Trade Center as long as he uses the elevator."

Coming down the stairs right in front of them was Ashley, this time not alone and talking intently with a chap in a short denim jacket, oversized tweed cap pulled low on his forehead and Dingo boots.

"Holy shit," said Danny. "That's John Lennon."

"Gotcha," said Lee quietly.

Ashley stopped right in front of them. "Hey guys, do you know John?"

"Wow," said Danny. "It's an honor."

"Yeah, nice to meet you, John," said Lee, trying to control himself.

"Don't be so sure," said the most familiar *Liverpudlian* accent in the history of the world. "I might turn on you, you know."

"So ... uh ... what are you doing, John?" asked Danny.

"What am I doing? I'm out getting fucked up," said John Lennon. "What are you doing?"

"We're uh ... well ... we're just uh ... my friend Lee Franklin here is a singer," said Danny. "You should hear him sometime. Got a voice like James Taylor."

"James Taylor?" said John. "You know, he was on my label once."

"I didn't know you had a label," said Danny.

"I hardly knew it myself until the bastards started suing me," said John. "It's called Apple Records."

"Apple?" said Danny, perplexed. "Isn't that the name of a computer?"

John Lennon looked to Ashley. "Where'd you find these guys?" Ashley just shook his head and shrugged his shoulders.

"Listen, John," said Danny, pointing his thumb at Lee. "My *client* here, Lee Franklin, is shopping for a label. Why not your ...uh ... Apple thing? Give a listen to his demo, let me know what you think."

"All right, you guys behave yourselves now," said Ashley, quickly guiding John Lennon down the rest of the stairs. "When you see Ray, tell him to come by the office later if he wants."

Lee and Danny just stood there speechless while John Lennon and Ashley Pandel disappeared into some inner sanctum.

"How could you say that?" Lee said finally. "Jesus, Danny, *I didn't know you had a label* – you never heard of Apple? Everybody knows Apple Records!"

"I guess I did, said Danny. "But I was so goddamn nervous I didn't know what the fuck to say. That was John Lennon for Christ's sake – that was the Beatles we were talking to right there, man. *Jesus,* Lee!" He hooted with delight. "John *fucking* Lennon!"

"Part of the Beatles anyway," said Lee.

"Hey, at least I tried to promote your career. You wait, now he'll remember your name and I'll get his number from Ashley, see if he'll come down to JP's catch your show."

"Ashley Pandel is *not* going to give you John Lennon's number. Didn't you hear what he said? *Tell Ray* to come by his office. He didn't invite us, did he?"

"Well ... didn't he mean all of us?"

"Keep dreaming, Danny."

"You sound like my brother. Don't forget what our friend John Lennon said, *I may be a dreamer but I'm not the only one ...*"

"'Imagine?'"

"Uh...I think so..."

"If you're gonna start quoting lyrics, Danny, you better at least know what song they're from."

"I'm just saying that only dreamers get anywhere in this world, Lee," said Danny defensively. "I may be a dreamer, but I got a plan and I'm not afraid to make a fool of myself to get somewhere. You'll see."

"I just did. Jesus!"

An hour later, Ashley's had started to thin out and the departing crowd split into two camps; one calling it a night and going home to set the alarm and wake up for that straight job early next morning. While the other, the *dawn patrol,* partied on in discos and after-hour clubs, sunglasses ready. Because nothing was worse than crawling home in the bright morning sun caught in the surge of rush hour commuters while having to shield your eyes like vampires with hangovers. Incongruously, each half was always wondering what they might have missed out on ...

By the mid-seventies, the hard-won freedoms of the revolutionary sixties, which were in some way identified with a liberal and free-spirited morality, had evolved into a wild and naïve flirtation with danger. Sex for nothing but its own sake had come out of the closet in every conceivable form, from gay bathhouses in Manhattan's meat-packing district to swinging hetero clubs, exemplified by the notorious Plato's Retreat on the Upper West Side. It almost seemed like everyone who stepped outside after dusk was doing drugs and having sex together in such places, from criminals to debutantes to bankers and their wives. And true enough, while snorting cocaine people weren't choosy about whom they got high with or what happened afterwards with very stoned consenting adults. Since cocaine was a drug that could be taken furtively in bathrooms or around dark back-room tables, New York City began to sprout the kinds of places specializing in that nefarious activity – seventies' *toxic mushrooms* popping up after the hard rain of the sixties. For years, according to mob informers and FBI surveillance, after-hours clubs would not only be tolerated, they would prosper. Looking back, one can only say that in spite of all its decadence and fiscal problems, New York City in 1975 never seemed so exciting, so enticing, so vibrant before; where everyone who wanted to was going to be famous and rich, or at least look that way, for a brief, shining moment. As David Bowie put it that same year in his hit *Fame*: "*What you want is in the limo ... What you get is no tomorrow ...*"

When Lee walked out of Ashley's into the brisk chill of the autumn air, there was a moment, as sometimes can happen on the New York *grid,* when all the cross-town traffic lights turned red and traffic stopped moving *en masse.* Briefly, the city held its breath and Lee stood in the middle of Fifth Avenue, looking downtown, and there beyond the Washington Square Arch arose the two silver monoliths of the World Trade Center, gleaming in the clear skies with a blinking red light on the soaring antenna that reached into the sky from the North Tower, like space-age lighthouses. The Washington Square Arch, a smaller version of Paris's Arc de Triomphe, was a monument to the country's heroic origins of sacrifice, dedication and unwavering ideals while the twin towers hailed excess, empire and sheer enormity as the bywords for New York's place in the universe. *Dead Center!*

"Can you believe that same guy we just saw tiptoeing down the handrail in Ashley's, strung a wire between those towers and walked right across, even sitting down in the middle of it all just to take in the view?" asked Lee. "I wonder what drove him to do it?"

"Publicity, free drinks, getting laid," said Danny. "Who knows? But you wouldn't catch me up there for anything."

"It's the right time for things like that now," said Lee. "Taking chances, crossing from one world to another with no net below, nothing to catch you if you fall. Doing the unthinkable just for the sake of doing it, just to show that it can be done!"

"Just the sight of those towers kind of makes you think that anything's possible now, don't you think, Lee? I mean, look at us – look where we are, man!" Danny laughed with glee. "We're gonna make it!"

"Then, I guess, anything *is* possible," said Lee, as the two young men stood alone. He wanted to say more, to tell Danny all about Lexi, but as he looked toward the door of Ashley's, Lexi, Ray, James Elliot and Kathy were putting on their coats and about to come out to join them. "So, we're going down to Madame Rue's, I guess?"

"Yeah," said Danny. "Hope I can get some time alone with Kathy. Maybe we can slip out while Ray's showing off the club to Lexi, I don't think she was ever in Madame Rue's before."

"Show off what?" asked Lee defensively. "There's not much that could impress her."

"She's too classy for that place, anyway," said Danny. "She won't last twenty minutes."

"Danny, tell me, what's the crowd like at Madame Rue's?"

"Oh, it's a mix, you got celebrities and just plain rich people slumming it and looking to get high."

"You can find drugs there?"

"You can find anything at Madame Rue's. That place has got an international reputation now - we get the *euro-trash*, the movie stars and the most *unfuckingbelievable* models you ever saw with skirts up to here. And there are a lot of people dressed to the nines who are there every night dropping hundreds, snorting blow, and you don't even know what they do – seems like all they do is party. Sometimes I ask Ray what some character does for a living, but he acts like it's none of my business, like only he's entitled to know the real inside dope. So then I ask one of the other bartenders who works with me, what some guy does who's throwing cash around like it's freakin' confetti, but I never get a straight answer. Just the phantoms of the night and who cares anyway? I mean, since Nixon resigned who's gonna look down their nose at anybody for making funny money? You think the Mafia is any worse than the government? I doubt it."

"So this is the *winter of our discontent* that followed the *summer of love*?" said Lee.

"Where'd you get that?" asked Danny. "Impressive."

"Somewhere between Shakespeare and Timothy Leary," said Lee.

Danny laughed. "They said *All You Need is Love,* but now I think it's more about money. Big money. And that never goes out of style, it's classic. Like The Beatles."

"And you, too, Danny, you're classic," said Lee. "Don't change."

"Change what?" said Danny. "My underwear?"

"Is this it?" said Lexi as the limousine pulled up in front of an overhanging marquee with Madame Rue's emblazoned in triple space letters. "It looks more like a movie theater than a disco."

"It was a movie theater, they showed pornos," said Ray. "Can you believe how I transformed it?"

"Then I'm not going in there," joked Lexi. "Especially if you're in one of the films, Ray."

Ray shook his head. "For your information, darling, in its heyday, this was the hottest vaudeville theater on the Lower East Side. Eddie Cantor played here – know who he was? And Buster Keaton with his parents – *The Three Keatons.* I'm going to have the city designate it as a historical landmark."

"They should designate you a historical landmark," said Lexi.

"Will you stop?" asked Ray, looking at James Elliot. "She loves to kid me."

"I just want to know how you know all this, Ray?" asked Lexi. "I never knew you were such a *vaudeville* buff."

"Ah, Maddy knows all this," said Ray. "He grew up down here, it's his neighborhood, his backyard. Anyway, the theater is totally renovated now, nothing like before."

"Maddy ... as in Maddy the Horse?" asked James Elliot. "The Mafioso?"

Ray just held his finger to his lips while Lexi looked away.

"Yeah," said Lexi," staring out the window. "My husband's best friend. Don't you read the paper? Ray's got all kinds of new friends." When Armando swung the door open, she got out of the car and walked to the club.

"I guess she saw that photo," James Elliot said slyly to Ray. "I thought you bought up all the New York Posts that morning and had them burned?"

"Don't even joke about that," whispered Ray. He hurried ahead to escort Lexi into Madame Rue's, where a thick red velvet rope was strung across the entrance. A bouncer and two security guards let celebrities and elite pass inside while dozens of hopefuls were held at bay. It was just a Thursday night before Christmas but the crowd in front of Madame Rue's was starting to spill out into the street. A light snow had started to fall, but this didn't discourage those waiting outside in the least; all pleas, requests and begging - *"It's me ... You know me!"* - were directed toward a six-foot two transvestite with a heap of lacquered ebony hair piled high on *her* head, held in place by a series of red and gold chopsticks. She stood stone-faced with her back to the crowd, a ferocious dragon embroidered on her remarkable kimono, holding an open compact mirror and dusting her nose with white makeup. This was *Madame Rue* herself and she surveyed the crowd with her mirror, while noting to her henchmen who shall pass and who shall wait forever.

Ray pushed his way to the front with Lexi and started shouting and one bouncer came over and asked him to keep it down.

"Hey, I own this place!" said Ray. "When did you start working here?"

"Today," said the burly bouncer. "And I'm a cop so when I say keep it down, I mean you. Now wait your turn."

Ray remained mute while he waited for the bouncer to back off.

"I see you got pull here, Ray," said Lexi.

"He's new, doesn't know me," said Ray. "Stanley," he yelled, waving his arms and smiling. "Stanley, it's me Ray!"

With that Madame Rue turned around. Layers of white pancake makeup and bright red lipstick still couldn't conceal the dark whiskers beneath, and the weight of *her* false eyelashes caused *her* eyelids to droop behind a mass of black kohl eye makeup. *Madame Rue* ignored Ray completely while addressing Lexi cordially.

"So nice to meet you, Ms. Langdon," he said in a deep baritone voice with a strong Brooklyn accent. "It's going to be a hot night – Halston just came in with Didi Ryan ..."

"Oh, I know Didi Ryan," said Lexi. "I met her at the NY Met ball. Her husband was related to the Aga Khan ..."

"Otto Khan," said Ray. "Robber baron like Carnegie or Rockefeller."

"You know everything, Ray," said Lexi sarcastically.

"Isn't that why you love me?" asked Ray.

"No," said Lexi coldly, turning to Madame Rue. "Can we come in now?"

He smiled at her. "Of course, Ms. Langdon. I'll have them set you up with a table near Didi and Halston, in case you want to visit."

"You're a sweetheart, Madame Rue," said Lexi. "Love your kimono, sugar." She kissed her on both cheeks.

"Let me know if you need anything out here, Stanley," said Ray as he followed Lexi in.

With that *Madame Rue* forcefully grabbed Ray by the arm.

"Don't call me Stanley, asshole! I'm *Madame Rue* out here."

"Jesus Christ," joked Ray to James Elliot once they were inside. "I hope they treat real customers better than me."

They walked down a long dark corridor where vintage silent movie posters lined the walls. At the end, just beyond a row of black double fire-doors which opened onto the *Bacchanalian* atmosphere of the club itself, was a coat-check room with three young, sexy girls, all dressed in kimonos, who were taking in coats, scarves and hats and giving back little plastic chips with numbers on them. This was the final frontier separating the grim reality of the street outside from the surreal fantasy of the club itself just steps away. Once you pushed through those black doors, a new world appeared, assaulting your senses with a myriad of bright lights, airplane level sounds and boisterous crowds, where all efforts at conversation were notched up to shouting level and people yelled into each other's ears.

Abruptly, Ray stopped at the coat-check and quickly gathered Lexi's and everybody else's coats in his arms, telling Danny to get everyone seated at a nice table with drinks, that he would be joining them directly. Danny understood when he saw Gloria glaring at Ray while she took five dollars per coat from the customers gathered in front of her, stuffing them into a cash box while her minions hustled the coats onto rows of hangers and passed out the chips. Ray tried to divert Lexi's attention, waving her quickly past the coat check. "I can put all our stuff down in the office. I'll catch up with you inside."

Boom. The intense, kinetic energy of the place hit you as soon as you pushed through those doors, like a storm on your senses, the swirling lights, the pounding music, the feeling of being in a *moral-free* zone. Half a dozen bare chested waiters dressed in nylon gym shorts and suspenders whipped through the crowd with trays of drinks while the bar itself was a *hive* of incessant activity; metal shakers held high overhead as bartenders mixed two cocktails at a time and a frantic clientele waved bills in the air, trying to get their attention, to get a *drink, please*! The dance floor itself, which took up half the club, was packed with well-dressed, sweating and gyrating bodies which ebbed and flowed en masse giving the distinct impression that everyone was dancing with everyone, men and women,

women and women, men and men, and even one blue-haired dowager who held her gold-collared Shih Tzu puppy out in front of her, barking to the beat.

Just outside, as Danny led Lexi, Lee, Kathy and James Elliot to a prime ringside table along the dance floor, Ray was standing at the coat check counter, his voice a whisper, pleading with Gloria as he handed her the pile of coats in his hands.

"I'm not alone tonight," he said. "We've gotta be cool."

"Don't tell me how to be," said Gloria.

"Just don't cause a scene or something. It won't be good for any of us."

"Why'd you bring *her* here?" asked Gloria.

"I don't know," said Ray. "I thought you weren't working tonight."

"You mean you thought I wouldn't know?"

"No, that's not it ... but she insisted on coming," Ray lied. "I tried to get out of it."

"Uncle Maddy said they needed help," said Gloria. "He doesn't like anyone else handling the money but family, even for the goddamn coat check."

"I'll make it up to you."

"You suck, Ray," said Gloria.

"I hope you mean that in a nice way," said Ray, heading into the club. He blew Gloria a kiss and she gave him the finger with a smile.

Ray found his table, checked his back to make sure Gloria wasn't following him, and finally sat down next to Lexi on a gold lamé sofa.

"So what do you think?" he asked Lexi. "Quite a place I've got here, eh? Everybody's having fun. Man, look at that crowd grooving out there on the dance floor. That's good – people dance and then they drink more and when they drink I make money." He turned to Lee. "Impressive, eh? Bet you've never been in a place like this before."

"Can't say that I have," said Lee. "Not in a while anyway."

"Welcome to the big-time," said Ray. "It's like magic in here. Anything can happen."

CHAPTER 18

I knew that kind of magic once before, such as I felt with Lexi Langdon, when anything could happen and did: Rome in the autumn of 1971, a time when my life seemed to be flowing so smoothly, so effortlessly, as if I were on the wave of destiny. Through Richard, I'd fallen in with a crowd of actors, photographers and models and we all liked to get high; that's what we had in common. Campo dei Fiori was our main stomping ground because everyone we knew seemed to live around there, and so we would meet there in the mornings, well ... afternoons, for cappuccino and cornettos, the Italian version of breakfast and then we'd just roam around the city, dropping in on friends, smoking lots of hashish in Moroccan pipes. The regular residents of the city just went about their business, going to work, shopping for groceries, raising kids, but we seemed to just float above their humdrum daily lives. Back then, Rome was a crossroads for the hip celebrities of the time, Italian cinema was winning over the world with the films of Fellini and Visconti. But me, I had dreams of dropping in at Keith Richards' villa in the south of France, "Nellecotte," totally unannounced, with my guitar, and I was sure that I'd get in somehow and end up jamming with the Stones. But that never happened and I ended up in jail instead. My plan was to return wealthy with all the money I'd make dealing hash back home and start cruising Europe in style, in wasted elegance just like the Rolling Stones.

In Rome I had a brief career as a DJ working at a posh disco, Scacco Matto not far from Piazza Navonna. I got the job through Eduardo, the son of the Chilean Ambassador to the Vatican, who introduced me to Gianni, the owner. I don't think Gianni was too hot on the idea, but his American wife loved it. An attractive, young, long-haired American hippie spinning the turntable, was sure to be a hit in her opinion, so I got the job. But from the start I did everything wrong. I should have listened to Gianni who told me to just play James Brown records and there'd be no problem. The clientele consisted of mostly middle-aged Roman playboys and their bored young girlfriends who hung on their arms and dragged them onto the dance floor. These men were like tired versions of Marcello Mastroianni and the girls like a young Anita Ekberg, La Dolce Vita twenty years later, you get the picture. But I wanted to be original so I went down to the basement of the disco and picked out all the cool albums I could find, the Stones, Pink Floyd, even Bob Dylan. But nobody could dance to it; they didn't know what to do when they heard that music come over the loudspeakers. So I started drinking more and more and bumping into the turntable and a few times I sent the needle skipping across the grooves, which was a definite no-no. After a few weeks of this, one day I walked in and there was a young black guy in a sharp suit rearranging the records. When I asked him what was happening, he told me to go see Gianni in his office who kissed me on both cheeks, told me to have a great life, gave me an envelope stuffed with Italian Lire and told me I wasn't born to be a DJ. I didn't know what to do with the money until I asked Richard and he told me exactly what to do.

I wanted a piece of the good life, didn't want to be another American hippie with a backpack and a Eurailpass sleeping in no-star hotels. I'd been to Capri and seen the yachts, and in Scacco Matto, I'd seen the girls and I knew what to order in fine restaurants and I figured this was the life I was cut out for. Even when I was sitting in that Rome jail cell, I thought there must be a reason or rhyme behind all of this, like this was taking me somewhere. No one abused me in there, it was no Midnight Express, and mostly I got stoned because there was as much shit in prison as out on the streets. Then one day a guard came to tell me to get my clothes, I was leaving, my father had paid my way out.

"Guess I'll see you guys down the road," I said.

"En Challah," said Merzad, my cellmate, touching his fist to his heart.

"En Challah," I repeated touching my heart.

"AREN'T WE GOING OUT THERE?" ASKED LEXI, GESTURING TO the packed dance floor. "Where everybody's dancing? I love to dance, you know that."

"Well, if you really want to, darling" said Ray. "But the place to be is the VIP room, down in the basement. That's where the real celebs hang out, not on the dance floor."

"You're just saying that because you're a terrible dancer," said Lexi laughing. "I've seen you!"

"Don't' start," said Ray. "This is my club, you know. I'll have you thrown out."

At that, everyone at the table burst into laughter and Ray smiled proudly, finally having succeeded with one of his jokes.

"Funny, huh?" he said to everyone.

"What's funny is that you could hardly get in your own club and now you're talking about throwing me out," said Lexi. "That's hysterical."

Everyone laughed but Ray.

For about half a minute, the flashing lights over the dance floor went dark and a huge chandelier descended over the dancers and neon stars dotted the ceiling, giving the impression of a surreal open-air ballroom. Donna Summer's latest disco hit "Love to Love

You Baby" was pumping through the system and up on *mount high* in his suspended booth a DJ danced along, conducting the dancers like it was his own symphony orchestra, sometimes pushing the bass frequencies so strong that your stomach moved in a sympathetic reflex. Smoky fog was pumped in at knee height on the dance floor, creating a white mist which rose to the ceiling and dramatically reflected the now pulsating strobe lights. Heavily muscled male bartenders, all in tight-fitting jumpsuits, flung bottles and glasses in the air while preparing drinks and waitresses in equally skimpy tank tops, braless with breasts bouncing wildly underneath, maneuvered their way around the dancers while holding trays on high. It was a euphoric atmosphere whether you were ready for it or not, infecting you the moment you walked in, rapturous party time chaos, throbbing to an unremitting and overpowering beat.

"All right," said Ray to Lexi. "We'll hang out here for a while. I'll check out the VIP action downstairs."

"Is it nice downstairs?" asked Lexi. "In this VIP section?"

"Not really," answered Danny, shaking his head. "More like some kind of storeroom in the sub-basement with a few dusty rows of folding chairs from when it was a movie theater."

"And that's the VIP section?" asked Lexi incredulously.

"Don't ask me," said Danny. "But that's where Jack Nicholson and Halston and Liza Minnelli like to hang out. Guess they like privacy. Ray had to hire a waitress just to serve the big shots down there and he made her sign a confidentiality agreement so she wouldn't be blabbing to the press."

Ray signaled to a waiter who dashed over with champagne on ice and plenty of glasses. He arranged the table and just before leaving pulled a small glass bottle with a tiny spoon attached to the top by a metal chain from the waistband of his nylon shorts and discreetly handed it to Ray while Lexi talked with Danny.

James Elliot leaned over and whispered, "Ray, don't let Lexi see that. You remember what happened at the party out east."

"Don't tell me how to handle Lexi," said Ray. "I'm her husband, aren't I?"

For now, thought James Elliot, looking at Lee.

The music had just reached another crescendo and white flakes of confetti were floating over the dancers.

"This is incredible," yelled Lexi over the music. "Come on, who wants to dance with me?"

"I'm a musician," said Lee. "So, I don't dance."

"I bet you could if I asked you nicely," said Lexi.

"Then please don't ask me nicely," said Lee. Then seeing that Ray was listening. "What about you, Ray, do you dance?"

"The owner of the club doesn't dance either," said Ray stone-faced. "Just like musicians."

"Well, Lexi, these *white bread* guys may not know how to dance," said James Elliot, standing and taking Lexi's hand. "But I'll take you for a spin if you're game."

"You bet I'm game!" said Lexi. "Lead the way, sugar."

"Oh, I want to dance too!" said Kathy.

"Then come on!" said James Elliot. "I love a *ménage-à-trois*."

The three of them stepped on to the dance floor and Ray and Lee could not keep their eyes off of them because James Elliot was nothing less than an amazing dancer, doing splits and twirls, a taller, thinner James Brown. While they were dancing, Ray ducked his head down and took a few hits of the coke before offering it to Danny who sat next to him and did the same. But when Danny passed it to Lee, he shook his head and got up.

"No blow for you?" asked Ray, sniffling back the residue in his nostrils. "That's good, a lot of artists get fucked up on this stuff, don't know when to stop."

"I don't know," said Lee. "Never liked it. Made my hands shake, couldn't play guitar."

"How's that going?" asked Ray.

"Oh, man," exclaimed Danny. "Haven't you heard? Lee's packing them in at JP's - everybody loves him. Who'd you say you were hanging out with, Lee?"

"I don't know," said Lee. "Billy Joel? He came in a few times, lives nearby, I think."

"Yeah, Billy Joel," said Danny. "You know him, Ray?"

"I met him at JP's," said Ray. "He asked me for some career advice and my answer was simple."

"What was that?" asked Lee.

"I told him to start playing guitar, the kids will get tired of the piano thing."

"Really? And what did he say?"

"I don't think he said anything, probably too blown away by my, uh, honesty. Nobody dares to tell stars the truth about their career, but I don't give a shit."

"I bet," said Lee, thinking that someone should tell Ray the truth, what a jerk he was.

"I wouldn't even sign him now," said Ray. "Him and Elton, piano guys like that, they'll be completely forgotten five years from now."

"I wouldn't count on it," said Lee. "They're both pretty damn good at what they do." He and Danny looked at each other. If it was anybody other than Ray, they would have been rolling on the floor in fits of laughter. But another thing that kept them from laughing, at least at Ray, was the ominous entrance of Maddy the Horse and Junior into their circle of chairs around the table.

"Got everything you need, Ray?" asked Maddy gravely.

"Sure, we're fine, Maddy. This is Lee Franklin, he's a rock singer."

Maddy nodded his head thoughtfully. "A rock singer?" he said, raising his eyebrows. "My niece Gloria, she's a rock singer, isn't she Ray?"

"Very different styles," said Ray. "Lee is more traditional and Gloria is into ..."

"Gloria told me you brought your wife here, Ray."

"Yeah, I did, Maddy," said Ray nervously. "She always wanted to see the club and I figured Thursday night, not too crazy, you know."

"Not too crazy," repeated Maddy. "What do you think, Junior? Not too crazy."

"I don't know, Maddy, what's crazy? Maybe Ray bringing his wife to the club is crazy."

"I hope Ray knows what he's doing," said Maddy, just as Lexi, Kathy and James Elliot returned from the dance floor and were trying to get by them to sit back down.

"Could you gentlemen let us sit down, please?" asked Lexi.

Maddy and Junior turned around and faced Lexi, neither of them knowing what to say.

"Aren't you going to introduce me to your lovely wife?" said Maddy finally.

"Of course. Lexi this is Maddy ... DiGeronimo, this is kind of his club."

"Not *kind of*," said Maddy, looking straight at Lexi. "It's my place, *definitely*. So, I finally get to meet Ray's wife, he's always talking about you."

"I hope that's a good thing," said Lexi.

"Says you do a lot of charity work just like me," said Maddy. "So, we have something in common."

"Well, then it's a pleasure to meet you, too ... Mr. DiGeronimo."

"This is Junior, he's my *beverage manager*."

"That must be quite a taxing job." Lexi smiled and Junior just stood there twitching his shoulders like he had a pain in his back. Maddy moved aside while Lexi, Kathy and James Elliot sat down. "I'm gonna let you kids get back to your party," he said. "Don't be a stranger, Mrs. Arthur, you're always welcome at Madame Rue's."

"I still use my family name, Langdon, Lexi Langdon."

Maddy looked at Junior. "These modern couples. Soon the husband will be doing the dishes." He looked at Ray. "Don't tell me you do the dishes?"

"Who's got time?" Ray joked. "I'm always here at the club."

"Good night, Mrs. ... Langdon," said Maddy. "Gotta say, that's one beautiful necklace you're wearing tonight. My compliments. I like fine jewelry."

"Oh, thank you, Mr. DiGeronimo, it was made especially for me by Tiffany and Company..."

Uncharacteristically, James Elliot interrupted her, "Hey, doesn't anybody introduce me?"

Maddy and Junior glared at him.

"Right," said Ray. "This is James Elliot, very famous fashion photographer."

"No pictures of me here, eh?" said Maddy. "I keep a low profile. Better to point your lens at the beautiful women here like Ms. Langdon." He smiled at her and then turned to Junior. "Hey, Junior, another bottle of champagne for Ms. Langdon."

"Right away, boss," said Junior scurrying away.

Maddy laughed. "Some beverage manager." He took Lexi's hand and kissed it. "Enjoy your evening, Ms. Langdon."

"Thank you, Mr. DiGeronimo. And thank you for the champagne."

"Call me Maddy," he said and then he smiled like a guilty little kid. "And you want to know a secret? Want to know what some people call me?"

"What's that?" asked Lexi.

"Maddy the Horse."

"Oh, do you ride?"

"You could say that," said Maddy.

James Elliot breathed an audible sigh of relief after Maddy walked away.

CHAPTER 19

I remember spending that Christmas alone and not really minding. I took a walk down to Rockefeller Center to see the Christmas tree because I once came here with my family when I was a kid for the holidays. But it looked smaller than I remembered, and I felt so out of place with all those happy families, loaded down with shopping bags full of Christmas gifts. Lexi had gone back to Houston for the holidays, I never really understood what for, some kind of formal family gathering and the Langdon Industries Christmas party. She said she needed to bring Ray with her or there'd be a "hole in the photographs," whatever that meant. But I knew she'd be coming back and we'd be together again, at least until she got bored with New York winter weather and I hoped that maybe next time she'd take me with her, wherever she was going. Anyway, it seemed so certain, our future together, that I wasn't too worried. We were as intimate as any couple could be even if most of our time together was in fine restaurants and fueled by champagne before landing at my flat and making love. When that was over Lexi would lie in my arms for a while before getting dressed and leaving, Armando always waiting down in the limo, so we never woke up to greet the morning together but still we were, at least I believed, in a real relationship, whatever that meant.

I was regularly playing at JP's and the place was really jumping during the holidays. One night, when Danny and Kathy came up to see my show, they seemed so much in love and Danny was beaming; I never saw him so happy. And I was feeling good, too. For some reason, the night Danny came might have been my best night there, best crowd I can remember. The place was full, and I got a nice round of applause and a solid encore, and Danny was on his feet cheering before I strummed the last chord on my guitar and then Kathy stood up and then everyone in JP's stood up. I mean, there were maybe seventy-five people, but still, this was something I'd never had before, and Danny was definitely leading the crowd. I held my guitar over my head and acknowledged the applause and cheers and that moment seemed to go on forever. There was one guy standing next to Danny, cool looking in a sophisticated European way with an impressive mustache totally covering his upper lip, in pressed Levi's and a button-down Brooks Brothers shirt and it looked like he and Danny were competing for who could clap the loudest. When I finally walked off that little stage, they toasted each other and started talking. Turned out the guy was French, Pascal Bernardin, and his father owned the Crazy Horse Saloon in Paris, a famous strip club that the Rolling Stones had sung about in their song "Live With Me." I rubbed a towel through my hair and then joined Danny and Kathy - and Pascal too - and we got to talking. In the music business himself, promoting shows all over France, Pascal was in town for meetings with agents at ICM and William Morris and had been told JP's was the place to hang out. He gave Danny his card and told him to call if we ever came to Paris and he could help us out. Later Danny gave me the card, writing, "Call this guy!" on the back. I don't know why he gave it to me, why he didn't just keep it himself, but I still have that card in my wallet to this day.

Maddy the Horse and Junior walked down 57th Street in the early dusk, a few days before Christmas, pushing their way through bustling crowds loaded down with brightly colored shopping bags. There was a freezing wind ripping down the street that cut to the bone. Maddy wore a thick camel's hair coat while Junior turned up the collar of his burgundy plaid sport coat and cursed the cold. They had left Maddy's white Cadillac parked in a construction site where a friendly union official kept an eye on it.

"I hate Christmas," said Maddy.

"Why's that?" asked Junior, picking his teeth with a toothpick.

"Because I gotta buy the wife a goddamn present and no matter what I get her she won't like it, but if I don't put something all wrapped up pretty under the goddamn tree, she'll give me shit all Christmas Day." Maddy stopped in the middle of the street. "And then her whole fucking family descends on my house to empty out the goddamn fridge. I'm like the fuckin' Salvation Army of Bensonhurst."

"Put a fucking lock on the freakin' icebox," said Junior laughing.

"I'd like to. But I'm telling you, if she gives me shit this Christmas about anything, I'm taking the next plane down to Miami, booking a suite at the Fontainebleau and calling in some hookers, Scotch and a bucket of ice. That's my idea of Christmas."

Junior laughed gruffly. "I'll come with you, boss. We'll get those hookers dressed up like Santa Claus while they're sucking our dicks, eh Maddy? *O Come, all ye faithful...*"

"Watch your fucking mouth, Junior." Maddy stopped on the crowded street again. "It's a religious holiday I'm talking about here."

"Will Gloria be there?" asked Junior.

"Where? In Miami? What are you fucking crazy?"

"Naw, I mean at your house in Bensonhurst for Christmas."

"Get the fuck outta here, of course she'll be there. She's my wife's brother's kid.

"What's her old man like?" asked Junior. "Deadbeat like the rest?"

Maddy looked down to the sidewalk. "He's dead. Been dead for a while."

"What happened to him?" asked Junior.

"Wrong place at the wrong time. You don't wanna know any more than that. I should have been watching out for him. Cops found him bent up like a pretzel in the trunk of a Caddy on a wharf in Long Island City."

"Must have been tough for Gloria, growing up without an old man. She's a cute kid, maybe I can help her out, you know? Make sure she's not screwing around with the wrong guy or something."

"She's family," said Maddy. "I know how you'd like to help her out. Hands off, Junior."

"Hey, whatever you say, boss. Just trying to help the *family*." Junior pretended to concentrate on whatever was hanging on the end of his toothpick. "Mind if I ask you something, Maddy?"

Maddy just nodded his consent.

"None of my business but ... you think Ray's screwing Gloria?"

Maddy lowered his voice. "Like I said, Junior, Gloria's family, so be careful what you fuckin' say ..."

"I was just wondering, you know, nothing ... but I mean, if she's going out with that scumbag Ray, I don't see why she couldn't hang out with me too sometime. I mean, I'm not cheating on my wife like that dipshit."

"You don't have a wife, Junior. Gloria's over twenty-one, what the fuck I got to say about what she does. For Christ's sake, she's got a fucking tattoo so I guess that means she's getting laid."

"She's got a tattoo? Where's she got a fucking tattoo?"

"Someplace you'll never see, asshole," said Maddy laughing darkly. "My wife's sister told me, wouldn't stop crying about it. I told her if that's the worst thing Gloria ever does, she'll be fucking lucky."

"What's it say on the tattoo?"

"What the fuck you think it says? *Junior's got a big dick* – is that what you think it fucking says?"

"I don't give a fuck what it says," said Junior. "All I know is nice girls like that shouldn't have tattoos. Or be fucking around with married guys like Ray."

Maddy looked at Junior. "You turn your collar up and you turn into a priest or something? What the fuck do *you* care what Gloria does? She's old enough to know her way around."

"Just wondering," said Junior. "Her being family and all. I'm family too, you know."

"You? Very *distant* family," said Maddy slowly. "I don't even know if Cleveland counts as family. Family ends at the Hudson River far as I'm concerned." He laughed. "Well, maybe Jersey counts too."

"Well, I'm more family than fucking Ray Arthur."

"Ray Arthur is not family," said Maddy sternly. "And if he fucks up with Gloria he's gonna have a talk with me. And he won't be able to talk when that's over, I'll tell you that."

"Forget about it," said Junior. "Or walk either. You ever want me to take care of Ray just give me the word. He's a scumbag."

"He's a scumbag, but we need him for now to put a legit face on the club." Maddy stopped at the corner of 57th Street and Fifth Avenue. "Well, this is it. Let's get the fuck in, outta the freakin' cold."

"What's this?" asked Junior. "Looks like some kinda fucking bank. We gonna rob a fucking bank, Maddy, do I need a fucking mask?"

"Do I look like I rob fucking banks?" asked Maddy. "I'm a fucking businessman and this is Tiffany, can't you read the fucking sign?" They both looked up to see the imposing letters carved in granite over the front door, Tiffany & Co. "They sell jewelry, expensive fucking jewelry. And I'm gonna get something for my wife for Christmas and you're gonna help me pick it out, Junior, and she better like it or I'm in Miami before the goddamn turkey is cooked."

"Fucking A," said Junior.

With so few shopping days left before Christmas, Tiffany was packed with shoppers, both serious buyers and wide-eyed tourists. The magnificent ground floor gallery with high ceilings was brightly lit with rows and rows of glittering display cases filled with fine watches, gold and silver jewelry, pearls, and gemstones. A commanding presence of well-dressed male and female Tiffany sales associates stood authoritatively at attention behind the showcases, looking as affluent as the very customers they served.

"Let's take a look around," said Maddy. "Tell me if anything looks good. I hate buying fucking presents. Last Christmas I gave her a roll of hundreds as big as my fist wrapped in a rubber band and she ran off crying to the bedroom. You believe that shit?"

"Fucking A," said Junior.

They strolled around the crowded store, bumping into customers and glaring with a menacing air. If there was something Maddy wanted to look at and a man blocked his view, Junior would get in the guy's face and stare him down until he moved aside. Maddy was fixed on the Rolex counter, trying gold watches on both wrists when Junior tapped him. "Over here, boss, you might find this interesting." He led him over to the other side of the store where a waist-high showcase displayed a series of gold necklaces, all dotted with diamonds in different numbers and sizes. A small card announced, Elsa Peretti - Diamonds by the Yard.

"Look familiar?" asked Junior. "Remind you of someone?"

"Peretti?" said Maddy. "Yeah, reminds me of Sal *Peressi* who owes me a lot of fucking money."

"Not the name, boss, the necklaces."

Maddy leaned down close to the glass, staring at the glittering diamonds. Then, with a start, he stood up, started pumping his head up and down and sucking his teeth.

"Ray's wife," said Maddy. "Lexi Langdon."

"Fuckin A," said Junior.

"Hers was even more fucking outrageous than these," said Maddy. "That fucking chain around her neck was covered with big fuckin' diamonds. Hey, Junior, get someone over here who knows about this shit."

Junior approached a slim young salesman, talking with a suburban couple and showing them sterling silver Tiffany key chains. He walked right in between the three of them.

"Over here, my boss needs some information."

The salesman raised his eyebrows, scandalized, but trying to keep his demeanor. "Sir, I'm occupied with this couple at the moment, but if you'll wait a few minutes I'm sure I can find you a ..."

"My boss doesn't like to wait," said Junior not moving.

The wife tapped him on the shoulder. "Excuse me, but we were here first." Junior turned around slowly, ignoring her and looking squarely at the husband. "You tell your wife to keep her hands to herself or you and me are gonna have a problem."

The husband was about to say something, but his instincts told him better. "Let's take a look around the store," he said to his wife and to the salesman, "we'll come back later." They walked off with her muttering how she had never seen such a rude man and the husband trying to move away as quickly as possible.

Junior faced the salesman. "So, you're free now. This way," pointing to where Maddy stood and following close behind.

"Is this all you got?" asked Maddy without looking up.

"All we've got of what?" asked the salesman.

"These necklaces, these ... Diamonds by the Yards things here. You got others out back or is this it? Bet you keep the good stuff out of sight, so nobody pinches it?"

"These are all the necklaces we sell in the store. Of course, we do custom pieces as well, depending on the customer's specifications."

"Like with more ice?" said Maddy.

"Ice?" repeated the salesman.

"Bigger diamonds. You know, something really classy."

"As I said, sir, we always try to satisfy the customer's desires," he said with a smile. "The custom order department is on the third floor, I'm sure they could help you."

"I don't need nobody's help, I just want to know what it would cost me for some piece like that, you know, something really classy, dripping with ice."

"I'm not sure I understand, sir."

"Don't play dumb with me," said Junior. "You work here right? You know what this stuff costs."

"I can show you the price list ..."

"Let's say with ten times more diamonds than ..." Maddy pointed to a very impressive necklace in the display case. "Than this one."

The salesman walked behind the counter and took out his key to unlock the cabinet while nimbly placing a black felt mat on top of the glass and carefully placing the necklace on top of it. "This necklace here is priced at ...." He peered down at a small white price tag on the clasp. "Nine Thousand Nine Hundred and Ninety-Nine Dollars, not including New York sales tax, of course."

"For Christ's sake, why don't you just say ten grand?" exclaimed Junior.

"They do that so he's gotta pop open the register and give change," said Maddy. "Or else he'd pocket the cash and walk out of this place." He smiled at the salesman. "Am I right or wrong?"

"I don't do the pricing," said the salesman.

"So ten times that would be over a hundred grand, right?"

"I suppose," said the salesman. "I really don't ..."

Maddy and Junior turned around and walked out of the store, not waiting for him to finish.

"A hundred grand hanging 'round her neck," said Maddy as they walked back down 57th Street, heading for his Cadillac.

"Fucking A," said Junior. "Hey, boss, you forgot to get something for your wife."

"Fuck it, I'll give her some cash. Then I'm flying to Miami."

"Fucking A," repeated Junior. "Fucking A, B and C!"

THE WEEKS LEADING UP TO CHRISTMAS WERE PARTICULARLY busy at JP's; crowds more rowdy as if every night were Saturday night with heavy drinking at the bar and bathroom stalls clogged by coke users crowding two and three around the toilet. It was as if everyone was already rehearsing for the great New Year's bash to come.

"Why do you close on New Year's Eve?" Lee asked JP.

"Amateur hour," said JP. "You got the night off."

Either way it didn't matter much to Lee. He was just gigging as usual and hanging out at the bar in-between sets, sipping a Scotch, hoping someone he knew would come in. When he performed, those sitting at the tables paid attention and applauded vigorously after each song, but those standing around the bar, just kept up an annoying hum of conversation that Lee was forced to sing over. Just as Lee came off the small stage, JP put his arm around him and escorted him to the bar.

"Great job, man, they love you."

"Some of them do," said Lee. "And some wouldn't know it if Bob Dylan was up there playing."

"Sing to the ones who listen," said JP. "That's my philosophy. You only need one right connection. No one listened to Dylan in the beginning either. Up at Columbia they called him *Hammond's Folly*."

"Why was that?"

"Because John Hammond was the A&R guy who signed him, but it took quite a while to get the rest of the label behind him. Then Dylan got a great *New York Times* review, and everybody wanted to jump on the band wagon."

"Well, when that happens, I'll tell them you were there at the get-go, JP."

"Still can happen," said JP. "Guy named Bruce Springsteen from out in Jersey took a bus into town to audition for Hammond and got signed on the spot. Now everyone is calling him the new Dylan, say he'll be the next big thing."

"New Dylan? Wow, that must be a tough one to live up to."

"Most don't," said JP. "But there are exceptions, so don't give up. If this guy Springsteen got signed maybe you can too."

"I'd like to meet him. Does this guy Springsteen ever come into JP's?"

"Not that I know of. They say he doesn't drink, no drugs, just music gets him off. Don't even know if he's got a girlfriend. Stays out in Jersey where they can't get at him.

"Smart move, saving his voice for his shows rather than bullshitting at the bar with some wanna-be producer."

"How's your voice holding up?"

"All right, I guess. That's four sets tonight. And last night, too.

"Don't worry, pal, I'll take care of you. Why don't you have a steak tonight?"

Lee laughed. "Wow, big time!"

"Just remember to send me that gold record when you get one – it will look nice over the bar. All you need, Lee, is a record deal and a few well-placed executives who are willing to put their ass on the line and get the machine rolling. Then it's up to you to get out there on the road and make it stick. That's what Billy Joel did and Bruce Springsteen is doing now, that's where the secret ingredient comes in."

"Secret ingredient?"

"*Charisma,* pal. Either you got it or you don't."

"So do I got it?"

"Lexi Langdon thinks so, that's a good place to start," said JP, smiling slyly and surveying the bustling crowd in his club. "You know, come January this city will start emptying out. Happens like clockwork, just like Labor Day out east."

"What was the wildest night you remember at JP's?" asked Lee. "Must have been a few."

"There've been great wild nights and wild nights I could have done without like the time John Bonham started waving around a pistol in the men's toilet."

"John Bonham, drummer of Led Zeppelin?"

"You got it. Biggest gun I ever saw, everyone retreated to the bar here or even out on the street. Fuck if I was gonna call the cops, so finally I made my way back there and talked him into putting it away before he shot himself, or even worse, me."

"Why the gun?"

"Craziest fucking thing you ever heard of. He said he was going looking for the guys that stole the Led Zeppelin 1973 tour money out of the safe at the Drake Hotel," JP explained. "Some low-life told him he knew who did it and gave him a name. I asked him why he didn't call the cops or let Peter Grant, *Zep's* manager, take care of it, but he said he was going to take care of it himself, stick his shooter in the guy's face and get the cash back. Fat chance of that happening. When I found out who he was going to see, I almost flipped. Told him if he stuck a gun in that guy's face, he'd end up in a trunk in the Jersey swamps in itty bitty pieces."

"Who was it?" asked Lee. "Who did he think took the money?"

"Some thug named Maddy the Horse, ever hear of him?"

"I think so," said Lee, thinking of Danny, thinking of Ray, and suddenly feeling very shaky.

JP DID INDEED KNOW HIS CUSTOMERS AND THEIR HABITS AND within a week of New Year's Eve the intensity of New York nightlife discernibly came down a few notches as the *crème de la crème* were drawn to the warmth of the Caribbean sun or the *après-ski* scene of Aspen and Vail. Anyway, it seemed that every big spender had skipped town. Or gone to Chicago to see the *chairman of the board* on New Year's Eve.

It was like three days after Christmas, the whole city still in holiday recovery mode, when Lee's phone rang earlier than normal. He put the receiver to his hear, coughed up a tired "Who is it?" and then Lexi started singing "Strangers In The Night". Amazingly, she knew the complete first verse even if her pitch was questionable.

"So what do you think, sugar?" she asked.

"What do I think what?" said Lee, squinting at his watch. "It's not night ... and we're not strangers ... or at least we weren't. Where are you?"

"Just 'round the corner ... well almost. I'm sitting in my apartment waiting for Ray to come back with my Christmas present."

"He must be doing some serious shopping - Christmas was three days ago."

"Tell Ray that. Says he got me a fur, but it wasn't finished in time. Says I'm going to need it where I'm going."

"Where's that?"

"Chicago, the - *brrrr* - windy city itself, on New Year's Eve no less."

"You're going to Chicago with Ray on New Year's Eve? What for? To catch the flu?"

"No sugar, I'm going to Chicago with Ray and *you* and the ever-fabulous Wes Edel on New Year's!" She giggled loudly. "Isn't that a hoot?"

"I repeat, what for?"

"Are you sitting down?"

"Actually, I'm lying down ..."

"Well get ready. We are all going to Chicago to see Frank Sinatra on New Year's Eve at Chicago Stadium. Is that amazing or what?"

"Frank Sinatra?"

"Frank *Strangers in the Night* Sinatra! Front row seats and back-stage passes because Wes knows Frank from the old days in Vegas. Says he's a bona fide, although honorary, *Rat Pack* member himself."

"And you like Frank Sinatra?"

"Sugar, who doesn't like Frank Sinatra? You know what my daddy use to say? It's Frank's world and we just live in it. Before you start passing judgment, hippie that you are, have you ever seen Frank Sinatra perform?"

"Do you mean on TV or in person?"

"In person, up close and personal."

"Well ... no."

"So, would you like to come? It's a one-time offer, *partner*."

"With you and ..."

"Ray and Wes Edel."

"Who got the seats?"

"I told you!" said Lexi exasperated. "Wes got the seats; says he knows Frank from the old days ..."

"Old days?"

"According to Ray, Wes started out booking acts in Las Vegas in the 50s. Booked the whole Rat Pack, including Liberace."

"I doubt if Liberace was in there, think it was Frank and Dean Martin ... maybe Sammy Davis Jr. and a few other drinking buddies. Yeah, Peter Lawford was in there too. So how did you include me in on this uh ... junket? I'm sure it wasn't Ray's idea."

"Actually, you can thank Wes. Seems that Alana can't come because she's getting an operation that day that can't be moved and Wes didn't want her to cancel."

"An operation? Serious?"

"Depends how serious you take tits." Lexi laughed. "Breast implants, it was her Christmas present to Wes. So last night we were all eating at Clarke's and Wes told Ray to invite a musician, someone who would appreciate listening to a real singer. He asked Ray if he knew anybody good, a real singer and I couldn't resist and mentioned your name and Wes jumped on it. So it was too late for Ray to nix the idea."

"So I'll be Wes' date?" said Lee. "That's funny ... I guess."

"Who knows? Maybe we can slip off somewhere for a few hours, catch up. Like I'll tell you to meet me at some bar or hotel and we can act like we don't know each other and just disappear ..."

"Like strangers in the night?"

"Now you're catching on."

Apparently, the real deal was that Wes got the tickets and Lexi supplied the plane. Lee got a call from Wes' secretary telling him to meet them at Butler Aviation, the private airport out by LaGuardia, on December 30th at six p.m. And she told him to bring a warm coat. Lee borrowed a wool Chesterfield from JP and was sitting there in the small waiting room of the private airport when two black limos arrived. One with Lexi, Ray and Wes and the other with an assortment of Lexi's initialed Louis Vuitton luggage for her three-day stay in Chicago. Lee had taken the subway.

Lexi kissed him on the cheek. "Oh! You're cold, sugar."

"I took the subway and walked. Guess I'm *persona non grata* when it comes to the limo?" asked Lee.

"Ray had to stop by Madame Rue's for something, said it would take too much time to go all the way uptown to JP's to pick you up."

"Thank you, Ray," said Lee, rubbing his cold hands together.

Opening the show for Frank was comedian Pat Henry.

"Jesus, this guy has been opening for Frank since the 50s in Vegas. I think I even booked him," said Wes. "Don't know how he puts up with it. Pre-show with Frank is not a fun place to be and the after-show party goes on forever.

"... Yeah, Frank's a great guy to play games with," Pat Henry was telling the audience. "I remember once during a game of charades; we were acting out song titles. When it came Frank's turn he got frustrated and picked up a clock and smashed it against the wall. I got it right away! *You're thinking of 'As Time Goes By' right Frank?*"

The audience applauded and laughed, and Pat Henry walked off stage and the lights went down, and the orchestra started up. And then came the main event, like when the President of the United States enters a room and the whole atmosphere changes, another dimension takes over and so it was when Frank Sinatra walked on stage, dressed in the most perfect blacker than black tuxedo imaginable, tan and sharp in a great toupee and holding a shot glass with ice and Jack Daniels, which he put down on the piano before grabbing the microphone off its stand, spreading his feet apart like a boxer, he began to belt out:

Chicago, Chicago, that toddlin' town
Chicago, Chicago, I'll show you around
Bet your bottom dollar you'll lose the blues in Chicago

"Can't believe it, it's just like a rock concert," said Lee. "Well, maybe not as loud but the same rush."

"You don't need to be loud when you got talent," said Wes. "Tell that to your friends down at *Webeegeebees*!"

"You mean CBGB? I never played there."

"Ray is there every night, scouting the talent. Isn't that right Ray?"

"It's a dirty job," said Ray. "But somebodies got to do it."

Wes looked askance at Ray. "Paying your limo bills is the dirty job."

Ray said nothing.

Frank ended with "My Kind of Town," another well-known Chicago anthem and then the concert was over after twenty-three songs by the sixty-year-old singer, who stayed on his feet the whole time, walking round and round that square stage to face every aspect of the stadium.

After the show, Wes led his party down the endless basement corridors toward the dressing room.

"Frank Sinatra stays down here?" asked Lexi shocked. "A star like him in the basement?"

"You'll see," said Wes.

They found their way to Frank's dressing room through a series of concrete halls, built like a military bunker. Wes said a word to the bodyguard standing at the door who told them it would only be a few minutes while Frank took a shower.

Wes turned to Lexi who leaned against the concrete wall holding her new full-length Fox coat tightly closed to her neck. "Don't worry, Lexi, Frank Sinatra stays at a suite at the Palmer Hotel, best hotel in town," he said. "But even Frank needs a dressing room. Say, how'd you like the show, Lee? Pretty Amazing?"

"Gotta admit it, still got his chops," said Lee. "And the band was incredible. Don't know why he does that theater in the round thing. Keeps walking around in circles with that mic cable trailing behind him."

"To sell more tickets, dummy," said Wes. "What do you think?"

"Yeah, but isn't it a pain to have to keep working his way around to face the audience."

"Hey," said Wes. "You know what they say in Vegas? It's Frank's world, we just live here."

"That's just what my daddy used to say," said Lexi.

The large bodyguard standing in front of Frank's dressing room door didn't say much, but just by his expression you knew when to move and when not to.

"How long are we going to wait?" whispered Lexi to Ray. "I'm getting cold and hungry."

"Didn't you hear, Lexi? It's Frank's world," whispered back Ray.

Then the door swung open and there stood Frank Sinatra himself, laughing and saying goodbye to the couple who was leaving.

"We'll see you down at the joint later, Jilli. Don't let the chef leave, you tell him I'll take care of him, no problem."

"Whatever you want, Francis," said Jilli.

"Just no goddamn photographers," said Frank.

The bodyguard whispered something into Frank's ear and Frank's bluer than blue eyes went immediately to Wes.

"Jesus Christ! If it isn't Wes Edel, the king of the ten percenters!"

"Actually, it was fifteen percent, Frank," said Wes.

"Don't tell me I still owe you a commission?" Frank took Wes' face in his hands and gave him a big kiss on the cheek. "This man was the best goddamn agent I ever had," he said to no one in particular. "And who's the beautiful dame you dragged down to this dungeon?"

"This is Lexi Langdon," said Wes. "She's from Texas. And this is her husband, Ray Arthur, who works for me at my label. Which is where you should be by the way.

"I got my own goddamn label!" said Frank. "Ever hear of Reprise Records?"

"Jimi Hendrix is on Reprise," said Lee.

"Good boy," said Frank. "And who are you?"

"I'm just a singer who was lucky enough to see your incredible show tonight."

"Finally, a compliment out of these stiffs," said Frank. "So, you're a singer? Do any of my songs?"

"Uh ... 'Strangers in the Night.' But not as good as you."

"That one's a bitch," said Frank. "I wanted a lower key, but Nelson Riddle kept it where it was. Bitch to sing." He looked at Lexi. "Langdon? I knew a Langdon down in Texas somewhere. Friend of LBJ? Think I did a benefit down in Dallas for Jack Kennedy that he was footing the bill for the whole damn thing. "Same family?"

"That was my daddy," said Lexi shyly.

"The man throws a hell of a party," said Frank. "Tell him I said hello."

"Actually, he passed away," said Lexi.

Frank shook his head. "All the good ones are gone, sweetheart, and your father was one of them." said Frank looking sad. "The Kennedy brothers, God bless them, LBJ, now only Nixon is hanging in there. Got to give him credit for that."

Frank's bodyguard entered and spoke loud enough for everyone to hear. "There's some guys out here want to see you. Say they're friends of Sam Giancana."

Frank looked over to the door to see Maddy the Horse and Junior peering in, goofy smiles and waves.

"What's the guy's name? Doesn't look familiar to me."

"Maddy the Horse," said the bodyguard.

"The horse! Where the fuck do these guys get these names?" said Frank. "Listen, nobody called me about any friends of Sam's. Tell them, but do it in a nice way, that I'm all tied up and ... wait a minute. I got an idea."

Frank called over to the banquet table at the other side of the large dressing room where a small black man was dishing caviar onto a cracker.

"Sammy!"

Sammy Davis Junior came running over, with the cracker in one hand.

"Frank baby, you have got to take a serious dip into this Beluga, it is for the Gods, out of this world, a trip and a half ..."

"I need a favor," said Frank.

"Baby, tell me what you need? A song and dance? You got it." Sammy punctuated his sentence with a quick *soft shoe* step.

"You see those two mugs standing just outside the door?"

Sammy looks to Maddy the Horse and Junior.

"Yeah, got 'em in my sights. What are they? Union guys - looking for overtime? Want me to call Mayor Daly?"

"Don't call him, I gave him enough tickets already. They say they're friends of Sam?"

"*Moi*?" says Sammy. pointing to himself."

"No, not you! Sam Giancana. But I never heard of them and Sam's been gone since last summer."

"They say he was ratting on his friends. You Italians don't like that one bit, do you, Frank?" Sammy laughed and waved his finger at Frank. "That's a no no!"

"What do you know from Italians? Do me a favor, get over there and take care of those guys, will ya. Give them a little star treatment and send them on their way. For all I know they could be packing."

"So, they could be packing and you're sending me?" Sammy looked around at Wes. "You got to love this man! Wants me to be his human shield."

"You're faster than me if they start shooting," said Frank.

So, Sammy walks out of the dressing room door and starts talking to Maddy the Horse and Junior and, after a few minutes of *shuck and jive*, managed to get rid of them even the whole while as Junior kept pointing inside the door to Frank, trying to move closer. Finally, as they walked outside the venue, past the trucks and limousines, Junior turned to Maddy:

"I can't believe Frank wouldn't see us. We flew all the fucking way out here and Frank won't see us."

"Too busy gabbing with Ray Arthur, to see goombahs like us," said Maddy. "Do you believe that Ray? Pretended he didn't see me. Who's he kidding? He's gonna hear about this, you can bet your ass. And you, Junior, it was your fucking fault! Why'd you mention Sam Giancana? The guy was a rat and they shot him while he was cooking sausages in his own house. Frank probably thought we were the guys that did it."

"So, he sends over a nigger?"

"I got nothing against niggers," said Maddy.

"Well, I know for a fact the guy's a Jew too."

"You can't be a nigger and a Jew," says Maddy. "It's like two different religions or something."

"Only if you're Sammy Davis Jr. Maybe, I should have told him we're cousins or some shit. Turn it into a family thing. That might have got us in."

"How do you figure that?" says Maddy."

"We're both called Junior, right?"

"Fucking moron."

By February, JP's was basically a sleepy East Side bar which came to life on weekends, when out of town rock fans wanted to see where Billy Joel and Carly Simon hung out, and sipped beers at the bar. Come the dark winter months, the tr*ust fund babies* like Lexi Langdon were nowhere to be found in Manhattan; streets covered in dirty slush didn't work well with high heels and a wicked arctic wind blowing off the Hudson River cut through even the warmest of fur coats.

Still, Lee would see Lexi from time to time. She popped in briefly for an event or shopping or a meeting with her lawyers and when she did, she always made sure to see Lee, keep him warm in his bed for a few hours above JP's.

"Where are you leaving me for now?" asked Lee with barely concealed disappointment when Lexi told him she'd be gone for much of what was left of the winter. She tended to tell him her plans after they were already made and too late to change or after they made love when Lee had no strength, emotional or sexual, left to protest. As usual, they were lying on his big bed, very close, their fingers roaming over each other's now familiar bodies.

"I don't know...might go to Aspen, we have a nice chalet there ..."

"We? You mean you and Ray?"

"Are you kidding, Lee? I mean Langdon Enterprises, my company. The only thing I share with Ray is ..."

"I don't want to know."

Lexi smiled. "Well, sugar, to tell you the truth I'm bored with skiing already. I could go for some sun, maybe start out in Key West or St. Bart's – take *The Yellow Rose* for a cruise all over the Caribbean. Maybe go someplace I've never been before – that's always a challenge. I have some friends who went to Brazil last year and just loved it, they built an incredible house in someplace called *Buzios* - they say it's the Hamptons of Rio de Janeiro and they invited me down for the Carnival this year. Sounds fabulous ... "

"Brazil, that sounds far."

"Nothing is far, Lee, for the jet-set! That's how the party travels, sugar. In fact, a lot of people I know are going over to see Dorothy Hamill skate at the Winter Olympics in Innsbruck and then hop on this new supersonic airplane, the *Concorde*, to fly down to Rio to warm up." She traced a spidery patch of skin on his back. "Where did you get that scar?" she asked.

"In prison," said Lee.

Lexi bolted upright. "You're kidding?"

"Yes, I'm kidding," he said right away, although he wasn't. A jagged pipe sharpened into a knife and a stupid argument in a Rome prison mess hall could have ended it all right there if his cellmate Merzad had not stepped in and saved his ass. But he was not going to tell Lexi about any of that, not now anyway.

"So, you just move along with it? Follow the party?" he asked. "What a life."

"I like to think the party follows me," said Lexi smiling brightly. "Wouldn't you if you could?" She hesitated. "Sorry, Lee, I didn't mean to..."

"You know I could follow you if you wanted me to, Lexi. What's to keep me from coming along?"

"You know I'd love that," said Lexi unconvincingly. "But it would be too messy. You know, there's so much family down there and business relations and just too many questions ... I really don't want to spend my time explaining things ... It's better like this. I always come back, Lee, don't worry."

"I'm not worried," said Lee just as unconvincingly.

"Better run," said Lexi. "Ray's coming home from somewhere, suppose I should be there waiting for him when he arrives."

"Why do you suppose that?"

"Because, sugar, as Walter Cronkite says every night at the end of the news, *That's the way it is.*" She dressed quickly, checked her makeup in her compact and kissed him on the nose. Lee lay still on the bed, watching her every move, wishing she could stay longer. "Don't forget, sugar, absence makes the heart grow fonder."

"That's what I'm counting on," said Lee.

IT WAS MID-AFTERNOON ON A GRAY MARCH DAY WHEN DANNY called Lee at the apartment, telling him he had a car for the day, describing it as *Ray's new set of wheels.*

"Let's go for a drive, man. I'll get you back in plenty of time for your show. Got to run some errands around the city. Want to come along?"

"Sure," said Lee. "Nothing else to do. So now your pal Ray is lending you his car?" he added with a trace of bitterness.

"Well, the car ... it's kind of his, but he hasn't even seen it yet. I'll tell you about it when I see you."

At two o'clock on the dot, Danny pulled up in front of JP's in a sporty late model foreign car.

"Ray's driving a BMW?" asked Lee, admiring the steel blue coupe. "Didn't he have a Mercedes last summer?"

"The Mercedes was Lexi's, leased through her business. That's gone now."

"Ray tells you everything?"

"Ray's a guy who likes to talk to someone who will listen to him."

Lee settled into the leather seat. "Nice set of wheels, but a little understated for Ray, don't you think? Thought he'd go for something more ostentatious like a *Jag*, something with a little more show for a guy like him."

"I don't know if Ray had much choice," said Danny. "He gets what Maddy offers him."

"What do you mean?"

"Maddy's got a piece of this luxury car leasing scam, kind of a scam for something else," he added laughing.

"What kind of scam?"

"From what I can figure, Maddy's main business is taking book all over town."

"You mean he's running numbers?"

"Numbers are up in Harlem; Maddy only deals with the high rollers who bet on the horses; never writes anything down and never forgets what they owe him - truly amazing to watch. It's all like between friends, calls everyone by their first name and never treats it like a business, so he gets to know the suckers whose bank accounts he's emptying. And you know what's the amazing thing? They actually *like* hanging out with him."

"Like you," said Lee.

"Hey, I just work at Madame Rue's. But, you know, these rich guys who think they're tough guys, they like palling around with a real gangster, telling their friends, all that bullshit."

"Sounds like Joey Gallo, friends with all those smart Broadway actors, eating down at Umberto's Clam House, until they blew him away."

"Yeah, everything's cool until it turns real nasty. And Maddy's good at that, too."

"What do you mean?"

"Here's how it works, let's say they go out to the track together, driving around in Maddy's Mercedes and they get to talking about cars and the *mark*, as Maddy calls them, says he likes Maddy's *fine* car, looking for something himself and guess what, Maddy's got a friend who leases Mercedes, BMWs, Jags, all that pricey stuff. So, without trying very hard, Maddy convinces them to lease a car from his friend, makes them think that they're getting some special deal he only does for his pals. But it's a load of crap - get it?"

"Get what? That gamblers like fancy cars?" asked Lee. "So what?"

"No," said Danny. "The thing is that the *marks* always lose in the end and Maddy gets them coming and going."

"You lost me."

"Come on, Lee, use your head, the guy leases a nice set of wheels from Maddy's friend – only it's Maddy who really owns the company – and then the guy's luck goes bad like it always does."

"It always does?" asked Lee.

"It always does when Maddy owns enough of the jockeys out at Aqueduct to make sure sometimes the favorite comes in second," said Danny.

"I don't get it, Danny. Maddy owns the jockeys?"

"I mean, he *owns* them as in he *bribes* them to throw the race. Jockeys bet too and sometimes they owe him money! It's a fix, everybody's in on it, and what was supposed to be a sure thing, the huge bet that was in the bag to get the guy out of the hole, turns into total disaster. So now, not only does the guy owe Maddy like a hundred grand for his gambling debts, but he's late on his payments to the leasing company for the snazzy car he's driving around, too."

"So, he's fucked."

"That's the whole idea. So early one morning when the guy is still sleeping, some goon who has a duplicate key to the car pulls it out of the guy's driveway and brings it back to Maddy who sends it to the car wash and leases it out to some other sucker. Once the car is officially repossessed, the guy is in really bad shit because the car lease is tied into everything he owns. His wife wakes up, looks out the window and starts screaming *Where's the freakin' car* and next thing you know the guy is signing over his house to Maddy or giving Maddy his business or his wife's jewelry...you see what I mean. It's a racket and once Maddy gets his fingers in you, he just keeps taking more and more until there's nothing left."

"Then what happens?"

"You don't want to know and neither do I."

"But where do you fit into all of this? Don't tell me you're the goon reclaiming the car!"

"Me? I'm just legally repossessing a leased vehicle, totally legit, and if I get stopped I got all the papers I need. I'm covered, like this morning, this BMW we're sitting in now was in someone's driveway in White Plains and now it's driving you and me around in style."

"Now you're one of Maddy's crew?"

"Give me a break, Lee. What am I gonna do? Tell him no? I'd lose my job at Madame Rue's and then I'm back tending bar at LaGuardia Airport."

"Sounds fucked up to me, Danny."

"I tell you what's fucked up, it's working as a bartender and breaking your ass ten hours a day for nothing. Maddy spotted me, sees I'm a good worker and he likes me, so he gives me a break and I make more doing this than in a week of bartending. And like I told you, I repossessed it. It's totally legit. What's the problem?"

"I thought you said it was Ray's car."

"Ray said he needed a car and *whada bada bing*! Tonight, he'll have one. That's what Maddy said anyway, maybe he'll change his mind if Ray pisses him off more than he should."

Lee said nothing, looking at Danny's boyish face smiling next to him, still full of freckles, looking more like a Boy Scout than a car thief.

"And you've been doing this for how long? Since you started working for Ray down at Madame Rue's? *Repossessing* Maddy's cars? That's your work?"

"I told you, this is the first one. Junior was busy doing something else, so when Maddy told me that I'm gonna do him a little favor today and pick up this car for him, I do it."

"And you plan on doing more *little favors* for Maddy?"

Danny paused. "Tell you what happened, I'm not used to these stick shifts and so I stalled out at the bottom of the driveway and the guy's wife came running out still in her nightgown and she's crying and she slips on the ice and then the husband runs out, and he's helping her up and they're both crying in each other's arms. I don't know ... didn't feel good."

"It sure isn't the music business."

"No ... but maybe it will get me there, Lee."

"Or Rikers Island Prison. Hope we don't get pulled over."

"I told you I got all the papers..." Danny fumbled in the inside pocket of his sports coat. "Ah, shit."

"What's up?"

"I forgot my wallet with my damn license."

"Shit, where is it?"

"Mind if we take a take a short detour into Queens? I've been staying at my brother's place in Astoria – it's right over the 59th Street Bridge. I must have left it there."

"I got time," said Lee. "Just tell me we're not going to jail together for driving a stolen car."

"I got it covered," said Danny as they nosed their way through the traffic to the 59th Street Bridge. "Besides, you know 'Jailhouse Rock?'"

Both Lee and Danny had an Elvis imitation ready to go and they started whooping and hollering all the way over the bridge. While they were stuck in traffic and still singing, one of the homeless "squeegees" crew who hung around the bridge entrance started cleaning their windshield with a dirty rag.

"Oh no," said Danny. "You gotta pay these guys just so they stop."

"Let's just sing louder, maybe that will stop him."

And they did, and it did.

"We're not in Kansas anymore," said Danny as they crossed the bridge.

"You mean we've left the land of Oz," corrected Lee. As usual, the 59th Street Bridge was being repaved, repaired, and striped plastic cones and brightly painted orange barrels diverted traffic every which way. Officially known as The Queensboro Bridge, it had enjoyed a short-lived celebrity thanks to the Simon and Garfunkel hit "Feeling Groovy (The 59th Street Bridge song)," but when you were jumping from lane to lane, trying to get onto the upper roadway with a line of trucks blocking your way, the vibe was definitely not *groovy*. Being one of the few conduits in and out of the city that didn't charge a toll, the 59th Street Bridge was the preferred gateway to Manhattan for trucks, local delivery vans and yellow taxis going to and from work. Just halfway across, Lee and Danny were frozen in traffic, moving by inches to a cacophony of beeping horns.

"Don't you just love this city?" said Danny with disgust. "Me and Kathy are thinking of moving out someday, maybe upstate, somewhere where you can breathe and not spend your life stuck in traffic or looking for a parking space."

"You mean the suburbs? Definitely not for me," said Lee. "So, how's it going with Kathy? How do you squeeze her in with all your nefarious activities at Madame Rue's? Stealing cars and all."

"Give me a break," said Danny. "I see Kathy all the time. If she's home and not off modeling somewhere I usually stay at her place. But she's got a roommate so that's why I keep my stuff out here at my brother's. Kathy's the best, never complains, and believes in me. First time I had a girlfriend like this, she's what keeps me going in a way. She's my future."

"Sounds like a bad song," said Lee scoffing.

"It's not a song," said Danny. "It's real life and we're always making plans for the two of us ..." Adding shyly, "That's what love is."

"I guess there's nothing wrong with that," said Lee, feeling a tinge of jealousy. The only plans he had ever made with Lexi were when she was coming over to see him at his flat. "Does Kathy hang out at Madame Rue's?"

"I definitely discourage her from coming down alone," said Danny. "There's Junior and the rest of Maddy's crew hanging around and I don't really want them to get to know her."

"How's her modeling career going? Making money?"

"She keeps working but she's smart, she knows it won't last forever," said Danny. "She puts it away. Calls it our *nest egg*."

"Who says models aren't smart?" asked Lee.

"Dumb guys like us," said Danny. "It's not like what you think."

"I never thought models were stupid," said Lee. "Just sexy."

"Tell me about it!" said Danny rolling his eyes. "You know what ... she wants to take me up to Westchester, meet her family, get them to start knowing who I am. Do you believe that?"

"That *is* serious, man. You better learn some table manners, so you don't pick up the wrong fork eating your *pâté* and be thrown out on your ass."

Danny looked at him. "I know which fork to use."

"Which one?" asked Lee.

"The clean one," said Danny.

Finally, the traffic started moving, and they slowly cruised over the slim roadway of the upper level. Danny knew his way around, taking the first exit down to Queens Boulevard and then zipping through the side streets of Astoria. Ten minutes later, he parked in front of a modest two-story house with green aluminum siding.

"So, I finally meet the loathed bridge *and tunnel crowd*," said Lee. "And I find out it's been you all along!"

"Steady," said Danny, stepping gingerly out of the car. "Cool, I don't see my brother's car parked in the driveway, so he's probably working. Let's do this fast."

They entered the house from the back entrance, a white screen door, and then up one flight of stairs where Danny unlocked another. "It's a two-family house here, don't know how my brother can stand it. But I don't think he'd move out of Queens if he won the lottery. Anyway, I've got my own room in the back," said Danny.

"You're so full of it," said Lee. "You told me that you had your own place in the city."

"Hey, my room is my *own* place and *this* is the city," emphasized Danny. "Where'd you come from? *Cow's Ass, Iowa*?"

"Ohio," said Lee. "It wasn't a bad place, I don't think about it much. Don't think I'll be going back anytime soon."

"You think Queens is a different country? A lot of famous people came from Queens."

"Yeah? Who?" said Lee teasingly.

Danny closed his eyes and concentrated, "*Ethel Merman*. My mother even knew her family."

"Never heard of her," said Lee. There were children's toys laying around on the floor and that lived in smell and feel. Last night's dinner dishes, pots and pans were still piled up in the sink.

"Smells like someone likes to cook with garlic," said Lee.

"My brother's wife is Italian," said Danny.

"Good cook?"

"Says that's why he married her, but I never eat here if I can avoid it. Him and me, we're not on the same schedule - or *planet* for that matter. And you know what, that's fine with me. *Don't explain – don'*t complain - that's my modus operandi around here. My brother and his wife working all day long while the kids are off to school and then everybody gets home and sits in front of the TV. So I'm the invisible man around here, by the time I get up they're all gone and then I make a point of getting out of *Dodge* before they get home and start hassling me."

"Hassling you about what?"

"I don't know, my plans, my future ... anything. But this is very temporary; soon Kathy and I will be getting our own place and I'll get the fuck out of *Archie Bunker* land. You want a coffee before we go, Lee?"

"No thanks, I'm OK ... what, you and your brother don't get along or something?"

"Good enough, but he's got ten years on me so there's always been kind of a, you know, a *generation gap* between us. *Summer of love* he was working his way through college becoming an accountant and I was wearing beads and getting stoned down in the *Village* so we never hung out or anything. Ken's all right, just kind of square if you know what I mean, doesn't understand what I'm trying to do in the music business at all."

"So, what does your brother do?"

"You're not gonna believe it – he works for the *IRS* – *Internal Revenue Service* - some kind of *bean counter*. Man, I could never do something like that no matter what."

There was the metallic sound of a key in the lock and then the door pushed open and Danny's brother Ken was standing there looking at them. Dressed in a gray suit and holding a briefcase, he was taller than Danny with thinning hair that would all be gone soon.

"Hey," said Danny.

"Hey," said his brother, not smiling. "What's up?"

"Forgot my wallet," said Danny.

"Yeah," said his brother stone-faced. "I saw it on the kitchen counter when I left so, I put it back in your room. I saw you had some of that spaghetti I left for you. No time to put your dishes away or what?"

"Sorry, the spaghetti was great, thanks ... Hey, Ken, this is Lee Franklin," said Danny.

At the mention of Lee's name Ken's face lit up and when he smiled, he had a bit of that same Irish charm and appeal as Danny. In fact, he looked like a different guy.

"*Lee Franklin* in the flesh! Been hearing a lot about you, Lee. You're the musician, right? The *mind-blowing* singer?" They shook hands.

"Yeah, I guess that's me," said Lee embarrassed.

"You *do* sing?" pressed Ken.

"Yeah, I do ... I guess I'm the singer around here. How you doing?"

"So, I finally get to meet you, Lee. I'm Ken O'Connor, Danny's brother. Come on in and sit down for a while, have a cup of coffee?"

"I already asked him," said Danny. "I'll go get my wallet and take a pee, we gotta hit the road, Ken."

"Do what you gotta do," said Ken, obviously disappointed. "Come on, Lee, at least we can chat for a few moments."

Ken sat down at the small dining room table and Lee followed him. He took off his tie and carefully folded it in half and then half again, putting it in his inside pocket.

"Hate these things," said Ken. "But what can you do?"

"Know what you mean," said Lee, although he owned but one tie himself, and Lexi had bought it for him.

"Danny's been telling me all about you, Lee, that is, when I can get him to sit down for five minutes. Sounds like you guys got something good going. Danny's a smart kid, just hard for him to get focused. But this may be the break he needs. And it couldn't come too soon. What's the plan?"

"No real plan," said Lee, not knowing exactly what Ken was getting at. "We're just going back to the city, I guess,"

"I meant with the music," said Ken. "And Danny being your manager and all."

"Oh that, yeah, well, we're just trying to get things going, I suppose."

"I'd say that getting John Lennon to produce you is really getting things going," said Ken smiling. "What's he like? Must be some kind of a far out guy, being a *Beatle* and all."

"John Lennon? What can I say? He's uh ... he's friendly," said Lee.

"Good to have a friend like that," said Ken. "That's all you need."

"Well, John Lennon said *all you need is love ...*"

"Love and a good accountant. So when you get that big royalty check, you put aside some money to pay your taxes. A lot of you show business people forget about that."

Danny hurried back into the dining room with his wallet in hand. "We better get going," he said to Lee.

"Where you going?" asked Ken. "Into the recording studio? You know, I wouldn't mind tagging along someday and meeting John Lennon. Lee says John's a friendly guy; think he'd mind if I hung out?"

"Sure," said Danny, avoiding Lee's glare. "I'll check it out ... but we're not going to the studio today, Ken ... I'm organizing this party down at Madame Rue's, better get going ..."

"Don't tell me you're still working at Madame Rue's?" exclaimed Ken. "I don't know what the hell you're doing down there, Danny."

"What I'm doing? How about making a living?" said Danny defensively. "Bringing in a little cash while we get Lee's career going. And besides that, Madame Rue's is like one of the biggest music business hangouts in the city and I'm making a lot of contacts."

Ken looked at Lee. "That's not what I hear about this Madame Rue's. From what I hear you got the jet-set rubbing shoulders with gangsters, men dressing up like women, all kinds of crazy shit. Not the kind of place I'd want my kids hanging out ... or my kid brother for that matter either."

"You don't know what it's like," said Danny. "You've never even been there."

"I don't need to go there to know what's going on. You should listen to me, Danny, I'm telling you there are bad people involved in that place and whatever kind of contacts you're making in that dump aren't going to help you, they'll only hurt you, believe me."

"How do you know? What, didn't they pay their taxes? Does that make them *bad people*?" said Danny.

"You don't know anything," said Ken heatedly. "Some guys down in the office were talking about it just the other day, what's that guy's name ... something *the horse?*"

Danny said nothing. So finally, Ken just laughed and looked at Lee. "Where do these wise guys find these names?

"We gotta go, Ken," said Danny. "I'll see you later."

Ken moved closer to Danny and put his arm on his shoulder. "Danny, just be careful, that's all I'm trying to say."

"Right," said Danny, backing away and leaving Ken standing there with his arm in the air.

"Nice meeting you, Ken," said Lee extending his hand, taking Ken's and shaking it.

"At least I hope you're not singing down at Madame Rue's." Ken said to Lee. "*Bad people*," he emphasized.

"Naw," said Lee. "I'm singing uptown at JP's on the East Side."

"Never heard of it," said Ken.

"'Cause JP probably pays his taxes," said Danny as he walked to the door. "Catch you later."

"Just be careful, Danny," Ken yelled after him. "That's all I'm saying."

"I'm always careful," said Danny loudly. "You know that."

"Right," said Ken sarcastically. "Always careful to ..."

"See you," said Danny, almost pushing Lee out the door. Ken O'Connor stood at the entrance, watching them walk down the stairs.

"Hey, where'd you get that snazzy car?" he yelled.

"Rented it from Hertz," Danny yelled back.

"Since when does Hertz rent BMWs?" Ken was saying to himself as he walked back inside his home and, seconds later, Danny took off, screeching his tires as he drove away.

They didn't say much until they were back on the 59th Street Bridge's upper deck with the city again in view, skyscrapers gleaming in the late afternoon sun.

"What the fuck was that all about?" asked Lee finally.

"I don't know," said Danny, exasperated. "Ken's a good guy but he shouldn't always be telling me what to do, especially with you there. And he doesn't understand crap about show business."

"Maddy the Horse is show business? Could have fooled me."

"Lay off," said Danny.

"Hey, what you tell your brother about yourself is one thing but what's this crap about John Lennon producing my album?"

"I don't know – I don't know where he got that idea. I probably said something about meeting John Lennon down at Ashley's that night and Ken got pretty excited. The Beatles are probably the only group he knows."

"I bet you told him more than that," said Lee.

"I don't know ... shit. Can't we just drop it? I hate going out there anyway ... now Ray's gonna be pissed, said he needed the car and here we are stuck in the goddamn rush hour traffic." Danny punched the steering wheel hard with the palm of his hand.

"It's always rush hour in New York," said Lee. "So where you taking me now?"

"I'd take you to see Kathy, but she said she was gonna go visit her folks up in Westchester today and tell them about us. I can't wait to get the hell out of my brother's place."

KATHY WALKED UP THE SAME DRIVEWAY SHE HAD PLAYED IN AS A kid when it snowed, learned to ride a bike on, and at the entrance, by the three-rail fence, gotten her first kiss when she was fifteen. She took smooth elongated strides on her very long legs and burst through the front door without ringing the bell. It was a very large house now which had begun as a modest 19th century farmhouse moved at a snail's pace to its current location thirty years ago and then set down to grow. The Muller family had added large and flawlessly matched side wings, a massive back extension and a pool, guesthouse and gardener's shed; and, most recently, a putting green so that Hank Muller, Kathy's father, could improve his game when he was off the links. Kathy came from a prosperous family, not super rich, but affluent enough and with the right Ivy League connections that guaranteed a certain *WASP* security in the rolling hills of Westchester County for generations to come. Her father, a partner in a *white shoe* Park Avenue law firm, handled estates and trusts for the same people he played golf with, often saying that he had secured more clients around the 9th hole than he ever did in his firm's conference room.

The Mullers were not city people, although the tiny village of Purchase, New York, where they lived was just a 40-minute train ride from Grand Central Station, less time than it took to get through one section of the *New York Times*. About once a month, Hank Muller and Cheryl, his second wife, would take the train into Manhattan, have dinner at the New York Athletic Club and take in a play if they could find one that wouldn't embarrass them both. Just a few years ago a friend had recommended *Oh! Calcutta!* and they found themselves *drop-jaw* mortified as they sat in the second row, staring at an assortment of completely naked actors prancing on the stage before them. Since then, Hank always checked in with the NYAC concierge before buying his theater tickets, asking him to recommend some *family entertainment* even if their children rarely accompanied them.

Since she began modeling professionally, apart from brief Thanksgiving and Christmas appearances when she happened to be in town, Kathy Muller rarely made it home herself. She'd been modeling since she was seventeen, was good at handling her money – maybe the one useful trait she had inherited from her father - and it didn't take long before she was sharing a studio apartment on the East Side with another model; finally, fully independent from her parents in both body and soul. When she moved out, her father had mentioned to her that there would be a trust fund for her someday and Kathy without thinking had responded, "Yes, if Cheryl doesn't spend it all before," which was answered by a stony silence.

She and her petite stepmother were not close in height, temperament or mutual affection. Her father had remarried one August when Kathy was sixteen and that September, she had gone away to boarding school and then off to sleep-away camp in the summer. Then there was the arrival of her stepbrother Harry Muller, born just a year later and Kathy's clear demotion to second-class citizen in her own family's hierarchy was sealed. The Muller family implosion had begun when Kathy's own mother, Charlotte, announced over breakfast, in-between bites of an English muffin, that she was moving out to Denver to live with a ski-instructor and aside from initial brief reunions the relationship between mother and daughter had dwindled to infrequent half-hearted telephone calls. Hank Muller, in the spirit of both revenge and efficiency, had married *Cheryl*, the tennis instructor from his country club; from *Charlotte* to *Cheryl,* an easy leap, a blip on the screen, and soft on the memory. Kathy could have been called a rebellious kid after that except that no one was really paying enough attention to her to be the object of that rebellion. Still, she was a *wild child* in her own way with an independent and fearless streak, getting into the modeling game when she shared a joint with a fashion photographer at a Soho party, she wasn't supposed to be at to begin with. High school ended with a yawn and Elite Models, her agency, wasted no time in sending her to Milan and then Paris for a year to learn her trade before coming back to New York to make her mark. Kathy was promoted as an all-American beauty, blond hair and wide smile with crinkly eyes. If the client couldn't afford Cheryl Tiegs, they'd settle for Kathy Muller at half the price. *Happy with Kathy*, that was her rep's tagline when selling her. And they were. She wasn't a superstar, but she worked steadily, and her American *cherry-pie* smile and bouncy blond hair made her a natural for shampoo and makeup commercials.

"Is anyone home?" Kathy called out as soon as she walked in the unlocked door. "Hey?"

"We're back here," came an icy voice from the kitchen. "Don't bother ringing the bell."

"I didn't," Kathy whispered under her breath. "Bitch."

Kathy walked on back through a butler's pantry hallway, lined with china cabinets and drawers for silverware, to the kitchen itself, a cozy lived-in space which used to be her favorite room in the house until Cheryl took cooking lessons in Aix-En-Provence and was now very concentrated on slicing celery into slices thin as a contact lens.

"Jean-Paul says the trick is to tuck the fingers of your left hand in and use your knuckles as your guide. That and a very sharp knife from Thiers, of course." For some reason totally lost on Kathy, Cheryl found this funny and chirped out a bit of squeaky laugher. She was an attractive self-confident woman, compact in an athletic kind of way, like an ex-tennis pro should be, and was entering her early forties as a classy suburban *object of desire* to her husband's golfing buddies. But she didn't feel that way about herself, sexy, beautiful and all the rest, when her 5-foot-ten model stepdaughter was towering over her and getting all the attention, something Cheryl avoided like the plague.

"Jean-Paul?" asked Kathy.

"Jean-Paul Grandcamp," said Cheryl without looking up. "Just got his second Michelin *macaron* this year ... *soooo* happy for him. He taught me the secret of how to make the perfect soufflé every time. Just that was worth the trip to France. It's all about the right eggs and ..."

"Is Dad around?" Kathy interrupted. "I have some news."

"Your father is probably at this very moment trying to dislodge his ball from a sand trap."

"Isn't it a little cold for golf? It's the middle of winter for god's sake!" said Kathy.

"For your father?"

"Yeah ... right."

"Listen, if we're going to have some kind of mother-daughter chat, why don't you pull up a stool and sit down so you don't hit your head on the beams."

"Very funny," said Kathy. She picked up a stool from the breakfast counter and pulled it close to where her stepmother was dicing celery. "What are you making?"

"Celeri roumalade."

"I met a guy."

"That's news?" asked Cheryl without looking up. "Isn't that what you do?"

Kathy ignored that dig, she was used to it already, but immediately ran through enough testy rebuffs that, if said out loud, would have ended the conversation right then and there. "He's a normal guy from Queens and he's funny and cute ... and I think he loves me."

"Queens?" said Cheryl. "Hmmm ... Forest Hills? I played there many times. Is he Jewish?"

"No, he's Irish, very Irish, the map of Ireland on his face ... and he loves me."

Cheryl looked up. "I heard that the first time. How do you know?"

"He told me," said Kathy.

"Well, that's something," said Cheryl with unabashed ironic enthusiasm. "What does he do?"

"Well, for now, he's managing a disco downtown."

"I'm sure your father will be thrilled to hear that."

"But he wants to get into the music business, he's managing this singer who's really good."

"The music business? Never knew anyone who was in that business ... if you can call it a business. Always heard it was run by crooks and cheats."

"Should I wait for Dad?"

"Suit yourself, dear. Sorry, but I can't entertain you. As you can see my hands are full. Oh, one thing, your *other* mother called a few days ago. You might want to give her a call before she goes off to Bali."

"Bali?"

"I think that's what she said."

"Maybe I'll bring him up to visit one of these days, so you and Dad can judge for yourself. His name is Danny."

"Better call first," said Cheryl. "You know how your father detests surprises."

"What do you mean?"

"I was referring to your mother."

"My mother?"

"When she served your father breakfast and then left him for her, what was it? Masseuse?"

"Actually, it was her ski instructor. That was a long time coming, anyway. No surprise, really."

"Depends who you talk to. I don't think your father would agree with your ... assessment."

"Right ... guess I'm gonna call a taxi and get back to the city then," said Kathy. "Try and see Danny."

"Who's Danny?"

"He's the guy I was telling you about. I just told you, his name's Danny."

"Oh ... the Jewish guy.'

"Irish," said Kathy exasperated. "Goodbye, Cheryl."

"Au revoir," said Cheryl, head deep in the oven and then madly consulting her cookbook. "Damn! Why isn't my soufflé rising?"

CHAPTER 20

Lee was nearly always alone in his apartment or hanging at the bar in JP's except on those blissful occasions when Lexi popped in to share his bed, couch or kitchen countertop for as long as she could or wanted. But on this especially slow Sunday night, he felt like he had spent half his life there, slouched in the same position, on that same sofa, watching the tube, drinking Scotch and hoping the phone would ring. Trying to put Lexi Langdon out of his mind, he made a feeble effort to concentrate on *The Sonny Comedy Hour*, a lame version of the now cancelled *The Sonny and Cher Show*. The "I Got You Babe" couple was no more and their prime-time TV slot had not survived the last TV season. When Sonny and Cher announced their divorce, the broadcast powers that be decided it just wouldn't be right for the U.S. public to continue watching the two of them, getting along uproariously on their TV screen, when the truth was that they were fighting it out in court. In a *Nielsen Ratings* version of Solomon's wisdom, there would be two shows: one for Sonny and one for Cher, although on whose show their only child *Chastity* would appear was left up to the court to decide. Alas, neither show clicked, and come next season the network would make an attempt at family unity to unite them again although, like most post-divorce reconciliations, the results (and ratings) were disappointing. Even a stab at divorce humor didn't work, example being when Cher gives Sonny a generous compliment and he replies by saying *That's not what you said in Court!* According to government statistics, after remaining steady for forty years, divorce in the U.S. had surged in 1974 and, well, it just wasn't so funny anymore. The joke was too close to home.

Lee was wondering if he had gone stale. He was hearing from Lexi so intermittently now; she traveled all the time and her nocturnal visits to their *love pad* became fewer and farther between. Had she found someone else to satisfy her when the need arose? Or even worse, had she and Ray reconciled? And at just that moment, with that thought in his mind, while Sonny was suffering through bad jokes and canned laughter, the phone rang. And it was Lexi.

Lee was always taken aback by Lexi's nearly total lack of remorse about anything she did, and the last thing she felt guilty about was leaving him hanging while she took off for parts unknown, *unknown* to him at least. She spoke to him as casually as if they had last spoken yesterday or mere hours ago, filling him in on her latest adventures while presuming he already knew the cast of characters involved, of which Lee knew practically no one. Lexi's world was *the only world that mattered* as far as she was concerned. If you didn't know that *Diana* was Diana Vreeland and that she was the editor of Vogue and that Lexi would be sitting next to her at the winter collections in Paris, don't bother asking because she wasn't going to stop to fill you in. The pertinent information that Lee did *kind of* glean from Lexi's rapid-fire delivery was that she was just off the plane, having taken a flight a day earlier than planned to New York from Denver because the snow was too wet and she was bored with skiing anyway.

"Ray's not back until tomorrow. So ... you want to come over and play?" Lexi suggested with little subtlety.

"Play what?" asked Lee. He couldn't resist.

"Play ... with me," she said with a giggle.

"Lexi, you sound a little, how should I say, tipsy," said Lee.

"Take my advice, sugar, get it while it's hot." And she giggled some more.

Lee hopped in a cab and arrived within minutes at Lexi's Fifth Avenue apartment building. When he stepped out of the elevator, Lexi was standing there in a cream crêpe de Chines robe, which she let fall open once the elevator doors closed. She was wearing high-heeled baby doll slippers, black seamed stockings, black garter belt and matching bra with her Diamonds by the Yard necklace suspended around her neck in just two long loops, reaching down to the puff of perfumed dark hair between her legs.

"I think I forgot the panties," said Lexi, wobbling slightly in her heels.

"But you didn't forget the champagne," said Lee.

"How'd you know that?"

"Took a wild guess."

"Well, you know, they were serving champagne on the plane, so much champagne that I thought it might be dangerous to switch to something else when I got home so I popped open a bottle of Dom Pérignon." She burped. "Whoops! Now that wasn't very ladylike, was it? I saved you a few drops but it's upstairs in my bedroom."

"I think I can make it up the stairs. How about you?"

"I'll give it the ol' Texas try, sugar."

Lee followed her upstairs to her bedroom, where she started pulling bits of lingerie out of her armoire: bras, silk and satin panties, corsets, garter belts and stockings and throwing them on Lee as he sat on the bed.

"Would you like me to try something on for you?" she asked playfully. "It's my *lingerie winter collection*, 'specially for Mister Lee Franklin."

Lee gulped. "Well, yeah, sure ... try on everything. What about some champagne?"

"Coming right up, it's in the bathroom staying cold. Armando filled one of the sinks with ice, clever boy."

Dropping her robe to the floor, Lexi strolled into the adjacent bathroom. Wearing no panties, the languid, intoxicating jiggle of her bare buttocks, punctuated by the dimples just above, was making Lee about as horny as he'd ever been. Through the open door he could watch her splash on copious amounts of *Chanel No. 5* from a very large bottle before returning with the green champagne bottle in one hand and two glasses in the other.

Bending down over him, she handed him the bottle and ran her tongue on his neck. "Do you like my perfume, Lee?"

"It's like a drug," he said.

"Did you know what Marilyn Monroe said when they asked her what she wore to bed?"

"Chanel No. 5?"

"You read Norman Mailer's book, too?"

"Only the good parts."

"You do the *pouring in* and I'll do the *trying on*. That's maybe the one thing I love about these northern winters, I can wear all my lingerie. Would you like a little fashion show, Lee?"

"Sure," he said as he slowly poured the champagne. "It takes so long for the bubbles to go down before you can start drinking."

"Yeah, it's a nuisance, isn't it, sugar? One of life's many hardships we just must endure if we ..." Her words trailed off as she pulled a stiff, underwired bra out of her drawer. "Oh, I forgot all about this, it only covers my boobs halfway, you think that will be okay?"

Lee just smiled as Lexi put together another outfit of black lace bikini panties, demi-bra and a garter belt she dexterously hooked to her seamed stockings, one leg at a time, while putting each foot on the bed right between Lee's thighs, her toes gently rubbing his crotch.

"What's that?" she laughed. "A pistol in your pocket?"

"Or am I just glad to see you?"

"Guess you know the routine."

"Guess so ..."

He pulled her to the bed and ran tender kisses up and down her back, her toes and her fingers, and then he was diving deeply with his tongue between her open legs. She was groaning and so was he, and then she was on top of him and riding him to an orgasm, which seemed to go on and on. But apparently it had ended too quickly for Lexi.

"I can't wait for the second act," said Lexi as she cuddled in his arms.

"Better give me some time to remember my lines."

"You do that, I'll be right back, sugar."

Lee dozed off for a few minutes, falling into that almost druggy post-orgasm sleep, until he heard Lexi come back into the bedroom and plant a kiss on his cheek and he awoke tangled in dark thoughts with an inexplicable sense of doom, like a dark cloud was coming over their affair, that something about this night was more about saying goodbye than welcome back. Still, he had scant evidence that anything was wrong except for a desperate need to talk to Lexi for real, to know what she was really feeling about him. He opened his eyes and touched her, rubbing his fingers high up on her inner thigh as she stood at a low dresser with her back to him.

"We make love ..." he began.

"You got that part right," said Lexi.

"But we never talk."

"What do you mean, sugar? We talk all the time. Didn't I call you just before you came over here?"

"Yeah, you call me, let me know when I'll be seeing you, but we never really talk about us," he said. "About what this all means."

"Talk about what *what* all means?" said Lexi, suddenly sounding irritated. She turned around from the dresser and he could see what she was doing. "You sure you don't want any of this coke? I found it in Ray's tuxedo pocket. He didn't think I knew where he kept it, doesn't want me to know about it, so I just took it. I doubt he'll say anything anyway; he's too big a coward for that."

"Naw," said Lee. "I don't want any, it never made me feel good, just more anxious than I already am."

Lexi took the small folded paper envelope from the dresser and placed it on the night table, carefully opening it and dipping her pinky fingernail into the pile of flaky white cocaine within and then carefully bringing it to her nose and inhaling it through one nostril, leaving little specks of white around her nose.

"I never used to do it either, but now it seems like everybody's doing it so why not me? Out in Aspen they were sniffing coke on the ski lifts! And I'm talking about the best people. But I won't do it with Ray, I hate how he gets when he's high, he's annoying enough already." Again, she dipped her nail and brought it to her other nostril. Then she handed the cocaine to Lee. "Come on, it's no fun doing it alone," she said.

Lee shook his head. "Then don't do it if it's no fun," he said obstinately. He didn't like seeing Lexi like this, high, slurring her words. It wasn't the image he had of her.

"Well, it's also hard to stop once you get started," said Lexi. "In fact, I think that may be the worst part."

"I just don't want any, Lexi. Maybe I'd become as annoying as Ray."

"That's impossible."

"Why don't you slow down on the blow and drink another glass of champagne so we can talk."

Lexi picked up her glass, watching the tiny bubbles rise to the surface. "I only took a tiny little bit. I could have all the cocaine I wanted if I cared about it. Maybe that's why I really don't care about it. Does that make sense?" She gave a little burp. "Oops! Hope nobody heard that." She laughed. "Ray hates it when I burp."

"Ray's not here," said Lee.

"Obviously," replied Lexi. "He's in LA, coming back on the red-eye tomorrow morning. So I guess I can burp all I want ..."

"Ray may not *be* here, but still you're always talking about him. You say you can't stand him, but you can't get him out of your mind."

"Ray Arthur is not on my mind right now, believe me, sugar. Not when you're here."

"But, sometimes, I get the feeling that he's more here than I am."

"Jesus, what do you mean by that?"

"I mean that, well ... that you know, really know, nothing about me except that I sing and play guitar."

"And are the most wonderful lover," said Lexi, moving closer to him.

"Okay, that too maybe." Lee smiled ruefully. "But you don't seem interested in anything except that either."

"Most men wouldn't complain."

"Guess I'm not most men."

Lexi ignored that and twisted around from Lee, clearly growing impatient and agitated. "Did I show you this amazing corset I bought in Paris at Chantal Thomas, Lee?" She started rifling through her drawers, finally pulling out a strapless lavender and white bustier, cut low in the front with Chinese silk embroidery. "Tell me this isn't the sexiest thing you ever saw?" She held it up to her, undoing the demi-bra she already had on and letting her full breasts fall free. "Help me put it on, Lee. It's got all these hooks up the back."

"You don't want to talk about me, do you?"

"I just hope it fits me," said Lexi. "It's a French size and ... "

"Lexi, can we just be still for a moment?"

Lexi went to yet another high dresser, a stunning flame mahogany chest, and started flinging open more and more drawers filled with lingerie, recklessly throwing everything behind her, piece by piece, not bothering to look where anything landed. Then she walked to her shoe closet, pulling out black patent leather Charles Jourdan pumps while dumping a dozen other pairs on the floor, then back to the cabinet to try on what was left, almost losing her balance once or twice as she stepped in and out of panties and garter belts. What had begun as an erotic ritual to turn Lee on had lost its rhythm; she turned more and more manic, silk and lace flying around the bedroom, shoes spilling out of her closet in a heap. Lexi was frenetic, pulling out drawer after drawer, emptying them out and moving on to the next, like she was going to go through every piece of clothing in every dresser in her room in as little time as possible and spread it all over the floor and bed. She grabbed half a dozen silk panties of every shade - pinks, pale blues, ivory, red and black - and tossed them in the air, oblivious as they gently landed all around Lee.

"I got this whole set in Neiman Marcus back in Dallas, and this was custom-made for me on Rue Cambon in Paris. I bet you'll like this, Lee, it's got some dirty words in French embroidered right on it. Can you imagine?"

She picked up an intricately embroidered push-up bra. "Oh, my God, I haven't worn this in years. I think my boobs are too big for it now."

She flung it over her shoulder, and it landed comically on Lee's head. He held it up in front of him before laying it down on the bedcover.

"Lexi, will you stop this?"

When she didn't, Lee stood up, and turned her around to face him, just then seeing the tears in her eyes. She stared at him wildly.

"Will you stop?" he whispered. "Please?"

"No, Lee, I won't stop. And don't you tell me to stop. If I want to throw all my clothes on the floor, then that's exactly what I'm going to do. Why not? Someone will clean it all up by tomorrow morning. What does it matter? Everything will return to normal in the morning, that's what my daddy always used to say no matter what happened." She kissed him savagely and he could feel the tears running down her cheeks. "I know what you want to talk about, Lee; you want to talk about *you*, and make me fall in love with *you* even more and then I'll love *you* ... totally, tenderly, tragically. Is that what you want, Lee? Just turn this into another one of your sad songs?"

"I just want to know where we're going, Lexi."

"Where *we're* going?" she yelled. "I'm twenty-five, my daddy died in the arms of a whore, I've got more money than I know what to do with and my husband's running around with some little mafia teenybopper. And now you want to know where we're going? What does it matter, Lee? We're just here tonight. We're not going anywhere."

"It matters to me," Lee protested meekly. "Because I need ..."

"Don't push me," Lexi said forcefully. "Or you're gonna ruin everything, Lee. I can tell you that right now."

"But don't we at least have to make some plans? Consider where we're going?" He stroked her back while trying to calm her. "Just tell me what you want me to do, Lexi. That's all I want to know."

"Don't you love to play music, Lee? Just keep doing that."

"Yeah, I love playing music ... but I love you too, Lexi." It was the first time he had said those words out loud and there was a painful stillness between them before Lexi spoke.

"Don't say that, Lee," she said coldly. "That's maybe the one thing I can't afford right now."

"So, you want to just keep going on like this and let months go by before we see each other? Is that what you want?"

Lexi let out a long sigh. "What I want has got nothing to do with it. You know I can't stand to be around Ray and yet I don't know how to get rid of him without causing an even bigger mess. And now I have you putting pressure on me. It's like everything is spinning out of control. That's why I have to get away, Lee. I have to figure this out all on my own." She took his face in her hands and kissed him gently. "You're precious to me, sugar. We'll survive, I'm sure of that."

"So, you're leaving again? Where are you going, Lexi?" Lee felt a twinge of panic, something that caught him short in his breathing and he suddenly wished he hadn't started this conversation at all. "And for how long ... this time?"

"Who knows ... I don't even know. I'm thinking of hooking up with *The Yellow Rose* down in the Caribbean, visit some friends, do a little island hopping. I tell you, just living in a *world without Ray* for a while would be a real vacation for me."

Lexi laughed while wiping the tears from her eyes as she started to pick up the scattered lingerie and stuff it back in drawers in no particular order. "Oh, God, my makeup must be running all over my face – I probably look like that rock singer we saw at Ashley's that night."

"His name's Alice Cooper," said Lee not wanting to joke. "So, I guess that's just the way it's gonna be for a while if that's what makes you happy."

Lexi picked up one panty and softly threw it at Lee and then a dark stocking and then a white bra.

"Lee, I married a man who was supposed to make me happy. I thought I knew all there was to know about him and now he makes me anything but happy."

"He was just the wrong man, Lexi. That's all. Probably couldn't handle all of this."

"All of what? You act like it's my fault."

"I didn't say that."

"No, you didn't, but how do you know the same thing wouldn't happen to you? It's not easy being *Mr. Lexi Langdon* and I'm not ready to call my lawyers and start signing papers and have people gossiping all over New York. If I know one thing about Ray, he won't go quietly. And you'll be dragged into it too, Lee, probably not the greatest thing for your career."

"You're more important to me than my career."

"Don't ever say that," said Lexi, letting out a deep, long breath. "So why not keep going just like we are, Lee, making each other happy? What's so wrong with that?"

"I don't know," said Lee. "I guess nothing is wrong with that."

Lexi sat on the bed but not close to Lee. "Whew, I'm tired now even with that wicked cocaine. Think I'll take off my makeup."

"Maybe I should get going," said Lee, hoping she would tell him not to.

But she didn't hesitate. "Maybe you should, Lee. It's late and Ray's coming home tomorrow." She kissed him. "Everything will be back to normal in the morning. Do you want me to call you a taxi?" She reached for the phone and knocked it off its cradle. There was a row of buttons along the bottom and Lexi started pushing them. "I can never get this damn phone to work, there are three numbers and an interphone ..."

The bedroom door was slightly open and when Lee looked up, he saw Armando, Lexi's gentle Philippine butler, standing in the crack of the door, looking at them as embarrassed as a schoolboy. Lexi was sitting on the bed half-naked, with most of her lingerie still on the floor, and the envelope of coke wide open on the night table. She swung her head up and when she saw him standing there, she turned livid, her eyes blazing.

"Get out of my bedroom!" she yelled at him.

Armando stood frozen in the doorway, trembling.

"I just thought you called me, Miss Lexi, my phone lit up and I came to see if you need something. I'm so sorry if I disturb you." He held his hands over his eyes, so innocently, as if to assure Lexi he hadn't seen anything.

"Just get out!" she yelled even louder.

"Yes, ma'am." Armando's voice cracked as he lowered his head and backed out of the doorway.

Lee said nothing and Lexi just took a deep breath and then went about picking up her lingerie.

"I guess you have to be very rich to afford to lose your temper like that," said Lee.

She stared at him. "Well, that I can afford then," she finally said with a pasted-on smile. "Love no but anger yes, I can afford as much of that as I want."

"I can't figure you out, Lexi."

"I'm not complicated, Lee. I'm just direct. When you don't need anything from anybody, you just get to the point. My daddy taught me to do that. Said I didn't need to treat people who worked for me like they're my friends. They're paid to give me what I want, that's the way it works – what do you think? Doesn't mean I'm always happy with what I get though."

"And Ray?" asked Lee. "Is he what you wanted?"

"Listen, Lee, I moved to New York to start a new life, too much history back in Houston. And I didn't want to be single anymore because then none of the wives will open their doors for you 'cause they're afraid you're gonna steal their husbands. And it's the wives who control the doors to ... society, or whatever you want to call it."

"I don't even know what that is," said Lee. "Society? What society?"

"I know you don't get it, but I can't just spend my *whole* life traveling around with ..."

"But that seems exactly what you do."

"Lee, I mean I've got to be fixed somewhere, a part of something ... something with roots. I couldn't just drop all that and run away with some singer nobody knows. I'm Lexi Langdon for Christ's sake, nobody would speak to me."

It was like she had shot him in the heart, but he couldn't show it.

"So I'm just like Armando, another one of the help."

"Don't be ridiculous, Lee."

"And you can treat the help however you like, whether they deserve it or not, just like Armando."

"Armando barged into my bedroom!" she protested.

"He was just trying to help you and you know it."

"That's what help are supposed to do, Lee. Help me," she screamed at him.

"So how can I help you, Lexi, tell me that."

She couldn't look at him. She got up and walked to the bathroom and stood in the doorway with her back to him. "Tonight you can help me by letting me get some sleep," she said, closing the door behind her.

Lee let himself out of the apartment and walked home slowly, in no hurry to get back to JP's and hang out with whoever would be left at the bar at this hour. From Fifth Avenue all the way to the East River, he crossed the East Side on 72nd Street where the traffic went both ways, and when he got to the river walk, stood above the dark water, looking at the lights of the distant bridges. He knew there was nothing to do but turn around, go back to his apartment and wait again for the phone to ring. He was good at waiting; he'd done enough of that already in that prison cell in Rome. Tonight could have been the night he would have told Lexi all about that time in Rome and bring her into his world, let her know who he really was, what he had been through. Tell her how he felt when his cell door slammed closed and he thought he might die of panic or something worse. For some reason he thought Lexi could have made all of that okay now. And all he had wanted her to say to him was that it was all right; that he was okay, that she would save him ... Was that what he wanted? But he hadn't told her any of that. Instead he had told her he loved her and that was a mistake because poor boys are always telling rich girls they love them.

When Lexi awoke the next morning, Ray was standing over her with his suitcase still in his hand, puzzling over all the lingerie, still in disarray and spread around the room.

"So what did you do last night?" he asked.

Lexi rubbed the sleep from her eyes and grabbed a cigarette from the night table.

"Not much," she said. "A few friends came over for drinks, welcome me home."

"What friends?" asked Ray a little too pryingly. "Anybody I know?"

"James Elliott and Lee Franklin, you know, some of my friends. Is that okay with you?"

"Lee Franklin?" asked Ray.

"He brought his guitar," said Lexi.

"Is that all he brought?" asked Ray.

Lexi made a face, got out of bed and put on her robe. "I'm taking a shower, Ray, little early for an inquisition."

She locked the bathroom door behind her and Ray picked up a pair of black panties that was lying on the foot of the bed and held it to his nose.

"Right," he said to himself, fingering the panties like a detective looking for clues. "A few friends ... and Lee Franklin."

CHAPTER 21

Nearly a week later, at ten o'clock in the morning Lee's phone finally did ring but it wasn't Lexi as he was hoping; in fact, it was the last person he wanted to hear from. But not knowing that, he dove for the phone from his bed, grabbed it in his hand before the second ring and almost made the, what would have been, fatal error of whispering *Lexi?* When he heard Ray Arthur's rough voice, barking at him, it was quite a shock. Ray spoke curtly, getting right to the point, asking or rather telling Lee to come down to Edel Records at noon that day because he had something important to discuss with him. The call left Lee more than rattled, wondering if Lexi had told Ray everything. Was this to be how his world would end, with some kind of showdown or confrontation with Ray? Not only that, Lee wasn't sure if it was wise to go meet Ray by himself, for all he knew, he could be surrounded by hoods from Madame Rue's. He would have liked to talk to somebody, anybody, but the only person he thought he could possibly call was James Elliott and really, what could he say even to him? That he'd been having sex with Lexi and was afraid Ray found out, afraid some heavies were gonna beat the crap out of him? Imagining James Elliot's bewildered reaction, he realized there was nothing else to do but to go meet Ray, face the music as it were, and find out what he wanted. For better or worse.

As ordered, Lee showed up promptly at noon at the Edel Records office, which took up the entire 23rd Floor of 1700 Broadway. Ray kept him waiting a good twenty minutes in the reception area and the young black receptionist with the huge Afro hairdo smiled at him with a sympathetic look on her face, like this is what always happens, although that hardly relieved his anxiety. He nervously thumbed through every old copy of *Billboard* magazine lying around, unable to concentrate on the *Hot 100* charts. His heart was racing, and he tried to prepare himself for whatever Ray might confront him with, attempting to come up with some sort of plausible defense. *It's your fault, Ray, the way you treated her,* or *You know, it wasn't me who started this,* knowing full well that nothing would really matter if Lexi had dropped him. He'd been having this affair with her since the end of the summer and his only regret was that he hadn't fucked her more, that he wasn't in bed with her at that very moment. Still, he was thinking that this could be really bad for him in a lot of ways, because if Lexi was leaving it up to Ray to end their affair, then he would come out the loser in a big way, losing Lexi, the apartment and his gig at JP's in one fell swoop. Not to mention what Ray might do to blacklist him in the music business. His downward spiral of doom and gloom thinking was only interrupted when the receptionist got a call and said that Ray could see him now.

"You can go on back," she said. "You know the way, right?"

"Yeah," said Lee, although he didn't.

Tentatively, he started walking down a long hall lined with gold records, past the mailroom and assorted executive offices. The place was bustling with activity while he himself felt like he was moving in slow motion and his instincts were telling him to turn around and get the hell out of there. Then, suddenly, Ray Arthur popped out of an office with his overcoat in hand. He walked briskly right toward Lee with his usual disgruntled look on his face, like he'd just had a fight with someone, a fight he had lost. Lee stopped dead in his tracks and braced himself, almost pushing against the wall, not knowing what was coming next.

"Hi, Lee," said Ray completely neutrally, without the least recognition of either having kept him waiting or any indication of an impending confrontation. "Let's get out of here, get something to eat," he said. Without waiting for a reply, he walked right past him and Lee let Ray get a few steps ahead and then turned to follow.

Their conversation was strictly one-way as Ray gabbed on about the music business and Madame Rue's and even his new BMW. They walked the few blocks around the corner to the crowded Stage Deli, a legendary Broadway restaurant with autographed photos of showbiz celebrities lining the walls and a small bucket of kosher pickles resting on every table. The owner, who sat behind the cash register, knew Ray, gave a nod to a waiter and they were quickly shown to a window booth. Before they even sat down, Ray ordered them both lean corned beef sandwiches on rye bread with mustard plus a side of coleslaw and another side of french fries without looking at a menu or asking Lee what he wanted to eat.

The waiter put a fresh bucket of pickles on the table.

"Drinks?" he asked.

"Give us two Dr. Brown's Cel-Ray Soda," said Ray. "Bet you never ate here before, Lee? That's why I ordered for you. I know what's good."

"Don't think so," said Lee. "Actually, I'm not too hungry."

"You will be when you see these fucking sandwiches," said Ray. "*Unfuckingbelieveable!*" he exclaimed, holding his hands six inches apart. "This thick!"

"You're the boss," said Lee.

The huge sandwiches soon arrived, overflowing with corned beef and impossible to fit whole into a human mouth. Ray talked incessantly through every bite, mostly about whom he was hanging out with at Madame Rue's - *Bowie, Jagger, Liza and Jack* - while Lee awkwardly tried to take a bite of the humongous sandwich. If he had any sense of dignity before, trying to eat that thing with mustard all over his mouth had taken away what was left. They ate quickly, neither of them finishing, and Ray wiped the mustard off his mouth, threw the paper napkins on his plate and leaned back to smoke a cigarette.

"You don't smoke do you, Lee?" he asked.

Lee shook his head while Ray lit up a cigarette, stretched out in the booth, and started talking enthusiastically about something that was the last thing Lee expected to hear from him.

"Great news for you, Lee. I got you on a tour."

"You got me on a tour?" Lee repeated.

"Yeah, out on the road as an opening act in big venues. Every baby act's dream," said Ray excitedly.

"But who am I opening for?"

"You ready?" said Ray. "Sha Na Na."

Lee said nothing.

"Did you hear me?" asked Ray pushing forward. "Fucking Sha Na Na, hottest act in the country. You saw them in the *Woodstock* film, right?"

"I think so," said Lee. "Lots of guys, dressed up in gold lamé singing hits from the fifties and jumping all over the stage. That's who you mean?"

"You know they blew everybody off that stage in *Woodstock,* including Hendrix."

Again, Lee said nothing, thinking that Ray might be kidding him and not wanting to fall for it. But he wasn't.

"The tour kicks off in northeast Canada, comes down through New England, and goes on from there - South, Midwest, all the way to the fucking West Coast. Probably gonna go right through the summer."

"Is Sha Na Na one of your acts?"

"You kidding? We don't do *shtick* at Edel Records, that's not our image. But Sha Na Na's agent is a really good friend of mine, hangs out at Madame Rue's – I can lock it up with a phone call this afternoon. If you want it, it's yours, Lee."

Lee sat back in his booth both dumbfounded, relieved and slightly insulted. "So, this is why you wanted to see me? Opening for Sha Na Na?"

"Yeah," said Ray, raising his eyebrows. "What else? To invite you to one of Lexi's *soirées*? She seems to be doing a pretty good job of that herself."

Lee thought it best to let that pass. "But, Ray, I'm not on your label either. Who's gonna pay for all of the expenses? The flights, hotels, car rental, all of that?

"We'll rent you a car when you need it, Edel Records has a corporate rate at Hertz and I'll even cover your flights. You get five hundred bucks a show in cash from the promoter to pay for hotels, meals, gas – all that shit. I'll write it off to artist development, even though you're not signed yet," said Ray. "Who else would you sign with anyway? I'm the only guy you know."

"I never thought about it," said Lee.

"So don't worry about it. I got a budget and I can make it happen. You might have to sign off on a few receipts for *float* even if you don't really get the money. Just between you and me, if you know what I mean."

"Float?" asked Lee.

"Float," repeated Ray. "Like cash."

So Ray's making money out of this too, thought Lee. "What about Wes? Does he know?"

"Didn't he say something to you about opening for one his acts at that dinner before Christmas? What's the difference? I can work it out with Wes. He does whatever I say he should do because I'm the one that's keeping Edel Records hot. He's not stupid."

"But, Ray, I'm a singer-songwriter, you know, a guy who writes *words* that are supposed to mean something, and you want me to go out there with a bunch of guys in costumes singing *doo-wop* hits in Canadian hockey rinks? Maybe I'm stupid, but does that sound like a great idea to you?"

"It's just important for you to get out there," said Ray. "Get some fucking exposure. Besides, with you out of New York for a while maybe my wife will start paying some attention to *me* for a change."

Again, Lee said nothing, astonished.

"Just kidding you, man," said Ray, reaching across the table and patting Lee on the shoulder a little too hard.

"Yeah, Lexi says she's a big fan," said Lee with as little emotion as possible. "You two should come to see me play at JP's sometime."

"I love JP," said Ray. "You know, I put that guy in business. Suppose he never told you that."

"I didn't know that," said Lee.

"Well, don't say anything about it to him, don't want to rub it in. But, you know, Lee, you can't sing at JP's forever, you got to get out there and let people hear you, people outside of New York, real people."

"Real people in Canadian hockey rinks?"

"Whatever, they're all the same, they buy records. That's all that counts."

"I don't know, Ray ... there's one thing I still don't understand."

"What's that?"

"Well ... I'm not on your label, you don't manage me or anything, so why are you doing this for me?"

Now it was Ray who looked insulted, or at least he played it that way. "Hey, Lee, you don't want to do it?" he said defensively. "No problem. I got a list of baby acts this long that would jump at this chance. It's up to you, man. You can spend the rest of your life at JP's or you can let me help you do something with your career. If I say you've got talent, you should believe it."

"No, I'll do it, Ray, could be good like you say." But all the time, Lee couldn't stop wondering, *why is Ray doing this for me?* "I guess I should say thanks or something."

"Don't worry about it," said Ray, as he scooped the modest bill off the table. "Lunch is on me. And next time you give a concert up at my apartment, I hope I'm invited."

Now Lee really didn't know what the fuck Ray was talking about, but he had a feeling the less said the better.

"Sure will," he said.

In a few weeks, Lee found himself freezing his ass off in northern Ontario, Canada, driving himself around in a rented red Cadillac and receiving polite applause from an audience waiting to hear Sha Na Na's hyped-up version of Danny and the Juniors' hit "At The Hop." The guys from Sha Na Na were easy enough to work with, no big egos, and intensely engaged in watching college basketball games on a backstage TV before they went on stage. Bowzer, a Columbia University graduate, was Sha Na Na's lead singer and front man, dressed as a gangly greaser in a black muscle-shirt and rolled up jeans. He was the one who taunted the audience while flexing his stringy muscles, ran around onstage, and introduced the other members of the band. As Lee walked offstage after his first short set, Bowzer was standing in the wings with his arms folded.

"Good show," said Bowzer. "At least what I saw of it."

"Wow, thanks," said Lee. "It's tough warming up the audience in these ice palaces."

"I heard the last couple of songs," said Bowzer. "You got a style, good lyrics, but there's something I can't figure out."

"What's that?"

"What the fuck are you doing on this tour?"

Lee laughed. "I don't know, Bowzer, I really don't know."

"I don't know either," said Bowzer, "and I graduated *magna cum laude* from Columbia."

"So, then what are *you* doing here?" asked Lee.

"I don't even know that myself, you know, show business..."

"It's your life, right?" Lee joked.

"Something like that. You know we started at Columbia as an a cappella group and it just took off. Me and the guys got a good thing going here, but let's face it, Lee, this is not the audience you should be aiming at. They're here to party not to listen."

"I'm beginning to get that," said Lee.

"Better get back to the game," said Bowzer, catching a glimpse of the TV and a few of his band mates cheering. "I got cash riding on this."

The hockey arenas where they played in Canada were strictly functional structures, devoid of the slightest pretense of architectural style, with little comfort for the fans and beat up locker rooms for the performers to change clothes and relax in. With numerous exits, these hockey *palaces* were drafty beyond belief, impossible to heat properly and uniformly plain and made even uglier when hundreds of sheets of beat up plywood were laid down to cover the frozen ice playing field. Bowzer complained that nobody in the audience was dancing because their asses were frostbitten from sitting inches above the ice beneath them. It was a soundman's nightmare with the music coming from the stage bouncing off every hard surface until it was more akin to a sports announcer's tinny echoed drone than melody, harmony and rhythm. Most nights, Lee played to half-empty houses because the majority of the public didn't arrive in time for the opening act. He filled up on tasteless cold cuts at the backstage catering, barely having time to eat in a decent restaurant and drove alone between cities in his blood red Caddy. So far, the high point of the tour had been having the tour photographer take a shot of him standing next to his Cadillac Coupe de Ville which he planned to send to Tony Hughes.

Normally, none of the promoters of the Sha Na Na concerts had much to do with Lee, his being just the opening act and not selling any seats in the house. His main purpose on the tour was to provide a pause between shows so the promoter could sell drinks, hotdogs and tour posters. But shortly after he arrived backstage at the New Haven venue, he was surprised to see Ron Delsner, who was promoting all the shows in the greater New York area, standing at his dressing room door looking very nervous indeed.

"Lee, right now there's an IRS agent in my office who wants to speak to you and I hope you know what this is about because I want that *fucking* guy out of my *fucking* office as soon as possible. You understand? Here, he gave me his card."

Ron Delsener handed it to him, holding it by two fingers, like it was a contagious disease. The card said *Kenneth O'Connor* with a downtown New York address.

Lee thought for a moment and then it clicked. "Oh yeah, I know him," said Lee. "His brother is a friend of mine."

"He's all yours, I'll have him brought down to you. And please, Lee, don't even mention my name to him, OK? If he asks you who the promoter is you say you don't know. Better yet, tell him it's Bill Graham."

"OK, Mr. Delsener, don't worry, it's not a problem. I don't think he's here to talk about you."

"So my heart can start beating normal again?" said Ron.

"I think so," said Lee.

In minutes, Ken O'Connor was shown to Lee's tiny dressing room. Ken walked in, looking around intently at everything there, from Lee's open guitar case to the backstage pass stuck on his coat, obviously very excited to be backstage at a real rock concert.

"None of the guys from Sha Na Na here?" asked Ken. "This must be kind of small for all of you, must be nine or ten guys in that band."

"This dressing room is just for me, Ken, they got their own dressing room, it's a lot bigger," said Lee. "But I think they're about to sound check anyway."

"Sound check?" asked Ken.

"It's like a rehearsal, make sure all the gear works."

"Oh, sure ... well, I'd love to meet those guys if I can, I still remember them from Woodstock. Christ, they put on one hell of a show, guys doing splits like James Brown and all of them really top-notch singers."

"You were at Woodstock, Ken, standing in the rain with the rest of the hippies?"

"You kidding? Me a *hippie*? I was studying my ass off at Queens College, getting my accounting degree. Never been to a rock festival in my life. I was talking about the movie *Woodstock;* my wife and I went into the city to see that film when it came out. And for me, Sha Na Na was definitely the best band in the film."

"Crosby, Stills and Nash weren't bad either," said Lee. "And it was their first gig."

"Don't remember them. But at least Sha Na Na played some songs I'd heard before."

"What about the "Star Spangled Banner" by Jimi Hendrix?"

Ken smiled. "I know I'm a square, Lee, you don't have to rub it in. I didn't come up here to talk about music. In fact, I bet you're wondering what the hell I am doing up here in New Haven, standing in your dressing room. I think your promoter freaked out when I showed him my IRS card. Only way I could get back here."

"If you came to see the show," said Lee. "You're early."

"I didn't come here for the show, Lee ... Truth is, I drove up here to talk to you about Danny. You see, I called JP's last week and someone told me you were on tour with Sha Na Na, wouldn't be coming back for months so I tracked you down, waited until you got within driving distance from New York, and here I am."

"What's up with Danny?" asked Lee. "Did something happen?"

"No, he's okay for the time being but I'm very concerned. In fact, I'm really worried."

"About what?"

"Mind if I sit down?" Lee cleared some clothing and his guitar case from the sofa and made room for the two of them to sit.

"You know I've been working for the IRS for a while," said Ken.

"Yeah, Danny told me something about it. Nothing wrong with that."

"I know he likes to make fun of me for that, but it's just my job, you know, it's how I support my family. Nothing wrong with that, huh? It's really a good job and could have a great future."

Lee nodded. "Yeah, he told me. Nothing wrong with that," he repeated.

"So, Lee, because of my job with the IRS I want to tell you right off that there's some stuff I can tell you now and there's some stuff I can't. Like I can't tell you how I know all this, but, believe me, I know it."

"All of *what*? Tell me, *what?*" asked Lee.

"OK, here it is, Lee. As you know, Danny is working at this place called Madame Rue's, some kind of disco and after-hours club, been working there since the summer, since you guys came back from the Hamptons. And what I know for certain is that this place, this Madame Rue's, is clearly run by the mob, by one of the *families*, bad guys who kill people all the time, we've got proof of that. And I don't mean they're taking a little kickback or protection money or something. I mean they're directly involved. In fact, the whole club is a front for illegal activities; they use it for money laundering from selling narcotics, gambling, grand auto theft, you name it."

"If they're doing all that down at Madame Rue's then why don't they get busted?"

"I'm not in *enforcement,* Lee, and they have their own agenda to follow, but I do have friends working there, *close friends*, and they tell me Danny's name is coming up all over the tapes."

"The tapes?" asked Lee. "What tapes?"

"Can't tell you that and don't ask me, but there's a whole slew of agencies interested in this wise guy, *Maddy the Horse*, who's running Madame Rue's for the mob. When the bust goes down, and believe me, it will sooner or later, it's not going to be just the IRS on their ass. It's going to be a major operation with every enforcement agency in this city trying to get credit and the net will be cast very wide and I don't want Danny getting locked up with all these guys and ruining his life."

"But, Ken, I don't think Danny is involved in any of that kind of stuff, illegal stuff. He's more like a glorified errand boy. At least that's what he told me."

"I don't think so either, but he's being used by these thugs and he's doing this creep *Maddy the Horse* favors. Danny's at that club every night until closing and he's not stupid, he knows what's happening, and those wise guys, these criminals, they don't like having witnesses around who aren't one of them, who can testify in court. And I hear that Maddy is some kind of psychopath, capable of anything. And it won't be any easier for Danny with the Feds breathing down his back because they're going to threaten him with jail time, squeeze him hard, and make him cooperate. I'm telling you; anything could happen."

"Shit," said Lee. "Did you tell him all of this?"

"Whenever I bring it up, he finds a reason to walk out of the house. I can't really talk to my brother about this, Lee. He just gets pissed off at me. Maybe I was too tough on him when we were kids, but you know with both parents gone and him running wild, I had to put my foot down."

"Both of Danny's parents are gone?" asked Lee. "I didn't know that."

"Long story," said Ken. "Dad went first, not even forty, cirrhosis of the liver, the *Irish virus,* never passed a bar he couldn't find an excuse to drop in, have a taste. And then mom just kind of gave up and ... like I said, long story."

"Sorry," was all Lee could say.

"That's all ancient history, as far as I'm concerned. I'm married, love my wife, love my kids, got a good job – not complaining. Losing dad and mom, let's just say I got past it. But I don't think Danny ever did. There's something inside of him that's still really hurting, something that pushes him away from me and toward all the wrong decisions. But maybe you could say something. You know he's my brother, but he looks up to you a lot more than me, Lee. We never really connected," Ken said sadly. "Not as close as we should be – probably my fault."

"I don't know what I can do, Ken. Sure, I could say something to him but I don't know if he'll listen to me anymore than you."

"It would mean a lot to me and my wife," said Ken. "We're all the family Danny's got. And family is everything as I'm sure you know."

I'm the last guy to talk about family, thought Lee. "Listen, Ken, when the show comes to New York I'll give Danny a call and we'll get together, have a talk, and I'll tell him to get out of Madame Rue's, but I don't know if that will work any better. Maybe he'll walk out on me, too."

"Thanks, Lee," said Ken. "That's all I'm asking. I just want him to hear it from you. And just don't tell him where it came from, OK? This is all between you and me."

"Don't worry," said Lee.

Ken O'Connor stood up, apologized that he couldn't stay for the show and shook hands formally.

"One other thing I wanted to ask you, Lee. Do you know who this guy Ray Arthur is?"

"Not really," Lee lied. "Why?"

"Nothing to do with you," said Ken. "But his name is coming up an awful lot on the tapes too, they say he's some kind of big shot in the music business."

"He's involved too?"

"Up to his ass," said Ken, as he started to leave the dressing room. At the door he turned to Lee.

"Tell me one thing; Danny never did meet John Lennon did he?"

Lee smiled. "Yeah, he did, Ken. I was right there with him. Danny spoke to him."

"Holy shit," said Ken. "I guess that's something."

"Yeah, it was really something," said Lee.

After the New Haven show the Sha Na Na tour moved west into upstate New York - Buffalo, Syracuse and finally Albany, where just after his forty-minute set ended the production manager called Lee into his office to take a waiting call. A call from Wes Edel.

"Are you just off the stage?" asked Wes.

"Yeah, maybe five minutes ago. Still carrying my guitar."

"How'd it go, Lee? Good response?"

"Yeah, went great, Wes. Closer we get to New York, the better the audience. Glad to be out of those hockey arenas."

"Good, happy to hear it, Lee ... didn't want to call you before you went on."

"Why's that?"

"Because Albany is about as close as you're gonna get to New York on this tour."

"Why's that?" Lee repeated.

"Because the tour is over."

"What's over?" asked Lee. "The Sha Na Na tour is over? They're doing great business. Why's it over?"

"The Sha Na Na tour is not over," said Wes awkwardly. "But Lee Franklin being the opening act for the Sha Na Na tour is over after tonight," said Wes.

"Why's that?" Lee said for a third time.

"Say that again and you got the chorus for a new song. Glad you had a good show tonight, Lee, always good to go out on a high note, leave them wanting more, that's what I say. So now you're leaving them a lot more." Wes laughed. "That's funny, I should have been a comedian."

Lee didn't laugh. "Out?" he asked stunned.

"*Out* as in I'm not underwriting a tour for an artist who's not even on my own goddamn label. *Out* as in that son of a bitch Ray Arthur has been spending my money like it's a free candy story. *Out* as in ..." Wes searched for another analogy but couldn't come up with anything.

"Out as in goodbye," said Lee.

"You're the songwriter," said Wes. "No insult to your talent."

"So, what do I do now, Wes?"

"Get that damn Cadillac back to Hertz...and send me your next demo."

"Thanks for your interest," said Lee ironically. "Does Ray know?"

"Ray Arthur no longer works for Edel Records," said Wes adamantly. "I fired his ass last week and cleared out his office, that *schmuck*. He should thank me for not calling the cops, there was some shit in his drawers ... I don't want to talk too much about that over the phone."

"I don't get it, Wes, didn't you tell me that I should open for one of your acts?"

"That I did and I'm a man of my word. But Sha Na Na is not one of my acts, so I don't know what the fuck you're doing on that tour or why I'm paying for it."

"It was all Ray's idea."

"Fucking Ray. And he had me believing that he had *ears*. You should thank me for getting you off this tour. What business does a singer-songwriter have opening for Sha Na Na?"

"That's what I said to Ray."

"One other thing, Lee. What about all this *float* you've been signing receipts for. There's a couple of grand in unaccounted expenses."

"The only money I got was from the promoters," said Lee. "Ray had me sign them; I don't know why."

"Guess what?" said Wes.

"What?" asked Lee.

"I believe you."

"So, I stay on the tour?"

"I said I believe you're not a thief like fucking Ray Arthur. But you're off the tour."

"Starting when?" asked Lee.

"Starting when I hang up the phone," said Wes. "Give me a call when you're back in town, when all of this has blown over. I'll take you to lunch, ever been to the Stage Deli?"

CHAPTER 22

Lee left the Sha Na Na tour in Albany the next day, checked out of his Holiday Inn and drove straight down to New York City, first calling JP from a roadside diner to see what he was coming home to.

"As long as I don't hear anything different from Ms. Langdon the apartment is still yours, pal," said JP.

"Thanks," said Lee.

"Don't thank me," said JP. "You gonna be in town for a while. Should I book some shows? Put you back on the calendar? You know people have been asking for you. Even Billy Joel was wondering where you disappeared to."

"Really?"

"You got fans, pal, better get back here. First rule of show business – if you want to be missed ..."

"Then you got to go away," finished Lee.

Lee dropped off the rented Cadillac at Hertz on East 48th Street, took a taxi up to JP's where he lugged his guitar and bags up the stairs to his apartment and plopped down on his bed. For some reason, he was not as down as he thought he might be, didn't miss the tour, glad to be in his own bed. Mostly, he was excited about the possibility of seeing Lexi Langdon again, although he had no idea when that would be or how he could make it happen. But against all odds, he believed it would happen and he had decided that when he did see her again, he would keep it light, no pressure and hope the spark was still there. Until then he would bide his time.

Being back in the city only buoyed his good mood, like this was the beginning of a new cycle for him and he felt a renewed sense of purpose. He'd been thrown off the tour, but Wes Edel left a door open for him, wanted to hear his demo... May was just beginning and Manhattan looked like it had been shined up and restored for the spring. Winter's gray piles of snow and the slushy smell of bus fumes had vanished, and trees were blossoming all over town. Central Park was green and welcoming again. And a new crop of cute young girls had sprouted as well, walking the wide avenues in miniskirts, talking enthusiastically to friends in groups of three and four and smiling at Lee when he passed, usually walking alone with no place to go but out and about the city. It all felt good and if there was a purpose to spring's renewing spirit, Lee was in sync with it this time. *Taking the bait again*, thought Lee cynically, floating high on pure unjustified optimism, where *anything was possible*. Once more he was sure he was where he should be even if Doctor John's New Orleans funk single, "Right Time, Wrong Place," had been topping *Billboard's Hot 100* charts and voodoo was in the air, even this far north.

In retrospect, even the Sha Na Na tour didn't feel so terrible. Ray Arthur might have used Lee to steal money from *Edel Records* to support his coke habit but not from Lee himself and true to Ray's word, he had gotten paid after every show. Not a fortune but he did come home with a fair amount of cash in his pocket, enough to take Lexi out to dinner when - and if - he saw her. That would be a novel experience, him picking up the check, but at least he was back, closer to Lexi, just blocks away on Fifth Avenue. Seeing Lexi was all he really cared about, he knew that now more than ever. There was no place else to go, *no direction home*.

JP had greeted him like an old friend, saying he could start gigging at the club whenever he wanted. "But please, no gold lamé outfits," he joked, more than once. His apartment had awaited his return, nothing had changed, and weeks went by until finally, Lee got sick of waiting by the phone. As a rule, he wouldn't call Lexi at her apartment, afraid that Ray might pick up, but at this point, he reasoned, what did he have to lose. Trying to pick a time when Lexi probably would be home and Ray probably not, he called that evening around seven and was very relieved when Armando answered the phone.

"Hello, Mr. Franklin," the butler said politely.

"Is Lexi there ... by chance?" asked Lee awkwardly.

"No, sir, Ms. Langdon won't be back until the end of the month."

"Do you know where she is?"

"She's gone to Houston and then St. Lucia to visit cousins, I believe. But Mr. Arthur is here, you want to speak to him?"

Lee was about to say *no* when he heard Ray's voice in the background coming ever closer. "Somebody's calling? Who's that, Armando?"

Armando replied, "It's Mr. Franklin ..."

"Well, then you can pass it to me," said Ray, mistakenly thinking Lee was calling for him. "Already tried me at the office?" he said to Lee. "I should sue that bastard Wes Edel."

"In fact, I didn't," said Lee. "Thought it would be better to call you at home. I guess you know I'm off the tour. Wes called me in Albany right after my last show."

"Then I guess you know I'm not working with Edel Records anymore," said Ray. "So, we're even."

"Yeah, Wes told me. So, what happened? Although it's none of my business if you don't want to ..."

"I'll tell you exactly what the fuck happened," interjected Ray venomously. "What happened is that I finally woke up and realized that I was doing all the goddamn work while Wes was taking home all the goddamn money. So fuck that, and him too! Now I got some guys with real money, silent partners, ready to back me on my own label, who will let me do things my way."

"So you're saying you quit?" asked Lee. "That's not exactly the way Wes put it."

"Well, Wes can put it up his ass for all I care."

"What about that business with the *float?*" asked Lee.

"More Wes Edel bullshit," said Ray. "Listen, Lee, we should talk. Lexi's not here, she's on some fucking island working on her fucking tan, left me here with her butler and not much else. I don't know what's her problem. But we can get together without her, huh? Is that allowed, Lee?" Ray laughed too hard, too long. "Come down to Madame Rue's tonight, before midnight or else it gets too crazy. James Elliot is coming by and of course your *manager* Danny will be there."

"So, Danny's still working at Madame Rue's?"

"When he's not managing your career," said Ray, laughing again. "I did more for your career in one phone call than Danny O'Connor will ever do."

"Right," said Lee. "How do I get past the bouncers? Past that huge transvestite?"

"Tell them you're a friend of mine."

"Does that work now?" asked Lee.

"Very funny," said Ray, not amused.

When Lee dutifully arrived at Madame Rue's before midnight, already a sizable crowd milled outside the club's entrance, held back by red velvet ropes hooked to chrome stands, desperately calling out Stanley's name, beseeching him to let them in. When Lee pushed his way to the front and asked for Ray, saying he was on Ray's personal list, the bouncers said they didn't know shit about any list, that Ray wasn't even there yet, and told him to wait on the side, not to crowd the door and turned their backs to him. When Lee insisted they should let him in, *Madame Rue* herself, in the imposing form of Stanley, the *grande dame* transvestite, outlandishly decked out in a short blonde wig, white chiffon pleated dress and matching heels, confronted him. *She* towered over Lee.

"Do you know who I am?"

"Marilyn Monroe in *The Seven Year Itch*?"

"Good boy," said Stanley lightening up a notch or two. "That gets you a few points, darling, but can you imagine how many people tell me they're a friend of Ray's, trying to get past me and into *my* club? Ray Arthur has got too many friends for an *exclusive* club. Sorry."

At Stanley's feet, aimed right up his legs, was a strong fan, controlled by foot switch, but each time he hit it the dress blew up way over his head and almost knocked his wig off. Not the desired effect at all.

"See what I mean? This was Ray's fucking idea," said Stanley. "And each time I turn it on my balls start hanging out. Asshole."

"Listen, I'm really more Danny O'Connor's friend than Ray's," said Lee.

Stanley smiled as he unhooked the red velvet barrier to let Lee pass. "Danny's a good kid," he said. "You should have said that up front. He's the only real man in this dump, besides *me* that is."

Dressed in a nice Armani suit and silk tie, reeking of Halston cologne, Danny was busy stocking the front bar with liquor. Lee leaned over the bar.

"Jesus, I could smell you when I walked in," said Lee.

Danny spun around. "Lee Franklin," he exclaimed. "Mr. Sha Na Na himself! Where's the gold lamé jacket?"

"Do you know how many times I've heard that?"

"So how did it go? They ask you to join the group?"

"Yeah," said Lee. "I'm the new Bowzer."

"So, Ray did you a real solid, eh? Got you out of the clubs and out on the road playing arenas?"

"Yeah, Ray got me out there and it's his fault I'm off of it now."

"What happened?"

"Turned out Wes Edel knew nothing about it and when he found out he flipped." said Lee. "And Ray was doing something funny with the accounting – I don't even want to know about it."

"I heard something went down with Ray and Wes Edel. So, when Ray left Edel Records I guess Wes pulled the plug on you, huh?" said Danny. "I'm not surprised."

"Ray didn't leave Edel Records, Danny, he got his ass fired. I think Wes caught him with his hand in the *cookie jar* or something."

"Typical Ray Arthur bullshit," said Danny with a smirk on his face. "He told everyone around here that he quit, that he's starting his own label and that Maddy's niece Gloria was gonna be his first signing. I think he's starting to believe his own bullshit."

"Answer me one thing, Danny?"

"You got it."

"Where'd you get that *perfume?* You put on the whole bottle or what?"

"Halston gave it to me himself, said I'm a good kid and that if I was six inches taller, I could model his clothes. I'll give you a bottle, he gave me six."

"I think you're wearing enough for both of us."

"So, what are you gonna do now, Lee?"

"I'm back at JPs, same old, same old. Listen, I know you're working now, but I really want to get together and talk sometime."

Danny smiled. "Don't worry, Lee, I'm still your manager, I'm working on something big for us."

"It's not just that, not just about *my* career," said Lee, looking around the club and already noticing a few guys in ill-fitting suits standing around, looking tough, not smiling, not partying.

"Hey, Danny," he said discreetly. "All these guys hanging around here, who are they?"

"Beats me," said Danny. "Sometimes, you don't want to know."

"You should come up to my place sometime, have a few beers. What about tomorrow afternoon? Stop by before you come down here?"

"Yeah, that's cool."

"Things still going strong with Kathy?" asked Lee, feeling a tinge of envy. "That last summer really started something."

"Best thing that ever happened to me," said Danny. "She's turned my life around completely. Wait until you hear about these plans we're making. I'll see if she's free tomorrow afternoon, she can come with me."

"Yeah, I want to hear all about that ... but tomorrow, you know, let's just make it me and you. Really, there's some serious stuff ..."

Ray and James Elliott entered the club, spotted Lee and Danny talking and Ray pointed them to his regular perch near the end of the bar.

"Danny, get us a couple of cold beers, will ya?" said Ray. "Or better yet, cold vodka – got any iced Stoli back there?"

"You got it," said Danny, opening the fridge behind him.

"Good," said Ray, as he scooted off, the pupils in his eyes as big as saucers. "I'll be right back, guys."

"What's up with Ray?" asked Lee. "Man, the guy hardly said hello."

"Elementary, *my dear Watson*," said James Elliot, tapping his nose. "We had dinner at PJ Clarke's or at least I did, Ray didn't touch his food, spent more time in the men's room than sitting at the table. Truth is, he hasn't been in a good way since Lexi went to the Caribbean and I don't mean like he's *pining* over her, more like partying non-stop with the *dawn-patrol*. Losing his gig at Edel Records might just have pushed Ray over the edge."

Ray returned even more coked up, lips twitching, clenching his jaw and with a cannibal look in his eye every time an attractive woman walked by. He spoke in a dry whisper and couldn't look Lee or James Elliot straight in the eye as they tried to follow his jagged conversation. Ray was in high paranoid mode, his eyes darting everywhere when he felt the thump of a firm tap on his shoulder. He literally jumped and swung around, startled to see Junior standing right there, inches from his face, not happy.

"Maddy wants to see you," said Junior.

"Tell him I'll be down in a minute," said Ray. "Just having a drink with my friends here."

"Why don't you tell him that yourself, Ray?" asked Junior. "That Maddy should fucking wait for you while you're up here at the bar shooting the shit with your buddies?"

Ray paused, looked at Junior. "Okay, so, where is he?"

"Down in the office, where he always is," said Junior. "Waiting for you."

Ray turned to Lee. "Give me a few minutes with Maddy, let me see what's up with him, we'll talk later. You guys finish your drinks, relax, and come downstairs when you're done. Anybody like to shoot pool?"

The office of Madame Rue's was a padlocked, windowless storage room where crates of liquor were piled on sagging shelves. A Pirelli Tire calendar hung on the wall, different shapely models in a skimpy bikini decorating each month, although the calendar was still open to December of 1975, already many months out of date. At the far end of the airless room stood a small pool table, cues and balls scattered around on green felt covered with dust. Maddy was leaning on a steel desk with an empty Scotch tape dispenser on it, picking his teeth with a letter opener when Ray walked in. Junior, who was following right behind, shut the door loudly and stood stiffly in front of it, arms folded across his chest.

"Hey, Maddy, what's up?" said Ray cheerfully. "Junior said you wanted to see me about something so, you know me, I dropped everything and came right down. It's getting busy up there, gonna be a good night, you can feel things buzzing already. Better get back up and keep an eye on ...uh, the store."

Maddy said nothing and continued picking his teeth while Ray grew more and more uncomfortable, finally turning his head to see Junior blocking the door.

"Couple of my pals are upstairs," said Ray. "I told them to come down when they finish their drinks."

"Nobody comes in until I say so," said Maddy, and Junior nodded.

Ray looked around nervously. "Hey, guys, we gotta fix this office up. Hottest club in town and we're using this ... what ... storage space for our office. Christ, that calendar is from last year. Know anybody with some furniture, Junior?"

Dropping the letter opener on the desk, Maddy turned around and studied the calendar on the wall, flipping through the months with his thick fingers, nails manicured and polished.

"No new calendar because Pirelli stopped making them," he said humorlessly. "Oil crisis or some shit. Who looks at the dates anyway? It's the tits and ass that sell these things." He stared closely at the month of March. "Nice knockers on this one." He let go of the calendar and sat down heavily on top of the desk. "Something wrong with this office, Ray? You want to change something? Not classy enough for a guy like you?"

"Well, I mean, to begin with, look at that desk, Maddy. Looks like something a school principal would sit at while he's handing out detentions." He laughed uneasily. "And the freakin' chair there – I wouldn't sit on it if I were you - the back's about to fall off. I don't know how Manny sits on it. He stays down here for hours doing the books and sits on that fucking chair. Man must have no backbone left."

"Manny says the chair is not the problem," said Maddy. "And Manny likes this desk, says if the office is too comfortable and the secretaries too good-looking, then when those bastards from the IRS show up, they'll want to hang out all day."

"So, Manny's an accountant, not an interior decorator – what does he know? The guy must weigh 250 pounds anyway, maybe it was him that broke the freakin' chair."

"Manny didn't break goddamn nothing, Ray," said Maddy standing up. "But Manny told me we got a problem here."

"If Manny's got a problem, why doesn't he come to me?" asked Ray tensely. "I'm the, uh, manager here."

"Manny doesn't come to you because Manny says you're the fucking problem."

Ray sucked his teeth and bobbed his head. "Me? I don't have any problems."

"Manny says the books don't add up," said Maddy. "Says they haven't added up for a while."

"Well," Ray said as calmly as he could. "They're not supposed to ... really, I mean, Maddy, you take your cut off the top from all the cash at the bar so, of course, the books aren't going to, as you say, *add up*. You know we're bringing in a lot more than what's showing up on Manny's ledgers. That's no secret among us, right?" He laughed and looked back at Junior who hadn't moved. "So what else is new? I mean ... business as usual!" Ray laughed again and Maddy kept staring at him.

"Yeah, I know that, Ray, and Manny knows that and even fucking Junior here knows that. But there's something that you don't seem to know."

"What's that?" said Ray quietly. "What don't I know?"

There was a moment of pure silence, like everything stood still, no sound of traffic or subways or the club upstairs. The only sound Ray could hear was Junior sucking in breaths behind him. Then Maddy the Horse bellowed at the top of his lungs. "I'll tell you what you don't fucking know! There's only one skimmer here, Ray! And it's me."

Ray, knocked back by the force of Maddy's voice, bumped into Junior who bruskly pushed him back to his place.

"Sure, I know that, Maddy - you're the boss," said Ray as he tried to regain his footing. "Everybody knows you're the boss. I'm just the front man, I may sign the checks but you're the boss here, Maddy. It's your investment I'm protecting here. Believe me, I never forget that."

"Investment? What the fuck do you think? Does this look like fucking *Wall Street* to you? This is the Lower East Side, you moron."

"I just meant that I'm not really the one running the business here or taking care of the money for that matter." Ray spoke fast, like his mouth was running in place. "I tell you, some nights, I can hardly get past Stanley or *Madame Rue* – whatever the fuck you call him – standing out front. He just ignores me - I'm kind of the invisible man here ..."

Maddy moved closer to Ray, now just inches away, pinning him between Junior and himself and staring him down. Ray shut up and stood still, his hands trembling.

"You're not invisible, you scumbag, and you've been taking cash out of the register and putting it in your pocket or whatever the fuck you do with it. You think I don't know, but I do. Your fucking coke habit is outta control and now you're losing at the track, heavy. What do you think, you can keep secrets from me? And you're even late on your fucking car payments!"

"Car payments?" said Ray. "I thought you gave me that BMW?"

Maddy looked to Junior. "Now he thinks I'm Santa Claus. Free car, free money ..."

"I can explain all of that," said Ray.

"I'm sure you can, Ray, you're a smart fucking guy. I'm sure you can explain your way out of any fucking thing you want to. So maybe you can explain something else to me, just so I understand."

"What? Explain what?"

"Explain to me why I shouldn't kill you for stealing from me?" said Maddy dead seriously. "Got an explanation for that?"

Ray looked around at the blank concrete walls surrounding him and began to hyperventilate for the first time in his life. "Maddy, come on - this is not a big deal," he said between forced breaths. "I didn't understand about the car. There's no problem, really, I'm gonna make everything right ..."

"Answer the fucking question," said Maddy.

"OK," said Ray. "Right ... what's the question?"

"Tell him the question, Junior."

"The question is why Maddy shouldn't kill your fucking ass for stealing from him?"

"Right," said Ray. "Right ... why you shouldn't kill me ..." He tried to smile but his lips were trembling. "How about because I'm your friend, Maddy? And friends don't kill each other over business ... they negotiate. I swear, I have not been stealing from you, Maddy. I give you my word."

Junior giggled, even Maddy snorted up a laugh and for the briefest moment Ray thought everything was cool, that maybe he'd handled these guys better than he'd feared and soon he'd be back at the bar flirting with Gloria, drinking vodka with James Elliot and Lee Franklin and taking out what was left of the cocaine in his pocket. Really, he would have liked to take that little bottle out now, take a few quick hits, get his head together, stop shaking and feeling like he was gonna pee in his pants. Maybe even offer some to Maddy and Junior, but he didn't think that was a good idea even if he *badly* wanted a few lines himself. Above all, he needed to stay cool and not piss these guys off, no telling what they might do if they got really angry. He knew guys like Maddy and Junior killed people, but he thought they only killed *each other*, guys like themselves, bad guys. But then he realized that maybe he was one of the bad guys too and it was the first time that thought had ever occurred to him.

Ray looked behind him and saw that Junior was smiling too, but he didn't like the way Junior was smiling with a deranged look in his eyes, like he was excited about what was to come next, something Ray thought he wouldn't like at all. His heart was racing like it was going to explode and he began to panic, looking for something to hold on to, to steady himself, afraid he might keel over right there.

"Yeah, Ray," said Maddy. "Because I like you, that's it. How come I didn't fucking think of that? What do you say we just shake hands on it, that you'll make everything right when you have a chance." He held out his hand. "You're my friend, right? Everyone wants to be my friend, don't they, Junior?"

Junior kept sniggering in a low growl, like he'd seen this movie before and couldn't wait to get to the ending again because that was his favorite part. Timidly, Ray put forward his own hand and Maddy grabbed it in his and the smiles disappeared from both of their faces.

Maddy's hand was fat, gold rings nearly disappearing into the folds of skin around them. When he started squeezing Ray's hand his eyes went dead and black as a shark and he kept squeezing it harder and harder.

"OK," groaned Ray, trying to pull Maddy's hand away from his own before Junior grabbed Ray's other arm and forced it high behind his back and held it there. "Jesus, Maddy, you're crushing my fucking hand. Come on ... for Christ's sake! You win, take the goddamn car, whatever the fuck you want – just tell me how much you want, and I'll pay you." Then Ray started crying.

Slowly, Maddy began to pull Ray's hand down toward the floor, like they were engaged in some kind of one-armed wrestling match. Ray was on one knee now and Junior, who still had Ray's other hand twisted behind him, put his own arm around Ray's neck in a *hammer-lock* while putting on more and more pressure with a demonic smile.

"Come on, guys! Christ, Maddy! This isn't funny," Ray cried, the words coming out in short painful gasps. "Give me a ... fucking ...chance ..."

"You shut the fuck up and listen to me, you fucking country club prick. You think you're my friend? I've killed guys that I loved like brothers, stuck ice picks right into their fucking brains. You think I give a shit? You're nothing to me. I'll leave your fucking ass rotting in some Jersey swamp and I won't even remember your name the next day! Nobody fucks with me and walks away."

Ray was crying. "OK! OK! What do you want?"

"I want a hundred grand by July fourth. That's what Manny says is missing and that's what you're gonna pay me on that day or the last July 4th firecracker you're gonna hear is my fucking piece blowing a hole in your head."

"Manny's made a mistake," said Ray. "I haven't taken a fucking hundred grand. He's out of his fucking mind! How would I take that kind of money?"

"You probably put most of it up your nose, you prick. Manny doesn't make mistakes, so if that's what he says you owe me then that's what you're gonna pay me and if you want to walk out of this room, I don't want to hear any shit from you denying it."

"I don't have a hundred grand," said Ray.

"Your wife has got that in spades."

"My wife hates my guts."

Maddy, over Ray's shoulder, looked to Junior.

"Junior, Ray says he doesn't have any fucking money. But I think he's holding out on us? What do you think?"

"I think he's a scumbag, Maddy," said Junior, twisting Ray's arm even more while cutting off his breath. "I think he needs to be taught a fucking lesson, that's what I think."

Maddy put his face just inches from Ray's own. "Diamonds, Ray, she's got diamonds, what do they call it ... Diamonds by the Yard. They sell 'em at Tiffany and she's got the biggest one they ever made. A fucking gold necklace covered with big fucking diamonds. It's like a goddamn rope around her neck, I saw it myself when you brought her around here."

"But I can't get that necklace, Maddy. Lexi hardly ever takes it off ..."

Maddy squeezed Ray's hand harder and Ray screamed in pain. "You gonna break my hand, Maddy?" Ray was sobbing. "For God's sake, stop please!"

"I can break his arm if you want," said Junior. He took his arm from Ray's neck and put his hand inside his jacket, touching the butt of his pistol while he twisted and bent Ray's arm high up on his back. "Or worse if you want. Just give me the word, Maddy. I don't give a fuck."

Maddy hesitated, looking straight at Junior without blinking. Then slowly, a smile returned to his face and he let go of Ray's hand and stepped away from him, twisting each gold ring on his fingers.

"Let go of him," said Maddy. I don't want him in the hospital or in the fucking morgue either. He's got work to do." He looked at Ray. "We got a deal, Ray, huh? You get that for me and we're even."

Junior let Ray's other hand free and stepped back. Ray collapsed on his knees, holding his aching hand and sobbing. There was a knock on the door and Junior opened it slightly, peering through the crack and saying nothing before pushing it shut again.

"It's his friends." Junior said to Maddy. "The spade and some other guy. What should I tell them?"

"Get up off the floor, you cunt," Maddy said to Ray. "Your friends are coming in. You want them to see you like this, crying like a fucking baby? Don't you have any pride, Ray?"

Ray struggled to his feet, straightened his tie, adjusted his jacket and wiped tears from his eyes. Maddy gave a sign and Junior opened the door. James Elliot walked in cautiously with Lee Franklin right behind him. The room smelled of fear.

"What's going on, guys?" said James Elliot, spying the billiard table in the corner. "Shooting pool?"

"Nothing going on," said Ray, his voice cracking. "Maddy and I just, uh, talking some business, that's all."

Lee remained silent and fixed his gaze on Ray. He had never seen him like this before, pale and shaken, scared shitless with his normal bravado nowhere in sight. Something bad had gone down, Lee could sense that even if he didn't know exactly what it was. Ray was cradling his hand, Junior standing at the door, his gun visible, stuck in the top of his pants and Maddy's face was red with drops of sweat dripping down his thick neck. Lee could see the panic in Ray's eyes and it was unnerving to see him scared like this no matter what he felt about him personally; he couldn't help but pity him. Maddy and Junior were both smirking, puffing their chests out and at that moment Lee understood exactly what Ken O'Connor was warning him about when called them *bad people*. Maddy kept his eyes on Ray, hardly acknowledging their presence.

"So now I'm gonna tell you why I don't kill you this time," said Maddy.

Ray nodded. "Okay," he groaned.

"Because it would break Gloria's heart and she's my niece and I don't want to hear her crying all fucking day."

"Thanks," Ray mumbled. "Guess I should thank Gloria for that."

"Guy's, like you always fuck up, Ray - you wanna know why?"

"Tell me," Ray whispered.

"Cause you're always trying to play it both ways. You're as big a crook as me and you snuck your way into the fuckin' country club set, but it's never gonna work for you 'cause you don't know who the fuck you are. But I always come out on top 'cause I know who the fuck I am."

"Who is that, Maddy?"

Maddy put his face close to Ray's. "I'm the kind of guy you should be very afraid of, that's who I am."

Maddy turned to walk out while Junior held the door open for him, he nodded to Lee and James Elliot but said nothing to them. Suddenly he stopped, pivoting around just as he was nearly out the door of the basement office.

"Give me your fucking piece," he said to Junior who readily obliged. Ray backed against the desk and James Elliot and Lee Franklin stood frozen as Maddy started screaming, waving the gun in the air.

"Let me tell you something else, Ray, shit rains down on the proud!" shouted Maddy. "Like that son of a bitch Jimmy Hoffa. Been gone for what, six months now? You think they're gonna find him someday sitting under a palm tree in Puerto Rico? What do you think, Ray?"

"I don't know," said Ray, terrified.

"You know what - you're just like Hoffa. You're one proud motherfucker. You think you got it made, Ray, with the rich wife from Texas with the mansion out in the Hamptons? You think I can't get to you? Is that what you think, you motherfucker? I'd be doing Gloria a favor by whacking you, but you're too pathetic to shoot." Maddy threw the gun on the pool table and grabbed a pool cue, cracking it in half on his knee. He was holding the heavy end of the cue in both hands and Ray was backed against the desk, trapped, unable to move. Maddy was breathing hard and hesitating, like he was either controlling his rage or deciding where exactly to crack Ray's skull with the butt end of the cue.

Then, calmly and seemingly without fear, James Elliot took a small step forward with his hands in the air and started talking very calmly and just the sound of his voice chilled out the tension in the room. He knew it was his moment to step in, that there was no other way out, even if Junior had his eye on him now with his hand on the gun he lifted from the pool table.

"Say, Maddy, did you ever see that movie *The Hustler*?" asked James Elliot. "That film with Paul Newman and Jackie Gleason playing ... who was it he played?"

Maddy, without looking up at him and still holding the broken pool cue said, "*Fats ... Minnesota Fats*."

"That's it," said James Elliot. "*Minnesota Fats.* Cool name, almost as cool as *Maddy the Horse.* In fact, I can't even remember what Paul Newman's character's name was, but they were both big time pool sharks with serious bets going down. You saw that movie?"

Maddy, still gripping the cue, the whites of his knuckles showing said, "I saw the fucking movie. So what?"

"So ... do you remember who the winner was in that last game of eight ball they played, Maddy?" asked James Elliot. "Was it Paul Newman or Jackie Gleason?"

Maddy kept staring at Ray, the veins in his neck popping out while Ray whimpered, frozen with fear. Then he looked up at James Elliot. "Gleason - *Minnesota Fats* – he was the winner, right? Why the fuck you asking me this now? Who the fuck are you?"

"I'm nobody," said James Elliot. "But I know why Minnesota Fats won that game."

"Get to the fucking point," said Maddy.

"Because Minnesota Fats never lost his cool, Maddy," said James Elliot. "He had class and he kept everything under control. Just like you're gonna do. Because everyone knows that *Maddy the Horse* never loses his cool and that's why he stays on top. That's what I hear them saying when they talk about you. Even up in my neighborhood, you got a name people respect."

Junior started laughing behind Maddy's back. "What the fuck is this spade going on about ..."

Maddy swung around and glared at Junior. "You shut the fuck up." Then he turned to James Elliot. "So, I never lose my cool," said Maddy. "That's what they say about me up in Harlem or wherever the fuck you come from."

"Hundred Twenty-Fifth Street and Amsterdam Avenue," said James Elliot, although he had never lived in Harlem his entire life. "That's what they say about *Maddy the Horse* up there.

Maddy laid the broken butt of the cue on the pool table and got in Ray's face. "Your spade friend there might have saved your ass today, but you're gonna pay me my money, Ray, or next time I'll rip your fucking throat out." Maddy smiled up at James Elliot. "And I'll be very cool when I do it."

"I'm sure you will," agreed James Elliot.

Maddy buttoned up his jacket and walked right out the door without a word with Junior trailing behind. Just as the door was about to slam shut Junior stuck his head back in to say, "Hey, Ray, better remember what Maddy said – there's only one skimmer here and it's me ... I mean it's him. Got that?"

"I got that," hissed Ray.

"Hope so, for your own fucking sake 'cause I'll be keeping a close fucking eye on you."

"I'll keep that in mind."

"Just business, Ray," said Junior. "I'm just taking care of business, nothing personal."

"Business, yeah. Thanks for not breaking my goddamn arm. I can hardly move it! It's gone numb on me."

"I'm your friend, Ray," laughed Junior. "Don't worry, if I wanted to break your arm, I would have made a clean break, couple of weeks in a cast and you'd be like new." He looked at Lee and James Elliot and smiled, and a toothpick appeared, hanging off his bottom lip. "I'm a fucking professional."

Once Maddy and Junior were surely gone, a thick silence filled the room. It was like a ferocious storm had passed, leaving a trail of wreckage and mute survivors. Ray moved around the desk and sat in the broken swivel chair behind it. He reached into his inside jacket pocket and pulled out a small bottle of sparkling white cocaine, swiping the desk top clean with the arm of his jacket and dumping its content on the surface. Then he took a credit card from his wallet, chopped up the pile of white powder and divided it into two thick lines before pulling out a hundred-dollar bill from his pants pocket and rolling it into a short straw. Lee could see Ray's hands trembling as he brought his head down toward the desk, quickly snorting up both lines.

"Maybe go easy on that, Ray," advised James Elliot.

Leaning his head back, feeling the cocaine drip down his throat, he asked, "Why?"

"Why?" said James Elliot. "I'll tell you why, because last time I looked there was a psycho in here waving a gun around like it was going to be the St. Valentines Day's Massacre all over again."

"He wouldn't have used the gun," said Ray. "I don't think they were serious."

"Looked pretty damn serious from where I was standing," said James Elliott. "He was ready to bust that pool cue across your head. Why does Maddy want to kill you? What's going on, why did he mention Lexi? And who's Gloria?" James Elliott shook his head in disbelief. "Man, what kind of deep shit have you gotten yourself into?"

"Gloria is Maddy's niece," said Ray. "She wants to be a singer, came up to hawk her demo at Edel Records and we got kind of ... close." He looked at Lee. "Nothing serious, but I see her sometimes – I'm not sure Maddy likes it. But that's how I met him, through Gloria."

"So that's why he pulled a gun on you? Because you're messing around with his niece?" asked James Elliot. "I don't think so, Ray."

"Well, there's more to it than that," said Ray. "Maddy thinks I'm skimming from the register, accused me of taking a hundred thousand dollars."

"A hundred thousand? That's a lot of money."

"I know it's a lot of money - you think I'm crazy enough to steal from these guys? I think Maddy just wants to fuck me out of my share."

"So what are you going to do now?" asked James Elliot. "How you gonna make all this go away?"

"How the fuck do I know ... I just hope he calms down. I'll speak to Junior – he's a psycho too, but he's not as crazy as Maddy, we hang out sometimes, and even get high together."

Lee remained silent; standing with Ken O'Connor's words going round his head.

"*Bad people*," he said mostly to himself.

"What?" said Ray. "Who are you talking about?"

"I'm talking about the two guys who just left, who were about to really fuck you up, Ray, if James Elliot hadn't stepped in. Man, when I saw that pistol come out it was like everything went into slow motion, like I couldn't move, it was terrifying. I'm telling you, it's not like the movies when there's a real gun in front of you."

"You don't meet guys like that up at JP's?" mocked Ray. "I can handle it."

"These guys are killers, anyone can see that, and you're in deep. I don't want to be there the next time someone pulls a gun. And he mentioned Lexi..." Lee stopped himself.

"I'll take care of my *wife*, Lee," said Ray pointedly. "I don't need you to tell me how to run my life..."

"Well, you need someone to tell you, Ray," said James Elliot. "Didn't seem like your life was running too smoothly a few minutes ago."

"I said I can handle it," said Ray. "Let's get the fuck out of this office. Gives me the creeps."

On the way up the stairs, Ray made a feeble attempt to regain his composure, straightening his tie and taking out a thin black comb and slicking back his hair. The three of them took their place again at the bar, ordering drinks as the cacophony of Madame Rue's blasted forth in full tilt. The club was packed now, and the party was surely on, but they stood apart, traumatized by what had gone down in the basement; they could barely keep the conversation flowing among them. Finding another vial of coke in his pants pocket, Ray fled to the men's room with an edgy wave over his shoulder. Soon, tired of waiting for him to return, James Elliot said he'd lost his urge to party and was calling it a night, asking Lee if he wanted to share a cab. As they pulled in front of the entrance to James Elliot's Greene Street loft, Lee put his hand on James Elliot's shoulder right before he slid out of the cab.

"*The Hustler* - I thought that Paul Newman won that game," said Lee. "Not Jackie Gleason."

"He probably did," said James Elliot. "Never saw the flick myself." He winked and got out of the cab. "See you around, Lee."

Just as the taxi was about to take off, James Elliot stuck his head inside the window again.

"One last thing, Lee," he said. "Keep an eye on Lexi."

"Why would I keep an eye on Lexi?" asked Lee.

"Well, a couple of months ago Ray asked me why I brought you up to her apartment with me while he was away somewhere."

"What did you say?"

"I covered your ass," said James Elliot. "Said we were hanging out at JP's that night, dropped by for a drink with Lexi. That's all."

"What did Ray say?"

"What could he say? He believed me. But he asked me if you brought a guitar with you that night."

"Brought a guitar? What'd you say?"

"Well, I figured if he mentioned a guitar then Lexi must have mentioned a guitar, so I said, of course you did and you played us some sweet music. But he smelled something was up because he said he was gonna get you out of the picture for a while."

"Wow! Sha Na Na – I get it."

"You catch on fast," said James Elliot, "for a white boy." He walked away from the taxi, laughing up to the doorway of his building. Lee shifted over to the other side of the cab.

"Thanks for that!" he yelled out. James Elliot didn't even turn around, didn't show Lee that he was smiling, just held two fingers up in the air behind him over his shoulder in a *Victory* sign.

CHAPTER 23

Things happen like that, thought Lee, everything at the same time, people coming back into your life. Months go by, nobody seems to know you and then there you are, right back in the thick of it. Like when he'd been sitting in that cell in Rome for weeks, waiting for someone to notice he'd been arrested. The police had said that the U.S. Embassy would be notified in due time and probably someone from the consulate would come by to see him. But a month had gone by and nothing, not a word. He was sharing his cell with an Afghani, Merad, also in there for smuggling hashish, although a lot more than Lee's amateur caper. He didn't know if the cops had done that on purpose, maybe they were listening in to his twelve by twelve cell; see if they could come up with any conspiracy between the two of them.

Finally, nearly six weeks after he was picked up in Campo di Fiori, a U.S. official did make an early morning appearance. There was a loud banging of a baton on his cell door and Lee was told to wake up, get his ass out of bed, somebody to see him.

"From the U.S. Embassy?" he asked.

"President Nixon himself," replied the guard. Guards speak English?

"Vaffanculo, stronzo," said Lee under his breath.

The guard stopped, about to whack him with the baton, but he broke out laughing instead.

"When you curse in Italian, it's funny. But next time I hit you where it hurts it won't be so funny."

The government guy didn't have much advice, mostly asking Lee his family information; said he'd contact them and then it would be up to them to decide what they wanted to do. The consulate could recommend an Italian lawyer but wouldn't pay for it. When Lee asked what would happen if he couldn't afford a lawyer, the embassy guy told him that then he'd wished he'd been arrested in America. When he asked how much this was all going to cost, the guy asked if his parents had a house, and Lee nodded his head. "Good," he said. "They'll be taking out a second mortgage."

And then, another two weeks of waiting before an Italian lawyer showed up, met him for ten minutes, gave him his card, said his stepfather had hired him. Asked if they were treating him all right in the jail. So far, said Lee. The lawyer said that was a good sign and asked him who his cellmate was and when Lee told him Merzad's name, the lawyer nodded gravely and told him to stay close to that man, he could protect him. So, Lee got to know his cellmate Merzad, who taught him about the ancient tribal system of Afghanistan, explaining his father was a chief and that his family had been smuggling hashish into Europe for years. When Lee asked why he got busted, Merzad blamed it on the new Afghani government headed by a prince who was calling himself President. They got me right off the plane, *he said,* but I'll be back on one very soon or a *shit storm* will go down in Kabul.

The lawyer told him one other thing, that since the package was addressed to his home in Ohio the FBI had picked up his parents and brought them in for questioning but after a day had let them go.

"After a day?" asked Lee. "Oh shit! You mean they spent the night in jail?"

"You send it to your home address?" asked the lawyer. "What did you expect? The FBI would bring them flowers from Campo di Fiori?"

FOR WHAT SEEMED LIKE HOURS, LEE HAD BEEN SITTING ON THE black leather couch at home, staring mindlessly at the TV while trying to focus on *The Edge of Night*, the newest of the afternoon soap operas. The show dealt with a steady onslaught of gangsters, drug dealers, psychopaths, and murderous debutantes and hardly soothed his frazzled nerves. He was still freaked out by the scene in Madame Rue's basement and was waiting anxiously for Danny to arrive; all the time, Ken O'Connor's warning kept echoing in his mind, *Bad People*. Then the phone rang. And this time, it *was* Lexi.

"Hey, stranger," she said. Just hearing her voice, the soft, southern curves of it melted away some of his anxiety and took him back to that first time he saw her on Indian Wells beach, so long ago. It still had the same intoxicating effect on him as that very first time.

"Lexi," was all he could say. "Lexi," he repeated.

"Well, at least you remembered my name," she joked. "Anything else?"

"Everything else," said Lee. "I was beginning to think these memories would have to get me by for the rest of my life."

"The rest of your life? You think I'd leave you hanging forever? Come on, sugar! I was just cruising around the Caribbean on *The Yellow Rose*, stopping at any port in the storm, just trying to think ... or better yet, not to think. Spent a lot of time with Captain Jack. He's good company when you want to be alone."

"Yeah, Armando told me something like that. Guess winter's no fun in New York," said Lee, still feeling the sting.

"Don't be silly, Lee. My aunt has a beautiful villa right on the beach down in St. Lucia and I just thought, among other things, it was as good a time to visit as any so ... *Packed up all my cares and woes, here I go, here I go, bye bye blackbird.*"

"You sing pretty well yourself," said Lee. "You should join me on stage sometime, next time you're in town, I mean."

"I know I should have called you, Lee, but it was

like, you know, leave quickly and don't look back for a while. Things were really getting bad with Ray. I couldn't be around him for another minute."

"So how are things with Ray now?"

"If anything, worse," she said laughing. "But I don't care anymore. Can you forgive me, sugar?"

Lee didn't know what to say. Probably better to say nothing, he thought, because the last time he pushed Lexi on their relationship, he hadn't heard from her for months and had passed a lonely winter indeed. If he asked too much, at the wrong time, she might just disappear again and despite what she said, *really* leave him hanging. Being in love didn't seem to have much to do with anything besides his own misery.

"You know, Ray put me out on a tour, but it didn't really work out."

"Sounds like Ray," she said. "Don't know why anyone would believe anything he says, least of all you. So...you still want to see me?"

"Sure" said Lee. "When?" The only word that mattered.

"How does tomorrow sound to you?"

"Tomorrow sounds very good to me, coming from you."

"I tell you what, *The Yellow Rose* is docked at the 79th Street Boat Basin and that's where you can find me. You know where that is?"

"I think so, the Upper West Side, right?"

"You got it, sugar. There's a little security hut at the entrance to the dock with a guard in it, I'll leave your name. It's the perfect place to be, the action is all on the river right now with the 4th of July celebrations and the President coming to town, tall ships cruising up and down New York harbor. It's exciting, we'll have a blast."

"If you're there, I'm sure it's the place to be, Lexi. Saw something about it on the news, didn't really pay much attention."

"Come on, Lee! Get in the spirit! Independence Day is just around the corner, in my case I'd say more ways than one, so it's time for some *fireworks*," she said provocatively.

WHEN DANNY FINALLY DID SHOW UP AT LEE'S APARTMENT AT twilight, Lee was sitting on his couch in near darkness still ruminating about his conversation with Lexi, trying to find meaning behind every word she had said and coming up empty.

"Man, turn on some lights here," said Danny, flipping up the dimmer on the wall. "Wow, you look like shit, Lee."

"Thanks, man. Not much sleep last night."

"Something bothering you?" asked Danny.

"Well, maybe a couple of things," said Lee, not wanting to get into it right away. "How's it going?"

"Great!" said Danny. "Things are moving fast. Maddy said he's opening another club on the West Side, and he wants me to manage it for him. At least that's what Junior told me."

"You like working for Maddy?" asked Lee. "I thought you were working for Ray? He got you the job, right?"

"Ray's nothing but the front man," said Danny. "Nobody takes him seriously down there at the club, but Maddy needs guys like Ray for the liquor license and all that legal crap because he's got a conviction for gambling or something on his record."

"What else do you know about Maddy?"

"I know all I need to know," said Danny. "And I know when to not ask questions. But Junior told me a lot about Ray."

"Like what?"

"Like all that bullshit about Ray being from this rich family down in Virginia or something? Saying he went to Princeton or some Ivy League place? Well, it's all a load of crap. Arthur isn't even his last name, it's his middle name."

"You're kidding me?" asked Lee astonished.

"I kid you not," said Danny laughing. "His real last name is Brown, *Raymond Arthur Brown*. That's what it says on the liquor license and when Junior calls him *Mister Brown* he flips." Danny laughed even harder. "And he's from Chicago, Junior found that out too."

"Wonder if Lexi knows that? Bet she never even saw the marriage license. Wow, I just thought of something, Danny."

"What's that?"

"Maybe Ray isn't even legally married to Lexi. Maybe he didn't use his real name and she could get the whole thing annulled."

"Why do you care so much if they're married or not?" said Danny.

"Not at all," said Lee, backing off. "Just thinking out loud, that's all."

They were sitting on the couch in the small rear living room of the apartment, their feet resting on the dark cherry-wood coffee table in front of them. Wooden venetian blinds were rolled down on the two back windows, which abutted a sooty airshaft. A series of recessed lighting fixtures discreetly illuminated the room.

"Ray might have it covered some way," said Danny. "Pretty swift at covering his tracks, gotta say that about him, started out in the mail-room of the William Morris Agency where he got caught opening some agent's mail. Then they found out he faked his college degree and he was about to get fired, but at the last minute Ray stole some big act from another agency and became a hero. Typical Ray! In fact, he became a major agent and about to become head of the music department when Wes Edel made him an offer he couldn't refuse and brought him to Edel Records as a *Vice President*, no less."

"How'd you know all this?"

"Ray told me himself! What do you think? By the time I start closing up the bar at Madame Rue's, Ray is usually so coked up that he's talking about everything to anyone who will listen. He even told me some stuff about him and Maddy's hot little niece, Gloria, said he's been humping her on the side. Where's the head around here? I gotta pee."

Lee pointed Danny down the hall to the toilet and sat there thinking about Ray, halfway wishing that James Elliot hadn't stepped in last night in the basement and had let Maddy and Junior pound the shit out of him. Finally, Ray had nothing on Lee, no family pedigree and now, no big record company job either. And he'd been cheating on Lexi at the same time. If Lee had only known all that, maybe he could have moved things faster with Lexi and really gotten Ray out of the picture, but instead he fell for that Sha Na Na tour. Ray wasn't stupid, he'd used that tour to get Lee out of the way while finding a way to pocket some cash for his coke habit, Lee finally deduced. When Danny came back from the toilet, he began to fiddle with the dimmer switch on the wall that controlled the overhead lighting, slowly changing the intensity of the recessed lighting.

"Nice touch," said Danny as he moved the switch back and forth. "I wouldn't have suspected there'd be a nice pad like this over JP's bar."

"Yeah," said Lee. "Nice touch, so don't break it. Listen, there's some stuff I want to talk to you about."

"I know what you want to talk about," said Danny. "But I'm telling you, Lee, you don't have to worry about your career. I'm on top of it - just give me a little time. Once I start managing Maddy's new club and Kathy and I get our place together, my next move is gonna be focusing on your career. I already talked to Maddy about putting some live music into the place and he seemed to like the idea. If that happens, you're gonna play on opening night and as much after that as I can manage. In fact, you're not gonna believe this, but Junior told me that him and Maddy are going in partners with Ray on his new disco label called, you ready? HooRay Records! Can you believe that shit?"

"Danny, I really got to talk to you about all of that."

"All of what?"

"All this business with Maddy and Junior and you working for them and getting more and more involved. Seriously, someday you could really regret that those guys even know your name."

"Listen, Lee, everything I do with them is strictly on the up and up," said Danny defensively. "I mean, Madame Rue's is a real business, right? Every week I get a paycheck like everyone else, signed by Ray Arthur. I don't even think Maddy's name is associated with the club at all. Even repossessing the cars, I told you, it's totally legit."

"I hope you haven't done any more of that."

"Just a couple," Danny lied. "It's hard to say no to Maddy. And I think the guy really likes me, sees I'm tough, busting my ass in that club night after night. Sometimes I'm the first one there and the last one to leave, always leave the bar spotless, all the bottles lined up with the labels showing, chairs all set right, you know, taking care of the details. Maddy respects that. It's guys like Ray that piss him off, you know, fucking phonies who never want to get their hands dirty. I'm telling you, Lee, you can learn a lot just from listening to Maddy. He fought his way up from the bottom, parents immigrated from Sicily right after the war, street fights in Brooklyn then he went pro, started fighting middleweight. Told me the smartest thing he ever did was throwing a fight when the right guy asked him to, said the winner ended up with shit and he got out of the ring for good and started hanging around one of those social clubs down in Little Italy, became a ... what'd he call it ... an *enforcer*, that's it, on somebody's crew. You wouldn't believe the shit that goes on down there."

Lee shook his head, "I can't believe you're becoming pals with this murderer."

"Who's the bigger murderer, Lee?" Danny asked defensively. "Maddy the Horse or Richard Nixon?"

"That's bullshit and you know it."

"The bottom line is, you know, like when everyone's busy or something I take care of some stuff for him, nothing heavy, just the cars or maybe keeping Junior company when he's gotta bring a lot of cash uptown."

"Don't tell me you're running around with Maddy's money?"

"It's not Maddy's money, it's the club's money, the bar take. I'm supposed to settle up with Ray at the end of the night although he's usually too stoned to pay much attention, so I just figure it out, tell

Junior the numbers and put the cash in a brown bag and hand it to him."

"Hope you get a receipt."

Danny laughed. "These guys don't like writing anything down. Junior stashes the cash up at Maddy's apartment and I go along for the ride, keep him company."

"You've been to Maddy's apartment?"

"I mean, yeah, a few times I've been up there in a cab with Junior but then I split, jump on the subway and go out to Queens or over to Kathy's. Hey, it's a good deal for me, this way I don't have to take the subway from all the way downtown at four o'clock in the goddamn morning. Looks to me like most nights Junior crashes there so I can't say who the apartment really belongs to, I've never been there with Maddy himself. Nice UpperEast Side building but it's decorated like crap *even* if it's really expensive crap. What these guys got in balls they don't make up for in decorating, I'll tell you that. Plastic slip covers on all the furniture and huge fucking lamps, look like they came out of the set of *Ben Hur*. Junior says Maddy's got a house out in Bensonhurst with the wife and kids, but his wife is always giving him shit about something. Junior said if it was him, he'd whack her." Danny broke up. "These guys are unbelievable, another fucking world. That's the thing with Maddy, nothing is like it looks, always covering himself, putting someone else between him and the law. He knows how to protect himself so when the shit hits the fan it's guys like Junior or even Ray who are gonna take the fall, not Maddy."

"Or guys like *you,*" said Lee. "I can't believe you're still doing the car thing for him. I thought you didn't like it after that time with the guy's wife falling on the ice or something."

"That only happened once ... I'm just thinking about my own future just like everyone else. I got plans and I'm crazy about Kathy so what if I'm cutting a few corners getting all this off the ground. I'm not breaking any laws ..."

"None you know about," said Lee.

"Whatever, I don't see the problem. I can walk away any time I want to."

"Not from Maddy you can't."

"Maddy's not as bad as you think, hangs out with politicians too, got a picture of him and Donald Maines, the *Queens Borough President,* standing together shaking hands, I saw it."

"Then that guy's probably a crook too, besides, I don't care if he's got his picture with the Pope ..."

"Wouldn't be surprised if he's got that too," said Danny. "Or at least the Archbishop of New York. Maddy gives a lot of money to the Sons of Columbus or some Catholic charity."

"I don't care who he gives money to," said Lee exasperated. "He's dangerous, Danny. When I was at Madame Rue's last night, I saw something go down between Maddy and Ray in that shitty basement office that you wouldn't have believed. Man, there was a gun and threats ... I was standing there with James Elliot and I didn't know if we were gonna get out of there alive."

"Ray had a gun?" asked Danny.

"No, Ray didn't have a gun, *Maddy* had a gun and he was waving it around and I'm not ashamed to say that I was scared shitless. I thought we were all going to end up dead in that basement."

"Maddy's got a temper," said Danny. "And Ray pisses him off with his high-class bullshit. But I know how to handle Maddy, we speak the same language, we're both from the street."

"That's what Ray thinks too," said Lee, raising his voice. "And I don't' give a shit about Ray, but you're my friend and I'm telling you ... you shouldn't be working with these hoods. If something bad happens, if the law gets involved, you won't be able to escape so easily. What if Madame Rue's gets busted and you're arrested and sitting in a jail cell with Junior. Who you gonna call?"

Danny smiled. "I'll call you, Lee."

Lee picked up his beer and took a big swig. "You know what? You're impossible. How the fuck could I help you?"

Danny got serious. "You don't need to help me, Lee. I know you think I'm some kid from Queens who doesn't know shit from *shinola* and sure, I got a lot to learn, but I'll tell you one thing, I believe in you probably more than anybody else around here. You're gonna make it big and I'm gonna be there when it happens. I got you that gig at the Talkhouse and look where you are now?" Danny stood up and gestured at the apartment. "You got a pretty nice place to live here, better than me, and a steady gig. Don't I at least deserve a little credit for that?"

Lee didn't know what to say. What *could* he say without bringing his affair with Lexi into it, and he wasn't ready for that yet. Not with Danny, because he felt ashamed, like he was a gigolo or something, that none of this was really due to his talent or Danny's maneuvering, as Danny liked to believe.

"We're going places, Lee," said Danny confidently. "You'll see, you and me."

"Hope it's not back to prison," said Lee.

"You've been to prison?" asked Danny, more in awe than shock.

"It's a long story," said Lee.

"Hey, Johnny Cash did an album inside a prison and it didn't hurt his career at all, did it?"

"Like I said, Danny, you're impossible!"

CHAPTER 24

The 79th Street Boat Basin consisted of a hundred and sixteen slips and eighty moorings with an angled protective wave wall jutting out into the Hudson River. An incongruous extension of Riverside Park, the marina almost had a resort quality compared to the gritty concrete reality of the city towering over it. It was the premier location in all of the city's five boroughs to harbor pleasure crafts and, even more so than in Sag Harbor, *The Yellow Rose* dwarfed all the boats bobbing at rest around it. Docked at the furthest extension of the small marina with its aft sticking out into the Hudson River, its imposing ebony hull gave the impression of being out of proportion to the calm river water it was floating upon. An odd fish to have found its way upstream, having crossed wide oceans and seas, repeating Henry Hudson's own journey made a few centuries before.

Most of the modest vessels at the 79th Street Pier belonged to city-bound day sailors who sailed the wide river on summer weekends with day trips up to Bear Mountain or West Point. But *The Yellow Rose* was an aberration to its surroundings, an eye-popping Caribbean island-hopping yacht that even experienced boatmen looked upon with awe and a fair amount of envy.

Lee arrived at the Boat Basin early the day after Lexi's call. An old guard with a crumpled captain's hat sat cramped in a small gray shack and checked his name off a clipboard with a stubby pencil and signaled him to pass through the gate. Lee walked down the pier to the furthest point where *The Yellow Rose* was docked and straight away saw Lexi, sitting alone on the aft deck reading *Vogue*, tanned, dressed in white short-shorts and a matching bikini top. Two black lacquered chopsticks held her hair on top of her head in a French twist as the sun reflected simmering golden red highlights. Lee saw her before she saw him and he was stunned; she looked more beautiful, more desirable, and more *perfect* than ever. He made a low whistle and slowly she turned her head to spot him standing at the foot of the gangplank. She jumped up and yelled with glee.

"Hey rock star - come on aboard!"

Almost embarrassed, Lee slowly descended the stairs that led to the lower floating dock, climbed the gangplank and stepped onto the yacht. Lexi put both of her arms around him and kissed him long and hard on the lips.

"Where's Captain Jack?" said Lee, surprised at this very public show of affection. "Or doesn't that matter anymore?"

"I imagine he's in town somewhere," said Lexi. "I nearly worked that poor man to death down in the islands, crisscrossing the Caribbean at a moment's notice. I told him to take some time off, take in the sights, although he's not really a city kind of man. But I suppose he'll find it interesting."

"Or terrifying," said Lee. "A real fish out of water."

"Oooh, that's corny!" said Lexi. "Anyway, he said he'd come back after dinner, wanted to eat a New York sirloin steak at The Palm. So, I treated him. He's just adorable."

"Not exactly yachting territory up here on the mean streets of Manhattan."

"No," said Lexi. "Not normally, but will you take a look out there and tell me what you see, sugar."

From where they were standing, they could look down the

Hudson River past the World Trade Center Towers and out to the Statue of Liberty and the harbor was truly swimming with boats of all kinds, large and small, all come to New York for the July 4th celebration.

"There are tall ships here from all over the world," said Lexi. "We'll never see anything like this again! And there's gonna be a fantastic fireworks display tomorrow night. Captain Jack says we'll be able to take it all in from *The Yellow Rose* without moving an inch. Won't that be *cozy*? Cook dinner ourselves and just hang out here on the boat with nobody bothering us. How does that sound to you, Lee?"

"Sounds ... perfect to me. So, you're staying here all by yourself?

"Well, Captain Jack is still officially here in his own discreet kind of way, but he sleeps in his cabin, checks that everything is ... shipshape, makes sure I have everything I need, but he rarely comes up top, respecting my privacy. I told him you might be staying over," she added with a giggle.

"You told him that?" said Lee, taken aback.

"Well, guess what, he seemed to like the idea, you must have made a good impression, Lee."

"And what about Armando?"

"He's back at the apartment."

"With Ray?"

"Jesus, Lee, do we have to talk about him," said Lexi exasperated. "*Yes*, Ray is up in the apartment, I suppose, and he can stay there for all I care ... at least, for a while, I mean. I wasn't back for ten minutes before it turned into another oh so *boring* fight, so I said screw that and walked out and came over here to *The Yellow Rose* just to try to get my peace of mind back. I had Armando bring over some clothes and shoes later, so I don't have to go back for anything until I'm good and ready."

"How do you know that Ray won't clean out the apartment while you're gone?" Lee laughed.

"That's not so funny! But I grabbed all the cash and jewelry when I left, and I don't think he'll take the furniture. Anyway, Armando is staying there to keep an eye on him and last I heard Ray hadn't even come home from wherever he was last night. God knows what he's up too and I don't give a good goddamn. He keeps badgering me for money, like I'm supposed to support his dirty little habits, plus he seems totally coked up every time I see him and that is just ... *insupportable.*"

"French?"

"*Oui,* for pain in the ass! I refused to give him any money at all and my accountant cancelled his credit cards, so Ray Arthur is on his own! At least *that* part of our relationship is definitely over," she said with finality. "So, Lee, that's the *Ray Report* for today. Can we drop that subject now and try to get on with our lives? Get with the program on this spectacular July 4th weekend? Maybe even get ... reacquainted?"

"Sounds good to me," said Lee.

"So," said Lexi, as she moved closer, so close that he could feel her sweet breath on his face. "We have everything we need here."

"We do," said Lee.

"And we don't really have any reason to go anywhere, for a while anyway, do we?"

"None that I can think of."

She put her hands on his cheeks and kissed him tenderly. "Me neither," she whispered. Then Lexi took Lee by the hand and led him down to the master stateroom where a beautiful gold leafed bed dominated the room. Without saying anything more, Lexi began to undress and in three moves she was naked. Lee did the same and they fell to the top of the bed and it felt so good, like this is what they were supposed to be doing all along, as they entangled themselves in each other, again exploring those most secret places, which they both knew so well.

Then they lay in bed, happily satisfied and exhausted, immobile, just kissing and tenderly caressing each other, staring into each other's eyes for a long time until Lexi went to take a shower. Lee stayed on the bed, as usual, thinking too much once she had gotten up. He sensed something had changed profoundly between them. When she returned, he sat up and shook his head in amazement.

"I think that's what I missed most about you," he said. "The pleasure of watching you walk around naked, how all those wonderful parts of you move as one. Never get tired of that."

"Hope not," said Lexi. "You look pretty good yourself."

"Really? I always think I need to change something. But when you say that, I feel all right."

"Don't change," said Lexi. She faced him, completely naked, her breasts pointing slightly to each side and the soft dark tuft of hair between her legs glistening with drops of water. "What are you thinking, Lee?" she asked.

"I'm thinking that looking at you makes me ..."

"Horny?"

"And hungry, too. Both at the same time," he replied.

"You're too much!" She took the towel from her head and playfully threw it at him. "My daddy would say that if a woman thinks the way to a man's heart is through his stomach then she's aiming too high!" Lexi laughed. "Guess that doesn't apply to you. We could go out somewhere ... or just stay on board and cook something up ourselves," said Lexi. "That way, we don't have to get dressed, do we?"

"Sounds good to me," said Lee.

"I told you, it would all be back to normal in the morning," said Lexi.

Very long morning, Lee thought. *And I had to get through so many nights alone to get back here.* He wouldn't let that happen again, no matter what.

"WHERE'D YOU GET ALL THAT?" ASKED GLORIA.

"I got my sources," said Ray. "And they save the good shit for me."

Ray and Gloria were down in the same basement office where Maddy the Horse had nearly broken his hand. Gloria was sitting on the pool table and Ray in the broken-down chair. He chopped up cocaine with his American Express Gold Card.

"This is about all that it's good for now," he said, without looking up.

"What do you mean?" asked Gloria.

"She cut me off," said Ray. "And this card was on her account, so now they're gonna take a scissor and slice it in two. I told her I don't need her fucking credit cards; I got my own."

"You do?"

"Of course, I do! What do you think? And soon I'll start my label with Maddy, Hooray Records, thought of that myself. Gonna be a winner. The hell with her."

"Maddy told me he's gonna call it Cavallo Records."

"Cavallo? What the fuck is that?"

"Italian for horse, as in Maddy the Horse."

"He doesn't understand the music business for shit," said Ray. "You can't have a record company with a name nobody understands what the fuck it means."

"What does Arista mean?"

"How should I know?"

"That's what Clive Davis is calling his new label. It means the best, like aristocrat."

"That's what Lexi thinks she is, some kind of aristocrat. But you know what happens to aristocrats, don't you?"

"No, tell me, Ray."

Ray had finished chopping up the coke and licked the edge of the American Express card, leaving it on the desk and rolling up a bill. He snorted two enormous lines with an almost howling noise, then tilted his head backwards, holding his nose, closing his eyes.

"I'll tell you what happens to aristocrats," he said to Gloria. "They get their fucking heads chopped off, that's what happens."

CHAPTER 25

Manhattan was dressed in red, white and blue everywhere you looked. American flags were flying wherever one could be mounted, on every streetlamp subway entrance and similarly colored banners hung over every intersection in the city. Street performers balanced on stilts were dressed in top hatted Uncle Sam outfits and tourists wore patriot hats. And red, white and blue popsicles were selling like crazy.

Lexi and Lee awoke late the morning of July 4th, to the incessant explosions of firecrackers and cherry bombs, bursting like grenades up and down Riverside Park, a narrow strip of parkland wedged between the Hudson River and gently curving Riverside Drive. From George Washington Bridge all the way down to the Battery, the Hudson River was congested with ships and boats of all kinds, blasting their horns and announcing Independence Day with a singular New York exuberance. Captain Jack had brought them *croissants* and *café au lait*, leaving the tray on the floor and softly knocking on Lexi's stateroom door before heading downtown to meet the rest of his crew and share in the city's celebration.

"Captain Jack's gonna have a blast down there," said Lee. "I'm sure half the city will be there. Maybe we should get out and celebrate, what do you think?"

"Ray gave me tickets to some big shindig tonight," said Lexi.

"Said I'd get to meet President Ford and even Elizabeth Taylor because her husband John Warner is organizing the whole bicentennial ... everything. He said he's friendly with John Warner's family down in Virginia, not that I believe a word of what he says anymore, he's so full of it. But to tell you the truth, Lee, I wouldn't mind just staying on the boat and watching the fireworks from here ... with you."

"Sounds good to me," said Lee. "Sure you won't mind missing that ball?"

"And not meeting President Ford? Hey, I'm a Texas Democrat! And I think Ray gave me those tickets just to try and get on my good side, or to show me that I need his help to get into a party like that. Do you believe him?" She snuggled up next to Lee in the bed, sipping her hot coffee and deciding whether or not to put some polish on her toenails. "I don't really feel like moving from The Yellow Rose at all, or from this bed, for that matter, either. Feels so good here, just the two of us."

"As long as it stays that way. Where will Ray be while all this is going on?" asked Lee. "Is he going to that party?"

"Believe me, he would love something like that, snorting coke with all the bigwigs – just his style. But he told me something about a big event at the club he's taking care of."

"And what would he say if he showed up here and saw us together?" asked Lee cautiously

"He *won't* come down here," insisted Lexi. "I told him to leave me alone for a while and Ray doesn't want to rock the boat any more than he has." She laughed. "That's funny!"

"What's funny?" asked Lee.

"Rock the *boat,* sugar! And we're *on* the boat!" Lexi laughed.

"That's not funny – that's corny. But I love to see you happy like this," said Lee, taking Lexi in his arms. "It looks like you're handling all of this pretty well."

"Handling what? Ray's just my husband, Lee, he's not my life, never has been, never will be. When I was down in the Caribbean, I made up my mind to live my life without him, to have a good time, and I didn't miss Ray Arthur for one single moment. And I had a blast! Let me tell you. The last thing I told Ray was that we should separate and live our own lives for now," Lexi continued. "He went kinda nuts, but I didn't really care, just told him he'd have to accept it. Maybe I was just a naïve little Texas girl to think that my own marriage could be so different from everyone else's."

"Like whose?" asked Lee.

"Well, like my own parents to begin with."

"Your mother died, that's not the same thing."

"There was more than that, a lot more. And it was part of the reason I came up north to begin with."

"You're losing me."

Lexi took a deep breath. "There was this Mexican woman, quite beautiful I'd have to say, Gabriella was her name, came to see me a few days after my daddy's funeral, knocking right on the front door of the house. I didn't really know who she was, never saw her around the house before and I was there with my cousins and my daddy's business partners so I couldn't really talk to her. Besides, I just thought she was a maid or something showing her respects and I said something about the servant's entrance being out back. She sure didn't appreciate that, gave me a look and said, *"I never came into this house through the back door and I won't start now."* Left a number to call her at, told me it was very important and turned around and walked away without saying good-bye. I didn't know what to make of her so a few days later I called."

"So, I take it she was not a maid?"

"Definitely not. Got maids of her own down in a beautiful house outside Tampico that my daddy bought for her, probably still living there. It's the oil capital of Mexico and Daddy was always going down there on business ... or so we thought. Said she needed to see me before she went back home so we met for coffee."

"Long lost sister?"

"Not quite," Lexi looked almost vulnerable. "My daddy's lover."

"That's heavy ..."

"Heavier than you'd think, lover *with* a family attached. Twin boys, my half-brothers, I suppose, Luis and Luca, never met them."

"Wow," said Lee. "What did you do?"

"What do you think I did? We finished our coffee and I called my lawyers and told them to write her a check and have her sign off on any claims on the estate. And to make it clear to her I didn't expect to hear from her or her sons ever again."

"And that was it? You didn't want to meet your half-brothers?"

"What for? So, we can cook burritos together at the family picnic? Case closed," said Lexi.

Captain Jack had left the *New York Times* folded neatly on the breakfast tray and Lexi spread it out in front of her while flaky bits of croissant fell on the sheets around them. They read the paper together, passing sections back and forth and commenting on the day's news. Doing that, waking up together, it felt so *normal* to Lee, as if this was how it should always be. They lingered over breakfast long past when the coffee got cold, Lexi's head resting on Lee's shoulder and he could not think of a time when he felt so calm, so at peace, so willing to be lost in somebody else's world.

"Here, they tell you everything that's going on tonight," he said, pointing his finger to a column in *The Times*. "Nine o'clock the *Gricci Family* fireworks start by the Statue of Liberty and they're gonna continue up both sides of the Hudson River, all the way to the George Washington Bridge. This *Operation Sail* is quite a big deal, something like fifty countries involved ..." Lee skimmed through the article. "What exactly is a Tall Ship anyway?" he asked. "And why isn't *The Yellow* Rose involved in all of this?"

"Well, how about because she's not a *sailboat* for one thing," said Lexi. "Or a Tall Ship for that matter, either. Captain Jack said to be a

Tall Ship you not only have to have sails, but the boat has to be kind of old fashioned looking, you know, three masts and all that, and *The Yellow Rose* is anything but that." She put her lips close to Lee's ear. "She's a *pleasure boat,*" she whispered. "Where would you rather be, Lee, out in New York Harbor shaking hands with the President of the United States ..." She let her hand slip down from where it had been resting on his chest and started rubbing between his legs in a small circular motion and his cock started to twitch and grow. "Or here shaking hands with me?"

"Take a guess," said Lee.

Lee was about to throw the newspaper off the bed and jump on Lexi when a small item in the entertainment section caught his eye.

"Now that's ironic," he said. "*The Ramones,* that punk band, are performing in London tonight on July 4th. Can you believe that?"

"I think Ray was supposed to fly over and see the show with Wes and Alana and I was going to tag along, go shopping with Alana. Now Ray says he's gonna start his own label, but I don't think he's got what it takes. He really blew it with Wes Edel."

"I'll tell you where he blew it, Lexi," said Lee, leaning across the bed and taking her into his arms. "He blew it when he lost you."

"Okay, now not another word about Ray Arthur," said Lexi. "Promise?"

"Promise."

"After all, this is Independence Day! And the very last thing I'm gonna say about ...*you know who* ... just so you understand, Lee, is that Ray never had *me,* I just had him for a while, that's all. And now I'm letting him go back to wherever he came from. It's as simple as that."

Hope it won't be as simple as that when my time is up, thought Lee. *Because where would I go back to?*

WHEN CAPTAIN JACK CHECKED IN ON THEM THAT AFTERNOON,

he was decked out in dress whites, looking like the admiral of the fleet, in a chipper mood and about to go out on the town. He smiled when he saw them together.

"Do you think you two will be leaving the boat this afternoon?" he asked Lexi. "If so, I'll lock things up and tell security to keep an eye on everything while we're gone. I'll be back in a few hours myself."

"Not going down to the Statue of Liberty?" asked Lee.

"Going down? The Captain only goes down with his ship, Lee," joked Captain Jack.

"No, that's okay," said Lexi. "We might take a walk somewhere, but mostly we'll be hanging around the boat. I think we'll do fine by ourselves, what do you think, Lee?"

Captain Jack looked at Lee and grinned. "I think you're in capable hands, Lexi. Just make him sing for his supper."

"I plan to," said Lexi.

They passed a lazy late afternoon walking hand in hand around the Upper West Side. When Lexi found a pair of shoes she particularly liked she bought them in all available colors, handbags to match, telling the salesperson that someone would come by later to pick up her packages. But they did fill shopping bags full of gourmet food at Zabars to get them through the weekend and then found themselves standing in front of the ominous Dakota on 72nd Street and Central Park West. Even on a hot summer's day the seven-story almost fortress-like residential building looked foreboding with its high gables and dark gothic façade.

"That's where they shot *Rosemary's Baby*," said Lee. "They say it's haunted, all kinds of weird stuff goes on in there."

"Well, then that's a relief," said Lexi with a laugh.

"What's that?"

"Well, that I didn't move there. I almost bought a condominium, but I got turned down by the board."

"You got turned down? That's unbelievable."

"Well, I blamed it on Ray. And besides it smelled like my old school in Switzerland, like nobody had washed the walls in a century."

Heading two blocks west on 79th, Lee tried to tempt Lexi into Papaya King for one of their "world-renowned" hot dogs and Papaya Daiquiris, but she needed some convincing before she was ready to cross that threshold.

"Lee, why should we eat here and probably poison ourselves when Warner Leroy's Tavern on the Green is just a few blocks away?" she asked. "I hear their Yellow Fin Tuna with truffles is extraordinary."

"I'm telling you, that tuna's got nothing on one of these hot dogs. Danny turned me on to them. You ever had one?" said Lee.

"No ... what are they made out of?"

"You don't want to know," said Lee. "Just try one. I'm buying."

They ordered two hot dogs on buns and slopped on mustard and chili. Lee wolfed his down with a Papaya Daiquiri while Lexi gingerly took small bites around the bun.

"It won't kill you," said Lee.

"Here goes nothing," said Lexi as she took a real bite, made a face and started chewing it and finally swallowed. She put the rest of the hot dog back on the paper plate and pushed it away from her like it was dangerous.

"So?" Lee asked.

"Well ... I'm still standing, so I guess that's a good sign." said Lexi. "Someday I'm taking you down to Houston and showing you my side of the world, eat some authentic Texas barbecue."

"You know, I'd love that," said Lee.

"You bet you would, sugar," she replied. "It would be a hoot."

THIS WAS THE FIRST TIME THEY HAD DONE ANYTHING LIKE THAT together, completely outside Lexi's illusory world of anything money can buy, just a normal Saturday, strolling around the city like any other young couple with no particular place to go on a hot summer afternoon. As the sun started to set over the Palisades cliffs on the New Jersey side of the river, they took a taxi back to the 79th Street Boat Basin and the guard at the security booth nodded cordially to Lexi, said Captain Jack had come back an hour ago. They found *The Yellow Rose* unlocked and open, champagne on ice waiting for them. "I bet Captain Jack is down in his quarters sleeping," said Lexi. "The man loves his naps."

They were sitting on the deck watching the sun set and picking from the stack of magazines they had bought that afternoon, French and Italian editions of *Vogue, Interview, Rolling Stone* and others when the security guard called to the yacht. It was Lee who stood up and took the phone.

"There's a guy down here who wants to see you," said the guard. "Said he's a friend of yours, but he's nowhere on my list."

Lee froze, thinking it must be Ray come to wreak havoc. "What's his name?" he demanded. "Are you sure he asked to speak to me?"

"You're Lee Franklin, right?"

"Right."

"Hold on a sec." Lee heard the bang of the telephone being put down, some talk in the distance and then the guard picking up the phone again. "Says his name is Danny O'Connor."

"I'll be right down," said Lee, both relieved and surprised.

"Who was that?" asked Lexi.

"You're not gonna believe it; Danny is here," he said to Lexi. "I don't know what he wants or how he even knew I was here, but I'll go find out."

"He probably just missed you, sugar. Wants to explode some cherry bombs together."

Lee found Danny in the parking lot entrance, pacing nervously back and forth, looking up at Lee with alarm.

"Are you all right, man?" was the first thing Danny said. "Is everything cool?"

"Yeah, of course I'm all right," Lee replied. "What's going on?"

"Whew, man, I was really worried."

"Worried about what? How'd you even know where to find me?"

"I know more than you think I know," said Danny slyly. "Finding you was the easy part. I had James Elliot call Lexi's place and her butler Armando told him she was on the boat and she'd be there all weekend." Danny smiled at Lee. "I put two and two together."

Lee ignored that last bit. "James Elliot? What the hell is going on here?" He was obviously agitated. "I still don't know why you're here, Danny?"

"Or why I knew you'd be here, either," said Danny. "Am I interrupting the honeymoon?" He smiled.

"What kind of question is that?"

"Relax, man, and I'll tell you what happened. I didn't come down here just to bug you, man, three's a crowd, right? Even I know that. But something happened and you're gonna want to know about it. You remember Gloria?"

"Gloria?"

"She's the punk singer, Maddy's niece, works down at Madame Rue's in the coat check."

"Ray's girlfriend?"

"You got it. She showed up at Madame Rue's about an hour ago. I'd just got to work, setting up for the night, you know, stock the bar all that shit, and in walks Gloria, looking like she hadn't slept all night. She pulls me aside and says she's got to talk to me. I thought it was something about the club, but she says no, there's some bad shit going down and I see she's very nervous."

"Get to the point," said Lee anxiously.

"The point is that Gloria told me that she was hanging out with Ray all last night and Ray was out of his fucking mind, coked-up beyond belief and going on and on for hours about Lexi, like he couldn't stop ranting about her and all her money and how she was not going to get away with dumping him like that, leaving him with nothing."

"Why was she telling you all this?"

"To tell you the truth, I think she was scared."

"What else did she say?"

"Well, she said she tried to calm Ray down, said he tried to fuck her on the pool table, but he was too coked up to get it up ..."

"She told you that?"

"Hey, she's a punk, what do you want? But she said after that, he really went crazy. Tried to break a cue in half and really fucked up his knee."

"What an asshole."

"She said she tried to keep him cool until he came down from all that coke, get him home somehow. But she said he lost her somewhere, it was like six in the morning and they were in some after-hours club, Acme I think it's called, another one of Maddy's joints ..."

"And?"

"And Ray disappeared, said he was going to the toilet and never came back, just left her there."

"Probably just went out to score more coke. So what?"

"Hold on, I'm getting to that," said Danny. "So, Gloria said she didn't know what the fuck to do, said she never met Ray's wife, really couldn't care less, but she didn't want to see anybody get hurt. And she knew you were a friend of mine and you were a singer. I think she was more worried about you than Lexi."

"Worried about me? Why?"

"Because Ray knows," said Danny, not needing to say more. Lee said nothing. "So, I called up James Elliot and he called Armando and here I am."

"Here you are," repeated Lee.

"When her butler said Lexi was on the boat down here, well, I figured you'd be here, too." Danny looked hard at Lee. "The thing I can't believe is that it's like everybody knew about this before me, James Elliot, Ray..."

"Danny, it's complicated...and there's not much to tell. So, what do we do now?"

Danny looked around to see that no one was watching them and then lifted his jacket to show the handle of a gun sticking out of his pants. "I thought I better bring this." The gun was so shiny it looked fake, like a toy.

"Jesus Christ, Danny, is that real?" asked Lee.

"Bet your ass it's real! Maddy keeps it hidden in the office, up in the ceiling, but I knew where to find it 'cause I saw him stash it once. And it's loaded - I checked."

"Why the fuck did you bring that?" asked Lee incredulously. "What the fuck is going on, Danny? Are you telling me everything?"

"It's just like I told you, Ray was really crazy last night and saying threatening things about Lexi. But that's not what got me up here with this gun, Lee."

"So, what are you doing here then?"

"It's because Gloria said that Ray was talking about you too, Lee, said he put you out on tour and you thanked him by fucking his wife and he was gonna get even real soon. Those were his exact words according to Gloria."

"That's not really what happened," said Lee. "You know that."

"So what did happen? Bet it started out in the Hamptons when I found you two sitting in the dunes at that party of hers. I should have figured it out then."

"Danny, there's nothing to figure out," said Lee, dropping his guard. "It just happened, that's all."

"And you couldn't tell me, your best friend?"

"I didn't tell anybody, afraid that would blow it. People start talking and Lexi getting scared."

"You're some piece of work, Lee Franklin," said Danny shaking his head. "Anyway, all that matters now is if Ray's got a gun, too. And if he does, you'll be glad you have this because then Ray will back off and no one will get hurt." Danny went to hand the gun to Lee.

"Jesus, I never even shot one before," said Lee. "You better keep it."

"All right," said Danny tucking it back in his pants. "I come from a tough neighborhood, if you're Irish you become a cop and if you're

Italian you become a wise guy. And both sides got guns so at least I know how they work."

"You think you're a tough guy," said Lee.

"I'm tougher than you think," said Danny defensively. "And I'm tough enough to look out for my friends."

Lee couldn't argue with that. They walked from the security hut back onto the dock, not saying much, while a boisterous atmosphere obliviously partied on all around them, bottle rockets were whistling overhead trailing a starry train as people stood on the decks of their boats, partying and drinking. Just before they reached *The Yellow Rose,* Lee turned to Danny.

"Listen, I've been thinking, don't say anything to Lexi about this, about Ray getting crazy and threatening her. And for Christ's sake don't let her see that gun."

"Whatever you say," said Danny. "This is your game."

"Say you just came down looking for me, to see the fireworks or something. We'll all go down to the end of the dock together, try to have a good time like none of this was going on."

"Who's on the boat now?" asked Danny. "Besides Lexi?"

"The crew's gone into town but the captain is around. And he's definitely not a fan of Ray's."

Lexi was taken aback when she saw Danny with Lee, getting up out of her chair, covering her bikini top with a cotton sweater.

"Room service," said Danny to Lexi. "Did you order a few jokes?"

Lexi was fine with him joining them because she liked Danny and thought him a funny, if not guileless character, with an accent straight out of *Saturday Night Fever*. And Danny knew how to charm Lexi too, cracking her up with his stories: "So I came down there into the VIP room, which is really like some storeroom filled with broken furniture, and I got three bottles of champagne on a tray and there in front of me are Halston, Liza Minnelli and, you're not gonna believe this, Jack Nicholson."

"Star-studded night," said Lexi.

"You're telling me. So, you know what I said when I walked in with the champagne?"

"Can't imagine," said Lexi.

"I said, *'Here's Johnny!'* And man, that cracked them all up. Jack said I did that line better than him and gave me a hundred buck tip.

"Are you hungry, Danny?" asked Lexi. "There's some stuff from Zabar's down in the galley, smoked salmon, shrimp salad ... just go help yourself."

Lee was impressed with how Danny had grown in sophistication since they had first encountered Lexi on Indian Wells Beach last summer. Now, he was much more than just the likable naïve kid from Queens tending bar at LaGuardia Airport; he was a *player* and he liked it. Working at Madame Rue's and rubbing shoulders with the *beautiful and damned* who hung out there night after night had widened his horizons considerably, making him a man of the world so to speak, even if it was just the small world of the New York downtown scene. But there was no nightlife in the world with the same juice as in New York City; everything else was minor league. Maybe Danny was the right one to back him up. Lee regretted that he didn't let him in on what was going on with Lexi a long time ago, from the beginning, in fact. And he felt ashamed to realize this only now. *Better late than never,* he thought, finally glad to have Danny there by his side, his manager, but more than that, his friend.

As the sun began to set, the action on the river was revving up with boats blaring their horns and even more firecrackers exploding. It was Lexi's idea to grab the bottle of champagne and stroll to the end of the dock. "Any minute now," she said, as they found a place among the small crowd gathered there and filled their glasses, ready to toast the first appearance of the Gritti fireworks display.

The 79th street Boat Basin was crowded with revelers, people literally jumping from one boat to another and the sea-going traffic up and down the river was intense. Dusk had suddenly settled, and nobody would have noticed anything out of place - even if anyone was looking that way, which nobody was - when a lone inflatable dinghy pulled up to the rear deck of *The Yellow Rose*. All eyes aimed skyward at cascading fireworks, which had begun at nine o'clock sharp and were still dancing up and down the river, a seemingly endless orgasm of flashing light and sound. Briefly, a shower of sparks highlighted two ski-masked figures getting out of the dinghy before they faded back into darkness as the concentration of light dissipated. Like actors in the wrong movie, out of place and time with the festivities around them, they climbed quickly over the low wall at the aft deck of *The Yellow Rose* and stealthily made their way down to the back stateroom.

"That's enough fireworks for me," said Lexi. "I think we can see them from the boat just as well. And I'm suddenly famished, what about you guys?"

Lee and Danny looked at each other. "Yeah, I could eat something," said Lee.

"Me, too," said Danny. "Hey, if you really want something good, I could get some hot dogs at Papaya King and bring them back? Wouldn't take long."

Lexi made a face.

"She's not a big fan," said Lee.

Back on board *The Yellow Rose*, Danny stayed up top on the deck while Lexi and Lee went down to get a sweater and fix some food. Walking into the stateroom, they surprised two masked figures crouching over the safe that was hidden beneath the floorboards. The safe door was swung open and one of the robbers was removing Lexi's Diamonds by the Yard while the other stuffed loose cash into a brown paper bag. When he saw Lee and Lexi, he instantly dropped the bag to the floor and went for his gun, pointing it directly at them.

"Don't fucking move," he said in a creepy Midwest accent. It was Lee who first saw them and slowly he put his hands up in front of him, but Lexi was startled and seemed not to comprehend the danger before her.

"Who are you?" she asked, her voice trembling. "How'd you get on this boat?"

"None of your fucking business," he said, waving them to the side of the cabin with his gun. "You two stand over there, away from the door and not a fucking word."

They did as they were told while the other ski-masked robber picked up the bag full of money and the two of them started to back out of the room together. But when they turned to the door, Danny O'Connor was standing there with the shiny gun held out straight in front of him. Everybody froze and the only sound was that of the fireworks, continuing to explode outside in the night sky. Finally, Lee spoke, without moving a muscle.

"Better just let them go, Danny. It will be all right. Just put the gun down and come over here with us."

Danny spoke to Lee, but kept his eyes and gun fixed on the guy in front of him whose own gun was now pointing right back at Danny. "I'm not gonna put down the gun, Lee," he said calmly. "I'm just gonna walk over there with you and Lexi and these guys are gonna walk out this door and that's it. No reason for anyone to get hurt." And very slowly, he started moving out from the doorway to go toward Lexi and Lee.

"You better do what your friend says," said the masked robber holding the gun. "Put the fucking piece down before you're the one who gets hurt, scumbag."

Danny got a puzzled look on his face. He recognized Junior's voice. "The voice ... I know you ... I know you."

Then there was a huge burst of exploding fireworks outside, but nobody moved until Captain Jack, who had just come up from his cabin, suddenly appeared in the doorway of the stateroom. Still in his dress whites he was looking down as he tucked in his shirtfront.

"I was woken up by the fireworks," he said. "And I thought ..." Then, looking up, he saw the two men in the ski masks and Danny with his gun. Junior swung his head wildly between Danny and Captain Jack; seeing someone in uniform had sent him into a panic.

"Who the fuck are you?" Junior shouted out, veering his gun wildly in front of him. "Are you a cop or something? What the fuck

..." He swung his gun back on Danny as the other robber started to bolt from the room and Captain Jack lunged at him and there were shots from both guns. Lee jumped sideways to cover Lexi while Danny fell hard to the floor with a surprised look on his face. The robber with the gun knocked Captain Jack out of the way with his pistol and ran out of the boat, but the other robber, apparently shot by Danny, was lying unconscious on the floor, blood pooling under his shoulder. Lee dropped to the floor and bent over Danny who was bleeding profusely from the chest. Danny reached up to Lee with his left hand, unable to talk, but grasping Lee by his collar like he was trying to say something. He was making gurgling sounds as he tried to breathe, and a line of blood came running down his mouth. Then his grip loosened, and his eyes went dead and there was no sound at all.

Lee was kneeling over Danny. "Danny! Danny! Jesus, somebody do something." He yelled frantically, tears filling his eyes. "Danny! Danny! Hold on, man!" He looked up to Lexi who was now backed up against the bed. "Lexi, call an ambulance!" But Lexi didn't move.

Captain Jack had pulled the mask off the wounded robber who was still clutching Lexi's Diamonds by the Yard necklace in his hand. It was Ray.

"That son of a bitch," said Captain Jack, putting his ear close to Ray's mouth. "He's still breathing." He took the necklace out of Ray's hand and handed it to Lexi.

"For God's sake call an ambulance!" beseeched Lee, but Lexi was looking only at Ray, lying next to Danny, unconscious on the floor. She spoke to Captain Jack evenly, without emotion, in an eerie new monotone level, one Lee had never heard before. Suddenly, there was no accent, no Texas; it was like she was possessed.

"Switch the mask," she said.

Captain Jack looked at her in confusion, not really understanding what she meant before it became clear and he quickly nodded his head, understanding full well what he had to do. With the mask still in his hand he stepped over Ray and came to Danny's lifeless body, bending down to put his ear on Danny's heart.

"He's dead," said Captain Jack to Lee. "Go with Lexi, let me take care of this." And he began to put the mask on Danny's face.

"Are you out of your mind? You can't do that," said Lee sobbing, trying to block Captain Jack's hands from touching Danny, but he had no strength and Captain Jack moved him firmly but gently to the side.

"Let me do what has to be done here, Lee," said Captain Jack. "Just back off."

Lee looked up at Lexi. She was squinting her eyes which brought her upper lip into a sneer, almost a snarl, like a dog guarding its bone, like a mean bitch you never thought would bite you before, but then you knew it would in a heartbeat to protect what was hers. Lee felt he was looking at a different woman than the one he had been making love with just that morning. He was alone in a room full of strangers, his best friend lying dead on the floor.

"Your friend is dead," said Lexi coldly, with a steel mask. "You can't change that. We have to move fast now, Lee."

"Yes, my friend is dead. And he died trying to protect you, Lexi! And now you want to make it look like he was robbing you? You think I don't know what you're doing? To protect that son of a bitch Ray?"

Lexi looked at Captain Jack, who waited with the mask over Danny. "Lee ... I didn't kill him and you didn't kill him. Even Ray didn't kill him. Why should we let this ruin all of us? Did Danny have a family? A wife?"

"No, not really, just a brother who lives out in Queens with his family ... I can't believe I'm even telling you this. What the fuck does that matter?"

"A brother with kids, right?" Lexi spoke rapidly to Lee. "Listen, I could help them, give them everything they'll ever need. It just can't look like Ray was the one who tried to rob me, Lee. You've got to understand that. If we don't do this now, make it look like Danny came here with that gun to rob me, there will be an investigation and everything will come out about my marriage, the drugs, that seedy club ... and even you. It will go on for years and I'll have to answer to the board of Langdon Industries, and who knows what they'll do?"

"Danny's still dead, Lexi! He's gone and your husband *did* try to rob you, and Danny died defending you. It's just not right what you're trying to do. Tell her, Captain Jack."

"I know what I'm doing, Lee," insisted Lexi. "We're gonna come out of this together and be fine. Everything will be back to normal in ..."

"Don't give me that bullshit!" screamed Lee.

"Lee," said Captain Jack. "Lexi's right. Let me do what I have to do. I'm telling you, don't try and stop me. Just back off like I said."

"I don't know," said Lee. "I can't let you do that to Danny." He was weeping with his eyes closed and didn't open them when Captain Jack pulled the black mask taut on Danny's head, covering his lifeless face, his still-open dull green eyes peering through the two slits. Captain Jack stood up and looked over the room. "Don't touch anything," he said with authority. "I'll go call the police."

CHAPTER 26

Lee sat in the back of a yellow Checker taxi dressed in the same dark Armani suit that Lexi had bought him months before when they went to Windows on the World, again crossing the 59th Street Bridge just as he had done with Danny. This time, on his way out to Brooklyn's Evergreen Cemetery, obsessively replaying in his mind the events of the last week, trying to undo the undoable. Captain Jack had indeed taken care of everything and as Ray was rushed away in an ambulance, he easily convinced the police that Danny had been mistakenly shot by his own accomplice as he was trying to escape from the boat. In fact, the way Captain Jack told it, he was the only witness to the whole event as Lee and Lexi had been on deck, heard nothing and saw even less.

"It's such a shame, I just would have told them to take my jewelry and leave," Lexi had told the police when she signed her statement. "But I guess my husband was trying to protect my honor or some foolish thing, trying to be a hero."

The only question the police had asked Lee on *The Yellow Rose* was his relation with the deceased.

"You knew this guy, right?" asked Detective Ryan.

"Yeah, he was my friend," said Lee.

"Some friend," said the detective.

Lexi and Captain Jack sat at the large dining table of *The Yellow Rose*, while the cops searched for evidence and shook their heads at the luxury of the boat and everything in it. It was all rather informal and routine until one of Lexi's lawyers arrived, still dressed in pajamas under his coat, and began dominating the inquiry, advising her what and what not to say. Lee went back up to the deck where an hour ago Danny must have been standing before he came down with his gun. It was beyond unreal. He just stared into the water off the side of the boat, fireworks over now, the city going to sleep. When he went back down, Lexi and her lawyer were gone.

Days later, ballistics tests showed that the gun they found grasped in Danny's hand, the gun he had taken from Maddy's office, was possibly linked to numerous unsolved shootings. That was enough to close the books on the whole case. Two detectives came by Lexi's apartment, apologizing for disturbing her, and handed her a sworn statement, which her lawyer had approved, with penciled *X's* marking where she should sign.

For days after Danny's death, Lee just sat up in his apartment above JP's, seeing no one until JP himself had come up to see him.

"Hi, Lee. Listen, just wanted to say sorry about your friend," said JP standing at the door. "What a goddamn shame."

"Yeah," said Lee. "It's just ... tragic. I don't know what else to say..."

"Hey, pal, got a few minutes?" asked JP.

"I guess, what's up?"

"Maybe it's better if I come in, got a few things I've got to tell you. In private." They sat on the same leather couch he had been sitting on with Danny weeks before and as he passed by the dimmer switch JP commented, "Nice touch."

"You haven't been down to the bar in a few days, not since this ... thing, happened," said JP.

"No," said Lee. "I just gotta be alone for a while, I guess."

"That's what I figured, no problem. Get over this in your own time. But I wanted to tell you about this, uh, guy who came by to see me this morning," said JP.

"What guy?" asked Lee.

"Well, you know, an older guy in a suit. Didn't say much, no card or anything, but I figure he had to be one of *her* lawyers. He was very discreet, never even mentioned her by name."

"Never mentioned *who* by name?" asked Lee, even though he knew very well the answer.

"Lexi Langdon," said JP. "Come on, you know what I'm talking about. When the shit hits the fan with people like her then the shit gets cleaned up pretty fast by their lawyers. Way of the world, pal, way of the world."

"So, what did he say?"

"Well, first he gave me this and told me to give it to you," JP handed Lee a sealed envelope. "And told me not to open it, so I didn't."

Lee popped open the thin manila envelope, peered inside and saw a check. Nothing else, no letter, no note, and no address or name on the envelope.

"He didn't give you anything else?" asked Lee.

"Well, first he gave me a lot of cash, what she would have owed me for the flat for like a year, and then some, and said his client was not interested in continuing to rent the property anymore and asked me if this was agreeable."

"What did you say?"

"What do you think I said?" asked JP, surprised. "I said *thank you*, of course. And then he brought out even more cash and told me that as far as he and I were concerned, his client had never even rented that property and wanted to know if I understood that. I said I did and he asked me if there was ever any lease or written agreement and I said *no* and he said, even better and put the cash on the bar."

"His client?"

"You know how they talk. Last thing he said before leaving, and this was kind of funny, he said that he had never been to see me and wanted to know if I understood that as well. I said sure. And then he said, and he was smiling while he said this, that if his client's name was ever mentioned in conjunction with this apartment then he'd be back with a New York City detective to investigate illegal drug use on the premises."

"Son of a bitch. Maybe he was a cop himself, the bagman."

"Cop, lawyer ... what do I care. I came out ahead of the deal," said JP. "So that's the official line, Lee, but speaking for me, I just want to say that the door is always open here at JP's for you, come back whenever you want to play or just hang out."

"And the apartment?" asked Lee.

"I'm afraid that door will have to close as soon as possible."

"How much time do I have?"

"What do you need?"

"I think they're burying Danny next Sunday; I can move out the next day if that's all right with you."

"Done deal," said JP.

JP LEFT AND LEE, AFTER SITTING IMMOBILE FOR A LONG TIME, moved into the bedroom and sat on the bed where he and Lexi had made love so many times he couldn't count, although he tried. Opening the envelope again and taking out the check, he saw it was from a corporation he had never heard of in the amount of twenty thousand dollars made out to his full name, *Leland James Franklin*. How she even knew that, he couldn't figure out. He folded the check in half, put it in the back pocket of his jeans and picked up the phone.

"It's Lee Franklin calling, Armando," he said. "Is Lexi there?"

"I'm sorry, Mr. Franklin, she's not here."

"Any idea when she'll be back?"

"Sorry, Mr. Franklin."

"And Ray?" asked Lee. "Is Ray there?"

"He's not here either, Mr. Franklin. But he's out of the hospital and you'll be glad to hear the doctors said he'll make a full recovery. We've all been praying for him."

"Listen, Armando," said Lee. "Can I give you a message for Lexi, a confidential message?"

"Of course," said Armando.

"Just tell her I'm going out to Long Island next week on Monday, and I'm staying at the Memory Motel – she'll

know where that is – and I'll be there for a week," Lee hesitated before adding, "and I'll be waiting there for her."

"I will tell her that, Mr. Franklin."

"You sure you've got it all?"

"Memory Motel, from...July 12th for a week, and she can contact you there, is that all correct?"

"I guess that's it," said Lee.

IT WAS NOT RAINING, AS ONE MIGHT HAVE EXPECTED, THAT SAD morning when Danny was buried at Brooklyn's Evergreen Cemetery, mid-July 1976. On the contrary, it was the beginning of a bright and shiny, summer day, a day that promised good times to come, just like the days Lee had passed with Danny on Indian Wells Beach a year before, a lifetime ago. Literally. As the taxi drove through Queens on its way to the Brooklyn cemetery, Lee was thinking that Danny must have known these tough city streets well, and yet for all his *street smarts* Danny was dead while he, an innocent from the Midwest who had been thrown into a Roman jail the first time he stepped outside the law, wasn't and none of that made any sense to him.

There hadn't been any kind of church service for Danny, Ken

O'Connor wanting to keep it quiet and protect his own reputation as best he could with all of the scandal that was swirling about. Surprisingly for an Irish family, there didn't seem to be many living relatives anyway; Danny's parents had married late, his mother past forty when he was born, and now they were both gone. The only ceremony to memorialize Danny O'Connor's brief time among the living would be a simple burial in Brooklyn with a handful of people to watch his coffin descend into the ground. When Lee stepped out of the cab and saw the casket suspended over the grave in the chrome winch that would settle it into Danny's final resting place, his knees almost buckled under him. Three gravediggers stood off to the side of the gravesite, smoking, leaning on their backhoes and talking low in Spanish. Lee looked over and saw Ken O'Connor in a black suit, standing with one arm around his wife and the other around Kathy Muller, a head taller than both of them, dressed in black as well, her head bowed down, and holding a white handkerchief to her eyes. His two small children were at his wife's side and, like all kids at a funeral, scared and ignorant. There was no one else except a white robed priest and a few gray undertakers with that well-rehearsed air of solemnity.

Lee paid the taxi and watched it drive away, not knowing what to do, where to go. With slow, guarded steps he took his place just behind Kathy, standing with his head bowed like the others while the priest read some scripture over Danny's casket. At that moment Lee noticed another man standing nearby, obviously there for the burial as well, but almost hidden by a large tree some yards away. He was looking right at him, and Lee looked away and then back again and the guy was still staring at him, even more intently and then, finally, he recognized him - Burt Bateman, Lexi Langdon's investment advisor whom he had met just once at her party in Amagansett. *What was he doing here?* Lee wondered. *Had Lexi sent him?*

After the priest closed the book, and made the sign of the cross over Danny, the casket was lowered down to receive the first shovelful of dirt thrown over it. Ken O'Connor and his wife busied themselves with the undertakers and Kathy turned around to face Lee, trying to smile but her lips would only tremble downward.

"Oh, Lee," she said as she put her arms around him and started sobbing uncontrollably. "This can't be happening. I don't understand anything. You knew Danny better than anyone, he was wild, but he would never do something like this. Robbing Lexi, carrying a gun... what got into him?"

"I don't know," said Lee.

"I'd never seen him so happy, we were going to find a place, move in together and he was about to start running this other club ... Oh, God," she sobbed and sobbed. "What am I going to do now, Lee?"

"I don't know," Lee repeated. "We're just going to have to move on, what else can we do? I know that's what Danny would have wanted," he said unconvincingly.

"I loved him so much, Lee. I never loved anyone like that before."

"You'll find ... "

"You don't understand. I'm pregnant, Lee," Kathy said frantically. "With Danny's baby. It's a boy. We knew that already, it's Danny's son, Lee, he'll be born in September. Can't you see?"

Lee looked at her swollen womb hidden under the flowing black dress. "My God," said Lee. "Danny never told me."

"Nobody knew but us. I didn't want my family to know. It was all going to be a big surprise, our marriage, our baby, and you were going to be the best man. Danny wanted to tell you that himself."

Lee felt the sky falling on him with nowhere to hide. He couldn't speak, could hardly breathe, he wanted lightning to strike him, for the earth to open up and swallow him - to just disappear. Kathy was crying hard on his shoulder and just putting his arms around her to comfort her made him feel like a traitor.

"I can't stand over his grave any longer today, Lee," said Kathy. "I have to go ... I'm going up to stay with my family for a while, I don't know how long I'll be gone."

"Some day we'll talk about Danny and ..."

Kathy put a finger to Lee's lips and just shook her head back and forth slowly, with tears rolling down her cheeks. "He loved you, Lee, just like he loved me. That's all we have to talk about. That's all we have now." Then she turned to get into a waiting black limousine.

Her car rounded a curve, passing close to Burt Bateman, who was still looking at Lee intently like he needed to talk to him. Once Kathy's car was out of sight, Burt furtively walked over to Lee, eyes to the ground. "I'm Burt Bateman," he said.

"I know. What are you doing here?" asked Lee. "Did Lexi send you?"

"Nobody sent me," said Burt. "I'm here on my own. But I knew Danny well, and I know you too, Lee. I met both of you at Lexi Langdon's party last summer and now you and I need to talk about something."

"You knew Danny well?"

"I'll explain."

"Not here," said Lee. "I can't talk now."

"But it's important," said Burt. "And it's timely, so it's got to be tomorrow at the latest. This can't wait, Lee, there are things that need to be taken care of right away."

"I'm going out to Montauk tomorrow," said Lee. "I'm taking the train in the morning."

"All right," said Burt. "Listen, there's a coffee shop up near where I live on Madison and East 74th Street, the New Wave; I eat breakfast there every morning. Can you be there at eight a.m. tomorrow?

"I can be there," said Lee.

"Don't be late," said Burt. "I don't want to miss the opening bell of the market."

"You're sure Lexi didn't send you?"

"I told you, nothing to do with her, whatsoever."

But in spite of Burt's assurances, Lee was thinking it must have something to do with Lexi, about when he would see her again, he was sure. Burt briskly walked away and drove off in his waiting black Lincoln Town Car just as Ken O'Connor approached Lee.

"Who was that?" asked Ken.

"A guy Danny and I met out on Long Island," said Lee. "Don't really know him well, surprised he was here."

"Oh," said Ken. "I thought it might be the police. This Detective Ryan came to see me at my office right after it happened, he knew some guys that I work with, guess the word got down that Danny was my brother. Asked me if I wanted him to follow up on anything or should he just drop it."

"I don't get it," said Lee. "What did you say?"

"Well, I told him to drop it," said Ken. "But I didn't tell him why."

"What do you mean?" asked Lee. "Why what?"

"You see my two kids standing over there?" said Ken. "They're burying their uncle today and everyone says he was a crazy thief, maybe dealing drugs, involved with the mob. But now, because of their Uncle Danny they'll definitely be going to college, anywhere they want, no student loans hanging over their heads when they get out, like me. You see, before Detective Ryan got to me I got a call from a lawyer, representing Langdon Industries, they owned that goddamn boat you know, and he came to see me at work, expressed his condolences and said it was better if we let this all go away, better for everybody and, he insinuated, my career too. First I was kind of insulted, like who the hell was he, and then he gave me an envelope with two checks, one for each of my kids, substantial amounts of money, six figures, and said I should invest it, put it in long term Certificates of Savings. I didn't tell anybody, not even my wife, just took the checks."

"So why are you telling me this?" asked Lee.

"Because I'm not a goddamn idiot, Lee. Don't think for a minute I believe the official story that Danny tried to rob that boat or that he was involved with all the crimes linked to that gun. That's a goddamn lie and a cover-up, and you and I know it. In fact, if anyone knows what really happened on that boat it's you, Lee." Ken looked at him intently. "And if there *is* anything else, you're going to keep it to yourself, right? Forever, I mean, until the day you die."

"Nothing will bring Danny back," said Lee. "That's all I know."

"No, nothing ... "Ken started to choke up and grit his teeth. "So, we're straight on that, Lee? You know I tried to warn Danny about these scums," he said. "And now, because of my crazy brother, my kids are gonna get a real break in life and I don't know what to think. But still, it doesn't add up to me, probably never will." Ken put his hand to his mouth, his eyes welling up but he stopped himself from crying. "I better get back to my wife and kids."

"I'm so sorry, Ken," said Lee. "I don't know what else to say." He held his hand out but Ken walked away without taking it.

THE NEW WAVE WAS A CLASSIC NARROW COFFEE SHOP WITH A spotless stainless-steel kitchen, run by an extended Greek family and squeezed between two art galleries, mid-block on Madison Avenue. A counter lined one side with trays of muffins and donuts across from a row of booths along the other wall, decorated with large color photos of the Acropolis and autographed eight by ten glossies of local celebrities who frequented the place. When Lee walked in, Burt Bateman was already sitting in a booth by himself under a signed photo of Roy Scheider of *Jaws* fame, finishing his poached eggs and wiping up the yoke with whole-wheat toast.

"Coffee?" asked Bert.

"Yeah," said Lee, signaling a waiter who promptly hastened to fill his cup to the brim. "So, what's this all about? If it wasn't Lexi who sent you, then why did you come to Danny's burial? You met the guy one time a year ago and now you come to his funeral? That's pretty strange," said Lee aggressively.

"Calm down, Lee, like I told you, Lexi Langdon has got nothing to do with this."

"Really? Well, what then? What do you want with me?"

Burt leaned in close to Lee and said what he had to say softly and clearly. "I knew Danny O'Connor a lot better than you think, Lee. Sure, I met him the same night I met you at that party, but you went off somewhere and Danny and I spoke quite a bit together. And like everyone, he asked me a lot of questions about the stock market, and again like almost everyone, he took my card. But you know what? Unlike most people, Danny actually followed up and many weeks later, gave me a call, must have been around Thanksgiving, asking even more questions and wanting to get together. He came down to see me at my office right after the Christmas holidays. Yeah...that was it, early January."

"What for?" Lee asked.

"What do you think? He wanted to invest like everybody who comes to see me," said Burt. "That's what I do, I'm an investment counselor."

"Danny wanted to invest in the market? With what?"

"That first time, he didn't have a huge amount of money, something like ten thousand and so I put together a modest portfolio for him, almost as a favor."

"I can't believe Danny even had ten-thousand dollars to invest," said Lee amazed.

"Finally, he had a lot more than that," said Burt. "Almost every week he'd bring me more, always in cash. You know, it was highly irregular and I shouldn't even have been doing it, taking in cash like that. My firm doesn't handle *currency*, but I liked Danny and I knew some tricks from Vegas about cleaning up cash so I did it for him. Never asked him where he got it, but I never knew it would get that big. I think Danny was as surprised as I was when I'd show him the figures. I remember him saying with that kind of money he could produce your album and that he had an in with John Lennon."

Burt shook his head and smiled. "I thought he was bluffing me, talking about John Lennon like they were buddies, but he was such a funny guy, always up, always making me laugh, always pushing me to invest in high risk, high return equities. So, it kind of became a game between us and it was fun for me too. Then ... this thing happened, couldn't believe it when I read it in the paper. Never would have thought that funny little guy from Queens would be capable of such a nutty act. Just goes to show you, you never really know what's going on in a guy's head. Guess he just wanted more, got greedy."

Lee didn't say anything to that. "How much is there now?" he asked.

Burt Bateman peered nervously around the New Wave to make sure no one was overhearing their conversation and then lowered his voice.

"He gave me close to a hundred-thousand," said Burt very quietly. "All in cash. And you know what? I nearly doubled it. And I bet it will double again before the end of the year."

"Are you telling me there's two hundred thousand dollars sitting somewhere in Danny's O'Connor's name?"

"Close to that," said Burt. "We got lucky with a few stocks and I sat on them and even bought more when everyone else was selling and then I sold when everyone was buying."

"Sounds like you have a good head for what you do," said Lee. "Guess Danny trusted you."

"Investing in the market is not about having a good head or even trust for that matter, it's about having a good stomach," said Burt. "So what do I do with all of Danny's investments now? Do I liquidate, write a check and close the account? You tell me."

"Why are you asking me?"

"Because it's in *your* name now, *Lee Franklin*."

"My name? What do you mean it's in my name?"

"Because Danny made you the sole beneficiary of the account in case anything happened to him."

"What?"

"Judging by the look on your face, I take it he never told you."

"No ... I didn't know anything about this account."

"There's more than enough there to record an album, I suppose," said Burt. "And a second one, too."

Lee sucked in his breath. "Oh God ... I don't want it, I don't want any of it."

"You don't? So tell me what you want me to do with it? Don't suppose you want me to give it away to charity?"

"Listen, Danny's gonna have a son, nobody knows this. Can you put it all in his son's name? Keep it quiet, wait until the kid grows up?"

"Yes ... I could do that," said Burt. "Establish a fiduciary trust account in his son's name. You just bring me his name when he's born and I'll do the rest. But after all of this robbery business I want to erase Danny O'Connor's name from this account and from me and my firm in every way possible so, if you have no objections, I'm going to move it offshore and bury this account so deep that no one will ever know it exists until that kid turns twenty-one. You'll have to trust me, Lee, because there's nothing in writing I can give you now."

"I don't think you would have gone to Danny's funeral if I couldn't trust you."

"There's one thing we have to be clear about, Lee. Lexi Langdon is my biggest client so she can never know anything about this. I'm sure you understand. Anyway, from now on, I only speak with you directly, Lee, about this matter."

"Right, this is just between us from now on. I'll make sure you get his son's name and any other information you need."

"Fine, I'll send you the papers, just in case something happens to me, and you make sure you put them somewhere safe. And for God's sake, don't bring me any more cash." He handed Lee his card and looked at his watch. "I'll be in touch." They shook hands and Burt Bateman dashed out of the New Wave.

Dumbfounded, Lee sat there, trying to figure out what he should do. The coffee shop was full and noisy, everyone eating breakfast and waiters yelling out orders to the busy short order cooks.

"I said with *skim* milk!" one of the waiters shouted out while he returned a bowl of hot oatmeal to the kitchen. Lee heard that and leapt up out of his seat, prompting a couple of customers to look at him askance. Suddenly it hit him like a ton of bricks, everything made sense and he wanted so badly to scream it out loud, although he knew he couldn't do that, not now, not ever.

Danny was the skimmer! Danny was the skimmer! Taking cash out of Madame Rue's *every week and bringing it down to Burt Bateman – that's what happened!* Lee's thoughts were colliding in his brain like a pinball machine gone crazy, all bells and whistles lighting up at once. *That nervy kid from Queens stole a hundred thousand dollars right under the nose of Maddy the Horse, big time Mafioso killer, and all the time Maddy's blaming Ray and ready to kill him for it. Danny Fucking O'Connor! What a set of balls that little guy had!*

After that, Lee sat quietly in his booth at the New Wave for quite a while. After the breakfast crowd cleared out, the place was nearly empty, and he just sat there, staring down at his coffee cup, thinking about Danny, remembering that day they walked down to Indian Wells Beach and Danny's fascination with the rich. When Lee began his affair with Lexi, he assumed he had left Danny behind with the rest of the *punters,* while he followed his own fantasy into the *lifestyle of the rich and famous.* But he couldn't have been more wrong, because now it appeared that Lexi Langdon was gone from his life, leaving him with a paltry sendoff check in his pocket while Danny had a few hundred thousand in his name and a son on the way. In truth, they both were thieves, Lee stealing Ray's wife and Danny going directly for the mob's cash. But what made him really feel humbled, what made him doubt himself even more, was that Danny O'Connor, whom he had never sufficiently taken seriously, had outsmarted everyone, even himself, and Lee didn't know whether to laugh or to cry about that and supposed he never would figure it out.

CHAPTER 27

I stayed at the Memory Motel for a week, maybe the worst week of my life, even worse than the months in that prison in Rome. Of course, once I was out there, I could have called Tony Hughes in Amagansett, maybe even played a gig at the Talkhouse, but I knew the first thing Tony would ask me was what had really happened to Danny on The Yellow Rose. And I couldn't answer that. The realization of what I had done, my betrayal, became more painful and permanent every day. I spent hours walking along the Montauk beach, looking out at the ocean as it changed colors with the light, from green to blue to gray, letting the days pass, waiting for a relief that wouldn't come. Sometimes I would stay out there on the beach until twilight, until I couldn't tell the ocean from the sky and then, reluctantly, I'd head back to the Memory Motel. I dreaded the nights in that motel room, lying on the bed alone, waiting in vain for Lexi to call.

In fact, I started finding any excuse I could to avoid going back to that room and began to hang out in the lobby with the blond surfer dude, the same night clerk who had given me the key that Labor Day weekend I checked in with Lexi. He was a small guy, about the same age as me, hair bleached by the sun, his surfboard lying right under the reception desk. Never saw him dressed in anything but a flannel shirt,

Hobie T-shirt, shorts and sandals. We didn't say much to each other but he seemed glad to have the company and when it got late enough, and he had given out all the room keys, he'd light a dooby, offer me a few hits and we'd sit back and watch the TV in the lobby, exchanging only a few well-spaced words about the surf and the weather and music.

The 1976 Democratic National Convention was in full swing back in New York City and it was all over the news, hardly anything else on the TV at all, couldn't get away from it. The Democrats had nominated Jimmy Carter, the former governor of Georgia, the non-Nixon, on July 15 and I watched it all, but it had no impact on me. Politicians gave speech after speech about opportunity and equality and a new way of government and it all seemed meaningless, less than meaningless, like a cynical joke played on us every four years. After Jimmy Carter's nomination acceptance speech, a huge crowd of people came to the podium to join him, his family, Vice-Presidential candidate Walter Mondale and his family, all holding hands, smiling broadly while confetti fell, the convention cheered and the band played "Happy Days Are Here Again." Behind Carter stood another large group of Democratic dignitaries, including Ted Kennedy and Lyndon Johnson's daughters, Lynda Bird and Luci Baines – what names! - and other big contributors to the Democratic Party, I suppose, all trying to squeeze into the limelight, grab some of the glory. As Rosalynn Carter was walking off the podium with her husband, I saw her take the hand of a young woman standing with LBJ's daughters and smile at her with great affection. It was Lexi Langdon.

One evening just around dusk, I strolled in from the beach and the surfer dude told me that there had been a call for me but no message. He said he told the caller to try again, but they never did.

"A woman's voice?" I asked. "Kind of a Texas southern accent?"

"That sounds about right," replied the surfer dude.

Later that night, when we were both pretty stoned, he asked me what I was going to do now and I said I didn't know.

"Don't worry, man," he said. "There's always another wave."

"I don't know if there will be another wave ... like her," I said. It was like I was talking to myself but I didn't care.

"Ain't no limit to the trouble women can bring," said the surfer dude. "Trust me on that one, partner."

My last day there, while walking for a final time on the beach, I started counting all the jet streams of the planes passing overhead, after taking off from JFK Airport. I imagined them all flying to grand European capitals and I thought I should follow and go back there, do it differently this time, try and start over if I could. I still had Lexi's check in my wallet and that could take me far away for a while. If there is any master plan to my life, any road map I'm supposed to be following, you could have fooled me, but that night at the motel I found Pascal Bernardin's card in my wallet right next to Lexi's check, the French guy Danny had met at JP's, and I thought I might just give him a call. That's what Danny told me to do. And he's my manager.

EPILOGUE

THE OLYMPIA THEATER, PARIS, FRANCE 1989

I was warming up my voice with not much enthusiasm, knowing after all these years that usually when you hit the stage everything miraculously came together, voice, band and public in some kind of energy vortex. My biggest fear was forgetting the words to the song and I had prepared a few "cheat sheets" to put at the base of my microphone in case I got stuck. Alone now in my dressing room, I glanced up at the clock on the wall, saw less than an hour to show time and sat down to write the set for the musicians. It didn't change much night to night, but we liked to keep it interesting for ourselves and throw in a few different songs each show, keep the fans happy and us on our toes. The same band, a mixture of French and Belgian musicians, had been backing me for almost five years now, and they knew about fifty of my songs. That included the three albums I had recorded since I came to France over ten years ago, plus some unrecorded stuff and a few covers. It was a band I could depend on and there wasn't much to talk about before the show, so I sat alone, sipping hot tea, and selecting a shirt to wear on stage. Pascal Bernardin, my manager, promoter and everything else, would normally leave me alone until he knocked on my door as we drew near to show time, asking me if I needed anything before I went on, more towels, aspirin, encouragement ... anything. But tonight, I was set and calm and even though it was the Olympia, probably the most prestigious venue in Paris, where Jacques Brel and Edith Piaf had sung, and Bob Dylan and the Rolling Stones too, I was proud to be there and ready to perform. The Olympia was very French with a nice bar backstage and a well-dressed staff who served musicians and their guests drinks and provided security, but it was my own crew and technicians who were really taking care of everything. I still spoke English to them after all these years, which they called cultural imperialism and I said, you got that right. Still don't know why things took off for me over here in France, maybe I connected with the right people, especially Pascal Bernardin and all his friends, who seemed to be the real French show business elite, running things in Paris with Pascal's father owning the Crazy Horse Saloon, classiest strip joint in the world. Even the Rolling Stones mentioned it in a song.

So when Pascal popped his head in and said there's someone here who wants to see you, I looked up because he, of all people, knew that you didn't see guests until after the show; that this time just before was sacred, when you go into a zone and need your space, all of that show business "respect the boards" crap.

"I'm trying to write the set, Pascal," I said impatiently. "Can't it wait?"

"It's someone to see you," he said. "It's a girl."

"Girl?"

"Well, perhaps not an ingénue but still, good looking, well dressed, around your age. I'm thinking it could be someone you would like to see, Lee," he explained, smiling through his thick mustache.

"If she gets your stamp of approval, Pascal, then tell her to come back after the show."

"She says she's not staying for the show, says she knows you from America. Must be American herself, rich American, never saw so many diamonds hanging on the neck of a woman."

I stared at him, startled, the pen stopping in mid-word on the set list.

"Is her name Lexi?"

"Yeah, that's it," he said. "Lexi Langdon."

ABOUT THE AUTHORS

ELLIOTT MURPHY

Singer-songwriter Elliott Murphy has released over thirty-five albums of original music since his debut AQUASHOW (1973) and continues to perform concerts in Europe, Japan, Canada and the USA. His journalism has appeared in Rolling Stone, Vanity Fair and other international publications. He is the author of three novels and numerous short-story collections. In 2015 Elliott Murphy was awarded the Chevalier de l'Ordre des Arts et des Lettres by the French Minister of Culture and in 2018 was inducted into the Long Island Music Hall of Fame by Billy Joel. www.elliottmurphy.com

MATTHEW MURPHY

Music business veteran and legendary tour manager Matthew Murphy has been living in Manhattan and the East End of Long Island his whole adult professional life, when not traveling around the world with major bands and artists for the last five decades. His resume includes Elliott Murphy, B-52's, Talking Heads, Eurythmics, Blondie, Bryan Ferry, Roger Waters, Kenny G, Patti Smith, Luther Vandross, The Blue Man Group, Incubus and Steve Martin & Martin Short.

facebook.com/diamondsbytheyardtheNovel

ALSO BY ELLIOTT MURPHY

Novels

Poetic Justice

Marty May

Tramps

Short Story Collections

Café Notes

Where the Women are Naked and the Men are Rich

The Lion Sleeps Tonight

Paris Stories

Poetry

Forty Poems in Forty Nights

The Middle Kingdom

Memoir

Just A Story From America

ELLIOTT MURPHY SELECTED DISCOGRAPHY

Aquashow (1973)

Lost Generation (1975)

Night Lights (1976)

Just a Story from America (1977)

Affairs (1980)

Murph the Surf (1982)

Party Girls & Broken Poets (1984)

Milwaukee (1986)

12 (1990)

If Poets Were King (1991)

Selling the Gold (1995)

Beauregard (1998)

Rainy Season (2000)

Soul Surfing (2002)

Strings of the Storm (2003)

Coming Home Again (2007)

Notes from the Underground (2009)

Elliott Murphy (2010)

It Takes a Worried Man (2013)

Prodigal Son (2017)

Murphy, Elliott.

Diamonds by the yard.

10/19
(3+2) TC: 5 9/20, 1/24

71252526R00231

Made in the USA
Middletown, DE
30 September 2019